STARSHIP FREEDOM

Starship Freedom

The Starship Freedom Series, Book 1

Daniel Arenson

Copyright © 2021 by Daniel Arenson
Illustration © Tom Edwards - TomEdwardsDesign.com

All rights reserved.

This novel is a work of fiction. Names, characters, places and incidents are either the product of the author's imagination, or, if real, used fictitiously.

No part of this book may be reproduced or transmitted in any form or by an electronic or mechanical means, including photocopying, recording or by any information storage and retrieval system, without the express written permission of the author.

PROLOGUE

Rubicon Space Station
18 Billion kms from Earth
Dec 24, 2199

Mike was trapped in the dark, so far from home.

It was too quiet out here. Too isolated. Too cold.

A shiver scuttled down his spine like a centipede. He missed Earth.

"Ah, relax, Mikey!" Boris leaned back in his seat, a grin spreading across his pasty face. "You Americans worry too much. You know that? You need to be more like us Russians! Kick back, have some vodka, and everything will be good again, ah?" He took a swig from his bottle and smacked his lips.

At least I'm not completely alone out here, Mike thought.

Though sometimes he thought being alone would be preferable. There was one other astronaut in the space station. Just one. Unfortunately, he happened to be a drunk Russian with a death wish.

"This ain't right," Mike said. "To be out here at the heliopause, the very border of intergalactic space. Just two men to guard the solar system. Just us. Alone before the darkness." He shuddered. "It just ain't right."

Boris leaned forward in his seat. He put down his bottle and stared at Mike. The smile faded from his face. He didn't even blink. Suddenly the pale Russian seemed entirely sober.

"I know," Boris whispered, his voice like wind through a

graveyard. "No men should be out here. Not so far from Earth. We are on the border of the unknown. Out there . . ." He gestured at a porthole that gazed out into space. "Out there is only the darkness. A realm of evil. What if . . . the dreaded *space goblins get us*?" He lunged toward Mike, eyes bugging out. "*Boo!*"

"Go to hell," Mike muttered, shoving the larger man away.

Boris roared with laughter. "Relax, my American friend! I am only teasing. I know what your American movies show you." The Russian snorted. "Giant drooling space bugs and bogeymen. Little green goblins who kidnap chickens and molest farmers." Boris waved dismissively. "Hollywood nonsense. There is no such thing as aliens, Mikey. Out here there is nothing but stars, long hours of boredom, and thankfully plenty of vodka."

"It's Mike," Mike muttered. "Not Mikey."

"What is that?" Boris was busy drinking again. "Here, have some vodka. Finish the bottle." He handed it over. Not much remained.

Mike shook his head. "I don't drink."

"Ah, what kind of American are you? I thought you guys are cowboys! Hard drinking. Scared of nothing."

Mike wiped his clammy forehead. Yes, he was scared. He was scared of everything. Scared of being so far from Earth. Scared of what might lurk out there in space. Scared of the next four years, trapped in Rubicon Space Station with Boris. He was told Boris was some esteemed scientist from Saint Petersburg University. But the man didn't seem like a scientist. He was always drinking, and he kept a loaded pistol tucked into his belt. At least when he wasn't firing it out the airlock, laughing between gulps of vodka. The man had actually built a vodka dispenser into his spacesuit.

None of this was right.

Mike missed home. He missed his wife. He missed his kids. He missed not being so afraid.

Sweat dripped down his forehead. Mike had arrived only a week ago, and his nerves were still frayed. How could he possibly survive *four years* here? He'd go mad within a month! Maybe he was already mad.

Calm down, he told himself. *There's nothing to fear. Dr. Boris Berezovsky is an accomplished astronaut and chemist—not some drunken lunatic. Interstellar space is nothing but a vacuum. There's no such thing as aliens. There's no such thing as monsters.*

He had always feared monsters. Even as a child. He would imagine them hiding under his bed, lurking in dark corridors, and waiting in his closet. It was the old fear of the dark, a gift from humanity's ancestors. Millions of years ago, the earliest hominids learned to fear dark caves, to tread carefully where bears and tigers might dwell. That instinct lingered on. Especially in Mike.

But now we don't face caves, Mike thought. *We face the great unknown. Space. The final darkness of man's soul.*

He approached the porthole and gazed outside. Rubicon Space Station was hovering at the heliopause, the edge of the solar system, the place where the solar wind met the resistance of the interstellar medium. That was the scientific description. But the heliopause was more than that. It was a border. A wall. A warning sign: *Go no farther!*

On the old maps, the ones from the Age of Sail, cartographers would name the unknown lands *terra incognita*. They would write dire warnings on those blank segments of parchment. *Here be dragons!*

Here was the new unknown.

Looking through the porthole, Mike saw antennae sticking out from the space station. He saw a survey drone orbiting the Rubicon like a moth. He saw *Pandora's Chariot*, the little starship Mike had flown here from Earth. The journey had taken a year.

He looked beyond them. He stared at space.

Not at the stars, no. He had counted those stars a million

times during his year aboard the *Chariot*. He stared at actual space—the darkness between the stars. The distance that went on and on forever.

Humans built great space stations and starships. Humans had colonized Mars and the moons of Saturn. Humans had fought wars in space, had conquered worlds, had explored the underground oceans of Ganymede, braved the firestorms of Venus, and charted the gaseous depths of Neptune.

But humans could not fly faster than light. Humans could not reach the stars. Here, where the Rubicon floated—here was the edge of man's reach. Here was the great barrier they could not cross. Here conquest ended and nightmares awoke.

"*Terra incognita*," Mike whispered. "Here be dragons."

A beefy arm slung across Mike, jolting him.

"You know what you need?" Boris said, squeezing him. "A good rousing game of chess! Come, I will set the board. We will get good and drunk and play the game of the gods."

"You're already drunk." Mike turned away from the porthole, shoving the Russian off. "Fine. We'll play. But I'm not drinking."

They sat down in the galley. The plastic table seemed too small for this cavernous room. Mike himself felt too small. Everything aboard the Rubicon seemed to be somehow the wrong size. The bunks seemed cramped, no larger than closets. The engine room towered, a cathedral for gods of machinery. The ladders that rose through the service shafts seemed built for dwarfs, while the industrial fridges clearly served giants.

Mostly, Earth seemed too small. Sometimes Mike thought he saw Earth through the porthole—a pale blue dot floating on the endless black ocean. Then he'd blink and Earth was gone. Maybe it was never Earth at all, just a floater on his eyeball, some memory of the sun. Even the sun was so far from here, just one more star among the billions.

"You play white," Boris said. "My gift to you. Go on. Make a move."

Mike blinked, pulling his attention to the chessboard. He moved a white pawn. "I'm not very good at this game."

Boris moved a black pawn. "No American is."

Mike allowed himself a shaky smile. He brought out his knight. "So that's what you've been doing here for the past eight years? Drinking vodka and playing chess?"

Boris nodded, moved another piece. "Vodka, chess, and sex are the three best things in life. Until you Americans send over a woman, well . . ." He took a swig of vodka. "How do you Americans say? Two out of three ain't bad."

"Eight years." Mike shook his head in wonder. "I can't even imagine. I've been here a week, and I've already got cabin fever."

Boris squinted at the board. "The American before you—he lasted only seven months. The one before him? Five months. You Americans. You are used to lots of noise and excitement and movies and fast food. You spend a few months at Rubicon and it breaks you. You, I think . . ." He scratched his chin, examining Mike. "You will last three months tops. You Americans are a weak people after all. No wonder we Russians beat you in the Greatest War."

"Actually, the Free Alliance, under the leadership of America, won World War III," Mike said, moving a rook.

Boris snickered. "More Hollywood nonsense. In movies, you are all cowboys. In space, you are just boys." He slid his queen across the board. "Check."

"Dammit." Mike bit his lip. He'd have to sacrifice a bishop. "Why is this even necessary? For us to be out here? The war is over, isn't it? It ended thirty-five years ago. Why are we here, one American and one Russian, guarding the galaxy from God knows what?"

"God?" Boris raised an eyebrow, captured the bishop.

9

"Mikey, I have flown from one edge of the solar system to the other. I chased Alliance brigades across the rings of Saturn. I plunged into the fiery hell of Venus just to plant the Red Dawn flag, take a photo, and watch it melt. I dug for ore in the gas mines of Triton. And I never saw a god." He leaned back, took a swig of vodka. "Now, as for goddesses, well . . . I have seen plenty of those. Have you ever seen a Russian woman, Mikey?"

Mike cursed at the board. He saw no way to salvage this game.

He saw no way to last four years here.

This tradition had begun thirty-five years ago. Right after the Alliance had won the war. And yes, dammit, they *had* won. After the peace treaties were signed, after the millions of dead were buried, the bloodied, weary survivors built the Rubicon. A station in the depths of space. A joint project. A symbol of peace.

Since then, two men had stood guard here. One of the Alliance. One of Red Dawn. One man representing democracy, freedom, and capitalism. The other representing equalism, the movement that had nearly conquered the world. Two men. Two opposing ideologies. Two allies. One species.

Them against the darkness.

The politicians spoke of aliens in the void. Of monsters waiting to strike.

"Let us stop fighting one another and face our common enemy!" they said.

Mike had never believed any of that. Aliens? Monsters from another world? Rubbish. It was the dawn of the twenty-third century, and nobody had ever seen an alien. Unless you counted those microbes they had found on that asteroid, which nobody did. Well, *Mike* did. He was a biochemist after all. But real aliens? Big nasty ones like from the movies? Just stories.

It was all a spin, Mike would tell everyone. Just a made-up bogeyman. A way to unite humanity after the worst war in human history. Aliens? Bah. Children's stories.

Well, maybe. Now Mike was here on the Rubicon, doing his part to unite mankind. Now he floated on the edge of interstellar space. Now he faced the void. And now he was no longer so sure.

A klaxon suddenly came to life, blaring across the galley.

"Goddammit!" Mike cried, leaping up. His chair clattered to the deck. He accidentally overturned the chessboard, and pieces flew everywhere.

Boris looked at the scattered pieces and sighed. He *tsk*ed his tongue. "Pity. I was three moves from beating you." He knelt on the deck and began collecting the pieces. "Calm down, Mikey! Just a false alarm. It happens all the time."

Mike covered his ears. The alarm kept blaring. Never stopping. And suddenly Mike was four years old again. Just a terrified little kid, huddling in a bunker as the Russian planes roared above, as the bombs fell, as the sirens wailed and wailed like wounded animals. He remembered pissing himself. He remembered the bunker wall cracking and dust falling from the ceiling. He remembered his grandfather having a heart attack and dying there in the bunker as little Mikey Bawden pissed all over the floor.

"Shut it off!" Mike cried.

Boris rose with a groan, abandoning the fallen chess pieces. "All right, all right! Calm down, you crazy American." The Russian grabbed his vodka bottle, took a swig, then swayed toward a control panel. "I forgot to tell you. The damn alarm is as sensitive as my ex-wife. Any asteroid that flies by, it goes nuts and starts screaming." With thick fingers, Boris tapped a few buttons. "Ah, there we go."

The alarm died.

Silence filled the space station.

Mike was trembling. Terror seized him. Not of any aliens invading the station, of course. But of his anxiety claiming him.

Of pissing himself here in the galley, as if he were four years old again. That old anxiety had always been the monkey on his back. Ever since that night long ago in that bunker.

Even as an adult, the trauma haunted him. At work, he'd go to meetings and freeze up, unable to speak, caught between all those staring eyes. After work, he would drive home, get stuck in traffic, and scream and curse and tremble, trapped among the cars like a prey animal among metal predators. At night he'd lie awake, agonizing over all the ways he had embarrassed himself during the day. Years later, he was still stuck in that bomb shelter, the walls cracking around him.

It was no wonder they had sent him here. He was a brilliant biochemist but a nightmare to work with. And what did you do with outstanding citizens of the Free Alliance you wanted off your back? Well, send 'em to the Rubicon! It was as far from Earth as anyone could fly, which his bosses figured was just a tad too close.

A symbol of world peace? Mike snorted. Maybe once. Today it was a goddamn penal colony.

The chessboard forgotten, Mike returned to the porthole. He wanted to see the asteroid that had triggered the alarm. After all, he was a biochemist. He studied the most basic building blocks of life. Or used to, before they sent him here. Asteroids sometimes contained carbon molecules, even—one time at least—the fossils of ancient microbes.

They said aliens didn't exist. But if microbes grew on other worlds . . . couldn't larger, smarter animals? The old stories returned to him. Monster stories.

He stared out the porthole, seeking the asteroid, and froze.

He stumbled back.

"Oh my God," he whispered. "Oh Jesus. Oh God. This can't be happening. Oh God above, save us."

At first he thought the alarms were wailing again. But it was a ringing in his ears. A pulsing, throbbing pain. A demon rising inside him. And Mike did it again. Thirty-five years later. A grown man, he pissed himself.

* * * * *

"Wake up, Mikey!"

Pain blazed on Mike's cheek.

"Wake up, you crazy American!"

Mike blinked. A blurred, pasty face appeared above him.

"You slapped me."

"You fainted," Boris said. "And you pissed all over the deck. What the hell is wrong with you?"

The Russian heaved Mike to his feet. For a moment the American stood swaying. He took deep breaths.

"We're dead," Mike whispered. "We're dead."

"What the hell are you talking about?" Boris demanded. "My God. The last American did not go crazy for a full six months. You come to my station, and within a week, you are raving like a madman."

Slowly, almost languidly, Mike raised his arm. He felt oddly calm, as if this could not be real. He pointed out the porthole. "Look."

Both men stared through the round pane into space.

The alien fleet was flying toward the space station.

It had to be an alien fleet. It could be nothing else. No human in the solar system had such technology. This was a terror from the darkness beyond the stars.

A nightmare.

Please, God, let this be a nightmare.

Mike must still be asleep. He must still be lying on the galley deck, dreaming the whole thing.

And in his dream, they flew there. Thousands of them. Thousands of gargantuan, spiky spaceships.

These were no sleek, angular machines like human starships. They were craggy, irregular, organic. One might mistake them for asteroids but for one damning feature. Claws grew from the ships. Massive metal claws. Each alien starship grew a dozen or more. These metallic blades all thrust forward, angling toward a central point, like a hand with all five fingertips pressed together.

All those claws were pointing at Rubicon Space Station.

Luminous letters appeared on the porthole's HUD. The station's computer was displaying stats on the glass pane. Mike could not judge the alien ships' size with his eyes, not without any point of reference. But the computer could, and it gave him the info.

Those starships were the size of skyscrapers.

Those claws were as long as city blocks, forged of dark iron. Each one could skewer the Rubicon like a saber through an apple.

"Boris, are you seeing what I'm seeing?" Mike said slowly, staring at the armada.

The Russian rubbed his eyes, stared out the porthole again. "It is impossible. It . . . it has to be a prank. Ha! I know how they did it. Somebody must have hijacked the porthole, covered it with a video screen. It is just some Hollywood movie!" He laughed, but the laughter sounded uneasy. "Come on, Mikey, is this your work?"

"We have to get out of here," Mike whispered. "We have to escape." His voice rose. "We have to get out!"

Boris shook him. "Calm down, dammit! Come with me."

The Russian dragged him off the galley. They passed through a round doorway, entering the engine room. A narrow bridge stretched over a sea of pumping pistons. Engines rumbled in the depths, and gears turned like battling metal nautiluses. Steam flowed through pipes along the walls, and gauges spun like the eyes of madmen.

The two men climbed a ladder, leaving the churning, grumbling engines, and entered an observation lounge. Here they faced a large bay window, six feet tall and almost as wide.

This was no electronic porthole. There was no HUD. No computer system. This was a normal window. Simple reinforced glass.

They saw the same view.

Thousands of clawed starships, dark and craggy and oddly organic. They were closer now. Red lights blazed on their hulls like arachnid eyes. They swam through the darkness like predators of the cosmic ocean, great barracudas ready to strike, to devour humanity.

Boris muttered curses in Russian. Mike didn't understand the words, but it didn't sound pleasant.

The Russian approached a communication panel, tapped a few buttons, and lifted a receiver. He returned to speaking English, his accent thick. "Attention, incoming vessels! You have reached Rubicon Space Station, an outpost guarding human space. You may advance no farther."

"You might as well speak Russian," Mike said. "They probably can't understand any human language."

Boris snorted. "Of course they know English. Your Hollywood movies have probably reached other galaxies by now, American." A joke. But his voice shook.

For a moment only the humming of the station's engines filled the observation lounge.

Then a sound came through the speaker.

A horrible sound.

A shriek. A cry of pure malice. A banshee cry. A ghost's scream. The howl of a demon clawing free from the womb of hell.

Mike covered his ears, grimacing. Boris cursed in Russian

again.

The sound grew louder and louder, higher and higher in pitch, until the control panel shattered. Sparks flew.

"It short-circuited the goddamn speakers," Boris said in a mixture of anger and awe.

The alien ships moved even closer, looming before the Rubicon. Their red portholes glared like wrathful eyes. They were so close now Mike could see movement inside their portholes. Creatures scuttled in the alien starships like maggots in rotten meat. Terrible creatures. Creatures with long legs, with strings of saliva between gleaming fangs, with staring, accusing eyes.

Mike couldn't see much more from here, only these snippets of nightmares. It was enough.

He turned and ran.

"Where are you going?" Boris called after him.

"To the hangar bay!" Mike cried. "I'm getting into my spaceship and flying the hell home!"

"Dammit, hold on!" Boris said. "We have to warn Earth."

But Mike was already running along the bridge, heart pounding, sweat dripping. The pistons pumped all around him, bang, bang, *banging* metal against metal, and they seemed like demons, like monsters from a dark forest. A pipe vented steam, the scream of a dying soul. The gauges spun like a thousand white eyes on an iron face, watching, mocking him.

A nightmare.

Just a nightmare.

This whole space station. This whole life. It was the anxiety again. Just the anxiety. It couldn't be real. Hell couldn't be real. Monsters couldn't be real. They were just the shadows under the bed.

Tears filled Mike's eyes. He cursed himself for being such a coward.

Words echoed in his ears.

We have to warn Earth!

Yes. Yes, of course. He wouldn't neglect Earth. He'd warn them. He'd send a message—from his starship! First Mike had to get out of here. He had to be flying home. There was time for warnings later.

As he ran through the station, Mike passed a few more portholes. Something was happening outside. Hatches like dark mouths were opening on the alien ships. Spiky spheres like sea urchins were emerging, rolling toward the space station. Bombs? Shuttles? Biological weapons? Or were those the aliens themselves? Mike wouldn't wait to find out.

He kept running.

Through a porthole, he saw a spiny pod racing toward the station hull. A second later, a thud reverberated through the station.

More spiky spheres flew.

Thud.

Thud.

Thud.

The monitoring drone was still hovering outside the station, filming the Rubicon's exterior. The drone broadcast the scene across monitors near the ceiling. Dozens of spiky vessels were attaching themselves to the station like barnacles. Circular saws emerged from the alien machines, spinning, buzzing, carving through the Rubicon's hull.

Mike ran faster down the corridor, heart hammering. The Rubicon was a labyrinthine station, originally built for a hundred occupants. Mike got lost, had to check a map on the wall, then kept running. He made another wrong turn. Damn this labyrinth! Damn this whole place.

As he raced down a tubular corridor, a circular saw burst through the hull.

Mike screamed.

Sparks flew across him, sizzling against his blue Alliance uniform. The station was breached! The air was not fleeing. The alien boarding vessels must be latched on tightly, sealing the openings they were carving.

Boarding vessels? Yes, it had to be. Mike had watched enough science fiction movies to recognize what was happening.

Aliens were real. And this was an invasion.

The saw pulled back. A circular piece of hull crashed down, leaving a gaping hole. Long black legs reached into the station, tipped with claws. Red eyes gleamed like drops of blood.

Mike ran down the hall, slammed a hatch shut, and locked it. For a moment he leaned against a bulkhead, panting. Sweat drenched him.

Screeches rose behind the hatch, deafening and furious, demanding blood.

Somewhere in the depths of the station, a human voice echoed. Russian curses. Mike felt a moment of guilt. He was running for his life, leaving the Russian behind. Well, it was every man for himself now. Mike would deal with his guilt later.

I'm a coward, not a hero, Mike thought. *But right now only cowards can survive.*

Finally he reached the hangar bay, a cavernous room strewn with crates, pallets, and scattered tools. The space station's shuttle awaited there, a boxy little vessel nicknamed the *Mouse*. It was no larger than an antique sedan. The *Mouse* would carry Mike to *Pandora's Chariot*. Once on the starship, he would fly right back to Earth and never look back.

Mike took a step toward the shuttle when spinning saws burst through the airlock.

He stumbled back. He felt the blood drain from his face.

The blades kept spinning. The sparks flew in fountains. Mike wanted to turn tail. To return to the corridors. To run and hide.

But he stood his ground.

There was no point running. The aliens were everywhere, swarming through the Rubicon. Their screeches echoed through the halls. Their clawed feet scraped along the decks. Their laughter echoed.

Mike knelt and lifted a wrench from the deck. He raised it like a club.

All my life, I was scared, Mike thought. *Of schoolyard bullies. Of my bosses. Of my own mother. No more.*

The airlock burst open.

For the first time in his life, Mike Bawden the coward refused to run.

The creatures entered the station.

Against every instinct in his body, Mike stood still, staring at them, holding the wrench. A single tear trailed down his cheek.

* * * * *

Spiders, was Mike's first thought. *They're spiders.*

Several aliens clattered into the space station. They reminded Mike of black widows, hairless and gleaming. But unlike Earth's spiders, these aliens were massive. They were as large as horses.

They scurried closer. Claws like katanas tipped their legs, scraping the deck. Their jaws unhinged, revealing rows of fangs. They had shark mouths. Hellmouths. Mouths that could swallow you whole if you were lucky. Mouths that were more likely to rip your flesh off the bones, killing you in slow agony. Each spider had eight eyes, round and red, the pupils slitted. Horrible intelligence shone in those eyes, calculating and vicious.

But the worst part was their bodies. Spikes rose from their

bloated backs, impaling a variety of heads. Every head belonged to a different species. Some heads still grew matted fur. Other heads sported scales or feathers. Some heads were mummified, and some were just skulls draped with strips of flesh.

Hunters, Mike thought. *They're galactic headhunters.*

He remembered, as a child, reading in *National Geographic* about tribal headhunters of Earth's past. One photo still haunted his nightmares sometimes, even now in adulthood. A photo of heads on spikes. The nightmare had risen from the page. Here it rotted before him.

"S-s-stand back!" Mike stuttered. He gulped and raised his wrench. It shook in his hand. "You c-cannot enter this place!"

One alien stepped closer, claws scraping across the deck, scarring the metal plating. The spider had unique colorings. While the other aliens were black, this one had a gray body and red legs.

A grin spread across the alien's face. A hideous grin full of teeth. A grin as wide as Mike's arm span.

And then the alien spoke.

"Hello. My name is Hel'rah of the Great Web. Are you . . . human?"

The alien had a voice like a trapped soul moaning in a dungeon. A voice like a storm on a lost world beyond a black hole. A voice like childhood's end. A deep voice. A masculine voice. The voice of the angel of death, calling you to your final home.

Strange. After all, they did speak English. Boris was right.

Mike forced a shuddering breath.

Be strong. Be brave. Be human.

"Go back!" Mike said.

Hel'rah began to laugh. A laughter like rolling boulders. Like shattering bones. His gray abdomen jiggled as he laughed, jangling the impaled heads. "I was hoping for a worthy adversary. Instead I find maggots. Just maggots. Your species will be so easy to devour."

Mike would never reach his starship. The aliens stood between him and the shuttle. He was going to die here, he knew.

But he could give his death meaning.

He could still warn Earth.

He glanced toward the back of the hangar bay. There—by the far wall. A control panel. He could send a message.

Earth was billions of kilometers away. Even at the speed of light, the message would take a day to reach Earth. But it was something. It gave Earth time to prepare. It gave humanity hope.

We need hope, Mike thought. *Hope is the only thing that can hold the monsters at bay.*

He took a step toward the control panel when another alien clattered into the hangar.

This one came from deeper inside the space station. The spider must have breached the hull elsewhere, then made its way here through the labyrinthine corridors. The creature was black, and rows of blinking eyes ran along its abdomen. It was smaller than Hel'rah but still the size of a piano.

"Master . . .," hissed the blinking beast. "Look what I found."

The alien was holding something. A bundle of silk like cocooned prey. Blood dripped from the bundle onto the deck.

The cocoon was wriggling. A hand burst out, tearing the strands of silk. A face emerged from the casing, covered in blood, unrecognizable.

"Blow the reactor, Mike!" the trapped soul cried, struggling inside the cocoon. "Blow this station up and take the bastards with you!"

It was Boris. Boris—wrapped in a cocoon. Boris—mutilated, bleeding, maybe dying.

"I-I don't know how," Mike whispered.

Blinking its many eyes, the black spider stepped toward its

larger brethren. It bowed, laying the cocoon down.

"A gift, Lord Hel'rah!" said the spider with many eyes. "I found this specimen in the engine room, trying to blow up the reactor core."

Mike guessed the spider was speaking English for his benefit. Nice of it.

Hel'rah, the gargantuan gray spider with red legs, leaned over the cocoon and sniffed. "These things stink. What kind of enemy is this? I bet they taste like tunnel swine."

"I ate one of its arms, my lord," said the spider with many eyes. "The taste is fine. This species will feed our empire. The ones on this station are not soldiers. There is no *eresh* in killing them. But once we reach their world, we will face true battle."

Hel'rah licked his chops. Saliva dripped down his fangs and hit the deck, sizzling. "I will judge their taste."

With his two front legs, the giant spider lifted the cocoon.

"Let him go!" Mike cried, swinging the wrench through the air.

The aliens ignored him. Hel'rah lifted the cocoon over his jaws. Boris wriggled, screamed, then begged.

Hel'rah gripped the Russian's head between two claws. Slowly, almost delicately, Hel'rah lowered Boris into his jaws. He bit down hard.

The bite ripped through Boris's neck. The spider gulped down the Russian's body. He kept the head in his claws.

Mike stared, frozen, unable to even breathe.

Boris's head was still alive. Still alive!

It stared at Mike. It blinked. The mouth moved, wordless.

Mike had heard that severed heads could live for a few seconds. As a child, he had read a book about the French Revolution. The author claimed that after a guillotine execution, the severed heads remained alive in the basket for a moment, blinking, trying to speak.

Well, apparently it was true.

Hel'rah swiveled his eight eyes backward, looking at his bloated abdomen. A forest of spikes rose there, impaling his collection of rotting heads. Hel'rah found one free spine near his thorax. With a swift, brutal movement, he slammed Boris's head onto the spike, adding it to his gruesome trophies.

Boris's head gave a final silent gasp, and then his eyes rolled back and gazed lifelessly.

Hel'rah licked the blood off his lips.

"The taste is . . . serviceable," the alien said. "Bring me the other one. I'll keep him alive for my mother. She might like these humans more than I do."

Mike finally snapped free of his paralysis.

He made a run for the control panel.

Boris had told him to blow the reactor, to take the spiders down with him. Mike didn't know how to do that. But he did know how to contact Earth.

Since he got here, he had been sending messages to his wife and children back home. He would send them one last message. A message of his love. And a warning.

Tears rolled down his cheeks. A lump filled his throat. He thought of them. His sweet wife. His two adorable daughters. They were the lights of his life. He thought that being away for several years was the worst thing he could imagine.

His mission at the Rubicon had turned out so much worse.

The aliens saw where he was going. They began to chase him. Their claws clattered across the deck.

Mike ran faster. He reached the control panel. He grabbed the receiver.

He had been calling Earth every day. He just had to tap a single button to call his most recent contact.

His wife.

The message would take a day to reach her. It would have

to do.

"Beverly, I love you. It's me, Mike." The claws were coming closer. He spoke faster, voice shaking. "Aliens are real, Beverly. Monsters are real. A fleet. An enemy fleet, heading to Earth. Tell the army! Tell them to get ready. I love you. I love—"

A claw drove into the control panel, shattering the machinery.

Steaming breath washed over Mike, reeking of rotten meat.

Mike turned around slowly. He found himself staring into the eyes of the beast. Hel'rah stood before him, his grin dripping blood.

"Please," Mike whispered. "I have a wife. I have kids. Please let me go."

A claw thrust and impaled Mike's belly.

He screamed.

The claw lifted him off the deck. Mike wriggled, skewered on the spider's leg. The pain pulsed from his wound, flowing across the rest of his body, a red supernova of agony.

"Oh, don't worry," Hel'rah said, his voice dripping mock concern. "A stomach wound is a slow death. You'll live for another few hours. Maybe even a few days. I would never dream of bringing my mother dead meat."

Across the hangar, the spiders laughed.

They carried Mike across the bloody deck, through the hole in the hull, and into their shuttle. They took him to their starship. They paraded him through a pulsing dark cavern full of watching red eyes. A cavern like a temple. Finally they laid him before a goddess of many claws, and she fed upon him. Slowly. Finger by finger. Toe by toe. Nose and eyes. But they left the ears. Maybe they wanted him to hear his own screams.

He would die eventually. He prayed it came soon. And as they ate him alive, Mike clung to one last comfort.

He had done his job. He had fulfilled his mission. He had

watched the darkness for monsters, and he had sent a warning to Earth. Maybe that gave Earth a chance. Maybe humanity could still be saved. Because monsters were real. Because terrors did lurk in the dark. And for a brief moment at the end of his life, he had shined a light on them.

His own light was fading now. The sun was setting on his life. He had lived that life as a coward. But perhaps Mike Bawden died brave.

CHAPTER ONE

**The Starship *Freedom*
High Earth orbit
07:00 Christmas 2199**

James "Bulldog" King, commander of the FAS *Freedom*, would miss his starship.

Today was his last day in uniform.

He passed his hand along a bulkhead, caressing his beloved ship.

"Forty years," he rasped. He could only speak with a rasp. "It's been a long ride, girl."

His throat hurt. Talking always hurt. The old war wound had never healed right. Even now, decades after the war, his throat ached whenever he spoke. But dammit, he would say goodbye to his ship.

"Farewell, old girl." He pressed his palm against the bulkhead, feeling the faint vibration from the engines, hearing the comforting hum of the machinery deep within the starship. "I'll miss you."

His eye twitched. The pain was bad today.

He walked across his cabin. Shelves covered most of the bulkheads, made from real wood, a luxury aboard a starship. Thousands of books topped the shelves—actual books, ink and paper. In the year 2199, paper was antiquated. Some of these books were centuries old, original editions, lovingly maintained over the generations. About half were novels, the other half history books. Literature and history were sisters, after all; both were forms of storytelling. Literature was the storytelling of the imagination. History was the grand story humans wrote upon the world.

Antique naval instruments nestled among the books. A brass astrolabe, a masterwork of gears and gimbals, rose beside a copy of *Moby Dick*. A telescope wrapped in leather, dating back to the nineteenth century, rested among parchment maps. A model sailing ship, a replica of the HMS *Beagle*, sailed inside a glass bottle. King had painstakingly built the ship himself.

He walked past these mementos, which he had collected during his decades of service, and faced his tall mirror. The scar was an ugly white today, a blazing streak across his neck like a comet's tail. He touched it gingerly. It hurt. The wound was thirty-five years old. And it still goddamn hurt.

"Maybe I should have died that day," he whispered. "Maybe I should have died by your side, Dad. You died a soldier. I lingered on. Look what I've become."

He examined the rest of his reflection.

On the surface, he still looked every inch the soldier. He wore a navy-blue uniform adorned with brass buttons, polished cuff links, and a braided aiguillette. Golden eagles shone on his shoulders—the insignia of a commander. Medals and service ribbons hung on his chest, earned during the third world war.

He was a tall man, powerfully built. His jaw was wide, and his steel-gray hair was buzzed short. His soldiers called him a bulldog. Partly because of his stubborn nature. Partly because he looked a bit like the animal, tough and mean but noble too.

Yes, in his heart, he was still a soldier. Despite everything.

He turned away from the mirror.

"They say you're a tourist attraction," he rasped, speaking to his ship. "They say I'm nothing but a carnival barker. But dammit, to me you're still a warship. And I'm still your commander. For one day more."

It was more than just Christmas today. It was an anniversary. Thirty-five years since he won the war. Since he lost his father. Since everything changed. Thirty-five years and the pain still lingered. And he didn't just mean the pain in his throat.

He approached his desk and lifted a model of the starship *Freedom*. The real *Freedom*, the ship inside which he now stood, was a full 1,500 meters long. Nearly a mile. This model in his hands was no larger than a newborn baby.

He spun the model over and over in his hands, examining the mighty exhaust ports, the broadside cannons, and the legendary railgun that thrust out from the prow. He remembered flying on this ship to battle long ago. He remembered the glory of victory, even if nobody else did.

"You're beautiful, girl. You made me proud. You're a museum now. But to me you'll always be a fighter."

* * * * *

A knock sounded on his door.

King put down the model starship. "Come in."

The door slid open. Lieutenant Commander Larry "Phantom" Jordan, XO of the *Freedom*, entered the cabin.

An XO was the second-in-command of a starship. King could think of nobody better for the job. Jordan was a tall, slender man with dark skin, white hair, and a strong jaw. He wore a meticulous dress uniform, the navy-blue fabric adorned with service ribbons and polished buttons.

He smiled when he saw King and, oddly, began to sing. "O holy night, the stars are brightly shining . . ."

His voice was deep and mellifluous. After all, Jordan was an amateur opera singer.

King snorted. "At least you're not singing the happy birthday song." He coughed. "I hate that damn song."

"You got lucky, old man," Jordan said. "To be born on Christmas is a special treat. You get to hear me singing far better music." He cleared his throat and kept singing. "Fall on your knees, O hear the angels' voices . . ."

It was funny, King thought. He himself could barely speak over a whisper. Jordan could sing like an angel.

"At least you're a better singer than you're an officer," King said.

Jordan laughed. "I see you're already embracing your role as a grumpy old man. Happy birthday, Jim. How does it feel to be sixty?"

"Everything hurts and I'm tired," King said.

"So business as usual. I've known you for . . . what, forty years now? I swear you've been a cantankerous old geezer this whole time. You probably came out of your mother's womb complaining about the thermostat in the delivery room."

"I was born on a farm, actually," King said. "In an old farmhouse in Nebraska." A wistful air touched his gravelly voice.

And I intend to die there, King thought. *Soon I'll be back home.*

The memories filled him. The swaying fields of wheat, spreading as far as the eye could see. The taste of corn right off the stalk. The smell of crisp morning air flowing over the prairies. He had been serving aboard this starship for most of his life. It was time to go home, to breathe the fresh air and wake up under the blue sky, not above it. He had earned this. Earned some peace.

Jordan nodded, and his smile softened. He understood. Jordan could always understand him.

The two men came from starkly different backgrounds. King had grown up on a sprawling ranch in Nebraska, the son of a prominent family that had fallen on hard times. Jordan had grown up in the hellscape of twenty-second-century Los Angeles, raised by a single mother. He had never known his father.

But the Alliance didn't care about your background, your family name, your race or creed. In the Alliance, you started equal to everyone else. Only your mettle mattered. Both King and Jordan had distinguished themselves as fighter pilots during the war, eventually rising to become senior officers, leaders of men. Some would call them war heroes.

And today we find ourselves stuck in a floating museum, King thought. *Two old war dogs banished to the doghouse. I've been rotting away here for too long. I grew old here. But I won't die here.*

Jordan held out a wooden box. "I brought you something, Jim. A birthday gift. It's also your Christmas gift. Thank God you were born on Christmas. I only need to buy you one present a year."

King accepted the box. "What is it?"

"Diapers for your old ass," Jordan said. "Open it, old man! Open it and take a look."

King couldn't help but laugh—a strained, hoarse sound. The pain flared. He winced. Ignoring the old wound, he opened the box.

Inside was a framed photograph.

A photograph of himself, a plucky young starfighter, standing by his father, the previous commander of the starship *Freedom*. Father and son both wore battle uniforms. They were smiling at the camera, guns in hand, two proud soldiers of the Free Alliance, ready to fight the Red Dawn for the freedom of humanity.

A date was scrawled below the photo. Christmas, 2164.

The day they won the war. The day they paid the cost of freedom.

The day the Russians took you from me, Dad, King thought. Pain clutched his neck as if the knife was slicing him again. *The day my heart broke.*

King looked up from the photograph.

"Where did you find this?" he whispered.

"My personal archives," Jordan said. "You know how I've always wanted to write a book about the war?"

"You've been saying that for thirty years," King said.

Jordan snorted. "Well, maybe if you gave me a day off now and then. I'm still doing my research. I was leafing through files from the war, studying our battles, analyzing our tactics. And I came across this photo. I took it myself. God, I was young and handsome back then. Even more than now. Pity I'm the one behind the camera. In the chaos of battle, I must have misplaced the photo, forgotten all about it. Well . . . here it is again. I figured it would make a good gift."

King stared at the photo. Him, just a young, cocky pilot. His father, the commander of the *Freedom*, the great general who had led the Alliance to victory against the Red Dawn. But there was more in that photo. There were older memories. His father taking him fishing by the river. Teaching him to box. Shaking his hand on his wedding day, then pulling him into a crushing hug. The photo depicted only one moment in one day, but it was like a single thread that unraveled a rug. The memories all came spilling out in a thousand colorful threads.

Look at that kid in the photo, King thought. *Look at me. Just a dumb hotshot. If I had known what the years would bring . . . If I had known what would happen to her . . .*

"Jim! Are you all right?" Jordan put a hand on his shoulder. "Does the photo disturb you?"

King blinked a few times. He looked up from the photo at his old friend.

"It's wonderful," King said. "Thank you, Larry."

He placed the framed photograph back in the box. He

wasn't ready to hang it up yet. Not here. He would hang it up at home among the fields of wheat. He would hang it in the house his father had built.

* * * * *

"And I have something for you, Larry," King said. "A little Christmas gift of my own."

Larry Jordan raised an eyebrow. "When did you turn into Santa? You never bought me a gift before."

"Well, I didn't *buy* this gift." King lifted the model of the starship *Freedom* off his desk. He turned it gently in his hands, smiling. "She's not exactly something you can buy in the store." He handed the model to the XO. "She's yours, Larry."

Jordan took the model, frowning. "This model? Damn, Jim, it took you a year to build this. It's been sitting on your desk since—"

"Not the goddamn model," King growled. "I'm giving you the ship. The real ship we're standing inside right now." He pounded a boot against the deck. "The starship *Freedom*. She's yours, Larry. I've decided to retire. I'm going to officially announce it tonight at the Christmas gala." His growl dropped to a whisper. "I'm giving you the *Freedom*. I know you'll take good care of her."

Jordan stared at him, silent for a long moment.

"Jim," he finally said, voice soft. "Are you sure?"

King's throat tightened, and it wasn't just the wound this time. "We fought a war together, Larry. We were two young officers, full of piss and vinegar. We flew starfighters into the Red Dawn fleet. We stormed the strongholds of the enemy in jungles and deserts. We lost brothers-in-arms. And we saved the world."

Jordan nodded. "Those were the glory days."

King heaved a sigh. "And then we grew old. We watched our warship turned into a floating museum, and we stayed here. We did not abandon our beloved ship. Even as we watched her degraded, shamed, turned into a pale shadow of herself—we stayed. Do you know why?"

"Because we're too dumb to get a job anywhere else?" Jordan asked, a bit of mischief sparkling in his eyes.

King snorted. "Speak for yourself." He chuckled. It hurt. "No, Larry. We stayed because the *Freedom* is special. This old girl won the war. She might be a museum now. But she's still the best damn starship in the fleet."

Jordan saluted. "I'll take good care of her, Jim. I'm honored. And I'll miss you."

"Ah, cut the sappy crap," King snapped. "You've been waiting for this day for thirty years."

Jordan laughed uproariously. "Yes, I admit it. It'll be nice to get rid of your cranky old ass." He squeezed King's shoulder. "How will you spend your retirement?"

"I'm going home, Larry. Back to Nebraska. Back to those golden farms. I . . . I was never a good husband. Never a good father. I neglected my wife, and . . . Well, that's in the past. Diane is gone now. And my son hates my guts. But I have a granddaughter, and maybe . . . maybe I can still become a family man."

Jordan's eyes softened. "Bastian doesn't hate you. Why don't you call him, Jim?" The XO's voice was warm and soothing like old whiskey. Somehow even when he was speaking it sounded like a song. "Call your son."

King turned away. "He doesn't want to talk to me."

"He's your son. He loves you. Maybe he doesn't realize it, but he loves you. Call him, Jim. It's Christmas."

King harrumphed. "All right. Anything to shut you up."

"Shut me up? You love my deep, beautiful voice. Admit it. You'll miss my singing on that farm."

"Ha! Finally I'll have some peace and quiet." King opened a drawer on his desk. "Before I call my kid, I need a drink. And you're drinking with me. I've been saving this bottle for a special occasion."

He lifted the spherical bottle. The drink swirled inside, stirring up whirlpools of amber, burnt sienna, and faded ocher. For a moment the round bottle became a miniature planet.

Jordan's eyes widened. "Martian ale. That's expensive stuff."

"Expensive and old. Almost as old as we are." King pulled two glasses from the cupboard. "Sit down. I'll pour you a glass."

Jordan checked the clock on the wall. "It's seven thirty in the morning."

"Come on, Larry. It's Christmas."

The XO nodded. King poured. They raised their glasses.

"To freedom!" King said.

"And to the *Freedom*, our beloved girl," Jordan said.

They drank. The ale was strong and sweet and burned down King's ruined throat. The war wound blazed.

As King looked at the bottle, at the amber liquid swirling inside, he remembered flying on this very starship to Mars. Remembered emerging from the hangar in his starfighter, roaring into a hellscape of enemy fire. Remembered trudging across the desert, fighting the enemy at every step. An old bottle. Old memories.

He refilled his glass. He drank again. That had been a long time ago on a faraway world. And finally now, a sixty-year-old man with a ruined voice and too much weight on his shoulders, James King was going home.

CHAPTER TWO

Buckingham Palace
England
07:45 Christmas 2199

Her Royal Highness Princess Emily, Duchess of Sussex, Lady of the White Rose, was about to see her Christmas wish come true.

At seventeen years of age, Emily was finally going to visit the starship *Freedom*.

She had dreamed of this all her life.

She walked through Buckingham Palace. Her dress swished, the cobalt fabric embroidered with sparkling silver stars, a suitable outfit for a day in space. She smiled wistfully. The palace was always resplendent, but on Christmas, a special magic filled it. Christmas trees shone with lights, adding to the majesty. Bells rang through the palace, and the smells of cinnamon, candy canes, and pine filled the air. Snow was falling outside, and the fireplaces crackled, filling the palace with warmth.

This was not only the grandest palace in England, arguably in the world. It was Emily's home. She had been born here. Raised here. She knew every corner of Buckingham Palace and the magical secrets it contained.

She had been born into wealth and royalty. And she wanted to see another life.

My grandfather was born here too, she thought as she walked through the festive halls. *But he joined the military, and he fought in a war. He served aboard the starship Freedom. It is thanks to him and his courage that we're here today.*

She paused by a towering painting framed in gold. Emily admired the artwork. The oil painting depicted her grandfather, Robert the Second, King of England. He was young in the painting, wearing a resplendent military uniform, standing by a porthole that gazed out upon the stars. All her life, Emily had found this painting fascinating. It was different from the thousands of other paintings that hung on the palace walls. In the other paintings, royals appeared standing inside palaces, or perhaps riding horses in the countryside. But the painting of King Robert II was unique. It was the only painting to portray a royal in space.

That painting depicts him aboard the Freedom, Emily knew. *And today I'll finally get to stand where he stood. Where he fought.*

"Emily, we should make haste," said Niles, her drone. "The shuttle is about to arrive."

"Oh shush." She waved the drone aside. "There are two crimes you should never commit against an Englishwoman. Never serve her cold tea, and never interrupt her navel-gazing."

The drone recoiled, floating backward in the air. "Serve cold tea? What do you think I am, a battle-droid? I would never!"

"Ah, but interrupting—that you're an expert at."

Niles floated a little higher, huffing. He was roughly the size and shape of an American football, though he would never admit it, referring to himself as a prolate spheroid. He boasted a silver shell studded with gemstones, and two blue cameras served as his eyes. To Emily, he looked a little like a floating Fabergé egg. She had mentioned that once. Once. Dear old Niles had sulked for a week, mumbling about being a fine work of English robotics, not an *egg*. And certainly not a *Russian* egg, thank you very much.

She admired the painting for a little longer, mostly just to annoy Niles.

Then Princess Emily continued walking down the corridor,

passing by suits of armor, more oil paintings, and Christmas trees. Finally she reached the palace gateway, a masterwork of iron and gold, adorned with rampant lions holding miniature crowns.

The King's Guards waited here, dressed in full regalia, complete with their tall bearskin hats. Emily smiled at the sentinels as they bowed. She stepped outside into the sunlit courtyard.

The Victoria Memorial rose ahead, a towering monument of marble and gold. Unveiled in 1911, it featured a Winged Victory standing majestically atop a globe, golden and resplendent. Other bronze statues, featuring ancient warriors and gods, rose across the palace grounds. King's Guards marched and rode horses. The Union Jack flew proudly. Some people called the British monarchy an anachronism. But to Emily, this was a symbol of pride. It was consistency in an era of rising, crashing tides of storming history.

"Over the past century, we fought a third world war," Emily said softly, perhaps speaking to her drone, perhaps to herself. "We joined the Alliance, the great union of free nations. We faced the Red Dawn and withstood them. We endured. Great Britain is the shield that guards civilization. But the starship *Freedom* . . . ah, the starship *Freedom* is the sword that strikes our enemy's heart."

"And here comes the *Freedom*'s shuttle now," Niles said. The drone rolled his two little cameras toward the sky. "Ugly machine, isn't it?"

"We can't all look like bejeweled footballs," Emily said.

Niles huffed. "I told you, Emily, I am *not* football-shaped, I am a prolate spheroid."

"Oh quiet, or I'll send you to America and they can toss you around at the Super Bowl."

The drone dipped in the air, his lights dimming. "Good heavens, don't even joke about that, Princess. Can you imagine me, as beautiful and sophisticated as I am, tossed around an arena full of sweaty Americans, fake grass, and cheap wine?"

"I think they drink beer at football games, Niles, not wine."

The drone shuddered. "Beer. The very word is loathsome. I hope they don't have beer aboard the starship *Freedom*, let me tell you."

They watched the shuttle descending toward the palace grounds. The vessel was boxy, loud, and covered with armored plates. The hull was raw metal, sporting no gold, no jewels. Its only decoration was a symbol painted onto the hull: a blue star with three red stripes on each side, spreading out like eagle wings. The symbol of the starship *Freedom*.

"Definitely an ugly machine," Niles said with a huff. "And that star-and-stripes symbol? Dreadfully American! Somebody ought to tell them that the Alliance includes Great Britain too, along with Canada, Australia, New Zealand, and many other English colonies. The symbol should have been a crown, perhaps. Now that would give the military some class! Do you suppose we can speak to the commander of the starship about replacing the symbol?"

"Oh, do be quiet, Niles," Emily said. "The shuttle isn't ugly. Oh, it looks nothing like the gilded chariots of the royal family, I know. But that doesn't mean it's ugly. This shuttle is a military machine. It's strong. And that's what matters."

Niles snorted. He didn't even have nostrils, but he managed to snort. "Military machine might be an exaggeration, Princess. The starship *Freedom* hasn't fought a battle since the reign of Queen Victoria II. Not since your grandfather served aboard her, may God bless his valiant heart. Today the *Freedom* is a floating museum. A tourist trap. This shuttle is nothing more than a glorified Ferris wheel pod."

"Quiet or I'll leave you behind," Emily said.

Niles raised the pointy front of his body, his way of raising his nose. "You can't. Your mother told me to accompany you, and that I shall do."

"I'm seventeen years old, and I have a fussy robot chaperone," Emily muttered. "Aren't I lucky?"

"I should say so!" Niles said, completely missing her sarcasm.

The shuttle blasted its stabilizer thrusters. The engine roared, and the exhaust ports glowed red. Heat bathed the palace grounds. The shuttle landed with a thump.

Her ride was here.

* * * * *

The shuttle door opened, and out stepped an Alliance Fleet soldier.

He was a tall, older gentleman with a wonderful white mustache. He wore a resplendent full-dress uniform, the most formal type of uniform a soldier owned. The fabric was purest white, dazzling with golden cuff links and polished buttons engraved with little wings. White gloves added an extra touch of class. A military cap completed the ensemble, sporting a blue star above the visor.

"Good morning, Your Royal Highness." The old soldier bowed before her. "I am Sergeant Major Oliver Darjeeling. It's a true honor to meet you. I am at your service, my princess."

Like her, he had an English accent. But Emily spoke with a posh upper-class accent, the highest form of the King's English. This soldier spoke with a working-class accent. From London, she thought.

Emily held out her hand for him to kiss, an anachronism that had been making a comeback in recent years. "The honor is mine, sir."

Darjeeling kissed her hand, then straightened. His eyes shone with tears. "I never imagined I would get to meet you, Your Highness. I remember the day you were born." He cleared his throat. "But please, no need to call me sir. I am neither officer nor nobleman, merely a humble soldier at the service of his princess." He gestured at the shuttle. "I'm here to accompany you to the starship *Freedom*, Your Highness. Please, after you."

"*Excuse me!*" Niles floated closer. "*I* shall enter first. I will secure the area for our princess."

Nose raised, the drone hovered into the shuttle. He emerged a moment later.

"Well?" Emily asked. "Did you defeat all the brigands and warlords hiding inside, Niles?"

The drone grumbled, "I did see a rip in the upholstery. I think we should turn back."

Emily turned toward Darjeeling and smiled thinly. "Forgive my drone, sir. I mean, um . . . Mr. Darjeeling." Her smile widened. "Can I call you Mr. Darjeeling?"

"You may, Your Highness."

"Thank you, Mr. Darjeeling. Oh, and . . . you don't need to call me Your Highness every time. Most people use that title when they first greet me, then simply call me ma'am. Or a simple Emily is fine too." She smiled.

"My apologies, ma'am. You are most kind to correct me. If you don't mind, I will call you ma'am."

"Of course. If that makes you most comfortable."

"Here, ma'am, watch your step." He held her hand, helping her climb the narrow stairs into the shuttle. "Welcome aboard. Please have a seat."

The shuttle contained six seats, all empty. Darjeeling sat at the helm. Emily hesitated, wondering if she should take a back seat. She decided to ride shotgun. Perhaps that was inappropriate for a princess, but she wanted to sit beside Darjeeling, to speak to him while they flew. The old sergeant, with his wonderful white mustache and polished cuff links, seemed a charming fellow. Emily already loved him.

She entered the cockpit. The back seats remained empty. She had taken no security guards on this trip, despite her mother's consternation.

I don't need guards, she had told her mother. *I'll have Niles with me. And besides, soldiers of the proud Alliance Fleet will surround me.*

Reluctantly, her family had agreed. Thank goodness.

She settled down in an upholstered chair. The one with the rip. This was clearly no royal carriage. And the military had not bothered to spruce it up. That was good. This was a military machine, all grit and gruff, as it should be. After all, when tourists visited the *Freedom*, they wanted the full experience. They wanted to feel like they were back in World War III, fighting the nefarious Red Dawn. In this cramped cockpit, the illusion was complete.

Well, aside from Darjeeling's resplendent uniform. Emily doubted that during the war, soldiers flew to battle with golden cuff links and parade gloves. The sergeant was clearly excited to meet her, so she would forgive him for overdressing. And after all, it *was* Christmas.

"Strap in, ma'am," Darjeeling said, taking hold of the yoke. "You might want to hold on to your robot."

"I do not need anyone to hold me," Niles said, his silver nose rising.

"Very well," said Darjeeling. "Three. Two. One. And—"

"Wait, perhaps I—" Niles began.

"Liftoff!" Darjeeling said.

The sergeant shoved down a lever, and the shuttle's engine roared.

They soared into the sky.

Emily inhaled sharply and clutched her armrests. Her seat belt suddenly felt ridiculously unnecessary. The g-force was pressing her so hard into the chair Emily thought they'd need a spatula to scrape her off.

Niles, who was hovering in midair, flew across the cabin. He slammed into a bulkhead and wailed.

"Why, you ruffian!" the drone cried. "Darjeeling, I order you to slow down! You're going to get us killed, scoundrel!"

The mustached sergeant ignored the drone. Holding on to the shuttle yoke, he glanced at Emily.

"Are you all right, ma'am?"

She nodded. "Yes. I'm fine. I spent the summers of my youth riding horses outside Windsor Castle. This shuttle is no more aggressive than a good English stallion."

Darjeeling smiled. "This is a Sparrow-class shuttle. At twenty meters long, with room for a pilot and five passengers, the Sparrow is among the smallest vessels the Alliance Fleet operates. But today, ma'am, you'll get to witness far more impressive machines. The fabled Eagle starfighters. The mighty Rhino-class heavy marine transporters. And of course, the grand old lady herself—the starship *Freedom*."

Emily listened but her attention was split. She kept gazing out the window, watching the land drop down below. Buckingham Palace soon looked like a toy, then shrank and shrank some more, becoming a mere stamp. Then all of London seemed small.

Emily had flown to space before. In 2199, anyone with some money could holiday on the moon, tour the rings of Saturn, or skydive on Titan. Some adventurers even flew near the sun in the heavy, ultra-thick Nightships that could withstand the terrible heat. Emily had done all those things. But she had never visited the *Freedom*, despite all those hours spent admiring the painting of her grandfather.

Nobody in her family had ever visited the *Freedom*. Not since her grandfather returned from the war.

He did not return the same man.

Emily had not known the young Prince Robert who flew off to war. She had not yet been born. But in the family stories, young Robert was a happy-go-lucky officer, quick to laugh, brash and brave. He came back a broken man. He had not laughed since. Not even smiled. It took two years for him to even speak again.

Some people said that Robert had done something terrible in the war. Something shameful. Something Emily didn't like thinking about. She didn't believe it. None of it. Vicious tabloid rumors! They said horrible things about her too. Robert had simply seen things. Seen too much. Some sights broke the soul.

Every year, thousands of tourists visited the starship *Freedom*. To the people, the ship was a symbol of hope. Of the Alliance winning the war. The *Freedom* was famous across the solar system. The legendary flagship of the Alliance fleet! The famous dreadnought that had broken the Red Dawn lines, liberated Mars, and won the war! Boys and girls across all Alliance nations, from America in the west to New Zealand in the east, from Venus in the dawn to Mars in evening's gloaming, knew of the *Freedom*.

But to the royal family, the *Freedom* was different. It was the place that broke their son.

Prince Robert had since become King Robert, and he was still a broken man. But Emily had seen the painting. She had heard the old stories. She wanted to visit the place of her family's greatest honor and darkest secrets.

She was almost there. Her fingers trembled.

Though it was morning down in Britain, the blue sky faded around the shuttle, and the stars kindled all around. The shuttle had breached the atmosphere. The pressure eased, and Emily felt weightless. Only the seat belt kept her from floating. They were in space.

* * * * *

"Well, I swear!" Niles said, glaring at Darjeeling. "I don't think this man has had a single flying lesson in his life."

"Niles! Be nice." Emily grabbed the drone and pulled him into her lap. "Calm down. We're fine."

"I am certainly *not* fine!" Niles said. "I banged myself against the bulkhead. It knocked out one of my sapphires."

Emily rolled her eyes. "You're covered with jewels. I'm sure you'll survive."

The drone gasped. "Princess Emily! The sapphire I lost is no less than the Tear of the Nile, a priceless jewel from the tomb of Nefertiti. Your great-grandmother, Princess Elizabeth III, wore it on her wedding day at Westminster Abbey. And now it's rolling around the filthy floor of a military shuttle!"

Emily sighed. "The floor isn't filthy, Niles. We'll find your gem. Calm down and enjoy the view."

The shuttle had a large viewport—as wide as a windshield on an antique automobile. It afforded a wonderful view. For a moment Emily simply sat and gazed in awe. No matter how many times she flew into space, the view always took her breath away.

At first they flew among other vessels. Thousands of shuttles, cruisers, and pontoons glided around Earth. Some ferried tourists from continent to continent; you could travel from Japan to America in half an hour if you hopped through space. Other vessels belonged to the Alliance Orbit Guard, a paramilitary force that defended their territorial space. A few rockets were rising into deep space, carrying passengers to other planets. Freighters and tankers lumbered in from deep space, hauling minerals and gasses from distant mines.

Then the shuttle flew by satellites. Thousands of satellites zipped back and forth, connecting the world. A few satellites streaked by so closely Emily recoiled, fearful they would hit the shuttle. Many drones flew here too, zipping around in complex orbits, seeking space trash like bees seeking flowers. With so much activity, space was full of random bolts, scrap metal, and garbage ejected from starships. The drones collected it, cleaning Earth's orbit as best they could.

"Look at those poor drones," Niles said. "What a dreadful existence."

"If you don't do your job right, I'll have you cleaning space junk with them," Emily said.

Niles gasped. "You would never!"

She cuddled the jeweled drone. "Of course not. Though I do think it would build your character."

The drone lifted his silver nose. "My character is impeccable. I am a paragon of high breeding and class."

"You were built in a little shop down on Oxford Street."

"Nevertheless, I've been groomed to aristocratic perfection. I wish I could say the same about you, young princess. Me, a junk drone! Ha! Can you imagine?"

Emily was preparing a retort when the clouds of satellites and drones parted, and she beheld the Milky Way in all its splendor. It took her breath away.

"It's beautiful," she whispered, tears in her eyes.

For a moment she, Niles, and Darjeeling all stared in silence. The spiral arm of the galaxy spread above, a silver river. Around it shone the countless stars, and Emily realized how small Earth really was. For all its starships and colonies and flying drones, they were just a speck in the cosmic ocean. She lived in a palace among priceless art collected over generations, but she had never seen anything as splendid as the night sky.

"It sure is something, ain't it, ma'am?" Darjeeling took off his cap and held it over his heart. "God has a mighty paintbrush, and the cosmos is his canvas. I've been serving in the Alliance Fleet for forty-two years, and the stars still take me breath away." He wiped a tear from his eye. "There's only one sight prettier than the galaxy."

Emily tilted her head. "And what is that, Mr. Darjeeling?"

"The starship *Freedom*, of course." The sergeant pointed. "And there she is now. Right off our prow."

CHAPTER THREE

Motherclaw *Hunger*
18 Billion kms from Earth
37th night of Hunter's Moon
576th Imperial Millennia

Skel'rah, Warweaver of the Great Web, enjoyed her first taste of human.

They were a tasty species.

She savored this meal, nibbling finger by finger, toe by toe, keeping the victim alive for as long as possible. When he finally died, still she just nibbled. She wanted to make this meal last. It had been too long since she had feasted.

I am so small.

She did not need to look at her body. She felt it. The shriveling up. Over this long year of hunger, she had been deflating, becoming a wet sack. That was the great curse and blessing of the rahs. *Sheertone ash keresh.* Constant hunger. Constant conquest. The eternal hunt.

"We do not domesticate." She bit off a rib, crushed it between her teeth. "We hunt. Or we hunger."

Before her on the deck, one of her many sons reared. His name was Hel'rah. He was large for a male and unusually colored, sporting a gray abdomen and red legs. The mutation was rare, seen only in the most vicious males.

"Mother, I'm still hungry!" Hel'rah screeched. "Give me a rib. Give me the spine."

Skel'rah snapped her teeth and lashed her legs, holding him back. "No! Back with you. You've eaten your fill."

"But I'm still famished!"

She stared at the new trophy on his back—a human's severed head, the face still locked in anguish. They had found only two humans aboard the space station. Just two morsels!

"You already devoured one," Skel'rah said. "This one is mine."

But she would need more food. Much more. One human was not nearly enough to rebuild her strength. She intended to lay many eggs on Earth. That planet was full of fresh wombs for her offspring. There, in human hosts, her offspring would grow strong. Grow into hunters.

But only if I eat more, Skel'rah knew. *Only if I devour enough protein to lay eggs.*

She scraped her claws across the metal deck of the *Hunger*, her motherclaw. Only one motherclaw flew in the fleet. Motherclaws were the largest starships the rahs built, far larger than the human dreadnoughts. One was enough. One motherclaw could shatter empires.

Her claws drew lines through the blood on the deck. She applied more force. The claws etched grooves into the steel plates. Sparks flew. That was the way of the claw.

Sheertone ash keresh. The sharpening of the claw. An endless cycle. It kept a rah forever on the hunt. For wombs. For flesh. It kept their claws sharp, their souls strong. Skel'rah would rather deflate to an empty sack of skin than grow plump and soft. Decadence was not the way of *Ishar*, the Right Path. And only *Ishar* could lead to utopia.

"I cannot wait!" Hel'rah announced. "I hunger too much."

The young male, the most violent of his clutch, knelt on the deck. He began lapping the blood.

Skel'rah leaped over what remained of the corpse. She

pulled her son to his feet.

"Stand straight!" she hissed. "You are a rah of the hunter class. You do not kneel and lap like a slitherpup!"

He snapped his teeth at her. "Silence! This is good blood."

She slapped him with her claw. The skulls of his back rattled.

"There is no *eresh* in lapping blood," she said. "There is *eresh* only in hunting, in devouring the flesh of live prey. We will be at Earth soon. Control your hunger!"

Hel'rah nodded, blood dripping from his mouth. "Yes, Mother. Forgive me. It's been so long since our last hunt."

Skel'rah looked at her son. He was large for a male, but he was still only half her size. Not many males were born into the hunter class. Most hatched as orbweavers, useful for building, cleaning, and maintaining the empire, but not for killing. A handful hatched as gazers, blessed with the holy sight. That was a prize greater even than hunters but incredibly rare.

But young Hel'rah here—his egg had grown in a great host. They had captured the mighty, furry female on a distant icy world, and her womb had given forth many hunters. It was true what they said. *Kalrosh hashel.* Strong host, strong egg.

On Earth, Skel'rah hoped to find some strong hosts. Her last clutch had contained a few hunters, though most of them were smaller, weaker males. On Earth she hoped for a strong brood of females, many of them huntresses, maybe even a gazer. No gazer had hatched in many years, not in all her conquests. If she could hatch a gazer on Earth, that was great *eresh*! Maybe even *eresh* enough to climb the web.

Maybe even someday to rule the web's center.

But she was getting ahead of herself.

Focus on your task, she told herself. *Focus on this hunt. Do not let your dreams of glory distract you.*

She returned to the human corpse. What was left at least.

The spine. A few ribs. Not much flesh remained on the bones. She would consume the last few bites, and it would give her strength for the battle.

She ripped off a rib, was about to crunch it, when she sensed something.

She spun her head toward the porthole. The skulls on her back, scores of trophies, clattered.

There it was.

A flash of radiation.

Just a streak of photons riding a radio wave crest.

It should not be there.

Human eyes would not see it. Orbweavers would not either. Even most hunters would be blind to such subtle electromagnetic disturbance. But Skel'rah was the daughter of a gazer, and maybe she had inherited some of the gift.

She scuttled toward the porthole, claws clattering across the deck. Other rahs—hunters and orbweavers alike—scurried aside. Skel'rah swiveled four of her eyes, gazing out into space.

There it was, flashing ahead.

She snarled, spun her other four eyes toward her son.

"Hel'rah!" she roared. "Did you allow the human space station to send a signal?"

The young rah was sniffing at the human remains. His saliva splattered the spine. He raised one eye toward her, keeping the rest on the bones.

"This one tried to send something." With a clawed leg, he rustled the human bones. "I cut him off before he could say much."

Skel'rah leaped toward him, grabbed the impudent hunter, and shook him. Several skulls rolled off his back.

"Even a few suspicious words could alert the humans. You fool." She bared her fangs at her spawn.

Hel'rah pulled himself free. Head raised high, he collected

the fallen skulls, reattached them to the spikes on his back. "Please, Mother, the hunger has gone to your head. These soft creatures pose no threat to the mighty rahs." He kicked some bones aside. "Besides, the message is only traveling at the speed of light. So slow!" He laughed. "Our fleet will reach Earth before the warning does."

"You stinking pool of maggot juice! Do you forget that we await the female phalanxes?"

Hel'rah snorted. "Please, Mother. We have warclaws full of hungry males. We'll do the job. Let us fly to Earth now, and—"

"We will await the huntresses!" Skel'rah swung her leg. She shattered one of the skulls on Hel'rah's back. Horns, fangs, and a long white beak clattered against the deck.

Hel'rah yowled. "That was the skull of an Eldurian bonebiter bird! I bested the beast in battle. Bonebiter skulls are rare."

"You led an entire phalanx of hunters to slay one bird," Skel'rah said. "There is no *eresh* in that. And you've gained no *eresh* since. This is your chance, young hunter. Prove yourself in this war, and you'll climb the web. Shame yourself, and I will feed your innards to the slitherpups!"

Hel'rah licked his lips, eying the dead human. "Can I finish your meal?"

Skel'rah hissed and pounced toward him.

She grabbed his abdomen with her eight legs. With her mighty jaws, she grabbed one of his legs—and bit it off.

Hel'rah screamed. Black blood spurted, spraying the deck.

Skel'rah spat the severed leg down. It clanged, still oozing blood.

"That is punishment," she said. "You almost spoiled our element of surprise. Now I must go clean up your mess." She looked at the blood on the deck. "You can clean up *this* mess."

Her son twitched on the floor, screaming in agony.

Disgusted, Skel'rah spun away.

She clattered across the deck. Her spawn had nearly ruined everything. She would have to mend the web he tore.

This mission must succeed. Earth must fall. I must ascend the web!

* * * * *

From the outside, the *Hunger* looked nothing like a usual starship. She looked like a bundle of claws. Thousands and thousands of claws sprouted from her hull, forged of steel, longer than any starship in the human fleet. All those claws pointed in the same direction. To Earth.

Thousands of smaller clawships flew farther back. Thousands more would soon join them, their hulls gravid with huntresses. The *Hunger* was a motherclaw, the largest class of starship in the rah fleet. She led the charge.

They were almost there. They dipped into the heliosphere, leaving the interstellar medium behind. The solar wind bathed them, glowing over their hulls, dancing an aurora dance of war.

The *Hunger* bloomed open. Her thousands of claws parted like petals in a steel flower, exposing a churning red maw.

From inside this cavity, this portal to hell, emerged a single shuttle. A mere sphere of spiked iron. Not much larger than Skel'rah herself.

She flew inside. She shot into the distance, chasing the signal from the Rubicon.

With a long claw tipped with a golden thimble, she nudged a strand of gossamer.

A dark portal appeared before her, and her shuttle leaped into the void.

For an instant that lasted an eternity, for an era faster than the beat of a heart, she flew in the shadowrealm. A place where time had no meaning. Where distance knew no bounds. A place of dark lights and swirling, colorful black holes, a place where strange whales roamed among nebulae of unknown particles, singing their astral song. It was a realm below the great web of reality. A place upside down and inside out.

That eternal instant ended, and her shuttle popped back into reality.

She had traveled a great vastness. She now flew past the innermost planets of this system. The rest of her fleet was far behind. So was the Rubicon signal.

To those watching from the motherclaw, Skel'rah seemed to have hopped forward in an instant. But to her, time seemed stretched, sagging like a web after too much wind. Her memories from only moments ago seemed dusty, barely more than dreams. She had never liked traveling the shadowrealm.

And there it came. The Rubicon signal, riding an electromagnetic wave. A human voice, crying out.

"Aliens are real, Beverly. Monsters are real. A fleet. An enemy fleet, heading to Earth. Tell the army! Tell them to get ready. I love you. I love—"

Skel'rah held her claws out wide, pulling sticky strands. Inside her shuttle, pulleys spun, tugging controls. Steel spinnerets emerged from the exterior hull, spreading blackness, weaving a web. She spun strands of dark matter and captured the Rubicon's photons like a spiderweb catching beads of dew.

She pulled the harvested photons into her shuttle, little beads of light trapped in her dark orbs. In the shadows of her shell, she consumed them. She devoured the energy like drops of honeydew. She ate the words of the human whose flesh still digested in her belly. With every photon she drank, she heard him.

"Aliens are real."

"I love you."

"An enemy fleet."

She slurped them all up. When Skel'rah flew back toward her shuttle, only darkness remained in space. His words were inside her. Nobody would ever hear.

The time is near, she thought as she reentered the motherclaw. *The fleet gathers. The strands unspool. The Great Weaving is about to begin. And when this web is complete, I will rule from its center!*

CHAPTER FOUR

The Starship *Freedom*
High Earth Orbit
08:32 Christmas 2199

The words echoed in King's mind.

Call your son.

He stood in his cabin, alone. Lieutenant Commander Jordan had returned to his own quarters, giving King privacy for the call.

It's Christmas, Jim. Call your son.

King wouldn't even have to lift a phone. Ten years ago, the Alliance had upgraded all soldiers with MindLink connections. The device was implanted inside King's skull, a piece of electronics the size of a stamp. He had been living with it for a decade, but it still gave King the creeps.

Back in the war, we didn't need to be more than human, he thought. *Today we're all goddamn cyborgs.*

It was a military requirement. A soldier had his uniform, his dog tags, and his MindLink. With these neural implants, they could talk telepathically, connect to the military intranet, and yes—even make phone calls. To talk to his son, King would just have to think about it.

"*I'll think about it* used to be an excuse to get *out* of doing stuff," he muttered to himself, then chuckled.

With a thought, he pulled up MindPlay, the implant's operating system. Luminous icons materialized before him, hovering in the cabin. They represented different applications. An image gallery. A calculator. A telemetry console. A connection to Wikipedia Galactica. And yes, the phone app.

The icons weren't actually there. Nobody else would see them. They were all in King's mind. Augmented reality. Hallucinations created by his implant.

Creepy.

He hated the damn thing. The instant he landed back on Earth, before he even took off his boots, he was getting the implant removed. Goodbye getting the news downloaded into his brain every morning. Hello rustling newspapers over a steaming cup of coffee. He couldn't wait.

With a thought, he opened the phone app. He hallucinated the application hovering in the cabin, translucent. He reached toward the icon of his son, prepared to call.

He hesitated.

The icon displayed a photo of his son.

Bastian King was a big, muscular guy in his thirties, covered in tattoos. He sported a mohawk and chinstrap beard. Damn silly hairstyle, if you asked King. The kid looked like a goddamn punk.

He hates my guts, King thought. *If I call him, he'll hang up. And why shouldn't he? After what I did . . .*

Pain gripped him. King rubbed his neck.

Ah, to hell with it.

He shut off his MindPlay. The hallucinatory interface vanished.

It was too early for this. Maybe he'd call at lunch. Once he got another drink or two in him. And he'd call with a real phone, goddammit. To hell with this hallucination crap.

He left his cabin.

He needed to walk off his nerves. It was his last day as commander of the starship *Freedom*. He needed to roam her halls one last time. To say goodbye.

*****

He walked down the corridors of the starship *Freedom*.

He normally spent his time in his cabin or on the bridge. He rarely walked like this through the prow's hallways. Some commanders prowled their ships, visiting department after department, speaking to soldiers, asking questions, connecting with their staff. Not King. He had never liked that aspect of the job. He respected his crew. He loved some of them. But he did not need to mingle among them—and certainly not micromanage them.

But today he walked the ship. Today he wanted to roam his beloved *Freedom*. This starship had been his home for most of his life. This was the final tour.

The corridors were utilitarian. The deck was diamond-plated steel, not carpeted like on some newer ships. Grates exposed views of crawlways and shafts. Exposed pipes and cables ran across the bulkheads, ladders led to service mezzanines, and motors hummed underfoot. The fluorescent lights were harsh and white, but with so much equipment everywhere, even they struggled to scatter the shadows. The place felt like a factory, and that's how King liked it. This was a warship—built for efficiency, not comfort.

That it now hosted more tourists than soldiers was beside the point.

Maybe his attitude was a little hypocritical. King's own cabin had a wooden floor, a crackling fireplace, and bookshelves across the bulkheads. But every man needed a retreat. The soldiers had their bars and lounges. He had his study.

As King walked, crew members bustled back and forth on their duties. But they all stopped when they saw him, stood at attention, and saluted. Yes, this was a museum ship now, and civilian companies owned half the decks, running the casinos, spas, magic shows, and other nonsense that had infiltrated the *Freedom*. But King still wore the Alliance uniform, dammit, and so did his crew. He insisted that they act like proper soldiers.

They turned my ship into a goddamn circus, he thought. *But they won't turn me or my crew into dancing monkeys.*

As he roamed the *Freedom*, he grieved at what she had become. He walked by the prow armory. But it wasn't an armory anymore. It was a gift shop now. Instead of guns, the shelves held plush toys, model starships, and even action figures of him, James "Bulldog" King, hero of the war.

It was only eight thirty in the morning, but many tourists already filled the starship. They stood in the gift shop, browsing the overpriced knickknacks. As King walked by, a child pointed.

"Look, Mom, look! It's him! The action-figure man!"

Other tourists looked at him. A few pointed. Some snapped photos. One old man limped forward, hand held out. He wore a baseball cap purchased from this very gift shop. The words FREEDOM FOREVER were embroidered on it. The price tag still hung from the corner.

"Gee, sir, it sure is an honor to meet you," said the old man. "I'm a big World War III buff. Didn't fight myself, unfortunately. Got this gammy leg since I was a kid. But I read every book about your battles, and it was glorious! I—"

"There's nothing glorious about war," King rasped, pausing in the hallway. "We did our duty. We fought for our country. And we still stand on guard."

The old man looked around, confused. "Um, in a museum, sir?"

King's upper lip twitched.

The Freedom *is more than a museum!* he wanted to shout. *She's still a warship, goddammit. To me she is.*

But he said nothing. The *Freedom* had been decommissioned thirty-three years ago. Just two years after winning the war. Since then, yes, that's all she had been. A tourist attraction. She had been a museum for longer than she'd been a warship.

"The honor of my life was to fly in this ship to battle," King said to the tourists. "The tragedy of my life has been to see her shamed. Merry Christmas."

He left them there at the gift shop. He heard their cameras snapping photos as he marched away.

* * * * *

"Sir! Sir! Commander King!"

King paused and turned his head. Mimori, the ship's loyal android, was running down the corridor toward him.

"What is it, Mimori?"

He frowned. Mimori running? That was new. She seemed downright flustered, which was damn near impossible for a machine.

The crew all knew that King hated using his MindLink. He refused to let them contact him through his brain implant. The younger spacers loved their MindLinks, and they often spoke telepathically. Not King. He detested the damn thing.

Unless it's World War IV breaking out, he would tell his crew, *you come to me in person, and you talk to me with your mouth. Like God intended.*

Mimori was running. That meant this was urgent. But at least it wasn't World War IV.

The android reached him and paused. Unlike a human, she did not pant, did not sweat. She straightened and saluted.

"Sir! I have news. High priority, highly classified." She

glanced around at the tourists walking back and forth. "Should I deliver it via MindLink?"

"No, dammit. Come here." He took her aside to a shadowy corner. "What is it?"

Mimori looked completely human. She was so lifelike, down to the pores of her skin and the mannerisms in her voice, that she could pass any Turing test. That is, aside from not needing to catch her breath after a sprint.

While most of the *Freedom* was built in America, a Japanese contractor had built the android. On the surface, Mimori looked like a typical Japanese girl. She was short, slender, and sported a black bob cut. Her smile was cherry blossoms blooming after a long, cold winter. Whenever he saw her, King felt a little calmer.

She wore a field uniform: smart trousers, a blazer, and a cap, all sewn of navy-blue cotton and jangling with brass buckles and buttons. But Mimori was not a true soldier. She had no official rank, and she wore no insignia. She was a physical interface to the starship's central computer. In a sense, she *was* the starship *Freedom*.

This android was just an avatar. The computer inside her skull was limited, a digital brain stem. The true mind was inside the starship's servers. When King spoke to Mimori, he wasn't just talking to an android. He was talking to the ship herself.

To King, Mimori was a goddess of freedom. A personification of the starship he loved. She was the most important woman in his life.

I'm going to miss you, my dear girl, he thought.

That was another reason he liked keeping his MindLink off. He didn't want to share every thought. The last thing he needed was the crew laughing about how he loved an android.

"Sir, one of my processors has been monitoring the Rubicon," Mimori said.

King frowned. "The space station? The one on the border

of the solar system?"

Mimori nodded. "Yes, sir. It's a light-day away, so I only get delayed information. But I like to keep a camera on the Rubicon. The space station is so isolated out there. Its central computer has been going a bit mad, I fear. We computers don't like isolation any more than humans do. These past few years, I've been trying to keep the Rubicon company. I've been sending him messages, and he answers. There's a full day lag due to the distance, but what can you do? We've been playing a game of chess, actually. A move a day. That's especially slow for computers—we think much faster than you humans—but it keeps the Rubicon happy, so—"

"Mimori, the news?" King said.

Mimori cleared her throat—one of the human mannerisms she had picked up. "Yes, sir. Sorry, sir."

It's funny, he thought, looking at the android. *We've been serving together for decades. She still looks young. And I've become an old man. But despite how she looks, Mimori is no young woman. She's a grand old starship. She's my starship. And I love her.*

Yes, it was definitely good he wasn't broadcasting his thoughts.

"Anyway, sir, the Rubicon didn't send me his chess move today," Mimori said. "He sends his move every twenty-four hours on the dot. It should have arrived two hours ago. And he always sends me a Christmas card too."

"Computers send each other Christmas cards," King said. "Who knew?"

She nodded. "Yes, sir, we do. We enjoy the holidays same as you. We *are* sentient beings, you know. As you can imagine, when the Rubicon went silent, I became worried. So I pointed the ATLAS system that way, and I examined that area of space more carefully. And ATLAS noticed . . . an anomaly. Strange gravitational waves."

ATLAS stood for Advance Telemetry Learning and

Analysis System. The system incorporated sensors, computers, and vast databanks. ATLAS was what the *Freedom* used to scan the universe for enemy ships, traps, defenses—any sort of trouble. The technology was fifty years old now, largely obsolete. These days quantum computers did that sort of work. But King refused to upgrade. ATLAS had won them the war. Sure, its processors were loud, its sensors were bulky, and the databases took up half a deck. But if you asked King, a good piece of technology should have some weight to it. If it was too small to kick when it broke, King didn't want it on his ship.

King furrowed his brow. "Gravitational waves? We normally only detect those from a serious spacetime disturbance like stars colliding."

"It's a puzzle," Mimori said. "But ATLAS sensors don't lie. Something disturbed spacetime at the Rubicon, casting out ripples that are hitting us here. I can't quite make sense of it. There are particles appearing in that sector of space that our science doesn't know anything about. There are all sorts of strange phenomena going on. ATLAS is going berserk."

"What if you point a good old-fashioned telescope at the Rubicon?" King said. "What do you see?"

"I already did, sir. At this distance, we can't see much. Normally, our sharpest telescopes can detect a speck of light where the Rubicon should be. Right now, well . . . we're detecting several smaller, fainter specks of light."

"What?" King leaned closer. "Mimori, what are you saying? The Rubicon is a guard outpost. What the hell happened to it?"

"I don't know, sir. I've never seen anything like this."

A chill washed over King. There was an old joke about the Rubicon. That the space station was there to guard the solar system from space gremlins and little green men. Hell, even the politicians spun it that way. *We fund the Rubicon to keep mankind safe!* In reality, it was a publicity stunt. A way to cooperate with Red

Dawn. There were always just two men aboard the Rubicon. One man of the Alliance. One of the Red Dawn. If they could unite against a bogeyman, the logic went, perhaps they could avoid another world war.

Well, for thirty-odd years that had worked. The Rubicon had never found any aliens, but perhaps it had maintained peace among men.

Was this peace now broken? Had somebody attacked the Rubicon?

We never should have trusted the damn Red Dawn, King thought. *What are they up to?*

"Mimori, I want a full report on my desk within an hour," King said. "Make the English simple enough for the politicians to understand. I'm passing this up the chain of command."

Mimori saluted. "Understood."

He nodded. "Dismissed."

He kept walking down the corridor, a chill in his belly. Suddenly he seemed to be walking down these corridors as a young pilot. Outside the portholes he saw the enemy ships, the torpedoes flying, the fire blazing. The wound on his neck flared with pain.

No. The war was over. He was just feeling nervous on his last day. Tomorrow he would be back on his farm, and instead of damn tourists all around him, it would be the birds.

He sneered, clenched his fists, and kept marching down the corridor.

CHAPTER FIVE

**The Starship *Freedom*
High Earth Orbit
09:00 Christmas 2199**

King walked down the winding corridors, determined to continue his farewell tour of the *Freedom*. But the news from the Rubicon gnawed on him.

Strange signals. A mysterious silence.

It's nothing, King thought. *Probably just an ATLAS bug. The system is showing its age. I'm just nervous because it's my last day.*

He tried to push the Rubicon out of his mind. Tried. He knew it was pointless.

You still have tonight to worry about, King reminded himself.

Tonight he would be hosting the annual *Freedom* Christmas gala. Every year, the *Freedom* turned its officers' galley into a glittering palace full of Christmas trees, music, and good cheer. This year was special. It was the thirty-fifth anniversary of the *Freedom* winning the war—not quite a round number, but just close enough to warrant a party. Many dignitaries would arrive for the Christmas gala, including prime ministers, generals, prominent writers, and esteemed artists. Even Princess Emily was visiting this year. Her grandfather, Robert II, had served aboard this ship in the war.

King would put on his finest dress uniform, the one with the white gloves and bow tie. He'd feel like a pompous fool, but he'd speak to the guests, make a toast. It was tradition. And then, with everyone there, he would announce his retirement.

So far, only Lieutenant Commander Jordan knew. Soon the world would know.

I have a few more hours, King thought. *Some time to walk through my ship and say goodbye. A last day with my dear old girl.*

One day would not be enough time to visit every deck. The *Freedom* was the size of a town. But there was one particular place he had to visit. It was his dearest place on the ship.

The *Freedom* had dozens of decks, scores of departments, and hundreds of corridors and chambers. But broadly, the ship was divided into three main parts, roughly of equal size. The prow. The midship. And the stern.

Right now King was marching through the midsection, nicknamed the Belly of the Beast. At 475 meters long and 300 meters tall, it was a big place. The prow was the brain, dedicated to science and command. The stern was the heart; it belonged to the engineers who kept the ship flying. Everything else lived in the Belly of the Beast.

King walked across deck 32, the midsection's uppermost deck. Great machinery filled the place, rising all around him. Gears. Winches. Twisting pipes. Hundreds of computers, screens, and terminals. From here, the top deck, officers commanded the fourteen Angels of Liberty.

The Angels were massive cannons mounted onto the top of the *Freedom*. Seven thrust out over the port bow, seven over the starboard bow. Each Angel was the size of the Statue of Liberty. They were built to cripple enemy dreadnoughts. Back in the war, they had terrorized the Red Dawn.

Of course, the Angels hadn't fired any torpedoes since the war. Since then, they'd only fired fireworks for the delight of the tourists. Some of those tourists were already flying outside the *Freedom* in their shuttles, waiting for the morning fireworks display. More tourists crowded the deck around King, oohing and aahing at the giant gears and cables that powered the Angels of Liberty.

Trying to ignore the tourists who were snapping photos of him, King approached an elevator. A few kids shot him with toy guns.

As the elevator descended, King thought about Mimori's warning again. Trouble at the Rubicon station. The distant outpost gone silent.

"I always told the suits that the Rubicon was a bad idea," he muttered. A sign of old age. He was talking to himself. "A station we share with the Red Dawn? Ha!"

He snorted. You couldn't trust the Red Dawn. All old soldiers knew that. But the younger politicians, well, they waxed poetic about peace, love, all that pie-in-the-sky treacle. They had never fought a war. They had never seen the Red Dawn soldiers on the field, slaughtering women and children. They had never charged through the fire.

For all King knew, the goddamn Russian out there at the Rubicon had gone mad, had blown up the whole space station.

A thought tickled King's mind, surprising him. It couldn't actually be . . . well, aliens, could it?

Ostensibly, the Rubicon was there to guard the solar system from an alien invasion. But that was just rubbish, of course. Absolute rubbish! King snickered. He had probably clocked more hours of spaceflight than any human, and he had never seen any goddamn aliens. They were just a myth. If there was trouble at the Rubicon, it had to be the Russians. Who else?

He was tempted to check the MindWeb, that sprawling telepathic database of human thoughts and knowledge, for more information on the Rubicon. But that meant activating the microchip in his head. And he'd be damned if he'd spend his last day like a zombie, brain plugged into the computers. No. He'd return to his desk before the gala. By then, Mimori would have a report waiting. A paper report. Good old paper and ink. When had they ever gone out of style?

* * * * *

Standing in the elevator, King watched the floors rush by.

Deck 31, right below the topmost deck, was dedicated to entertainment. The sprawling promenade contained a variety of attractions. A wooden pirate ship moved on rickety rails, its masts scratching the ceiling. A robotic pirate with a scraggly beard leaned over a balustrade, inviting tourists to come in for some rum and gambling. Animatronic dinosaurs roared in a minigolf course, their creaky tails knocking aside golf balls. A magician stood on a stage, dressed like Dracula, sawing a woman in half. Several androids in slinky outfits stood nearby, inviting tourists into their spas for a massage. A water slide snaked around the complex, eventually dropping down to a wave pool on a lower deck.

In the old days, deck 31 had contained a chapel where soldiers could pray before battle. Today deck 31 was a joke. Today the tourists flocked there to waste their money on blackjack, robot hookers, and goddamn Dinogolf.

Decks 30 and 29 were no better. They contained a holographic movie theater, restaurants ranging from fast food to fine dining, a wax museum featuring historic warriors, bumper cars shaped like little starfighters, and of course a shopping complex. King missed the days when deck 30 was a mess hall for his troops.

Later today, he would be hosting Christmas dinner in one of these restaurants. It used to be the officers' galley, but now rich tourists dined there. A world-class chef was flying in from France.

A far cry from the battle rations King used to eat there as a young soldier.

The elevator had large glass windows. As it descended, King viewed the luxury of these upper decks. A giant Christmas tree rose from the food court. Acrobats were leaping from the mezzanines, dipping toward the fountains, and delighting the onlookers. A few employees were dressed as Freedom the Frog, the starship's lovable mascot. They were dancing for the children and signing autographs.

They turned my ship into goddamn Disneyland, King thought.

Finally, blessedly, the elevator descended into deck 28, leaving the garish entertainment district. It kept going down. For a while, King passed through the living quarters, which spanned a full sixteen decks. Officers lived in the upper decks, enlisted soldiers in the lower decks. At least that used to be the case. Ten thousand soldiers had once served and lived aboard the *Freedom*. Today only a skeleton crew remained, crowding into one deck. The rest was a hotel.

The tourists delighted in staying in bunks where terrified marines had once flown to battle. Those bunks had carpets now, entertainment sets, and minibars. Not quite the old military experience. But tourists demanded their luxuries. And they tipped well.

King suddenly wondered why it had taken him so long to retire.

The elevator kept descending, passing into the lower decks now, approaching the underbelly of the ship. King looked through the elevator windows at the cavernous warehouses and armories. Thousands of missiles, torpedoes, and plasma barrels used to fill this place. Now the armories serviced the tourist industry. Here was where robots washed the linens, built the souvenirs, and fixed whatever the teenagers broke.

He passed by deck 9. The entire deck was dedicated to

powering, loading, and firing the Fist of Freedom, the ship's enormous railgun. It was a major tourist attraction. Come see the gun that beat the Russians! Hundreds of tourists crowded the mezzanines, pointing at the Fist's smoldering reactor. Electricity crackled in the air, raising everyone's hackles. Several kids were yawning. They wanted to return to the higher decks where Freedom the Frog was walking around.

Then King passed into deck 8, and he breathed a sigh of relief.

He felt better at once. Now he was descending through the hangar bays. Deck 8 contained the Sparrows, little shuttles used to ferry dignitaries. Decks 7 and 6 contained the Rhinos, bulky troop carriers; they had been rusting away here since the war. Finally he reached the lowest four decks.

The Eagle hangars.

His favorite place on the starship.

Four entire decks, spanning the midsection of the *Freedom*, housed the Eagles. The best damn starfighters in the galaxy.

He exited the elevator on deck 1. The lowest place in the starship. He walked upon the humming, vibrating ventral hull of the ship. Just below spread the vastness of space.

And there they were. Resting on the deck before him.

The Eagles.

King allowed himself a rare smile.

* * * * *

S-35 Eagle-class starfighters. The best damn starfighters in the galaxy. King walked among them, smiling softly, lost in memory.

A few mechanics were working in the hangar, maintaining

these metal birds of prey. As King approached, they dropped their tools, stood at attention, and saluted. King returned the salutes. The Eagle mechanics were the backbone of the *Freedom*, maintaining her superiority in battle. They were not officers. They received no fame from the public. But to King, they were heroes.

"Merry Christmas," he told them, every man and woman in turn. He knew them all by name.

The pilots weren't there right now. They were probably relaxing in the lounge, preparing for the big stunt show later today. Two hundred pilots served aboard the starship. Known as Freedom's Flock, they were the ship's biggest tourist draw, delighting the crowd with daredevil aerobatics.

Yes, the Eagles—these mighty birds that had won World War III—now flew stunts.

King ran his hand along one Eagle, caressing its curves. Back in the war, the eagles had been dark gray. Today they were painted red and blue and lined with blinking lights. They needed to stand out in space for the tourists, not hide in shadow. But King didn't mind their new colors. To him, the red and blue did not diminish their beauty. They enhanced it for all to see.

Each Eagle was seventeen meters long, which often surprised the tourists. People thought the Eagles were smaller, since they were single-pilot machines. From afar, it was easy to misjudge their size. But each starfighter was larger than a semitrailer. They needed to be large. They carried a lot of weaponry. At least they used to. Their wings contracted in space, expanded in atmosphere. Their engines brought light to the darkest shadows, hope to those who despaired.

King had flown one during the war.

He smiled as he walked between the Eagles. Just a thin smile. Not a smile that showed his teeth. He didn't smile big smiles anymore. He rarely smiled at all. Laughing hurt. Even smiling too wide stretched the wound on his neck. He kept his emotions deep inside, crushing them with clenched fists and gnashing teeth.

But today he allowed himself this small smile. This was a good place. This was home.

He remembered himself as a young pilot, known then by his call sign, "Bulldog." Just a kid from Nebraska. Just a young punk full of piss and vinegar, eager to blast away his enemies. He remembered himself running across this hangar, heading to the starfighters with his fellow pilots. With Larry "Phantom" Jordan, who was now his XO. With Prince "Charming" Robert, who was now the King of England. With Yehuda "Lion" Levy, whose daughter was now a pilot on this starship. With so many pilots who never returned home, who never grew old.

Good memories. A good place. The war had been the worst time of his life, but in some ways, also the best. A time of death, despair, of losing friends, losing his father. But also a time of laughter, courage, and brotherhood.

Look at me, he thought. *I've become a nostalgic old man. I used to mock nostalgic old men. Maybe that's both the curse and blessing of life. We all eventually become the people we deserve to be.*

He walked among the Eagles, heading toward the back of the hangar.

And there he saw her.

S-35 Unit A1. The Golden Eagle.

His personal starfighter.

* * * * *

Stanchions and velvet rope separated this starfighter from the others. The Golden Eagle flew no stunts. She was not painted red and blue. Her hull was still its original gray, covered in battle scars. Stars were painted onto her hull, one for each enemy starfighter downed. No fewer than sixty-seven stars shone on the Golden Eagle, an Alliance record.

King had earned those stars as a young pilot. Decades later, the record still stood. As King looked at his starfighter, a lump filled his throat. His eyes stung. Those were horrible days of war. But also days of glory and so much promise.

A voice came from behind him.

"She's one ugly bird, sir. All scratched up and dented and old. Just like you."

King turned around, snorting.

Colonel Gal "Spitfire" Levy stood there, hands on her hips, a mocking smile on her face. She was a tall brunette with mischievous eyes. Freckles were strewn across her nose and cheeks. Her baggy flight suit could not hide her slender grace.

"And like me, the Golden Eagle is a tough killer," King rasped.

Spitfire laughed. "That she is. Best damn bird in my fleet. If only you'd let me fly her now and then."

She was fluent in English, the *lingua franca* aboard the *Freedom*, but she spoke with an accent. Spitfire had been raised in Israel, the daughter of a famous fighter pilot. Her grandfather had been a fighter pilot too. And his father. It went back seven generations. Flying was in her blood.

King growled at her. "So long as I'm commander of the *Freedom*, nobody flies the Golden Eagle but me."

Spitfire raised an eyebrow. "Sir, you haven't flown the Golden Eagle since before I was born. When are you going to let somebody fly her again? By somebody I mean me, of course. The lovely commander of your starfighter fleet."

Gal Levy was only thirty-five years old. But despite her young age, she commanded the Freedom's Flock, the starship's complement of starfighters. Spitfire was young and cocky, yes, but also fiercely intelligent and brave. She had been flying starfighters since she was twelve years old, and she was the best damn pilot in the fleet.

A stunt pilot, King reminded himself. *Spitfire has never flown in battle. She was born after the war. Just a few days after it ended. After her father died in battle.*

"Spitfire." He hesitated, then put a hand on her shoulder. He gazed into her eyes. "I wasn't going to tell you yet. I'm going to announce it officially at our Christmas dinner. But I'll tell you now. I'm retiring. Today is my last day in uniform. I'm leaving you the Golden Eagle. She's yours now. Take good care of the old bird."

Spitfire took a step back. Her eyes dampened. Her arms dropped to her sides.

"No, sir!" she whispered. "No, you can't retire!"

"Try to stop me."

She sniffed, then dropped all decorum and pulled him into a hug. "It's so sudden. I'm going to miss you, sir." Tears flowed down her cheeks. "You took me in when I was just a young pilot. You trained me. Mentored me. I can't let you go. After my father died, I . . ." She pulled back a little, stared into his eyes. "You're like a father to me."

King could not speak, suddenly worried he'd shed a tear.

My own son rejects me, he thought. *But I have Spitfire.*

He brushed back a strand of her brown hair. "And you're like a daughter. Your father was a good friend. He never got to meet you, but if he's looking down, he's proud of you. And I'm proud of you, Gal."

"Does that mean you're giving me command of the entire starship *Freedom*?"

"Don't push your luck," he growled. "That job is going to Jordan." He barked a laugh. "Nice try though."

She laughed too, wiped away her tears, and winked. "Maybe

someday. A girl can dream."

"Just don't tell anyone," King said. "Not until after I announce it officially. I wanted you to know before the others."

Spitfire took a step back, stood at attention, and saluted. "It's been the honor of my life to serve you, sir."

He returned the salute. "The honor has been mine." He lowered his hand. "All right, all right, enough sentimental crap. Princess Emily is due to arrive by shuttle soon. Before she flies into the *Freedom*, she'll be touring space around the starship. A prime spot to view starfighter stunts. I want your team to put on a damn good show for her."

Spitfire's smile faded. "With all due respect, sir, Emily is not my princess. I'm Israeli. My people fought to free ourselves from the British empire."

King snorted. "So did half the world. My country did too. But that was long ago. Today we're united under the Free Alliance banners. Princess Emily is a symbol of the Alliance. She's a symbol of what we all cherish."

Spitfire bit her lip. "All right. I disagree with you, sir. But I respect you. And I'll respect the little princess. We'll put on a damn good show." She winked. "Don't we always?"

"Nobody showboats as well as you," King agreed with his own wink. "Is the flock ready?"

"My pilots are relaxing in the aerie," Spitfire said. "Lazy bastards. Probably getting drunk already. I'll go fetch 'em." She made to walk away, then hesitated. "Sir . . . why don't you fly with us today?"

King frowned. "What, perform stunts?"

She placed her hands back on her hips, raised an eyebrow. "Oh, are stunts beneath you, mighty starfighter ace?"

He chuckled—a hoarse, raspy sound. "Yes. But it's more than that. I haven't flown a starfighter in years. I'm rusty."

"I've watched the old videos of you flying in the war,"

Spitfire said. "I've studied those videos over and over again. Your raid on Mars. Your attack on Titan. Your triple butterfly spin maneuver in the asteroid belt, diving from the sun to break the Red Dawn lines. You're the best damn pilot I've ever seen, sir."

"That was when I was much younger. But thank you for kissing up to an old man. It still won't get you the job of ship commander."

She sighed. "Well, I better start buttering up Lieutenant Commander Jordan. I suppose he'll be Commander Jordan now. The old bastard is going to outrank me by *two* ranks now. Oh, he's going to love that."

King sighed too. "Try not to make his life miserable, Colonel. He's a good officer."

She stuck out her tongue. "I make everyone miserable. It's my greatest talent. After flying, that is. Now let's go fetch those lazy pilots. It's time to perform for a princess."

King walked across the hangar deck, heading toward the pilots' lounge. Spitfire walked a step behind him. The lounge, where the pilots spent their free time between performances, was known as the aerie. A nest for eagles. An appropriate name. Though King had always thought the name a bit ironic too, given that they were on the ship's lowest deck.

As they neared the aerie, King frowned.

Music was playing in the lounge. It sounded dim from here. But King recognized it.

He growled, clenched his fists, and his scar blazed with white fire.

Red Dawn's national anthem.

* * * * *

King burst into the aerie, the blood roaring in his ears.

It was coming from here. The damn music! Red Dawn's anthem!

"What the hell is going on here?" he demanded.

Dozens of pilots filled the lounge, relaxing in armchairs, playing pool, and drinking at the bar. At once they snapped to attention and saluted.

The anthem kept playing. The music was bombastic, far too loud, and full of trumpets. A marching song. A battle song. The choir was singing in Russian, but different Red Dawn nations sang the anthem in their own languages.

The Red Dawn. An axis of evil.

King hated the bastards.

A century ago, a movement called equalism had swept across the world. The ideology worshipped the government, oppressed the people, and crushed freedom. Fascism and communism had a baby, and its name was equalism.

Nation by nation fell to the revolution. First equalism seized Russia. Then China, North Korea, and Vietnam. From there, it spread across the Pacific and consumed all of South America. Several countries across Africa and the Middle East bowed before them. Together, these nations formed the Red Dawn. A grand cabal of evil. United, Red Dawn tried to conquer not just Earth—but the entire solar system. First the moon, then the asteroids, finally Mars—they fell to Red Dawn, and still the empire spread.

But some nations resisted.

The free nations of the world formed the Alliance. The United States led them. Britain and the Commonwealth joined the battle. Japan, South Korea, Israel, India, Western Europe—they joined too, answering the call of freedom. They all hoisted the Alliance flag.

They stood up. They fought back.

It took half a billion lives to defeat those red bastards, King thought, the anthem playing in his ears. *And now their anthem is playing here on my ship!*

King had heard the Red Dawn anthem many times during the war. The enemy blasted it from their tanks, their infantry brigades, even their starship transmitters. He had silenced them all with the *Freedom*'s guns.

He glowered at the holoscreen that hovered near the deckhead. The anthem was coming from there.

The holoscreen was streaming a live video from the Kremlin. Red Dawn troops were marching, rifles in hand. They wore the dress uniforms of their cruel army. The fabric was red, adorned with many brass buttons and buckles. Their coats were long, their boots tall, and elaborate aiguillettes adorned their chests.

The Red Dawn didn't celebrate Christmas; religion was outlawed in their lands. But December 25 was still an important day to the entire human species. Today World War III had ended, and the Russians were out en masse. King imagined that it was the same in the other Red Dawn nations.

They put on the same damn show every year.

The camera panned toward Saint Basil's Cathedral. Its teardrop domes scratched the clouds, painted in dazzling colors. The Tsar Cannon stood below the cathedral, a masterwork of bronze, adorned with reliefs of lions, serpents, and horses. Built in 1586, the Tsar Cannon remained the largest gun in the world until the age of spaceflight.

A familiar figure stood atop the cannon's bore, smiling a crooked smile at the camera.

Premier Katya "Katyusha" Petrova, the leader of Red Dawn.

The woman who had slashed King's neck.

* * * * *

Her name was Katya Petrova, but everyone, both her people and her enemies, simply called her Katyusha. It was what she called herself.

King stood in the pilots' lounge, staring at the video from Moscow. Staring at the woman he hated most in the world.

Like him, Katyusha was sixty years old. But she barely looked thirty. Nobody knew how the Russian premier kept her youthful looks. Some believed she simply had good plastic surgeons. Others claimed she was an android. Some defectors whispered of horrifying medical procedures. They said that Katyusha grew her own clones in underground labs. Once they were old enough, she sawed open their skulls, scooped out their old brains, and implanted her own brain instead. With every brain implant, they said, she became crazier and crazier.

And that was saying something. King remembered her well from the war, and she had been quite unhinged then too.

She wore the field uniform of Red Dawn. A long red coat. Leather boots that rose to her knees. Her chin-length black hair spilled out from under her fur cap. A pin on her lapel showcased the symbol of her ideology—an equal sign inside a circle.

"Hello, people of Red Dawn!" she said, still smiling crookedly. Her Russian accent was thick. "Today is Victory Day. Today we celebrate our great triumph against the evil Alliance!"

Fighter jets soared above her. Red fireworks blazed. The people cheered. At least the people watching in Moscow. Here aboard the starship *Freedom*, nobody was cheering.

"Turn that damn screen off," King growled.

One of the pilots, a big guy with the call sign Meatball, rummaged through a box of remote controls. "Right away, sir. Sorry, sir, the holoscreen has been acting up lately, and . . . I just need to find the right remote, and . . ."

"Hurry before I shoot the damn projector," King said.

Despite his rage, he couldn't resist looking back at the screen.

Katyusha was smiling at the camera. She seemed to be smiling right at him. That deranged crooked smile, her eyes dripping mockery.

"The cruel Alliance butchered our children," Katyusha was saying. "They raped our women. But we fought them. We defeated them!" She drew her saber and swung the blade, slicing the air. "If they ever threaten us again, Katyusha will cut them down to size!"

The pain on King's neck blazed. But worse was the pain in his heart.

He remembered. The Battle of Mars. The blood pouring over the red desert.

Katyusha had looked exactly the same. He could see it all again, as vivid as the hologram. His father, Ulysses King, leading the troops from the trenches. Katyusha—charging at the general, wrestling his knife from him, and slitting his throat.

"Dad!" the young James King had cried, running toward the old man.

He grabbed his father. But it was too late. The general was dead.

And then—the pain.

The blazing agony in his neck.

Katyusha, laughing and slicing, and—

King growled, gnashed his teeth so hard he cracked a crown, and pulled himself back to the present.

"Of course, the silly Alliance claims they won the war," Katyusha said, standing atop the cannon. She tossed back her head and laughed. "Silly capitalist weaklings. They might have conquered Mars, yes. So what? Everybody knows that the glorious

Red Dawn won the war! Even if little Commander King refuses to admit it." She stared at the camera, smiling crookedly. "Are you watching Katyusha now, little commander?" She pouted. "Does your little neck hurt? Katyusha should have cut deeper, perhaps. But Katyusha does rather enjoy knowing you lived to run a museum. Just an old man in a floating tourist trap. So sad!"

She laughed again. As billions watched.

"Get this crap off my ship's screens!" King roared. He almost never shouted. His throat would ache all night.

"Ah, here we go," said Meatball, finding the right remote. He clicked a button, and blessedly the damn hologram vanished.

King took a raspy breath, then turned toward the pilots. They all stood in the lounge, staring back at him.

King glared at them, one by one.

For a moment silence filled the aerie.

Then King spoke.

"You are stunt pilots. You put on shows for tourists. You've never flown in battle. The war ended long ago. Some of you were little kids. The rest of you hadn't even been born. But despite what you might hear elsewhere, the war never *truly* ended. Not for me! Not for this ship! Today the war is not fought with guns. But with words. And that is a good thing. I would rather suffer ten thousand insults than have to fly to a single battle."

The pilots stared at him, solemn. Meatball lowered his eyes, cheeks red, perhaps feeling guilty for letting the video run for so long.

"You all know what really happened on Mars," King said. "I was there. I saw it. The women—defiled. Their children—murdered. The Red Dawn troops carried out those crimes. The same crimes they blame us for now. We defeated them then. We liberated Mars. We liberated half of Earth. *We* did this—the Free Alliance. You are officers of the Alliance. And I want you to be proud of the uniforms you wear. You stand for something. You stand for justice. For democracy. For freedom."

One pilot, a young hotshot they called Curly, cleared his throat. "With all due respect, sir, we're just stunt pilots. We're glorified circus performers."

"You wear the uniforms of the Alliance Fleet," King growled. "That still means something. To me it does. You might think you're just performers. Just acrobats dancing for the crowd. But to me, you are pilots as fine as any from the war. I'm proud of you. Every last one of you."

A few pilots glanced at one another. This was, King knew, uncharacteristically sappy of him. He was normally the guy chewing out soldiers, not waxing poetic about how proud he was of them. They didn't know this was his last day. Only Spitfire knew. She stood nearby, a sad, knowing smile on her freckled face.

"The echoes of Red Dawn's national anthem still fill this room," King said. "Sing with me a better song."

He had never been a great singer. Not even before Katyusha had sliced his throat. Jordan had always been the officer with the golden voice. But as King began to sing in a raspy, pained voice, the others joined. They sang the "Song of Freedom," the anthem of their beloved starship.

> *Let all free souls salute her flight*
> *Let her engines bathe the dark with light*
> *Let her cannons sing the song of freedom*
> *The fleet will gather; she will lead them*
> *Our flagship sails into the flame*
> *As poets weep and sing her name*
> *For liberty's light! For glory's hymn!*
> *Praise the Freedom, she will win!*

CHAPTER SIX

Sparrow Shuttle *Freedom*-A1
High Earth Orbit
09:33 Christmas 2199

Emily squinted through the viewport.

"The starship *Freedom*?" she said. "Where? I still can't see her."

Darjeeling pointed. "There, ma'am. Do you see that slender blue light?"

Her eyes widened. "Yes! It's still so far."

Darjeeling nodded. "The starship *Freedom* is a dreadnought-class warship, among the largest machines humans ever built. She cannot anchor too close to Earth. She awaits us in deeper space."

The *Freedom* was dim. Some starships shone like stars. Others glittered with neon. Some starships were floating casinos, and their dazzling lights lured gamblers like flowers lured bees. Other starships were pleasure pontoons, speed racers, and luxury yachts, their particolored lights projecting the wealth of their masters.

The *Freedom* was different. Despite her massive size, she was hard to see. Her hull was dark gray tinged with blue. The starlight limned her form, painting her with azure highlights. As the shuttle flew closer, Emily squinted. At this distance, the ship seemed rough, irregular. If Emily hadn't known any better, she might have mistaken it for an asteroid.

"That so-called starship is positively ghastly," Niles said. His two camera lenses spun on their little stalks. He was probably zooming in, could see more details than Emily.

"I think she's beautiful," Emily said.

The legends returned to her.

The starship *Freedom* rising from the ashes of the Red Dawn's assault.

The great dreadnought rallying the Alliance Fleet.

The *Freedom* charging toward the final battle, cannons booming.

Emily had watched the movies over and over, read the books, the poems, listened to her grandfather's stories. And there she was before her. Not a hologram or words on a page but the real starship.

A tear rolled down Emily's cheek, and she whispered an old poem.

Let all free souls salute her flight
Let her engines bathe the dark with light
Let her cannons sing the song of freedom
The fleet will gather; she will lead them
Our flagship sails into the flame
As poets weep and sing her name
For liberty's light! For glory's hymn!
Praise the Freedom, she will win!

Flying the shuttle, Darjeeling removed his cap.

"Praise the *Freedom*, she will win!" the mustached sergeant repeated, eyes shining with tears.

The "Song of Freedom." It was a poem her grandfather had written long ago. A poem they taught in schools today. A poem Emily had etched across her heart and soul.

*****

They flew closer. And finally Emily appreciated the sheer size of the *Freedom*. Her eyes widened.

By God! The *Freedom* dwarfed Buckingham Palace, and that was no small palace. Place the *Freedom* down in London, and she'd cover the entire Mall—from Buckingham to Trafalgar Square. From there, the *Freedom*'s legendary railgun would extend even farther, crushing half of Covent Garden.

In other words, she was big. Damn big.

"She's a full fifteen hundred meters," Darjeeling boasted, noticing how wide her eyes had grown. "When she was christened forty years ago, she was the largest starship ever built. The first dreadnought. And if you ask me, still the greatest."

"Are there larger starships today?" Emily asked.

"Well . . ." Darjeeling squirmed uncomfortably in the shuttle's pilot seat. "There are some that are larger, yes. The Red Dawn flagship *Lenin* is larger. But no ship is grander than our beloved *Freedom*. And none are so legendary."

"I meant no offense," Emily said. "She's truly a grand old lady."

"That she is, ma'am. That she is. We're almost there. Shall I fly the shuttle around the ship, give you a tour of the exterior before we enter?"

"That would be grand. Thank you, Mr. Darjeeling."

As the shuttle flew closer, more details emerged. From afar, Emily had thought the *Freedom* craggy like an asteroid. But those were no random crags on her surface. A host of machinery and equipment covered the *Freedom*. She spotted mighty cannons, telescopes, hangar bays, armored plates, machine-gun nests, antennae, radio plates, magnetic field generators—it was all too much to take in at once, a veritable forest of technology. The

Freedom wasn't graceful and smooth like modern starships. She was not built for beauty; she was built for war.

"Let us begin our tour from the stern," Darjeeling said, yawing the shuttle.

They flew toward the back of the starship. The stern rose before them, a sheer cliff of metal. Three exhaust pipes gaped open like caves.

Emily giggled. "Mickey Mouse."

Darjeeling tilted his head. "Pardon, ma'am?"

"The three exhaust ports! It's the way they're arranged. One big one at the bottom. Two slightly smaller ones above. Like mouse ears. The stern of the *Freedom* looks like Mickey Mouse." She giggled again, then blushed and lowered her head. "I'm sorry. I don't mean to mock your ship."

"No need to apologize, ma'am. You have a delightful imagination."

Another shuttle glided by the stern, perhaps ferrying tourists. Emily and Darjeeling still flew a distance away, but that other shuttle was close to the *Freedom*, giving her some perspective. Emily gasped. The shuttle seemed *tiny* by the dreadnought's stern! Like a fly buzzing by an albatross.

"How large are those exhaust ports?" she said, eyes wide.

Darjeeling smiled. "The size of football fields. Or as the Americans call it—soccer."

Her jaw dropped. "Each one of those ports—the size of a football field? My goodness."

Darjeeling nodded. "You could fit the London Eye into those exhaust ports. In fact, if you placed just the stern of the *Freedom* inside London, it would dwarf every skyscraper in the city. I don't mean the entire starship. Just the stern."

Emily leaned back as if too awed to even sit upright. "Wow. Why is it so *big*? The ship must have massively powerful engines!"

Darjeeling nodded. "Indeed she does, ma'am. Indeed she

does. In fact, a full third of the starship *Freedom* is dedicated to the engines. Take the engines out of *Freedom*, and put them down in London, and they would stretch for several city blocks, and they would rise higher than Big Ben."

Their shuttle flew past the stern, then began flying alongside the starboard bow. Emily gazed at the hull passing by, yard after yard of armor and machinery. She tried to imagine that gargantuan engine churning inside. An engine the size of an entire neighborhood! Incredible.

"Does she fly on regular rocket fuel?" she asked, hoping it was an intelligent question. She wanted to appear educated when speaking to the military, to prove herself more than a pampered princess.

"The starship *Freedom* uses a Talaria drive, an advanced propulsion system," Darjeeling said. "Talaria technology utilizes particle physics to propel starships much faster than conventional engines could." His cheeks flushed. "To be honest, ma'am, I ain't no engineer, and I don't fully understand the technology. But I've flown aboard the *Freedom* many times. With the Talaria engines fully primed, the *Freedom* can reach one percent the speed of light."

Emily tilted her head. "Just one percent the speed of light? Oh dear. That doesn't sound very fast, does it?"

"Certainly not!" Niles interjected. "May we go home now?"

"Hush, Niles," Emily said.

Darjeeling ignored the drone, God bless him. "To answer your question, ma'am. One percent the speed of light does not *sound* very fast, as you say. Yet I assure you, it is a very fine speed indeed. Before Talaria drives, when starships only had conventional engines, it would take a year to travel from Earth to Mars. But with a Talaria drive, the journey only takes a day. That's how fast even one percent the speed of light is."

"Fascinating, Mr. Darjeeling," Emily said. "It's truly

counterintuitive. I realize now how blisteringly fast that one percent is. It reminds me of how it used to take sailing ships months to circle the globe, but the steam engine cut that time back to mere days." She frowned, thought for a moment. "Can the *Freedom* reach the stars with a Talaria drive?"

"Lamentably not," said Darjeeling. "You see, even the nearest star to us, Alpha Centauri, is over four light-years away. Even with Talaria drives—flying blisteringly fast, as you so aptly put it—the journey would take centuries."

"Centuries! Oh my." Emily deflated. "Pity. That too is counterintuitive—just how much farther the stars are compared to our neighboring planets."

"Indeed, ma'am. Our mortal brains struggle with distances and speeds on this scale. As far as our solar system's planets are from one another, they're all very close compared to the stars."

"So I suppose somebody would have to invent faster-than-light engines to reach the stars," Emily said. "Like in the science fiction films from America."

Darjeeling chuckled. "Yes, well, according to dear old Einstein, traveling faster than light is impossible. I'm afraid it's only possible in films. With the *Freedom*, we have conquered the solar system. But space is so unimaginably vast, and the stars are so incredibly far away, that interstellar space is simply impossible to cross. Not unless you have centuries to spare."

"Maybe that's a good thing," Emily said. "I'd have loved to fly to other stars, see worlds beyond our solar system, and explore the galaxy. Like in my favorite films. But other films portray alien invasions." She shuddered. "If there are aliens out there, I'm glad space is so vast. If one cannot travel faster than light, perhaps Earth is safe."

Darjeeling nodded, smiling politely. "Quite right."

She laughed. "Don't tell me, Mr. Darjeeling. You don't believe in aliens. I know, I know! Most people don't. But I'm a silly girl with an overactive imagination. And a large library of science fiction films."

"I assure you, you're perfectly safe from aliens here. And if any beasties from deep space should appear, the *Freedom* will beat them back. Ah, but I've been chattering away! We're still flying along the starboard hull, and there are sights to see. Let us continue our tour."

* * * * *

The shuttle glided along the *Freedom*'s starboard hull. Past the stern, they flew alongside the midsection of the ship. Armored sheets of metal soared like cliffs. Rails along the armor could generate magnetic fields, adding an extra layer of protection against enemy ordnance.

Darjeeling spoke as they flew. "The midsection, located between the stern and prow, is sometimes called the Belly of the Beast. It contains three hotels, several spas, world-class casinos, a wax museum, a wave pool, three dance clubs, and even a minigolf course."

Emily cringed. "It's all rather . . . American, isn't it?"

Darjeeling laughed. "The *Freedom* has many Americans in her service. But this is truly an Alliance-wide cooperation. Soldiers from sixteen countries serve aboard the *Freedom*, and tourists visit her from around the free world."

"But not from Red Dawn," Emily said.

Darjeeling shifted uncomfortably. "Not often. We do get some tourists from Red Dawn countries, now that there's peace. But the commander, he . . ." He cleared his throat. "Well, he . . . how should I put this . . . ?"

Hates Red Dawn, Emily thought. *Of course King hates them.*

Katyusha herself slit his throat.

She thought it best to change the subject.

"There are no portholes," she said. "I find that so odd. I've been on cruise starships, and they're lined with portholes so the tourists can see the galaxy."

Darjeeling seemed relieved. He continued prattling on. "Quite an astute observation. You see, while the modern *Freedom* contains many amenities for tourists, she still maintains the facade of a military starship. Those are the original shields on her hull from World War III. Now, as we fly by here, you'll see an actual scar on the hull from the Battle of Mars. We've decided to keep it there. It serves as a reminder of the *Freedom*'s great flight."

Emily saw the scar. It was the size of a city block, denting the mighty hull. She imagined the *Freedom* during that great battle, leading the Alliance fleet to victory. She wondered if her grandfather had been very scared. She wondered if, when the enemy scarred the hull, her grandfather had fallen to the deck, if the fire had washed over him, if he had screamed and prayed.

A shadow fell over the shuttle. Emily leaned toward the viewport and looked upward. A massive cannon thrust out from *Freedom*'s dorsal hull, casting a long shadow. A few other shuttles were flying nearer the cannon. They could have easily flown into the muzzle.

"One of the Angels of Liberty," Darjeeling said. "Great torpedo launchers. Each cannon is as large as Big Ben. Fourteen of them top the *Freedom*. Each one can destroy an enemy frigate with a single blast."

"I never imagined cannons this large," Emily said. "My dear!"

Darjeeling smiled. "Ah, but the Angels of Liberty are small compared to the *Freedom*'s primary weapon. Let's take a look."

He nudged the throttle, and the shuttle flew faster. They glided by the midsection, and now they flew alongside the prow.

The sergeant explained that the prow contained science labs, command stations, and observation facilities. He described it as the brain of the ship. But Emily found it difficult to concentrate. She kept thinking of her grandfather aboard this ship. Back when it had been a real warship, when it had fought in a terrible war that had claimed half a billion souls. A war worse than any war in history. Maybe worse than all previous wars combined.

I pray that the Freedom *never fights another war. That none of us do. I'm so lucky to be born in an era of peace.*

"Mr. Darjeeling," she said. "Did . . . did you fight in the Great War?"

The sergeant major lost his smile. He looked at her. He nodded solemnly. "Indeed I did, ma'am. Indeed I did. I was just a young corporal then. Just a scared boy from Whitechapel, the son of a factory worker. He commanded me in battle. James King. He's the finest officer I've known. And indeed the finest man." He cleared his throat. "Aside from our true king, of course. Meaning King Robert, your grandfather. Forgive me, ma'am."

She laughed. "There's nothing to forgive. You too are quite a fine man, Mr. Darjeeling. I've not known you for long, but I can tell."

He beamed. "You honor me, my princess. Your kind words are a gift I'll never forget."

Emily was about to say more when the shuttle flew beyond the prow. She gasped.

There it was.

There—the famous twin rails!

"The Fist of Freedom," she whispered. "I've read about it."

For a moment she and Darjeeling stared in silent awe.

The Fist of Freedom. The starship's fabled weapon.

"It's a railgun," Emily said. "It uses electromagnetic energy to propel projectiles at hypersonic speed. Those two rods thrusting outward? The projectile travels between them like a train between two tracks. Am I right?"

"Quite right, ma'am. The Fist of Freedom has only been fired a handful of times and not once since the war. The Fist takes a full day to charge, but when it does fire, it can obliterate any enemy, even the largest dreadnought. Did you know each of those rails is five hundred meters long? They're taller than the old Twin Towers in New York City, the ones from the old still photographs. These prongs are the two fingers in the Fist of Freedom." He held up two fingers. "Between them, they can launch projectiles powerful enough to destroy worlds."

Emily grinned. "Did you know, Mr. Darjeeling, that during the Hundred Year War, English soldiers would hold up two fingers to taunt our French enemies? A sort of reverse V-sign. The gesture symbolized the two fingers an archer used when drawing a longbow, the weapon which was devastating the French lines. I think that today we can give the gesture a new meaning. Two fingers for the fabled Fist of Freedom!"

"A proper lady should not hold up two fingers!" Niles interjected.

"Oh shush, drone," she snapped. "My grandfather served aboard this starship when it was actually firing that railgun. Surely I can hold up two fingers. And if you don't be quiet, Niles, I'm going to stick these two fingers up your sockets."

Niles gasped. "Well, I never!" The drone flew to the back of the shuttle, huffing and muttering to himself.

* * * * *

"We're about to enter the starship *Freedom*, ma'am," Darjeeling said. "Once aboard, you'll be treated to a grand tour of the interior, culminating with a fabulous Christmas dinner.

Commander King will be hosting. But first I would like to show you one more thing."

He shoved down the throttle. The shuttle jolted forward, flying at incredible speed.

"Slow down, you ruffian!" Niles cried from the back.

But Emily only laughed. This was fun. The only thing missing was the wind in her hair.

The shuttle flew under the *Freedom*'s belly, then rose again by the port hull. Darjeeling took them a little farther out into space, then spun back toward the *Freedom*. They now faced the side of the starship. From here, Emily got a view of the entire length of the beast, stem to stern.

Darjeeling checked his watch.

"Just about . . . now."

Just then, the Angels of Liberty sang.

The great cannons of *Freedom* fired!

But they did not fire torpedoes like in the war. Fireworks flew from their muzzles instead, streaking forward and then exploding in space. A dazzling show of lights illuminated the starship and shuttle. It was so bright they could probably see it from Earth.

"They're shooting fireworks!" Emily breathed. "How lovely."

"Aye, ma'am," Darjeeling said softly, the fireworks painting his face. "May they shoot fireworks every Christmas, and may these guns never fire torpedoes in battle again."

It was a nice sentiment. Emily wondered if the famous James "Bulldog" King, commander of the *Freedom*, felt the same way. They said the old officer was a real war dog. That he resented turning the *Freedom* into a museum. That he was miserable commanding a tourist attraction. That war was in his bones. The tabloids painted him as a grumpy, quarrelsome character, a bulldog chained to his doghouse, barking and snapping his teeth at the world.

Well, and the same tabloids portrayed Emily as a pampered brat who cared more about her nail polish than the concerns of her planet. Surprising nobody, tabloids lied. She quite looked forward to meeting this Commander King.

After a few dazzling fireworks, the cannons darkened. For a moment nothing happened.

Then all the Angels sang together. A great finale rack of fireworks flew into space.

This was no normal fireworks display, no random explosions of color and light. This was something special. These fireworks were blue, red, and white, forming a crackling, shining Union Jack the size of Hyde Park.

Emily gazed in wonder. She wanted to say something sophisticated. She could only manage, "Wow."

"They prepared these fireworks for you, ma'am."

She covered her mouth. "I'm just a girl. I'm nothing special."

"You are a princess. You are *my* princess. We're proud to host you aboard the *Freedom* this special Christmas. Look, ma'am. Look back toward the *Freedom*. There they come! The mighty Eagles."

Airlocks opened near the *Freedom*'s underbelly. Starfighters emerged.

Emily leaned forward, gasping with delight.

"Eagle starfighters! Like my grandfather flew in the war."

A dozen flew out, painted red and blue and lined with lights. They were long, slender vessels, as graceful as true eagles. Their wings were folded inward now, but Emily knew that they could extend those wings for atmospheric flight. Their exhaust ports shone, leaving luminous trails through space.

The Eagles flew closer to the shuttle, then branched out, drawing arcs of light ahead of Emily. She grinned, the light dazzling her.

The starfighters flew closer again, then whipped around in spirals, painting helices of light. They performed for her like male birds seeking to impress a female. They charged toward one another, then yawed, barely avoiding crashes as Emily gasped and clutched the armrests. Some flew upside down, one over the other, cockpits almost touching. They performed barrel rolls, flips, swoops, and dives. One even drew her name in space with its glowing trail.

As Emily watched the show, she clapped. Other shuttles hovered nearby, full of delighted tourists. Cameras flashed. More cameras flashed from the *Freedom* herself; there was an observation lounge near the top, and a crowd must be watching from there.

But Emily knew this show was for her.

"I don't deserve this," she said softly when the show ended. "I'm not some heroic warrior. I'm not my grandfather. I never fought in any great battles."

"That's a good thing," said Darjeeling, voice soft and kind. "The age of wars is over. Do not lament its end. It's a far, far better world that celebrates fireworks over bombs, that adores princesses over warriors. We fought for freedom in the war. Now let us enjoy our freedom."

She kissed his cheek. "Thank you, dear Mr. Darjeeling."

He blushed, removed his cap, and saluted her.

Still a little flustered, he flew the shuttle toward the *Freedom*, a hatch opened to welcome them, and Emily's life changed forever.

CHAPTER SEVEN

Fort Liberty Marine Base
Headquarters of the Freedom Brigade
Nebraska
10:07 Christmas 2199

It was sad to wake up alone at Christmas.

Captain Bastian King was a typical marine. He woke up every morning at the crack of dawn, ready to face the day. Most days, that meant hitting the gym. On Christmas, it meant opening presents with his family.

But not this Christmas.

This Christmas his family wasn't with him. This Christmas he was a divorced man. This Christmas he woke up on a military base, alone.

It sucked.

He wanted to stay in bed till noon.

His MindLink buzzed in his skull. Somebody was trying to call him telepathically. Probably what woke him up. Screw that. It was Christmas. They could get lost. With a thought, he shut off the microchip. The ringing faded from his mind.

Bastian tried to fall back asleep but could not. Finally his bladder, full and aching, got Bastian to his feet.

He glanced at his watch. Jesus, was it really past ten?

He trudged across the room, wincing. The floor was too damn cold. Nobody else was around. His fellow marines had all gone home for Christmas. They were probably opening presents with their families now.

But my family kicked me out, Bastian thought with a grimace.

He shuffled out the room, down the hallway, and into the communal washroom. He splashed some water on his face, shook his head like a wet dog, and stared at his reflection.

He was a big, beefy man, built like a tank. Tribal tattoos covered his muscular arms. A mohawk ran across his head, a strip of bristly black hair, and a chinstrap beard hugged his jawline. Bastian took out his trimmers, began shaving the sides of his head. He did this every morning, keeping the unusual hairstyle neat and groomed.

His wife said he looked like a meathead. Like a big dumb brute. He supposed he did. He supposed he was. But at least he had great hair.

Well, ex-wife now. Bastian was still getting used to thinking of Stacy as his ex.

Music sounded from down the hall. His minicom, a computer the size of a playing card, was back in his bunk. It was blasting "The Eagles' Last Flight" by Powertron, his favorite band. The bombastic song, full of electric guitars and pounding drums, indicated that a fellow soldier was calling. When his family called, the minicom played "The Dunes of Mars," a soothing ballad.

Bastian ignored the music. It was probably the same person who had buzzed his MindLink. Persistent bastard. Whoever the hell it was, they could get lost. It was Christmas. Yes, he was stuck here at Fort Liberty, a marine base in the middle of Nowhere, Nebraska. So what? It was still his day off.

He rubbed the sleep from his eyes, stared again at his reflection.

"Cheer up, buddy," Bastian told himself. "This afternoon, you get to pick up Rowan. The judge herself said you can. Christmas morning might suck. But Christmas afternoon—that's daddy and daughter time."

That brought a smile to his lips. Whatever life threw at him, Rowan was still his daughter. She still loved him. Maybe Bastian couldn't open presents with her this morning, but they could still spend the afternoon together. That was a ray of light in a dark year.

He checked his watch again. Three more hours. Then he could drive home and pick up Rowan.

Well, not my home anymore, he reminded himself. *I built the damn house. And I can't even step inside.*

He heaved a sigh, buttoned up his fatigues, and wandered down the corridors of Fort Liberty. The base normally bustled with activity. Marines marched, drilled, and chanted in the courtyard. Soldiers rushed up and down the hallways. Voices came from every room. Well, not today. Almost everyone was home with eggnog. Only a skeleton crew remained, a few unlucky souls chosen to hold down the fort during the holiday. The base was eerily silent. Bastian wasn't used to hearing his footsteps echo in these corridors.

A private wandered down the hall, looking utterly miserable. The poor kid had pulled Christmas duty. Bad luck. When he saw Bastian, a captain, the boy stood at attention and saluted.

"Merry Christmas, sir!" the private said.

Bastian returned a lazy salute, mumbled something that sounded like "Mury 'mas."

He walked on by. He just couldn't wake up fully this morning. Okay, he was also a little hungover. Okay, very hungover. Not professional for a marine officer, he knew. But dammit, last night had been rough. His first Christmas Eve without family around. So he had hit the bottle. Hit it hard. He was paying for that now.

Fort Liberty, Nebraska. Headquarters of the Freedom Brigade. Normally, five thousand soldiers served here. Bastian, a captain with over a decade of experience, commanded two hundred of them.

Over a decade of experience. Bastian liked that. It sure sounded better than *stuck in a rut for thirteen years.*

The Freedom Brigade had a proud history. Posters hung on the base walls, displaying its past glory. During World War III, the Freedom Brigade had flown aboard the starship *Freedom*, serving as the dreadnought's marine force. From the *Freedom*, they had deployed to the mines of Titan, the methane jungles of Europa, and the deserts of Mars. It was on Mars that they finally beat back the Red Dawn and won the war.

Well, that was ages ago. Bastian hadn't even been born. The starship *Freedom* was now a museum. The bunks aboard the dreadnought, where the space marines used to live, now served as a hotel. Tourists bunked in the homes of heroes. And the modern-day Freedom Brigade was stuck on Earth.

So much for heroics in space.

None of today's Freedom Brigade marines had seen combat. Few of them had even been to space. Hell, half of them had never left Nebraska. They spent their time stuck here, training for God knows what. After countless generations of bloodshed, culminating in the worst war in history, humanity had finally achieved world peace. That was great. That was a miracle. It was also incredibly boring.

Bastian paused by a poster on the wall. It depicted the great Battle of Mars. Marines were racing across the red surface, firing their guns. Starfighters streaked above. More troops kept deploying in shuttles. Far above flew the starship *Freedom*, wreathed in light, delivering salvation. It was the most famous photograph from the war.

My dad is flying one of those starfighters, he thought. *The famous James "Bulldog" King, the greatest war hero of them all.*

Bastian turned away.

Sorry, Dad, for being such a disappointment.

Those glory days were long gone. Times were good. And maybe that made men soft. Sometimes Bastian wished he could fight a great war too, could become a hero, could be something more than who he was.

A fat, depressed meathead who can't afford child support. Some hero I am. He glanced back at the poster and snorted. *But at least I don't run a tourist trap, Dad.*

Bastian rubbed his temples. His head was still pounding. He wandered into the executive lounge, looking for a strong cup of coffee.

"Dude!" Alice leaped from her seat. "I've been calling you all morning. You turned off your MindLink. And you're not answering your minicom either." She ran toward him. "I need to—"

"Shh." He put a finger on her lips. "No talking yet. First coffee."

"But—" Alice began.

"Coffee. First."

He shuffled by her. Alice grumbled, hands on her hips.

It was probably a mistake to antagonize her. Master Sergeant Alice Allenby was *not* somebody you wanted to piss off. Especially not on Christmas morning.

Nicknamed "the Viking," Alice stood over six feet tall, even taller in her military boots, and boasted impressive muscles. Her hair hung in two blond braids, and her eyes were blue fire. She had grown up on a Nebraska farm, chopping wood and lifting bales of hay. In high school, she became captain of the wrestling team. When she wasn't stuck on the base, she still wrestled competitively. Which she frequently reminded people of.

"You know, I went to the Olympics last year," she said. There she went again. "If you're not careful, Bastian, I'll kick your ass."

He waved her aside. "You finished twelfth place. I'm not

scared of you." He reached for the coffeepot, found it empty. Dammit. He began to rummage for coffee beans. "And you know, Allenby, it wouldn't hurt you to call me *sir* every now and then. I *am* your commanding officer."

Alice snorted, hands still planted on her hips. "Oh please. I've known you since I was two years old, back when you would pull me along in your wagon."

"Yeah, well, you weighed a ton back then too. My arms still hurt." He lifted a bag of ground coffee. "What the hell is this crap?" He sniffed. "French vanilla? Where's Sergeant Aydemir? I told that idiot to buy Columbian beans."

Alice stomped closer to him, grabbed his arm. "Listen to me, meathead. I've been looking for your dumb, hungover ass. My grandfather called this morning. He's in trouble. I need to leave the base and check on him, so sign my damn exit card, *sir*." She draped that last word with a good dose of mockery.

Bastian watched the coffee brew. He tried to ignore the vanilla smell. It contained caffeine, and that was what mattered now. His stomach gave a sickening churn. His head was still throbbing.

"Alice, you know your grandfather." He rubbed his temples. "He calls every day about something. Bigfoot trampling over his rhubarb. Aliens molesting his chickens. Vampires sucking blood from his cows. What now? Did the Loch Ness monster pop out of his bathtub?" Bastian rinsed a chipped mug. "Or was it a ghost in his underwear drawer?"

Alice bit her lip. "He said a giant spider kidnapped my grandmother and trampled over their cornfield."

Bastian sighed. "Giant spiders. That's a new one." He finally filled his cup and took a sip. The hot brew burned down his throat. He barely noticed the vanilla. "Your grandpa is crazy, Alice. Tell him to call the police and leave us alone."

"The police told him to stop calling them."

Bastian gave a sarcastic grin, holding up his cup of coffee. "Gee, I wonder why." He sipped. Ah, blessed caffeine.

"I better go check up on them," Alice said. "I just need you to approve it. Don't make me go AWOL, Bas."

Bastian rolled his eyes. "Alice, you're stuck here for Christmas with the rest of us losers. You lost the draw fair and square. So suck it up. I assure you, a giant scorpion did not drag your grandmother away."

"Giant spider," Alice said. "My grandfather was quite specific."

"Your grandfather is quite senile. He needs to be in a nursing home."

Alice frowned. "He's a proud Allenby. We Allenbys do not belong in nursing homes."

"You're right. You Allenbys belong in loony bins."

"*Sir.* Can I go check on him? I promise to be back by lunch." She looked around the lounge. "It's not like anything else is happening around here today. Or ever." She muttered those last two words under her breath.

Bastian checked his watch yet again. Stacy, his ex-wife, still had their daughter for three more hours. Ah, hell. Bastian had time to kill. And maybe some fresh air would clear out this hangover.

"Fine," he said. "But I'm going with you. We'll take the buffalo. I'm driving, and we're listening to *my* music."

* * * * *

Bastian left the lounge with Alice. With two cups of coffee in him, he felt a little more like a human, a little less like a zombie. Soon Rowan would be here. He had a present waiting for her.

Maybe she would even bring him a card.

She was the light of his life.

His marriage had collapsed. His military career, if you could call it that, had slammed into a wall. His father was the commander of a starship, and his uncles had all been legendary fighter pilots. And him, Bastian King? Well, he had the famous surname. But he was nothing but a meathead. A grunt. Too dumb to fly. Stuck on Earth. The black sheep of a famous family.

Yes, he was feeling sorry for himself this morning. He blamed the booze from last night.

But he had Rowan. His little girl still loved him. She was five years old and the only good thing in Bastian's mess of a life.

He couldn't wait. He needed a dose of Rowan now.

As he walked down the corridor, he activated his MindLink implant with a single thought.

MindPlay, the implant's operating system, hovered before him in the hallway. Glowing buttons, scroll bars, and drop-down menus floated in the air like holograms. If anyone else walked by, they would see none of it. It was all in his mind. The implant sat inside his skull, plugged into his brain tissue. Slender cables connected directly to his visual cortex. He was hallucinating the interface. The neural implant simply controlled the hallucination.

As he walked, Bastian raised his hand, scrolled through a few options, and pulled up an old video of Rowan.

In a sense, it was a memory. A memory experienced with his own senses, recorded by the MindLink, and stored inside the microchip. Memories stored on MindLinks were always so much crisper, more detailed than "wet memories," which were what people called memories stored in the ancestral brain.

Walking down the hallway, Bastian no longer saw the white tiles and concrete walls. He was watching Rowan racing through a cornfield maze, giggling as she tried to find her way out. Bastian could even smell the crisp air.

"Daddy, Daddy, I'm lost!" Rowan ran toward him, grinning. "This maze is too big."

"I guess we'll have to stay here forever," he said in his memory. And the present Bastian, walking in the base, mouthed the words silently. He had replayed this memory many times.

"Dude, careful!" A strong hand grabbed his arm. "You almost walked into the wall."

Bastian blinked and minimized the memory. The hallucination shrank into a little floating sphere like a soap bubble. He was back in the base. Alice gripped him, glaring. Indeed, he had almost walked right into a wall near the commissary.

"Oops," he said.

"Are you hungover? Or were you watching MindLink videos again?"

"Both," he confessed.

Alice sighed. "You were watching those catgirl cartoons again, weren't you?"

"It's called anime, and no." He felt his cheeks flush. "And how do you know about that?"

"I know everything. Come on, here's the exit door." Alice gestured. "Try not to trip."

Before Bastian could step outside the base, his minicom rang. Somebody was calling. He pulled the device from his pocket. The caller ID appeared on the small screen.

James "Bulldog" King, commander of the starship *Freedom*. Bastian's father.

"Crap," Bastian said.

* * * * *

He stepped into a utility room, leaving Alice in the hallway.

He wanted some privacy.

He had not spoken to his father in over a year. What did the old man want?

Bastian wanted to hang up. To ignore the bastard. His fists clenched.

Maybe it was the hangover weakening his resolve. Maybe it was the Christmas spirit. Maybe it was the divorce still messing up his mind. For reasons he could not understand, Bastian said to hell with it, and he took the call.

He held his minicom to his ear.

For a moment—silence.

Finally James King's voice emerged from the minicom's speaker.

"Hello, son."

With his wounded throat, King's voice was sandpaper and gravel and creaky old leather. Ironic. The old man *could* be calling over the MindWeb, communicating with Bastian telepathically. No need for speaking. Both men had the neural implants installed. All soldiers did. Telepathy was easy, fast, safe.

But King hated it. A few years ago, he had reluctantly undergone the implant surgery. It was an Alliance requirement. But he avoided using his MindLink whenever possible. To the old man, telepathy was akin to witchcraft—mysterious and unholy. So he had called Bastian on a goddamn *phone*, ruined throat and all.

"What do you want, *sir*?" Bastian said. "Aren't you busy overseeing your museum?"

Yes, King was calling from the starship *Freedom*. Bastian was sure of that. The old man never visited Earth. Not even for Christmas. Not even for birthdays. Bastian remembered that quite well.

"Son," the commander rasped. Then paused.

Bastian waited. He wanted to hang up.

Finally King continued speaking. "I called to say Merry

Christmas."

"You said it. Goodbye."

"Wait." His father coughed. "Bastian, I know we haven't talked in a while. I know you're still angry. But we don't have to—"

"I'm not angry, Dad. All right?" Bastian made a fist, facing the wall. "You called, we talked for Christmas, you're off the hook for another year. Happy?"

"No, I'm not happy!" King snapped. "I'm trying to fix this, dammit."

"Fix what?"

"You know what!" King roared. "The fact that my son won't talk to me. That my granddaughter barely knows me."

Bastian laughed. A cold, mirthless sound. "I get it. When I was a kid and you were the famous starship captain, you ignored us. Your family didn't matter. Suddenly you turn sixty, you realize you're an old man, you're lonely on Christmas, and you want to make amends. Well, Dad, it's too late."

King was silent for a moment, just breathing raggedly. "I deserve that," he finally said. "But dammit, Bastian, our family is falling apart. Stacy and you got the divorce. And with what happened to your mother—"

"Don't you talk about Mom!" Bastian said. No—shouted. He was trembling now.

The memories flooded him.

His mother—packing her suitcase, leaving home.

Gone for weeks.

Bastian, only eighteen years old, flying to Prague. Entering that little hotel room. Seeing the blood. The bodies.

He closed his eyes, his throat locking up. He was thirty-three now, a captain in the Alliance Marine Force. But often he still felt like that boy, that scared teenager making that horrible discovery.

For another moment, King was silent. Then the commander spoke in a soft, grainy voice. "I just want to fix things, Bas. Come to the *Freedom* for Christmas. Bring Rowan, if Stacy lets you. We'll have a nice dinner. We'll be a family."

Bastian placed his fist on the wall. He wanted to punch through the concrete. "You don't want me on the *Freedom*, Dad. I'm just a grunt, remember? A dumb marine. I flunked out of your fancy flight school."

"You know I don't care about that. I'm proud of you, son. No matter what your career is."

Bastian snorted. "Bullshit. You were a fighter pilot. Your dad was too. And his dad. I'm sorry to be such a disappointment."

"Stop sulking like a little kid!" King said, anger filling that grainy voice. "You are an officer of the Alliance Defense Force. Act like it!"

Bastian laughed. "That's all you care about, isn't it? Your precious Alliance Defense Force. That's why you drove Mom away. That's why—"

"Bastian, stop it."

"That's why she left! That's why she ran to Prague, and why . . ." Bastian couldn't say any more. The words caught in his throat.

For a moment neither man spoke.

Finally King growled, "Merry Christmas."

The commander hung up.

Bastian remained standing there, facing the concrete wall. Words appeared on his minicom.

CALL TERMINATED

"No kidding," Bastian muttered.

He returned to the hallway. Alice was waiting. She looked at him with soft eyes.

"You okay, boss?"

"Fine," Bastian said. His throat felt tight. He could barely speak. Maybe that was how his father felt all the time.

Alice put a hand on his arm. "You wanna talk?"

"I said I'm fine." He marched toward the exit. "Come on, Alice, move your ass. Let's go check on your grandfather. We'll kill that giant spider for him."

CHAPTER EIGHT

The Starship *Freedom*
High Earth Orbit
10:40 Christmas 2199

The words echoed in King's cabin.

"Merry Christmas."

Harsh words. Bitter words. King still clutched the phone, though he had already hung up on his son.

It took a long moment for King to relax his hand, to release the phone. He took a deep breath.

It hurt. It hurt so goddamn bad.

King had fought wars. He had charged into enemy lines. He had held dying soldiers, and he had lost his wife. But this pain, in many ways, was worse.

I'm leaving the Freedom, he thought. *All I had left were my son and granddaughter. And I've lost them too.*

King knew that Bastian still blamed him. And maybe he was right to.

"Maybe it *was* my fault," he said to himself. "Maybe I drove Diane away. Maybe I drove my wife into the arms of a killer. Maybe—"

He began to cough. He was talking too much today, straining his broken throat. Dammit, he needed another drink. He reached into his cupboard, pulled out the bottle of Martian ale, and drank deeply. Right from the bottle. It burned his throat, but he didn't care. Physical pain was good. It drowned the emotional pain. King would gladly suffer the pain of ten thousand bullets to forget the pain in his heart.

He put down the bottle.

He stared into a mirror.

"Look at yourself," he growled at his reflection. "You've gone soft in old age. Whining about problems at home. Pitying yourself. Drowning your sorrows in a bottle. It's pathetic. Stop it! You are a soldier."

He straightened. He raised his chin. He stared at his reflection with hard, dark eyes. Yes, there he was again. The soldier. The tough guy. The commander who felt no pain, who could fix everything. Who could win world wars.

That's all he knew how to be. The other James King, the man outside the uniform, the man with vulnerabilities and fears, well . . . he didn't know how to be that man.

He would have to learn. He had the rest of his life to figure it out.

Hopefully Rowan would be part of that life.

Maybe he had lost his son. But goddammit, King would not give up his granddaughter. There was at least one little girl in the world who loved him. And that mattered. She mattered. Right now Rowan mattered more than anything in this universe.

He returned to his desk, a heavy piece of furniture carved from real oak. Yes, it was his last day, but he had work to do. In a few hours, he would be hosting the annual Christmas dinner. Until then, he had paperwork to catch up on.

Literal paperwork.

As promised, Mimori had prepared a report on the Rubicon, printed it, and placed it on his desk in a neat binder. People thought him crazy to still read on paper—like some old sea captain from a bygone era. But paper books filled the shelves in his cabin, and paper reports covered his scarred oak desk. In the age of telepathy, he relished the physical feel of the world.

And it wasn't just that. Something about paper reminded him of home. His father had collected paper books.

King leaned back in his seat. The leather creaked. He placed on his reading glasses, another anachronism in this era of bionic eyes, and began leafing through Mimori's report.

He leaned forward. A frown creased his brow.

"What the hell?"

He flipped a page, and his frown deepened. A chill flooded his belly.

He reached for his comlink. He held the device to his mouth.

"Mimori, report to my office please."

She answered at once. "Be right there, sir."

They could, of course, have an entire telepathic conversation over the MindWeb. King could hallucinate the android right in front of him. No need for her to walk over. King snorted. Let the kids use that tech. He preferred to speak to his crew face-to-face. Hell, if they were all going to live in a virtual world, why even build an android in the first place?

A moment later, a knock sounded on his door.

"Enter," King said.

Mimori stepped into the office, snapped her heels together, and saluted. The android was wearing her parade whites, a finer uniform than what the crew normally wore aboard the *Freedom*. Her outfit included white gloves, a black bow tie, and a golden aiguillette. King himself still wore the simpler service uniform of the Alliance Fleet, the fabric blue, the buttons brass rather than gold.

King glanced at the pin on the android's lapel. It marked her as *Mimori Unit 1*. There were seven Mimori androids aboard the *Freedom*, serving different parts of the ship. Three androids worked here in the prow. Two supported the midsection, and two more worked the great engine rooms in the stern.

Each Mimori was ostensibly the same. They certainly all looked the same—sweet young women with Japanese features. But over time, King had noticed differences in their personalities. The three prow Mimoris were prim and professional; they were used to dealing with senior officers. The midsection Mimoris tended to smile shyly, to lower their eyes, even giggle; they were used to handling tourists. Meanwhile, the stern Mimoris loved to complain, crack sarcastic jokes, even curse. It came from so many years in the greasy engine rooms, no doubt.

Each Mimori connected wirelessly to the starship *Freedom*'s central computer system. When King spoke to this Mimori unit before him, he was conversing with his starship. Mimori was simply a friendly interface. At least that's what the engineers said. But over his years here, King had seen each Mimori develop as an individual. Perhaps they were the *Freedom*'s multiple personalities.

"Can you explain this report?" King said. "In plain English. If I'm reading these numbers right, a catastrophic explosion struck Rubicon station yesterday."

Mimori nodded. "Yes, sir, that was my conclusion as well. ATLAS has picked up traces of the blast. But it's more than that, sir. ATLAS also detected too much gravity at Rubicon. The graviton count around the space station skyrocketed. As if thousands of asteroids were flying there. Asteroids the size of towns."

King stared at the numbers on his report, then into Mimori's eyes.

"Could asteroids have destroyed the Rubicon? We should have seen a cloud of asteroids approaching from a mile away."

Mimori frowned. "A mile, sir? ATLAS sensors can detect asteroids several trillion kilometers away, with the observable distance depending on the asteroid's mass and surface reflectance."

"A figure of speech," King said. "So something big is at the

Rubicon, maybe an asteroid cloud, and it's generating gravity. Why didn't we spot it coming?"

Mimori never lost her composure. "I don't know, sir. Whatever we're detecting at the Rubicon, well . . . it simply appeared. Overnight. Blinked into existence. I admit, sir, the numbers don't make sense."

King rose to his feet. He paced the cabin. "Well, we certainly have a mystery on our hands. A space station seems to disappear. And strange unidentified objects, big and heavy, appear at the same time. What about incoming transmissions from the Rubicon? Are they still radio silent?"

Mimori smiled sweetly. "Sir, may I direct your attention to the last chapter in my report?"

In other words: *Read the damn manual, asshole.*

"I'm sorry, Mimori." He opened the binder again. "I called you before I finished reading your report."

"You tend to do that, sir."

"Hey!" He pointed at her, glaring over his reading glasses. "Watch the attitude."

Her smile widened. "It's all right. I'm flattered. It means you miss me."

So much for the prow Mimori units being prim and proper. This one could have come up right from the engine room. Sassy little machine.

Yes, I do miss you when you're away, he thought. *And I'm going to miss you on Earth.*

Mimori didn't yet know that he was retiring. He hadn't told many people yet—just Jordan, who was like a brother, and Spitfire, who was like a daughter.

But Mimori . . . Mimori was somebody special. She was his closest confidant. His hope in the dark. She was the *Freedom* herself, a goddess of the stars. Android and starship were one woman, and she was the great love of King's life. He didn't know how to say goodbye to her.

It's no wonder I drove Diane away, he thought with a sudden pang of guilt.

Well, enough sappiness. He was still a soldier. He still had a job to do. Starting tomorrow, he could spend the rest of his life relaxing on the farm, waxing poetic about grand ladies of the stars and lost loves.

He flipped to the last few pages in Mimori's report. He stared at the words, scarcely believing.

"A dark blot in space." He looked up over his glasses. "That's what it says in your report. What do you mean by a dark blot in space, Mimori?"

"Just what I wrote, sir. A dark blot in space."

"I read that," he growled. "Elaborate."

"Space isn't nearly as empty as people think. Human eyes can't see everything that's out there, but I can. First of all, space is *full* of radiation. It's mostly just random chatter. Distant pulsar stars, nebulae, supernovae, and so on—they all release a lot of electromagnetic noise. And the cosmos, of course, is still awash with radiation from the Big Bang. Then there's solar wind, solar dust, neutrino showers, Higgs boson particles, magnetic fields, cosmic rays—"

"I get the idea," King said. "Space looks like a Pollock painting. Get to the point."

Mimori nodded. "Sorry, sir. Anyway, when I aimed the ATLAS sensors at the Rubicon a second time, an hour after the first event, well . . . I detected nothing."

King placed his hands on the desk and leaned toward her. "What about the first chapters in your report? All about the gravitational fields and explosions and general mayhem at Rubicon?"

"That's the thing, sir. It all suddenly vanished. One hour ATLAS saw chaos. The next? Nothing. Not even cosmic radiation. Space appeared *empty*. It's as if somebody took a giant eraser to space and simply wiped away the Rubicon."

"Or somebody is jamming their signal," King said.

Mimori nodded. "That seems to be the more likely explanation. Somebody might be intentionally blinding us."

The temperature in the cabin seemed to drop ten degrees. King struggled not to shiver.

"What the hell is going on here?" he rasped. "I don't need this on my last day."

Mimori tilted her head. "Your last day, sir?"

King cursed himself for his slip. "Ah, hell. I wasn't going to tell you until dinner."

The android frowned. "Tell me what, sir?" She took a step closer to him. "Are you all right? Are you . . .?" She gasped. "Are you ill?"

He groaned and rolled his eyes. "For chrissake, Mimori, I'm not dying, if that's what you mean. I'm retiring!"

Mimori froze. She stared at him. Then she whipped around the desk, grabbed King, and pulled him into an embrace.

"Sir, you can't!"

He stood stiffly for a moment, then embraced her too. "It's time, Mimori. Beyond time."

She looked at him. Her eyes sparkled with actual tears. Yes, she was an android. But the starship *Freedom* had real artificial intelligence. True emotions. The ship felt pain. And Mimori felt it too. Her makers had given her the ability to feel, to love, even to cry.

"You've been my commander for many years, sir," Mimori said. "But you're more than that to me. You're a friend. My best friend."

"Ah, hell," King said. "Don't make an old man cry on his last day as a soldier."

Mimori grinned. "Oh, I will! Because you have to say

goodbye to the other six Mimoris too. In person. One at a time. One of us will get you! You'll shed tears yet, old man. We know that deep down you're a softie." Then the android shed her own tears and pulled King back into a tight embrace.

"I wish I could take one of you seven with me," he said, holding her.

But of course that was impossible. The Mimori androids had personalities of their own, some individuality. There were computers inside their skulls with some basic artificial intelligence. But the androids were tethered too strongly to the starship *Freedom* herself. To remove a Mimori android from the ship, well . . . that was like removing a whale from the ocean. Over time, trapped in an aquarium, the whale withered and died. The android would too.

Maybe that's what happened to me, King thought. *They took a soldier. They stuck him in a museum. And I've been withering.*

Suddenly he wanted to say to hell with the report, to let somebody else handle it. He would head to the bar and get good and proper drunk. How about that for ringing out a career?

But the binder, lying on the desk, haunted him.

Somebody had erased a blob of space. Somebody was hiding something going on at the Rubicon. That was not normal. King would normally bounce this up the chain of command, but everyone was off for Christmas.

And this felt important. King had never seen anything like this. Not in all his years in space.

"Mimori, I have an idea," he said. "Have you pointed ATLAS at Pluto?"

The android frowned. "No. Should I have, sir?"

"Indeed you should have," King said. "The Alliance maintains several telemetry satellites in orbit around Pluto. They point toward deep space, then relay the data back to Earth. They're purely there for scientific research. The astrophysicists down on Earth use the data."

Mimori's eyes widened. "And Pluto is significantly closer to the Rubicon! One of those satellites might have seen something."

King nodded. "Get ATLAS on it."

"I will right now. Pluto is five light-hours away from us, so I can't get you any real-time data. But if those satellites are regularly transmitting, I can get you a transmission from five hours ago." She winked. "For a human, you're not too dumb."

"For a fancy toaster, you're not too bad yourself."

Mimori got a faraway look. She seemed to be gazing past King. She raised her arms, held out her hands, and closed her eyes. Gently she swayed, pirouetted, and moved her arms. A soft smile touched her lips. She looked like a mad conductor with an invisible orchestra.

Deep inside the starship, motors rumbled. Gears turned. Machinery hummed. The deck vibrated beneath King's feet.

King hesitated for a moment. Then, reluctantly, he turned on his MindLink. What the hell. One last time for the road.

With a thought, he summoned a hallucination of the *Freedom*'s schematics. A translucent diagram of the starship hovered before him. It looked like a hologram, but he was hallucinating it. His implant connected to the ship's computers, pulled the data, and painted the image directly into his brain tissue.

King saw glowing yellow parts moving inside the *Freedom* schematic. Parts of ATLAS were rearranging themselves. The telemetry system spanned several decks in the prow. Sensors extended from the ship's hull. Radio plates turned. Sensor panels unfurled like great sails. *Freedom* was a museum, a retired warship, but also a scientific station. The instruments were decades old. The technology was obsolete. But ATLAS still did its job.

Mimori, controlling the machinery from her trance, was gazing toward Pluto.

For a moment she just listened.

Then she gasped.

The android screamed and grabbed King's arms.

"Mimori!" King said, turning off his MindLink. The hallucination vanished. "What is it?"

Her eyes snapped open. They were pure white; they were rolled so far back the irises were gone. She clung to him, trembling. King knew that androids had emotions, but not that they could feel terror. And there was no misreading Mimori's body language. This was sheer terror.

"I hear it," she whispered, voice trembling. "The signal from the Rubicon. Most of it was erased. Blotted out of space. But some radio waves reached Pluto. The satellites heard. They are afraid too. They can feel fear."

King gripped her arms. He shook her. "Mimori! Look at me. Look at me, dammit."

Her eyes rolled back down. She stared at him, face pale.

"Sir, I'm scared."

"What was in the signal?" he demanded.

"A voice. A human voice. Only a few seconds. But sir . . . it's so horrible."

King grunted. "Play me the audio. I can handle it."

She nodded, and her eyes glazed over. Sounds emerged from her mouth. Scrapes. Hisses. Rumbling motors. A clatter like claws across a hard floor.

The background noise of Rubicon station, King realized. *She's producing it from the speaker in her throat. What the hell is that clattering?*

Then Mimori began to speak. But not with her voice. With the voice of a man. The voice of an astronaut on Rubicon station.

"Beverly, I love you. It's me, Mike." The clattering grew louder. It definitely sounded like claws. "Aliens are real, Beverly. Monsters are real. A fleet. An enemy fleet, heading to Earth. Tell the army! Tell them to get ready. I love you. I love—"

Mimori let out a terrible scream.

Then she collapsed.

King had to catch her, to carry her to the armchair by the bookshelves. The android sat there, trembling. Finally she seemed to calm down. She looked at him.

"That's the end of the transmission, sir," she said.

King took a deep, raspy breath. The air burned his throat.

"Who the hell is Beverly?" he said.

"His wife, sir. I think the Rubicon astronaut was trying to call his wife."

"We gotta get the admiral on the line," King said. "This is going up the chain of command—today—and I don't care that it's Christmas."

CHAPTER NINE

Nebraska
11:02 Christmas 2199

The mechanical buffalo raced over the fields of Nebraska. The tall grass whipped its metal hides, and the engine rumbled in its bowels.

Bastian rode the beast. The ride was surprisingly smooth. A real buffalo, he imagined, would bounce up and down and side to side, tossing him around in the saddle. But the robotic buffalo had state-of-the-art stabilizer technology. Its legs regularly adjusted their length, matching the terrain. The beast's back remained steady, offering a luxuriously smooth ride. Its metal hooves kicked up dirt, but riding on its back, the robot almost seemed to be floating.

Bastian loved the machine. Robotic animals were more expensive than hover-trucks, which most folk rode here in Nebraska. But robots were *way* cooler. Bastian had saved up for years to buy this buffalo. At this price, he probably could have bought an actual atmocar, fast enough to break the sound barrier and sturdy enough to skim the stratosphere. But Bastian didn't like flying. Maybe it was still the trauma of flunking flight school. He liked remaining on the ground.

He enjoyed riding his buffalo, feeling the wind in his hair, seeing the fields stream by. Sometimes he would take the buffalo out into the wilderness, and he would just ride for hours, exploring the wild beauty of Nebraska. Despite all the pain he had suffered here, he loved this land. He was part of it, and these golden fields and grasslands anchored his soul. His family had always flown in space, brave warriors of the stars, but not Bastian. He was different. He was a man of Earth.

"Can't you go any faster?" Alice cried, clinging to him from behind.

"This is as fast as a buffalo runs," Bastian shouted over the wind.

Riding behind him, Alice peered over his shoulder at the speed dial, which was embedded into the buffalo's neck.

"Just seventy miles per hour?" she said. "They should have shaped this like a turtle, not a buffalo! It'll take ages to reach my grandfather."

Bastian laughed, the wind streaming over him. "Maybe if you weighed less, the buffalo would run faster."

She reached around him, poked his belly. "You're no Slim Jim yourself, big boy."

"Hey, I'm all muscle."

She snorted. "And I'm the princess of England."

"You're a Viking, not a princess," Bastian said. "We're almost at your farm. Be patient. I'm sure your grandpa is fine."

As a kid, Bastian would sometimes sneak onto the Allenby farm. He'd snatch some apples, scare some chickens, maybe grab an ear of corn. Just a dumb kid getting in some trouble. Even back then, a good twenty years ago, Farmer Allenby had seemed terribly old, his hair white and wild. He would chase little Bastian off the farm, firing his shotgun into the air.

Well, that was then. And now Chester Allenby, who was pushing ninety, was getting his revenge. Every day, the old man called Fort Liberty.

"There are aliens on my farm, I'm telling ya! And the police won't do nothin'."

"Honest to goodness, I saw Bigfoot walking in my field.

Send over the marines!"

"It's alligators in my sewer again. Goddamn alligators in my pipes, I can hear them grunting. I need a marine squad here, stat."

But every time, it was nothing. The aliens turned out to be coyotes. Bigfoot was nothing but a wild boar. The alligator was just a banging pipe. Bastian would normally ignore the kook, but Alice loved the old farmer. So here they rode again.

"A giant spider kidnapping his wife," Bastian muttered to himself. "We'll probably just find a daddy longlegs on his pillow."

But it was okay. The ride was on the way to Bastian's house. Well, what had been his house. Before Stacy got it in the divorce. He'd step on a spider, ride a little farther, and be with his daughter again. A few hours with Rowan, his little angel, would make everything seem right again.

They finally saw the Allenby farm ahead.

It was a small farm, as far as they went. A cornfield. A soy field. A chicken coop and some cows. The farmhouse was a humble home, the roof missing a few tiles, the walls needing a coat of paint. It was a far cry from the King ranch farther west, with its Neo-Colonial manor and sprawling fields.

The Kings came from old money. The family had fallen on hard times, losing its fortune in the war, but they still had their land. Bastian had grown up in that manor. Of course, it legally still belonged to his father. Even though Commander James King had spent the past four decades in space, the ranch was still his. Someday Bastian might inherit it. Or might not. For now, he refused to set foot there.

Not after what happened.

Not after what he saw in that hotel room.

The ranch belonged to Commander King, and Bastian wanted nothing to do with the man. As far as Bastian was concerned, he had no father. Even if that meant he had no home.

He slowed the buffalo down. They rode onto Allenby Farm,

and Bastian took deep breaths, trying to calm the turmoil inside him.

* * * * *

"Thank goodness you're here." Old Man Allenby burst out the front door, wearing overalls and nothing else, even in the cold. He was barefoot, and his white hair stuck out every which way. "It got her! Alice, that darned giant spider got your grandma!"

Bastian stifled a laugh. Ah, same old Chester Allenby. He was senile, and laughing wasn't nice. But Bastian couldn't resist a little chuckle.

Alice glared at him. "Stop laughing at my grandfather."

"You're right." He nodded. "I'm sorry. Let's find the spider that spooked him and step on it."

The two marines walked along the cobbled path. Patches of snow lay scattered across the garden, and icicles hung from the roof. Christmas lights dangled from the crooked eaves, half of them burned out.

Maybe I've been working Alice too hard, Bastian thought. *She lost her parents just last year. And her grandparents are getting too old to maintain this farm.*

He should give her some time off, he knew. Time to clean up the place. But Alice was the best damn soldier in the Badgers Company, which Bastian commanded. Hell, she was probably the best damn soldier in the entire brigade. Bastian had promoted her to master sergeant, making her the senior NCO in his company. She was his right-hand woman, his liaison with the enlisted troops he commanded.

Unfortunately, that meant she didn't get a lot of time off. Now Bastian felt guilty about that. He liked Alice. And he had been working her too damn hard.

Since his divorce a year ago, Bastian had been spending all his time on the base. Weekends. Holidays. Working and training nonstop. That meant Alice was there nonstop too. As his master sergeant, she went where he went. At Fort Liberty, he sought refuge from his broken home life. Was he keeping Alice away from fixing hers?

Now I really feel like shit, Bastian thought, looking at the sorry state of her farm.

He vowed to start treating Alice better. A week or two vacation would give her a chance to fix things around here.

Old Man Allenby grabbed his arm, eyes wild, interrupting Bastian's thoughts.

"You gotta find her, Captain!"

Bastian frowned. "Find who? The spider?"

"My wife! The spider took her, son. Dragged her off into that there forest."

The old man pointed with an arthritic finger. Bastian stared past the farm to the forest. Snow draped the trees.

He sighed. "Mr. Allenby, you see, spiders are very small. Far too small to lift an adult woman."

"Don't talk to me like I'm a child," Allenby snapped. "I babysat you when you were still shitting your diapers. Hell, I babysat your father too. I know what I saw. A giant spider. A spider the size of a goddamn horse. First it ate one of my cows. Then it dragged my dear Hannah into the forest." He sniffed. "She's the love of my life. You gotta find her. Please."

Alice embraced her grandfather. "We'll find Grandma. I promise you."

"Mind if we take a look around the house?" Bastian said.

"I told ya, goddammit, the spider took her into the forest," the old man said.

Alice patted his arm. "I know, Grampa. I know. But we just

want to check the house, okay?"

The old farmer snorted. "Oh, all right. If you must. I see you don't believe me. You think I'm crazy, do ya? Well, come on in!" Sarcasm draped his voice. "Make yourself at home. Have a cup of tea, why don't ya?" He harrumphed. "You'll see I ain't crazy. You'll see the goddamn cobwebs!"

As they approached the front door, Alice leaned toward Bastian.

"He's getting worse," she whispered.

Bastian wondered what they'd find inside. Maybe Hannah Allenby was simply in another room, maybe doing the laundry or lost in a good novel, and Chester got confused. At his age, his mind was going. It was sad. Bastian hoped he never reached ninety. He would prefer to die in glorious battle than fade into senility.

Some chance of that happening, Bastian thought. *The wars are long gone. My primary antagonist as a marine seems to be a house spider.*

When they entered the house, Bastian covered his nose. The place stank. It was also a right mess. The kitchen table and chairs lay overturned. A pot had spilled porridge across the floor. The stuffed moose head had fallen, and two cats hissed atop a pile of fallen books.

"Grampa, what happened here?" Alice said. "Did you fall down again? Did you knock these things over?"

"Mrs. Allenby?" Bastian cried, coning a palm around his mouth. "Are you here, Mrs. Allenby?"

He began searching the house, worried that something had fallen on her.

"Grampa, what happened?" Alice repeated. "Was there an earthquake?"

"A spider!" he said.

Alice gasped. "Did you knock over all this furniture trying to catch a spider?"

"No, goddammit! The spider knocked it over." The old man harrumphed. "Aren't you listening to me, Alice? The spider was the size of a goddamn Clydesdale!" He pointed at Bastian. "Almost as fat as that meathead."

"Hey!" Bastian bristled. "I'm all muscle. Mostly muscle." He glanced down at his belly. "Okay, I put on some weight during the holidays. Sue me."

"Bastian, stop obsessing over your weight for once," Alice said. "Help me look for my grandma."

They moved into the dining room, which was in bad shape too. The cabinets had been yanked off the walls. Shattered plates and cups lay across the floor. A heavy white curtain draped across the entire back wall.

Alice gasped, went very pale, and pointed at the curtain. "Bastian!" She grabbed his arm. "Look."

"I see it. A giant curtain across the wall. Or is that a bedsheet? I—"

Then it clicked.

That was no curtain. No sheet either.

Those were cobwebs.

Cobwebs covering the entire dining room wall.

* * * * *

Bastian stepped outside the farmhouse, squinting in the sunlight.

"Mrs. Allenby!" he shouted.

"Grandma!" Alice cried.

Old Man Allenby hurried out of the house, still barefoot and wearing only overalls. The elderly farmer pointed at the forest.

"The spider took her thataway. Into the old woods. Please. You have to save her."

Bastian glanced at his watch. He was supposed to pick up Rowan soon. He didn't have time for this.

"Alice, I gotta get going," he said.

She looked at him, eyes full of tears. "My grandmother. Won't you help me?"

Bastian grumbled under his breath. "Hold on."

He turned aside, activated his MindLink, and did what he hated to do.

He called his ex-wife.

For a long moment, nothing happened. Finally her MindLink accepted the call.

A hallucination of Stacy appeared before him, standing in the snowy yard. In real life, she was back home, several miles west from here. But her avatar filled his mind, seeming to stand here in the flesh.

"What is it, Bastian?" She was folding a shirt. "I'm busy packing my suitcase. Make it quick."

Only he could hear her voice. He was hallucinating the entire thing. But the illusion was complete, indistinguishable from real life. Aside from the absurdity of a woman folding laundry in a snowy field, that was.

"Merry Christmas to you too, Stacy," he telepathized.

Telepathizing was a strange art. When Bastian had first gotten the MindLink installed, he had struggled to get it right. You had to think up the words, direct them to the right part of your brain, and send them over the MindWeb. Early on, Bastian would get confused, would accidentally transmit private thoughts. He had embarrassed himself quite a few times during those early years. But it got easier. By now, he knew how to keep some thoughts private, how to send others over the neural network. Eventually, they said, it became second nature.

He found that speaking aloud helped. Often, he spoke the same words he was transmitting telepathically. It was unnecessary. Stacy was miles away, could not actually hear his voice. But *speaking* the words helped Bastian distinguish the private from the public. A good trick for dumb meatheads like him.

Stacy groaned. "Bastian! What do you want?"

"I might be a little late picking up Rowan. Just a little! No more than half an hour late."

She tossed down the folded shirt. "Bastian! I have to leave my house in exactly seventy minutes, or I'll miss my flight. I'm heading over to Bemidji for the weekend. If you don't show up here in seventy minutes to pick up your daughter, I'm taking her with me."

"Stacy!" he whispered between clenched teeth. "I get Rowan for half of Christmas. You heard the judge."

"Only if you pick her up on time."

"Why the hell are you going to Bemidji anyway? That's all the way in Canada."

"It's in Minnesota, dumbass. Hunter has family there. Not that it's any of your business."

Ah yes. Hunter. Her new boyfriend. The organic food salesman. Bastian had never met the guy, only heard stories of how sensitive, kind, and handsome he was, and how his health food store was booming. The local farmers raised good food here on the farms of Nebraska—wheat and beef and corn, honest American fare. But apparently Hunter's customers preferred avocados, sprouts, and seeds from overseas. All organic and free-trade, apparently. Whatever that meant. To Bastian, it all looked like animal feed. He wanted to smash Hunter in the face with a bag of quinoa.

"I'll be there," Bastian growled and hung up. He turned toward Alice. "We gotta hurry."

Alice was kneeling, examining the snowy ground. "I see

some tracks. Look. See that? Those are footsteps. Strange footsteps. Holes." She shuddered. "Giant spider feet."

Bastian looked. He saw them. Holes the size of apples in the snow. What kind of animal could leave such tracks? Maybe it was a mechanical beast? A robot spider, similar in construction to the buffalo? But that didn't explain the cobwebs. Why would a robot, even a spider-shaped one, spit out cobwebs?

He didn't have time for this.

"Bemidji," he muttered. "Goddamn Bemidji with Hunter and his avocados."

Alice didn't hear him. She was already racing toward the forest. "Bastian, come on!"

Reluctantly, he followed, cursing every minute that passed.

* * * * *

They lost the trail five minutes later.

Following the tracks through the garden was easy enough. But once they reached the forest, they encountered hard, icy ground strewn with stones. Fresh snow was falling, hindering their efforts. At one point, Bastian thought he found more footprints, but Alice pointed out that those were hoof prints. Just a deer.

"I don't have time for this," he muttered, checking his watch.

Alice looked at him, biting her lip. She was a big, powerful woman, almost as big as him, but tears rolled down her cheeks, and her bottom lip quivered. Despite her size, she looked so vulnerable standing there in the snow.

"You can't help me?" she whispered, breath frosting.

Bastian pursed his lips. "No. But I know who can. Come

on, back to the buffalo. I have a friend who can help. And let's *hurry*."

Two minutes later, they were back on the mechanical buffalo, galloping across the plains. Bastian knew that every minute counted. Not just because Stacy was going to take their daughter to goddamn Bemidji. If Alice's grandmother was out there in the snow, she was in danger. With all the stress today—about his daughter, his father, and Hunter the Quinoa King—Bastian had nearly forgotten what truly mattered here. There was a woman in danger. Alice's grandmother. No, Bastian could not abandon the old lady.

He shoved the throttle down to the metal. The robotic buffalo gained speed, legs kicking up snow and chunks of ice. They didn't need to take any roads. The buffalo roared over the wilderness at breakneck speed.

Even so, the journey seemed agonizingly long. Every minute lasted an eternity.

Finally Bastian saw the place ahead.

Meskwaki reservation. Home to the last few dozen members of the Meskwaki tribe.

"Bastian, why are we here?" Alice shouted over the wind, riding behind on the buffalo.

"Charging Bear will help us," he said. "He's the best damn tracker in Nebraska. Hell, probably in the world."

He slowed the buffalo down. For a moment he and Alice rode in silence, staring around them.

Meskwaki reservation was a humble place. Pickup trucks and tractors rusted along dirt roads. Trailers, huts, and even a few tents stood on the plains, home to the last survivors of the tribe. The little gardens and farms didn't produce much food. The locals did what they could to survive. They wove bracelets, embroidered rugs, sold whatever they could. They were too proud to beg. The landscape around them was wild and beautiful, but here in the valley was a hard life, an ancient people clinging to survival. World War III had been hard on everyone. But the Meskwaki had suffered more than most.

Riding the buffalo at a slow clip, Bastian rode through the reservation. The tribe came out to greet him. They knew him well. Smiling shyly, a woman offered him and Alice bowls of stew, which they gratefully accepted. The meal was rich with venison and wild mushrooms.

"They don't mind seeing Alliance uniforms here?" Alice asked, sipping from her bowl. Both she and Bastian were wearing their olive drabs, the standard fatigues of Alliance marines.

"Many members of the Meskwaki tribe fought with the Alliance in the war," Bastian said. "Half of them gave their lives. They are a proud, free people, and their tribe is thousands of years old, but they honor the Alliance."

They found Charging Bear outside his trailer. He was a towering man, close to seven feet tall. Bastian was a big guy, but next to this giant, he seemed small.

On his birth certificate, his name was Chuck Baker. But he preferred to go by Charging Bear, his traditional name. He stood in the snow, holding a chainsaw. He was busy carving a log, sculpting the rough shape of a wolf. He was a sculptor by trade. Completed works stood around him in the yard. With his chainsaw, Bear could carve logs into eagles, wolves, bears, and other proud animals. Some of the logs were carved with the faces of the tribe's elders.

Charging Bear sold some of these sculptures to support the tribe. Bastian himself owned one, a mighty eagle. It sat back in his home. Well, Stacy's home now.

"Hey there, Bear!" Bastian cried over the roaring chainsaw.

The giant shut off the chainsaw and turned toward Bastian. He wore faded old jeans and a leather jacket. His face was gaunt and weatherworn, and his black hair hung in two braids. The two men were the same age, thirty-three, but Charging Bear seemed older. It wasn't just the lines on his forehead, carved by wind and bronzed by sunlight. It was an old sadness in his eyes, a weight on his broad shoulders.

Despite the sadness he carried, when he saw Bastian, the giant smiled. "Hello, Bas. How are you?"

Bastian dismounted the buffalo and hugged his friend. "Hey there, bud. I like the new eagle you're working on."

Alice waited on the mechanical buffalo, wringing her hands and biting her lip. Bear noticed her distress.

"What's wrong?" the giant asked.

"We need your help and quick," Bastian said. "Can you spare an hour?"

"Of course," said Bear. "For you—always."

"Then come on. Onto the buffalo. We gotta ride hard. I'll explain on the way."

"On that contraption of yours?" Bear snorted. "You guys keep your buffalo. I'll take my horse."

"Your old nag?" Bastian said. "We gotta move fast, bud."

"Oh, don't worry. I got a new ride."

The giant walked toward a rickety shed, opened the door, and revealed a gleaming new robot. It was shaped like a horse, forged of dark steel, as graceful as the real thing.

Bastian whistled. "That's a beauty."

"Built her myself." Bear grabbed a shotgun, slung it across his back, and climbed onto the saddle. "Try to keep up, buddy."

Not a moment later, they galloped out of the reservation. Bastian and Alice rode the buffalo. Bear rode his robotic stallion. Indeed, the buffalo struggled to keep up.

They galloped hard across the plains, heading to the forest to hunt a spider.

CHAPTER TEN

**The Starship *Freedom*
High Earth Orbit
11:51 Christmas 2199**

"Off for Christmas." King grunted. "The admiral—off for Christmas! I'm sitting here on the most credible threat the Alliance has faced in years. And he's off for Christmas."

King stood in his quarters, nearly crushing his comlink in his hand. That hand began to shake with rage. He had called the admiral's office. His personal assistant. Even the man's wife. They were all stonewalling him.

"Jim." Jordan's voice was deep and soothing. "It's all right."

King's upper lip rose in a snarl. "They're blowing me off. You know they are. This wouldn't have happened before the *Freedom* turned into a goddamn theme park."

Something cracked in his hand. He opened his fist. He had crushed the comlink.

"Jim." Jordan placed a hand on his shoulder. "You're stressed. It's your last day. You're looking for enemies to fight."

"What do you think I'm doing—trying to recapture the glory of war before retirement?" King snickered. "You know me better than that."

"Yes, I know you, Jim." Jordan smiled soothingly. "We go way back. And I've seen the report on the Rubicon. I know this is serious. Go blow off some steam, Jim. Hit the gym or bar. I'll keep trying the admiral, and if I can't get him, I'll try the other generals. I might have better luck." He winked. "After all, I'm far more personable than you, you cranky old bastard."

King glared at his old friend, then barked a laugh. "I can't argue with that. All right. You try it. Before I break any more expensive equipment and get it docked off my first retirement check."

He left his office, stood for a moment in the corridor, and gazed at the hustle and bustle of the ship. Crew members hurried back and forth, busy at their tasks. A guide was showing Japanese tourists the uniform of Prince Robert, which hung in a glass display case. When they noticed King emerge from his office, the tourists pointed and took photos. An elderly woman with thick glasses approached King, spoke excitedly in Japanese, and snapped a selfie with them.

King forced himself to smile, but he suspected it looked more like a grimace. Struggling not to pummel somebody, he marched down the corridor, into an elevator, and ascended toward the upper deck.

Blow off steam, Jordan had told him.

There was something King had always wanted to do. In forty years aboard this ship, he never got the chance.

Hell . . . why not? It was his last day. What could they do? Fire him?

The *Freedom*'s primary weapon was the Fist of Freedom, the enormous railgun whose twin prongs thrust out from the prow. But the *Freedom* had other weapons too. Fourteen cannons topped her dorsal hull. Seven along the starboard, seven along the port. The Angels of Liberty.

Back in the war, these cannons had fired Maccabee torpedoes. The legendary Maccabees were among the largest torpedoes ever built, their warheads the size of houses. Launching those devastating missiles, the mighty Angels of Liberty could destroy an enemy frigate with a single hit.

During his days as a starfighter pilot, King had fired only small missiles, which could fit onto his Eagle's wings. He had always wanted to fire one of the Angels, a cannon the size of a redwood.

King rarely smiled. But right now a mischievous smile tugged at his lips.

A retirement present to myself, he thought.

He took the elevator into a cavernous control room. The chamber would not shame a church nave. Gears covered the walls, their teeth as large as men. Pipes ran along the deckhead. From this chamber, gunners controlled the Libertas, one of the fourteen Angels of Liberty. The Libertas was the most famous of the fourteen; she had taken out the great dreadnought *Mao* during the war.

A colossal chute dominated the room, slanting from the hull toward the floor. It looked like a water slide for giants. The gunners used to load the Maccabees into this tube, which then delivered the torpedoes into the cannon's bore. Today the gunners loaded barrels of fireworks, but the principle was the same.

To lift torpedoes and fireworks this big, every Angel of Liberty came with several loader mechas. Well, they used to. Today most of the giant robots were on Earth, working in factories. One had apparently been gutted and turned into a playground, complete with swings on his metal arms. But a few mechas remained aboard the *Freedom*.

One mecha stood here in the control room behind velvet ropes. They called this one Samson. Tourists like to snap photos of him. If they paid extra, they could even climb into the cockpit for a photo.

The loaders were essentially human-shaped forklifts. Samson was forty years old now. His yellow paint was peeling off his steel frame. His motors, pistons, and gears were all outdated. Today, people used graviton lift plates to carry heavy loads. But

Samson remained, an enduring symbol of the *Freedom*.

King had always wanted to operate him.

The gunnery crew was on break. They wouldn't be firing more fireworks until the Christmas gala tonight. The fireworks awaited in cylindrical containers the size of buses, stacked together like giant metal logs.

King's mischievous smile grew. He was the commander of this ship, but suddenly he felt like a young ensign again, pulling pranks and getting into trouble. Those had been good days. More innocent days. Before the loss of his father. Before the death of his wife. Before he got old.

King pulled aside the stanchions that cordoned Samson. He climbed a ladder to the mecha's torso, where he slid into the cockpit. An array of joysticks and levers thrust out from a control panel. Pedals controlled the mecha's heavy metal feet. A crude but effective machine.

King flipped a switch, turning the mecha on. Samson's motors rumbled. Lights flashed in the cockpit. King grabbed the joysticks and placed his feet on the pedals.

He moved his legs. Hydraulic pistons moved. And Samson began to walk, thumping his way across the deck. The machine weighed thirty tons, and King knew they could hear these footsteps several decks down.

Try to stop me, he thought.

So far, so good. No dismayed gunners came running into the control room. King still had the place—and the mecha—to himself.

King kept moving the joysticks and pedals. Motors rumbling, Samson thundered toward the pile of firework barrels. King pushed two joysticks. Samson extended his hands, which were shaped like forklift prongs.

Gently King manipulated the mecha's hands. The metal fingers closed around one of the firework barrels. King pulled back the joystick, and Samson lifted the tubular container.

This was fun. King hadn't had this much fun in ages.

He placed the barrel into the loading chute. With one of Samson's fingers, he tapped a button. The barrel began rolling up the chute on magnetic tracks. The chamber vibrated. The barrel vanished from view, moving toward the Angel of Liberty, which thrust out from the hull.

King climbed out of the mecha, approached a huge lever, and paused.

He connected his MindLink to a camera on the starship's exterior. A video feed floated before him, featuring a view of the Libertas. The legendary cannon pointed at the stars.

This was one time King didn't mind using the implant. It gave him eyes outside the ship. And he wanted to see this.

A green light appeared on a control panel on the wall. A message appeared below it.

READY TO FIRE

"Here goes," King said, gripped the lever with both hands, and shoved it down.

With a deafening boom that shook the entire starship, the Libertas fired.

King stumbled back, grinning. The deck swayed beneath his feet. The entire starship jerked in space.

On his MindWeb video, he saw it happen. The cannon fired the barrel into the distance. A few klicks away, the fireworks exploded.

Red and blue lights blazed in space, forming the shape of a great eagle. Its wings spread a mile wide. The bird of light soared, spun, and opened its golden beak to silently sing.

Across the ship, they were probably scratching their heads. This wasn't on the schedule! King chuckled to himself.

There. Now I've done everything on the ship, and I can retire in peace.

"Not bad!" came a voice from behind him. "Next time, can

you fire Darjeeling out the cannon?"

King turned around.

A girl sat on a pipe, one knee pulled to her chin, chewing an apple. She spat out a seed.

"Hello, Stowy," King said. "Were you watching the whole time?"

"Nah." The girl shrugged. "I was relaxing in the ducts, minding my own business, when you raised a holy racket. Had to come see what the noise was about. I thought it was a goddamn alien invasion!"

The girl wore a ragged dress with many pockets sewn on like patches. She wore no shoes and only one striped stocking, which was pulled up to her knee. Her messy brown hair hadn't seen a comb in years, it seemed. Freckles lay strewn across her impish face, especially on the upturned nose. There was something a bit off about the girl. Elfin. She seemed like a creature from the lands of faerie, risen into the world. Sometimes King wondered if she was just a MindLink hallucination.

"Has Darjeeling been giving you a rough time lately?" King asked, suppressing a smile.

Stowy laughed. "Nah, not really. He chases me a lot, but he's slow and fat. I can always escape him. He yells and waves his fists and it's really funny." She put a finger atop her lip like a mustache, shook her fist, and spoke with a fake British accent. "Oi, you girl! Get out of that pipe, you pipsqueak!"

A fit of giggles seized her. Stowy laughed so hard she fell off the pipe. She rolled around the deck, laughing hysterically.

King couldn't help but smile. Nobody knew her real name or where she came from. Three years ago, the girl had sneaked onto the ship. A stowaway. She had no home on Earth, no family that anyone knew of. So they called her Stowy. They accepted her. She spent her days sneaking around the ductwork, crawling all over the ship, popping out from vents anywhere between the stern and prow. Nobody knew where she slept. They left out trays of food for her. Sometimes Stowy even popped out of a vent in the aerie, where she joined the pilots for beer and poker.

King would have given her a proper bunk to sleep in, but they all belonged to the civilian company that ran the hotel. So in the ducts Stowy remained, spending her days sneaking around, popping up everywhere like a mole, and mostly tormenting poor Darjeeling.

"Hey!" Stowy said once she stopped laughing. "Commander King, are the rumors true? Are you going to retire?"

King lost his smile. "And how do you know a secret I've only shared with my senior officers?"

Stowy grinned. "I know everything that goes on around here. Hey, when you retire, you should name me commander. I know this ship better than anyone."

King snorted. "That I don't doubt. But you have to be eighteen to join the Alliance."

She rolled her eyes. "Oh my, look at you, judging me for being young and cute. It's not my fault I'm only seventeen. I would have been born earlier, if I wasn't so lazy and just stayed in my mother's womb for a full extra two years! Yes, *two years* I stayed in the womb. My mother said I was just sleeping in there, eating apples, singing tunes, not wanting to come out. She'd hear me giggle from inside, you know. True story. That's probably why she abandoned me." She shrugged. "Go figure."

King brushed some ashes off her shoulder. "Stowy, when I'm gone, look after this ship, will you? You might not be an officer of the Alliance. You're not even supposed to be on this ship. But you're right. You know this ship. You know it better than any map. Look after the place when I'm gone."

Suddenly Stowy was sniffing. Tears rolled down her cheeks, drawing lines through the soot. She saluted. "Yes, sir! And the first thing I'll do once you're gone is shoot Darjeeling out the cannon. Kidding, kidding!"

She let out a huge sniff, then pulled King into a hug.

King grumbled. Stowy was getting soot all over the uniform. But gradually he loosened up and hugged her back.

"Goodbye, Stowy. Don't get in too much trouble while I'm gone. And if you ever find yourself back on Earth, swing by Nebraska. I'll cook you a meal."

"No thanks. I love the *Freedom* too much to ever leave. This is my home." She smiled shakily. "Thanks for letting me stay. You da best, boss."

She hesitated, then stood on her toes and kissed his cheek.

Then, giggling, the girl spun on her heel and ran off. Quick as a chipmunk, she vanished through a vent into the ductwork. King smiled wistfully. Whenever Stowy left a room, it always felt like waking up from a dream, as if a bit of magic had just left the world. You were left wondering if she had ever really been there. The only signs of Stowy that remained were the apple core on the deck and the soot on King's uniform.

CHAPTER ELEVEN

**The Starship *Freedom*
High Earth Orbit
12:27 Christmas 2199**

Emily walked through the starship *Freedom*, eyes wide, gaping at the wonders.

"Oh, Niles, isn't it marvelous?"

The drone hovered beside her. His silver shell glittered with sapphires, rubies, and diamonds. He seemed woefully misplaced among the starship's metal bulkheads, diamond plate decks, and rattling pipes.

"It's positively ghastly," the drone said. "We've been exploring this starship for two hours, and I haven't seen a single decent work of art on the walls. Not one original oil painting or statue to be seen! I miss Buckingham Palace."

"Oh come, Niles." Emily slung an arm over the hovering drone. "Where's your sense of adventure?"

"Adventure? Bah!" Niles turned from side to side. His cameras took in the twisting, metallic corridors that snaked through the *Freedom* like a maze. "I'm liable to catch a horrible computer virus in this place. It's positively oozing with viruses. I can hear them scurrying through the walls."

Emily rolled her eyes. "You can't hear computer viruses in the walls, Niles."

The drone gasped. "There! There goes one now! A virus!"

A tiny hatch opened on the drone's shell. A slender rod emerged, pointing at a ventilation grate above.

Emily looked and frowned. She *did* see something. Something fast moved behind the vent. Emily glimpsed a flash of brown hair or maybe fur. Thumping and banging sounded above the deckhead, and then it was gone. Whatever it was.

"Mr. Darjeeling?" Emily turned toward the sergeant major. "I think I spotted a mouse in the vents. Do you have mice here aboard the starship *Freedom*? Not that I'm complaining, of course. I rather like mice." She bit her lip. "I hope it doesn't sound like I'm complaining."

"Well, I *am* complaining!" Niles said. "This whole starship is infested."

Darjeeling, the kindly sergeant with the wonderful white mustache, acted as tour guide. Two hours ago, they had begun the tour in the upper decks, which contained casinos, wax museums, and various other tourist traps. Emily had found those areas disappointing.

"I want to see the real ship," she had told Darjeeling. "The place my grandfather had served in."

Darjeeling had nodded, accompanied her to an elevator, and taken her to the lower decks. This place was more like it. The corridors twisted and turned like a medieval dungeon. Hatches led to old armories, engine rooms, and war rooms. And real soldiers served here! In the upper decks, Emily mostly ran into tourists, and when she did see an employee, it was a civilian. A waiter, perhaps, or a blackjack dealer. Or sometimes somebody dressed up as Freedom the Frog, signing autographs for the kids.

Not down here. Here served real soldiers in real uniforms. Here were the men and women who kept the ship running. They cleaned the engines. They maintained the cannons, even if those cannons now fired fireworks instead of torpedoes. They honored the *Freedom* and her legacy.

Every once in a while, Darjeeling would stop a soldier, inspect them, and harrumph.

"Polish those boots, Corporal!" he'd tell one man.

"Iron that shirt, Private!" he'd tell another.

"Shave those cheeks."

"Trim that hair."

Soldiers gulped when they saw the old sergeant, nodded as he critiqued them, and hurried off. Emily realized that Darjeeling was more than just a tour guide. He was an active-duty NCO aboard a working starship.

To Emily, this aspect of the ship—seeing the military machine below the glittering casinos and spas—seemed wonderful.

Even if there were mice.

Darjeeling stared at the vent above. Until now, Darjeeling had been all kindly smiles around Emily. Even when he was correcting his soldiers, he remained calm and professional. But now he scowled and shook his fist at the vent.

"Dammit, get back here, you little urchin!" he cried. "I'm going to catch you and give you a beating."

Emily gasped. "Mr. Darjeeling! It's only a mouse."

Darjeeling lowered his fist. His cheeks flushed. "Forgive my outburst, ma'am. I sincerely apologize." He glanced back at the vent, and his mustache bristled. "Begging your pardon, ma'am, but that was no mouse. That was a menace I've been chasing for three years now. She almost never shows herself. She must find you curious."

Emily placed her hands on her hips. "What is going on, Mr. Darjeeling?"

Darjeeling took a deep breath and smoothed his uniform. "My apologies, ma'am. My deepest apologies. Just a little problem we've been dealing with, but we'll solve it." He smiled. "Now—

we're almost at deck 9. The control deck for the Fist of Freedom. You were curious to see the mighty Fist, yes?"

Emily hopped in excitement, forgetting all about mice in the vents. "Yes. I can't wait."

* * * * *

They took an elevator down. As they descended, Emily unfolded her map of the starship *Freedom*. A paper map. How quaint. They handed them out when you docked, and you could take them home as souvenirs. Looking at the ship's schematic, the eyes were immediately drawn to the Fist of Freedom.

According to the brochure, the Fist was the largest gun ever built. Its twin rails thrust out from the prow. An illustration appeared on the back of the map, showing the Fist of Freedom standing erect in Manhattan. The two prongs stood as tall as the tallest skyscrapers.

The base of the prongs was attached to the ship's midsection. From there, they flanked the prow, and finally thrust out into empty space. Emily was heading toward the base of the rails—the control room where gunners operated the grand railgun.

She emerged from the elevator into a massive chamber. It was the size of an airplane hangar. Cold wind blew through the void, ruffling Emily's golden hair. Mezzanines surrounded the cavern, crowded with tourists. The balcony where Emily stood was empty aside from her, Darjeeling, and Niles.

The perks of being a princess. You got your own private showing of everything.

She leaned over the railing, gasping.

"Would you look at that," she whispered.

The rails thrust out—one along the chamber floor, one along the ceiling. Two fingers the size of office towers. She could only see their bases from here. Most of the rails were outside the hull. But enormous screens hung on the cavern bulkhead, displaying a view from outside. It felt like looking directly out to space. Emily could see the full length of the rails pointing at the stars. The illusion was perfect.

"Emily, don't lean over the railing!" Niles said.

"Oh shush, I'm fine." She leaned even farther over the railing, just to irk him, and pointed downward. "Mr. Darjeeling, what is that below?"

She squinted, staring at it. Enormous machinery filled the base of the cavern. Pistons rose and fell. Gears turned. Tubes glowed with pale blue light. A glass sphere churned, full of searing, crackling light like a star trapped in a snow globe.

"That's the reactor that powers the Fist of Freedom, ma'am," Darjeeling said. "We can only see part of it from here. The reactor produces enough electricity to propel a projectile between the rails." He pointed. "Do you see there below, by the engines? That's one of the projectiles."

Emily gasped. "But it's huge, Mr. Darjeeling!"

He nodded. "Yes indeed. We call them Goliath missiles due to their size. That projectile is the size of a whale. Of course, we haven't fired the Fist of Freedom in thirty-five years. Not since the war."

"How many Goliath missiles are on the starship?" Emily asked.

"Just the one, ma'am. And . . . I'll let you in on a little secret. Even that Goliath below is hollow. It's there for the tourists."

Emily bit her lip, staring at the enormous Goliath below.

"Is it true the Fist of Freedom can destroy planets?" she asked.

"I don't know about planets, but it can cause some serious

damage," Darjeeling said. "You see, using electricity instead of a propellant like gunpowder, a railgun can hurl projectiles at incredible speed. That magnifies the projectile's kinetic energy. Goliaths don't have warheads. They carry so much kinetic energy they don't need warheads. A humble bullet fired from a railgun will be far deadlier than a bullet fired from a regular pistol. Increase the size and speed, and you keep increasing the kinetic energy. The Fist of Freedom can easily destroy an entire city. Not to mention the most heavily armored enemy dreadnought. In fact, it was the Fist of Freedom that destroyed the RDS *Mao* during the war, crippling the Red Dawn's fleet."

Emily tried to imagine it. The massive gun booming, destroying enemy starships. Like in the stories.

"The *Freedom* must have been unstoppable with this weapon," she said.

Niles flew up to them. "Not that unstoppable. I read the specs. The Fist of Freedom takes a full day to charge." The drone snorted. "How much use is a weapon you can fire only once a day?"

"Useful enough to win the war, Sir Drone," said Darjeeling.

"And useful enough that if there's ever another war, Niles, the *Freedom* will win that too," Emily said, annoyed with her jeweled companion.

Darjeeling smiled soothingly. "Ah, the *Freedom*'s days of fighting are over. Maybe the days of all humanity fighting are over. I pray we forever have peace, though we honor our heroes."

"Like my grandfather," Emily said softly. "He was a fighter pilot here."

Darjeeling nodded. "And a most honorable man. I did not know him well during my service here. Ten thousand soldiers served aboard the *Freedom* during the war, and back then, I was only a humble corporal, and he was a prince and officer. But I saw him fly in battle, and I admired his courage. He's a great man, our dear King Robert." He bowed. "And you are a great princess, Emily, and a source of pride to both your family and kingdom."

Emily smiled and patted his arm. "Thank you, Mr. Darjeeling. Brave soldiers like you honor our kingdom. Indeed, you honor the entire Alliance."

The mustached sergeant beamed. He wiped away a tear. "Thank you, ma'am," he whispered. "Your words touch me more than you can know."

Niles rolled his camera eyes. "Are you two quite finished patting each other on the back? The saccharine is clogging my sockets."

Both humans ignored the drone.

"Mr. Darjeeling, do you think it would be possible to meet the Freedom's Flock?" Emily said. "The pilots who put on that marvelous aerobatic show for me?"

Darjeeling hesitated, his smile vanishing. "I . . . Well . . ."

Emily frowned. "Oh, I'm sorry. If there's a problem, we don't have to—"

"Oh, not a problem per se," Darjeeling said. "It's just . . . the flock can be a rowdy bunch." He lowered his voice. "They're not English like us."

"They sound like savages!" Niles said.

Emily laughed. "That's quite all right, Mr. Darjeeling. Many nations are part of our Alliance. I don't expect them all to bow before me."

"There better not be any American pilots," Niles said. "You know I can't abide Americans."

Emily shoved him. Hard. "Niles! Rude!"

One of his jewels dislodged and flew into the pit, where it clattered among the engines and vanished. Niles looked down dejectedly. "That ruby cost more than this entire starship."

"Go get it," Emily said.

Niles gasped. "And get engine oil all over me? No, thank

you." He raised his silver nose and floated away.

* * * * *

As they headed back toward the elevator, they passed by another vent, this one near the deck. Once more, Emily caught movement from the corner of her eye.

She paused. Leaving Darjeeling, she knelt by the vent.

A face stared through the grate.

Emily gasped and stumbled back.

A human face! A girl's face!

"There's somebody trapped down here!" Emily said.

Darjeeling rushed forward, face flushing. "I've got the ragamuffin this time." He reached toward the grate and yanked it off.

The girl inside the vent blew him a raspberry. "You'll never catch me, old man!"

Laughing, she vanished into the duct and scurried away. Clanking sounded under the deck. The girl must be crawling right under their feet.

Darjeeling reached into the vent, but he was too big to follow. His white mustache bristled, and his eyes bugged out. "Get back here, miscreant! I won't be having you on my ship."

Emily frowned. "Mr. Darjeeling! What is going on?"

"Please ignore her, ma'am," Darjeeling said. "She's a stowaway. She's been tormenting me for three years now. The crew call her Stowy. They see her as something of a mascot. But she's the bane of my existence, she is."

Laughter sounded from another vent—this one above their heads. Stowy's pale face appeared at the grate.

"Hey, Princess Emily! Did you know that Darjeeling is a big

poo-poo head?" The stowaway laughed and vanished again into the ducts.

"Why you!" Darjeeling raced toward the grate on the deckhead, jumped, but could not reach it. He began dragging a crate over, grumbling about how he's going to catch the girl this time.

As Darjeeling tried to reach the grate on the ceiling, Emily stood on the deck, confused.

"Psst!"

The sound came from behind her.

"Psst! Hey! Princess!"

Emily turned around. Stowy's face now appeared in another grate, this one on the bulkhead. Darjeeling didn't notice. He was busy trying to unscrew the grate on the deckhead vent.

Emily knelt by the bulkhead. Stowy stared at her from inside the duct. She looked about seventeen, same age as Emily, maybe a year or two younger. Her face was elfin and freckled, her hair light brown and messy.

"Why, you're a regular Whac-a-Mole, aren't you?" Emily whispered.

Emily glanced over her shoulder. Darjeeling still hadn't noticed. He was reaching into the ceiling grate, muttering about how he'll toss Stowy out the airlock.

"Princess." Stowy reached from the duct and grabbed Emily's arm.

Emily recoiled. Suddenly Stowy seemed less silly, more menacing, like a ghost haunting the ship. The girl's eyes lost all their mirth. They now stared with burning intensity.

"Be careful, Princess," the stowaway whispered. "I hear everything. I know all that happens on this ship. Something is coming. Something dangerous. Something from beyond the stars. Beware!"

"I got you now!" Darjeeling roared, reaching toward her.

Stowy yelped and vanished into the duct.

Within an instant, the girl was gone and did not return. As Emily continued her tour of the ship, Stowy's warning echoed in her mind.

Something is coming. Beware!

CHAPTER TWELVE

Nebraska, Earth
13:28 Christmas 2199

Charging Bear knelt on the forest floor, staring at the frozen ground.

"I don't know what left these tracks." The giant's eyes were dark. "No animal I've ever seen. Not a machine either. Something unholy walked here. I can smell it. The stench of evil fills this forest."

Bastian knelt beside his friend. He stared at the ground too, squinting. "I don't see anything." He sniffed. "I don't smell anything either."

Bastian had no skills in tracking. That much was obvious. There were some things he was good at. He was a decent enough shot. He could lift big weights at the gym. He sometimes won a round of poker. But it seemed that where it counted, Bastian kept failing. He tried flight school, only to flunk out, breaking a long tradition of King pilots. He tried marriage, only for Stacy to dump his ass for Hunter and his avocados. And now, when Bastian needed to save an old lady from this forest, he couldn't even find tracks in the snow.

Luckily, Bear was there. The giant could probably track an ant across concrete.

"Sight is not just what your eyes see." Bear straightened to his full height, towering over the others. "There are many senses. Come, we need to hurry. There's great danger here. Great need."

"Can you tell if my grandmother is still alive?" Alice said, standing beside the tracker.

At over six feet tall, Master Sergeant Alice Allenby stood taller than most men. She could also wrestle most of them to submission. But standing beside Bear, she seemed downright petite.

"I don't know," said the giant. "I don't know magic, Alice. I just have strong senses. Come, hurry."

Pretty soon they had to abandon their buffalo. The quadrupedal robot was too bulky to move through the thickening forest. They kept the robotic mustang, which was slender enough to walk between the trees. Unfortunately, the mechanical horse was just large enough for one rider. Alice climbed onto the saddle, beating Bastian to it.

Bear ran ahead, leading the way. He said he needed his feet on the ground to track his quarry. Bastian had no idea how Bear could follow a trail while running, but apparently, the giant could.

Bastian ran behind the tracker, breathing heavily. He could barely keep up. Bastian spent a lot of time in the gym, but that mostly involved lifting weights and drinking protein shakes. He wasn't much of a runner. He was like a tank—big and brutish and deadly at short distances, but send him cross country, and he'd break down before long.

"Alice, come on, share the horse," he panted.

Alice rode nearby on the mechanical stallion. "Both of us won't fit. You're too fat."

"It's muscle!" he said.

"Sure. Keep running, meathead. You could lose a few pounds."

So Bastian kept running. He needed to get this over with fast.

I'll be there in time, Rowan, he thought. *I promise. I ain't letting your mother take you to Bemidji to spend the rest of Christmas with Hunter.*

They kept moving through the forest, heading uphill. Perfect. If there was anything Bastian hated more than running, it was running uphill.

Soon enough, he could smell something ahead. An oily stench. A smell like an old deep fryer abandoned outside, still sticky with grease, flaked with burnt meat and covered in bugs.

"Stinks like your feet, Bas!" Alice said, riding beside him.

Bear stopped running and pointed at a forested hilltop.

"It's coming from there," the giant said. "The stench. There's something evil here."

Bastian stopped running too. He leaned over, clutching his side. His heart pounded. Alice had ridden on the horse, but she didn't look happy either. Her cheeks were flushed, her lips purple, and frost clung to her eyelashes. Bear, meanwhile, wasn't even out of breath.

As he struggled to catch his own breath, Bastian drew and charged his pistol. "Yeah, well, let's find whatever grabbed Granny Allenby and fill it with bullets."

He walked toward the stench, boots cracking frozen twigs. The others followed, their own guns drawn. A gust of wind blew icicles off the trees. The icy blades sliced into the snow around them.

The friends wormed between maples and pines. The smell grew. Bastian nearly gagged, wishing he had brought a gas mask. He walked, gun pointing the way, and reached the hilltop.

Gnarled pines rose among patches of snow, crowning the hill like astral sentinels guarding a kingdom of ice. A cobweb stretched between the trees, as large as a sail. Halfway up the web hung a cocoon. It was roughly the size of a person.

Alice gasped, dismounted the robotic horse, and ran toward the cobwebs.

"Granny!" she cried.

"Alice, wait!" Bastian shouted, aiming his pistol at the

cobweb.

She ignored him. She reached the web, leaped up, and her fingertips grazed the cocoon. It didn't budge. Alice jumped again, pawing at the cocoon, trying to pull it down. It hung above her like a piñata.

"Bear, cover me," Bastian said.

The giant nodded, eyes dark, and hefted his rifle.

Bastian rushed toward the cobweb. Alice was still reaching for the cocoon, tears in her eyes. And then Bastian saw it.

A strand of white hair stuck out from the webbed bundle. Somebody was inside.

"Bas, boost me up!" Alice said. "I can't reach on my own. It's too high even for Bear."

Bastian obliged. He hefted Alice upward, elevating her toward the center of the web. She grabbed the cocoon with both hands and tugged, but it wouldn't budge.

"It's glued on tight," she said, hopping back down.

"Hang on," Bastian said. "Let me try something."

He drew his knife and began sawing at the cobwebs. Maybe he could bring the whole structure down, cocoon and web alike. The strands were damn sticky. Several times, the cobwebs caught his hands, ripping off little hairs.

Impatient, Alice began to climb the web. Not too smart. She quickly found herself glued in place. She had to wriggle out of her coat, then hopped back down, leaving the jacket stuck to the web. She shivered in the cold.

"Brilliant, Allenby," Bastian said.

Alice hugged herself, teeth chattering. "Shut up."

Finally Bastian cut enough strands that the entire web sagged. The cocoon drooped toward the ground. With Alice pulling the cocoon, and with Bastian cutting through cobwebs, they managed to free the bundle. They laid it on the snow.

Bastian slipped his blade into the cocoon, then carefully

sawed it open. It was like sawing open a cast.

And there she was, lying inside.

Hannah Allenby.

"Granny?" Alice whispered. "Granny, wake up!"

But Bastian knew the old woman was dead. Her skin was pale blue. Her eyes were open and still. She was frozen solid. It was not the cold that had killed her, though. A hole the size of an apple gaped open in her chest.

Bastian frowned. "There's no blood. There's no blood anywhere." He touched the corpse. "Not on the cocoon, not even inside her. She's been drained."

Alice wept, holding the dead woman's hand.

Charging Bear knelt by the body. He looked up at Bastian, eyes cold. "I've heard of such things."

Bastian shuddered. "What the hell did this, Bear? What could drain a woman of blood?"

"My people tell stories of a demon who comes from the dark," Bear said. "For many eras, she sleeps. She awakes in winter to feed. We call her Sowuti."

"A giant spider," Alice whispered, looking up from her grandmother.

Bear nodded. "Yes, you're familiar with our mythology? In my tribe's stories, Sowuti appears as a great arachnid, though in some tales, she—"

"A giant spider!" Alice cried again, raised her pistol, and fired.

Bastian spun around.

God above.

It came charging through the forest, coming right at them.

A spider the size of a cow.

Bastian shouted and opened fire.

* * * * *

The spider raced toward them. The bullets didn't faze it. It charged over the ice, opened its jaws, and shrieked.

Bastian kept firing. His bullets glanced off the enormous arachnid.

"What the hell is that thing?" he shouted.

The spider leaped over a fallen log, vaulting toward him. Its eight legs shone like katanas. Fangs filled its gargantuan mouth. Those jaws could put a shark to shame.

Bastian stood his ground, firing his pistol with both hands. Bullets hit the spider's abdomen, dented the exoskeleton, but did not penetrate. One bullet shattered something on the spider's back. Fragments of bone flew.

Skulls, Bastian realized. *There are skulls on its back.*

Then the spider slammed into him.

Bastian howled and fell. It was like a train plowing into him.

The hideous creature raised one leg. A gleaming claw tipped it. The alien brought the leg down hard.

Bastian rolled. The claw punched into the frozen ground, digging several inches deep. Another leg rose, fell. Bastian rolled again, nearly impaled.

Charging Bear and Alice stood nearby, firing at the creature. But they couldn't penetrate its thick shell.

"What are you?" Bastian shouted.

The spider laughed. Its eight eyes shone, red gemstones full of fire. Saliva dripped onto Bastian, sizzling hot. The creature opened its hellmouth wide, revealing a quivering gullet.

"Death . . .," the beast rumbled, voice like steam.

Bastian fired his last bullet into the open mouth.

The spider recoiled.

Bastian seized his chance and kicked hard, hitting the

creature in the face. The spider screeched and stumbled back.

Bastian rose to his feet, reached into his pocket, and pulled out his spare magazine. He reloaded. Meanwhile, Bear and Alice kept pounding the creature with their own bullets, knocking it a few steps back.

The spider lunged toward Bastian again.

He fired.

A single shot into one eye.

The eye burst, splattering red juices.

The spider screamed.

Bastian fired again and again, pounding the creature. He took out a second eye. And still the spider leaped forward. The mighty jaws closed around Bastian's arm.

He bellowed.

His blood spurted.

"Bastian!" Alice cried.

She ran, vaulted off a boulder, and landed on the spider's back. The creature's spikes rose around her. Alice began screaming, stabbing the spider with her knife. She sank the blade into another eye. Charging Bear drew his own knife, began stabbing at eyes. One of the spider's legs slammed into the giant, knocking him into the snow.

All the while, the spider kept gripping Bastian, chomping on his arm.

But inside the creature's mouth, Bastian was still holding his pistol.

He fired.

His bullet plowed through the spider's palate and burst out the back of its head.

The spider opened its jaws to scream. Bastian fell to the forest floor, his arm a bleeding mess. Tooth marks ran along the forearm.

The spider was still alive. A hundred bullets filled it, and the damn thing was still screeching. The creature was down to a single eye. Alice leaped off the spider, her blond braids fluttering, and reloaded her pistol. The spider turned toward her, limping, bleeding. She fired. The spider's last eye exploded, and the beast crashed down.

Still it twitched, legs kicking blindly. One leg caught Charging Bear, ripping his jeans, cutting his thigh. The giant roared. He was out of bullets, but he began pounding the blind creature with his rifle.

"Goddammit, die already!" Alice shouted, stabbing the wounded creature.

Bastian limped forward, groaning in pain. Blood flowed down his arm. He had one bullet left. He had to make it count.

Even without eyes, the creature sensed him. It seemed to stare at him with empty sockets.

"You cannot stop us . . .," the spider hissed.

"Great, it speaks English," Alice muttered.

"We . . . are . . . the rahs," said the spider. "You . . . are . . . meat. Humanity will fall!"

The enormous arachnid chuckled, spraying saliva and blood from its mouth.

Bastian fired into that open mouth. This time the bullet drove into the brain, and the spider finally thumped down dead.

Bastian spat on the corpse. "Bastard."

Then he fell to his knees, and his blood speckled the snow.

* * * * *

Bastian looked at his arm. What a mess. Gingerly he tried to pull up the sleeve, then grimaced in pain.

"Let me help you," Alice said. She raised her knife.

"Get that blade away from me," Bastian said. "It's covered with spider eyeball juice."

"I need to cut off your sleeve. Shut up." Alice gripped his arm, then began sawing the sleeve off. Roughly.

"Be gentle!" Bastian roared.

"Be quiet!" She got the sleeve off, looked at his injury, and *tsk*ed her tongue. "That's all you've been whining about? A few tiny little tooth marks?"

"Those teeth were the size of box cutters." Bastian looked at the wounds and grimaced. They were still bleeding.

"Good thing your arm is so fat," Alice said.

"It's muscle!"

She pulled a med kit from her pouch. They were combat soldiers of the Alliance Marine Corp. They always carried basic medical supplies. There had not been a war in decades, but now Bastian was thankful they stayed ready.

Are there any more of these damn spiders? he wondered.

"I'll patch you up for now," Alice said. "You're lucky I took all my first aid classes. But you'll need to see a proper doctor back on the base."

She tended to his wounds. Her eyes were still damp with tears, and her grandmother's body still lay nearby. But she dedicated herself to her task, cleaning the bite marks one by one, then applying auto-stitch strips. God bless her. She busted his balls a lot, but she was a damn loyal sergeant. More than that—a loyal friend.

"Thanks, Alice," he said. "When you leaped onto that spider and began stabbing eyes, you saved my ass."

She splashed antiseptic into his wounds. "You'd have done the same."

Bastian winced at the fresh explosion of pain, then took a deep breath. "I'm sorry for your loss, Alice."

She sniffed, and a tear rolled down her cheek. She said

nothing more.

As Alice worked at bandaging his arm, Bastian looked at Charging Bear. The giant stood by the dead spider, examining it.

"What do you make of it, Bear?" Bastian said.

The tracker looked at him. He suddenly seemed a decade older. Bastian had known the guy for thirty years. For the first time, Bear looked afraid. And it took a lot to make a seven-foot, rifle-toting giant who collected chainsaws look afraid.

"In my tribe, we tell stories of Sowuti, the spider goddess," Bear said. "Centuries ago, long before white men reached America, we spoke of her in whispers. We fought her in the winter forests. It's said that Sowuti had many sons. This dead creature, I believe, is one of those sons. The spider goddess has risen from her long slumber, and she's spawning again. An ancient evil has returned."

When his arm was bandaged, Bastian walked toward the spider. He kicked it. It felt like kicking solid steel. Spikes rose from the spider's back, impaling various skulls. Some skulls with horns. Some with four eye sockets. Some long, others triangular. Bastian didn't recognize any of them.

"Well, an old demon is one possibility," Bastian said. "But if you ask me, this thing hatched in a Red Dawn lab. You know those damn equalists. They're always doing genetic experiments, trying to breed supersoldiers. How do you think Katyusha stays young? She keeps cloning herself, killing the clones, and implanting her brain into their bodies. People who'd do stuff like that, well . . . I wouldn't put breeding giant spiders past them."

Alice chewed her lip, looking at the dead spider. "Maybe it's an alien."

"There's no such thing as aliens," Bastian said.

"Sure there are," Alice said. "My grandfather has seen a bunch of them."

Bastian rolled his eyes. "He claims to have seen little green men probing his chickens. Not the same."

Bear remained dour. He never removed his eyes from the dead creature. "Maybe Alice is right. In the legends of my people, Sowuti came from beyond a great darkness. A creature of the night sky. Maybe . . . an alien."

"This creature called itself a *rah*," Alice said. "Bear, are there any legends of demons called the rahs in your tribe?"

The giant shook his head. "No, but demons often go by many names."

"Whatever that bastard is, we better haul its corpse back to Fort Liberty," Bastian said. "We can find a lab to—"

His MindLink rang, interrupting him.

Stacy appeared before him—a hallucination standing on the hilltop. A very pissed-off hallucination. She crossed her arms.

"Bastian! You were supposed to be here three minutes ago. I have to leave now. I'm heading to Bemidji, and I'm taking Rowan with me."

"No!" Bastian blurted out, speaking aloud as he telepathized. "Ah, crap. Look, Stacy, I'm running late, but I'll be there in five minutes. Okay, ten minutes, fifteen minutes tops, just—"

"What the hell is that near you?" Stacy said, grimacing.

Dammit. Bastian had forgotten to turn his eyesight link off. With the feature switched on, Stacy could see what he was seeing. Damn MindLinks.

Bastian switched off eyesight sharing, but it was too late. Standing in her kitchen, Stacy would have seen what he saw. The giant dead spider.

"It's nothing," Bastian said. "Just . . . please wait, Stacy. Please. We agreed I can spend half of Christmas with Rowan."

Stacy's eyes shot daggers. "She's better off at Bemidji. To spend Christmas on an army base? With whatever the hell creature that was you got over there?"

"I wouldn't be living on an army base if you hadn't taken

my goddamn house!"

"Oh, is it about the house again, is it? Well—"

"Please let's not do this again, Stacy. Okay? Just please hold on. I'm racing over right now."

She groaned and rolled her eyes. That meant okay.

Bastian hung up.

He looked at his friends.

"Bear, mind if I borrow your horse?"

The giant gave him the thumbs-up. "Not at all. Go get Rowan. Alice and I will drag this creature back to the base. We'll build a litter."

Bastian nodded, slapped his friend on the arm, then mounted the robotic stallion. He galloped as fast as the machine would go.

CHAPTER THIRTEEN

The Starship *Freedom*
High Earth Orbit
14:25 Christmas 2199

King slammed down the phone. For a moment he just stood at his desk, jaw clenched.

"Another dead end," he growled. "General Forester is away for Christmas too. Vacation on his ranch. MindLink turned off."

He turned away from the phone. He looked at the two officers in his cabin.

Mimori stood by a framed parchment map, a treasure from the eighteenth century. The android was wearing her fancy parade uniform, complete with white gloves, a black bow tie, and golden aiguillettes. She was all decked out for the Christmas gala, though the event was now in question. The android stood very still and silent, holding the Rubicon report she had prepared. For the past hour, she had been sending this report to Alliance admirals and generals on Earth.

So far, nobody read it.

One general said he'd get to it right after Christmas dinner. The others didn't even answer.

Lieutenant Commander Jordan stood by a bookshelf. He too wore his parade whites, looking like some fairy-tale prince. King had always thought the Alliance dress uniforms looked a little silly, even pompous. But they were standard at military ceremonies. King himself still wore his blue service uniform, a simpler outfit. He hadn't bothered changing into his own parade whites. He wasn't thinking about the upcoming Christmas dinner now.

"We should call High Commander Archer," Jordan said.

Jordan was normally calm, collected, more liable to sing than shout. But now the XO's face was hard, his eyes dark.

"And go over the heads of the admiralty?" King said.

The high commander was, as his name implied, the head of the entire Alliance, the leader of the free world. Even as a dreadnought commander, King did not report to him directly.

"Jim, we've already contacted every admiral." Jordan heaved a sigh. "They're all out for Christmas."

King barked a laugh. "Well, we left messages with their secretaries. I'm sure that will help."

Jordan pursed his lips. "Is this really what's become of the Alliance? Have three decades of peace made us so complacent? Back during the war, we could get anyone on the line within moments. Even the high commander."

King eyed the bottle of Martian ale, which still stood on his oak desk. "Back then, we were a warship. Now we're a joke."

Mimori raised her chin. "Sir, I'm no joke!"

"No, you're not," King said, a kindness in his rasp. "You're a damn fine ship. The best in the galaxy. But when the admirals look at me, they don't see the commander anymore. Hell, some of the officers down at HQ hadn't even been born when we stormed the Red Dawn strongholds." He sighed. "They look at me, and they see a carnival barker. The crazy old man who runs the flying spa, casino, and resort." He gave in to temptation and poured himself another drink. "I used to fight enemy fleets. Now I book magicians and stand-up comedians."

Jordan smiled, accepting a drink too. "Well, I've always wanted a career in entertainment. I do hope to sing at the gala tonight."

King harrumphed. He lifted the model of the *Freedom* from his desk, ran his hand along the railgun. "Such a beautiful ship. She was always beautiful."

"Please don't rub my rails while I'm standing right here, sir," Mimori said.

King snapped his head toward her. Jordan raised an eyebrow.

The android winked.

Jordan laughed—a deep, mellifluous sound. "You're leaving me with one sassy android, Jim."

King snorted. "All right, enough sass. We'll call the high commander. Mimori, make the call. Connect it to my MindLink. Going over the admiralty is a breach of protocol. But hell, what are they gonna do, fire me? I'm retiring tomorrow. Let me break one last rule."

Mimori nodded. "Calling right now, sir."

The android closed her eyes. Semitransparent screens, dials, and progress bars floated around her head, a visual interface. It looked like holograms, but it was a hallucination. King's MindLink was turned on, connected to the starship. While Mimori worked, King was able to see what she was working on.

Funny, King thought. *On my last day, I'm finally using my MindLink. I'm still getting the damn thing removed tomorrow.*

The android scrolled through her contact list and chose High Commander Archer, who worked in Alliance Headquarters down in Washington, DC. King had visited Alliance Headquarters many times. The building was roughly shaped like two hands pressed together in prayer. At least if you squinted and used your imagination.

They had built that building quickly during the war. Everything happened quickly back then. The United States and other democracies scrambled to form an alliance against the rising tide of Red Dawn. As millions were dying, as cities burned, the free people of the world gathered in the ruins. They united. They formed a great wall to break the tidal wave of equalism.

Some people complained that Alliance Headquarters was based in the United States, one country, while the Alliance comprised dozens of nations. But back then, everything happened so fast. The United States had led the coalition, so the headquarters remained on American soil, and the current high commander was an American.

Still, Americans formed only half the staff. Many officers from great nations served in the headquarters on the ground, and they served here aboard the starship *Freedom*. King and Jordan, the *Freedom*'s two most senior officers, were both American. But Sergeant Major Darjeeling, the senior NCO aboard the *Freedom*, was English. And Colonel Gal "Spitfire" Levy, who commanded the starfighter fleet, was Israeli. Mimori had been built in Japan. There were officers and NCOs from twenty-three other nations aboard.

All swore allegiance to the Alliance high commander.

Who was not answering his phone.

Finally an android down on Earth answered the call. She materialized here in the cabin aboard the *Freedom*. Another hallucination. The android appeared as a pretty young woman in a white uniform, her blond hair held in a sensible ponytail.

"Welcome to the office of the Alliance high commander! Please be aware that our office is closed for the holidays. Have a Merry Christmas and—"

"Get Archer on the line," King growled. "This is Commander James King calling."

The android smiled sweetly. "Oh, the hotel manager! Yes, of course." She tilted her head. "Going over the heads of the admiralty? I'm not sure that's according to protocol. I'll have to file a complaint. If you're willing to sign a form, I—"

"Get me Archer on the line."

"I'm afraid he's on holiday, sir. If you don't mind filling out a request form, I can queue you in for a call in early February. Would mornings or afternoons work better for you?"

King hung up on her.

Goddammit.

He looked at Jordan and Mimori. His second-in-command and the personification of the ship he stood in. They stared back, silent.

"We've done all we could to raise the alarm," King said. "Only to be dismissed. Mocked. Turned away. Us, the soldiers who won the war." He clenched his fists, and his lip peeled back in a snarl. "We're alone."

Jordan placed a hand on King's shoulder. "Not alone. We have one another. Us in this cabin, and the thousands who live and work aboard the *Freedom*."

"And you have the *Freedom* herself," Mimori said. "Me."

"Whatever is out there at the Rubicon, if it comes here, we'll be ready," Jordan said.

King shook his head sadly. "I wish I could agree. But we have no ammunition aboard this ship, aside from a few personal pistols. No Maccabee torpedoes for the Angels of Liberty. No missiles for our Eagles' wings. No bullets for our machine-gun turrets. Our single Goliath projectile is hollow—just a fake for tourists to photograph. We're no warship. We're a museum."

"No," Mimori said. "We're heroes. From the ashes of defeat, when the war seemed lost, we rose and brought hope to mankind. If new darkness falls, we will shine our light again, and we will ring the bells of freedom."

"I never knew you were a poet, Mimori," King said.

She smiled. "I've studied your old war speeches."

"Our old bulldog does have a poet's soul," Jordan said, smiling too.

But King did not smile. His frown only deepened. His old

war wound ached.

"This is probably nothing," King said. "Probably just an astronaut too deep in space, too lonely, imagining monsters in the dark. Odds are we're safe. But soldiers do not win by playing the odds. They win by preparing for any eventuality. They win by expecting the worst—and facing it head-on. We are still soldiers. They might call us showmen, carnival barkers, entertainers. But I know that we're still soldiers, and we will not ignore this danger. The *Freedom* was a military ship once. We still remember what happens to those who do not prepare for war."

Jordan lost his smile. He had grown up in Los Angeles. He remembered what had happened to his city. He nodded solemnly. "We're still soldiers. A bit older. A bit slower on our feet. But soldiers still."

"My hull is still thick and strong," Mimori said. "I don't mean the synthetic skin of this interface. I speak to you now as the starship *Freedom* herself. I am unarmed. But I am armored. And I'm ready to shield the people inside me—whatever danger might come."

King nodded, satisfied. The commander of a starship was only as good as his crew and his ship. And King had an excellent crew and ship.

"I'm going to start contacting the senior officers and NCOs," King said. "I'm implementing a complete lockdown of the starship *Freedom*. All civilians, tourists and staff alike, will report to their cabins. All military personnel will enter a state of yellow alert. I'll be closing down all tourist facilities. And the Christmas gala is canceled."

"Grinch," Jordan quipped.

Mimori nodded at King. "Should I begin to relay your orders to the ship's officers?"

"I'll do it myself," King said. "This should come from me."

Jordan leaned closer and spoke in a low voice. "Jim, if

you're wrong about this, if this is just a false alarm . . . there will be a lot of very angry people down on Earth. Christmas is the busiest tourist day of the year."

"I won't compromise the security of my ship to make a buck," King said.

"Still, the backlash could be severe," Jordan said. "Both from our bosses and from the public. Not to mention the civilian contractors who run the spas, casinos, and the other entertainment facilities. They have powerful lobbyists. To close a premier tourist attraction on Christmas because of a cryptic message from the Rubicon . . ."

"That's what the Rubicon is there for. To warn us of threats to the solar system."

"On paper, yes," Jordan said. "We both know the Rubicon was always a publicity stunt. Just a way to get one American and one Russian to sit in a room together without killing each other."

"Nevertheless, the Rubicon sent a warning. And military protocol demands that I take it seriously." He put a hand on Jordan's shoulder. "If this is a false alarm, I'll take the heat. I'm retiring anyway. You'll begin your command with a clean slate."

Then King remembered. He had planned to officially announce his retirement at the gala tonight. The same gala he just canceled.

I guess I'm staying on board for a little longer, he thought. He heaved a long, raspy sigh. It hurt.

CHAPTER FOURTEEN

The Starship *Freedom*
High Earth Orbit
14:42 Christmas 2199

The aerie was famous, at least among British royalty. Located on the bottom deck of the starship *Freedom*, it was an exclusive lounge for starfighter pilots. Emily, the granddaughter of a starfighter pilot, had heard many stories about it. King Robert—back when he was Prince Robert the intrepid pilot—used to drink, play, and socialize there.

When Emily entered the aerie, she expected to find a sophisticated club. Oil paintings would hang on the walls, she had imagined. A chandelier would glow. A butler in a tuxedo would be serving wine, while the pilots reclined in giltwood chairs, smoking pipes, stroking their mustaches, and discussing the issues of the day.

After all, her grandfather used to haunt the aerie. Naturally, Emily had imagined a place worthy of a king, a club of class and sophistication.

Of course not.

This was the *Freedom*, after all.

"I don't think we're in Buckingham Palace anymore, Toto," she told her drone.

"I should think not!" Niles said. "This place is positively ghastly. Do you think there will be a bar fight? Oh dear."

"I think it's wonderful," Emily said. "We need a place like

this in the palace."

"Heavens no!" Niles bristled, his gemstones clinking. "We certainly don't want Buckingham Palace to become a hive of ill repute."

Standing at the doorway, Emily admired the aerie. The smell of beer and cigar smoke filled the air. Pinups covered the walls, depicting scantily clad women lounging against starfighters. Emily blushed to see them.

The lounge was packed, and nobody had noticed her yet. The Freedom's Flock, the starship's complement of stunt pilots, filled the place. At least she assumed those were the stunt pilots. They wore blue flight suits, so it seemed a safe assumption.

A few pilots were shooting pool. Others were drinking at the bar. A couple of men were arm-wrestling while one slipped a coin into an old-fashioned jukebox. "Thunderstruck" by AC/DC began to play. The song was centuries old, but Emily, a buff of historical music, recognized the tune.

"We put on a good show today, didn't we?" one pilot was saying, examining a pool table. He bit into a pickle. It *snapped*.

Nobody had noticed Emily yet. The cigar smoke was apparently concealing her.

"*I* put on a good show," said another pilot, a portly man with pink cheeks. "You, Pickles, flew like a one-winged chicken."

Pickles snorted. The origin of his nickname was clear. The pilot reached into a jar, pulled out another pickle, and bit with relish. "Me, a one-winged chicken? You, Meatball, fly like a one-legged elephant."

Meatball, the beefy pilot, gulped down beer. "Ah, whatever. You're full of crap as always." He wiped suds off his lips. "Hey . . . they say the princess of England was watching from one of those shuttles. You believe that?"

Pickles snorted. He tapped the side of his head. Suddenly his left eye glowed red. A bionic implant. Laser beamed out from the eye, tracing angles between several billiard balls.

"Yeah, Meatball, whatever you say." Pickles squinted, adjusting the laser from his eyeball, plotting his pool shot. "And I heard the queen was watching from the whorehouse porthole."

A third pilot, an Asian woman with long black hair, stomped forward and crossed her arms. "Hey, Pickles! It's cheating if you use your bionic eye like a laser pointer."

"Shut up, Katana, it's part of my body," said Pickles, looking up from the pool table. The laser from his bionic eye swept upward, blinding a few pilots. People cursed. A dart went wide, hitting a pinup girl over the bar.

Everyone started arguing and laughing. Emily watched with wonder from the doorway. She had spent her life among prim and proper royalty. Seeing these daredevils in their natural habitat seemed so alien and marvelous. Granted, these pilots were officers of the Alliance, themselves something of royalty aboard the starship. Not many soldiers became officers, let alone pilots, let alone starfighter pilots. But Emily supposed that when you were the princess of England, anything short of tea with the queen seemed a bit lowbrow.

If *she* found this place a bit rough, Emily couldn't even imagine what Niles was thinking. The drone just hovered there silently. Probably too mortified to speak.

Darjeeling, who had accompanied Emily here, stepped forward and cleared his throat.

The flock all looked up.

Emily smiled hesitantly and waved.

A few cigars fell from a few mouths.

"Ah, shit," said Pickles. "The princess *is* here."

He turned off his bionic eye and managed a clumsy bow, knocking over his jar of pickles.

"Sirs, ma'ams, officers of the fleet!" boomed Darjeeling. "May I introduce to you a special guest aboard our starship." He removed his cap. "Her Royal Highness Princess Emily, Duchess of Sussex, Lady of the White Rose."

"Hi." She smiled and curtsied.

Pickles bowed before her. "Pardon, Your Majesty! Or is it Your Highness? I'm from New York. I don't know shit about royalty, but— Hey, welcome aboard!" He grinned, scooped up his jar, and held it out. "Want a pickle?"

Meatball, the heavyset pilot, shoved the smaller Pickles aside. "Don't offer the princess of England a pickle! She's not a peasant like you." He held out a beefy hand for Emily to shake. "The name's Bob. But the boys call me Meatball. It's because I cook good meatballs."

"It's because you look like a meatball," Pickles said.

Emily shook Meatball's hand. He had a warm, crushing grip. "Hello. It's nice to meet you. Nice to meet you all."

* * * * *

A few more pilots introduced themselves. Katana was petite but fierce, and her eyes gleamed with savage intensity. Snoopy, a young female pilot with blond hair, only smiled shyly, too meek to even talk. Curly winked and kissed Emily's hand. Honey Badger and Babyface strutted around, trying to impress her, while Tenderfoot only blushed and nursed a beer. There were a bunch more, each boasting a silly nickname. Emily didn't know their real names. Around here, the pilots went by their call signs.

My grandfather was known as Charming, she remembered. *Appropriate for a prince.*

Soon Emily was laughing with the flock, refusing the beer (and pickles) but laughing at the jokes. Honey Badger, the tiniest pilot in the crew, began to croon. Meatball grunted and tossed an apple core at the diminutive singer.

"You'll really teach me to fly a starfighter?" Emily said, laughing.

Pickles nodded. "Sure, babe. Anything for the princess of England. I tell ya, the boys back in Brooklyn ain't gonna believe me."

"Ah, don't fly with that putz!" said Meatball. "I'll give ya a flight in my bird. You'll see what real flying's like. And I don't even need a bionic eye to find my way."

Pickles blew cigar smoke at him. "That's right, Meatball, 'cause you always just follow my wake."

The larger pilot laughed. "Whatever, Pickles, we all know that your mother—"

"What the hell is going on here?"

The voice boomed from the back of the aerie.

Everyone scrambled up and snapped to attention. Even Darjeeling, who had been enjoying a cup of tea at the bar.

"Commander on deck!" Darjeeling cried, saluting.

Emily rose too, though she wasn't sure why. She stared toward the shadows at the back of the lounge.

A tall woman stepped into the light. Her brown hair was pulled into a ponytail, freckles adorned her nose and cheeks, and her eyes burned with fury. She was a pilot too. She wore the same blue flight suit as the others. But five golden bars topped each of her shoulders. She was a colonel, outranking everyone else in the room.

She's young to be a colonel, Emily thought. *She looks like she's still in her thirties.*

Darjeeling stepped toward Emily and bowed his head. "Your Highness, may I introduce Colonel Gal Levy, known by her call sign Spitfire. She commands Freedom's Flock." He turned toward Spitfire. "Ma'am, may I introduce Princess Em—"

"I know who she is," Spitfire said. "And I don't give a

damn. I didn't come here to grovel or curtsy or kiss ass. Pilots of the Alliance do not bow before royalty. Let alone a teenage girl." She glared at the rest of the flock. "Pickles! Meatball! You get that?"

The younger pilots gulped.

"Um, yes, ma'am," Pickles began. "It's just that—"

"Quiet!" Spitfire roared. "No excuses. I'll have you scrubbing space barnacles with your bare hands."

Pickled loosened his collar, cringing. "Yes, ma'am."

Emily stepped forward. "Miss Levy, if I caused any trouble, I apologize. I didn't mean to step on any toes."

Spitfire spun toward her, eyes flaring. "You will call me *Colonel* Levy, or you will call me by my call sign. Is that understood? This is a military vessel, not your precious palace."

Emily stepped back again. "I'm so sorry, Colonel Levy. I just wanted to come and thank you. For the show you put on for me. For—"

"For you?" Spitfire laughed. "We didn't put on a show for *you*. There were thousands of tourists watching. Most who didn't need to book an entire shuttle for themselves. You're nobody special, *Princess*."

Emily's eyes stung. Surprisingly, she found herself close to tears. She wasn't used to being scolded like this.

"How dare you besmirch the princess's honor?" Niles demanded, flying toward the colonel. A hatch opened on his body, and his slender pointer emerged. "Now stand down, ruffian, lest my rod finds your backside!"

Spitfire stared at the drone in disgust. "Will somebody get this jeweled football off my deck?"

Niles bristled, jewels rattling. "A *football?* I assume you mean the crude American game, the one where hulking brutes toss so-called pigskins." The drone shuddered. "I shall have you know that I'm a prolate spheroid, and my jewels are worth more than your life."

"Shut him up or I shoot him down!" Spitfire said, reaching for her sidearm.

"Pardon, Colonel," Darjeeling said, stepping closer. He held out his hands in a placating gesture. He was twice Spitfire's age, but she outranked him, so he was treading carefully. "Now let's be fair. Princess Emily isn't to blame for what happened. She wasn't even born back then."

Emily wasn't sure what the sergeant was talking about. She would ask him later. Right now she wanted to make amends.

"I don't know why you're cross at me, Colonel Levy," Emily said to the tall pilot. "If I've offended you—"

"Don't flatter yourself." Spitfire snickered. "It takes more than a spoiled princess to offend me. Did you really think you could prance in here after what your grandfather did?"

Emily tilted her head. "What did my grandfather do? He's a war hero."

Spitfire snorted. "Is that what they teach you at your fancy princess school? That Runaway Robert was a war hero?"

"Everyone knows King Robert is a war hero!" Emily said. Finally some anger rose in her. To insult her was one thing. But to insult her family was far worse. "He earned many medals in the war. King Robert has his problems, yes. He can be sulky, moody, withdrawn. The war was hard on him, and he never fully healed." She raised her chin and squared her shoulders. "But he's an honorable man, a fine king, and a proud veteran."

Emily took deep breaths, reeling after her speech. Truth be told, she had always found her grandfather intimidating. But she also loved him, and she would defend him wherever he was besmirched. Darjeeling, bless his heart, pressed his cap to his chest and nodded his agreements.

But Spitfire was not swayed. She poked her finger in Emily's chest. Right on the collarbone.

"Don't you play innocent li'l princess with me. You're just like him." She turned toward Darjeeling and raised her voice. "Sergeant, I want her off my deck!"

Darjeeling turned red. Clearly he was fuming. But Spitfire was a senior officer, outranking everyone on the deck. There was little Darjeeling could do.

He took a deep breath, steadying himself, and bowed his head. "Colonel, certainly. Forgive us."

Emily and Darjeeling walked toward the exit. Niles flew at their side, rattling with rage, muttering something about how he'd never been so insulted in his life.

As they walked past an antique pinball machine, the princess leaned toward the aging sergeant.

"Mr. Darjeeling, during the war, did my grandfather do something . . . upsetting?"

"Well . . ." Darjeeling cleared his throat. "Those who know him well don't believe it. And I myself do not. But it was Spitfire's father who died in the fiasco. And . . . ah, well, perhaps it's not my job to tell you."

"Tell me what?" Emily said. She walked around a foosball table, heading toward the door. "What fiasco? Please tell me."

"Well, all right," said Darjeeling. "It was the winter of 2158, and—"

The aerie door banged open.

James "Bulldog" King, commander of the starship *Freedom*, stood before them.

* * * * *

"Commander on deck!" Darjeeling boomed—the loudest Emily had ever heard him.

Darjeeling stood at attention, raised his chin, and gave Commander King a brisk salute. Across the aerie, the flock abandoned the pool table, the dart board, and their beers. The pilots formed two neat lines along the walls, snapped their heels together, and saluted too. An empty bottle of beer rolled across the deck. The jukebox was now playing Iron Maiden's "The Trooper." Pickles kicked it, killing the music, then stood at attention again.

Emily wasn't sure what to do. She wasn't a soldier, and she didn't think it proper to salute. So she simply stood there, trying to appear respectful, and examined the fabled old commander of the starship *Freedom*.

He was a tall man, his shoulders broad, his jaw wide. His steel-gray hair was cropped short. His skin looked like old leather, beaten and dried in the sun. An angry white scar stretched across his neck.

Katyusha gave him that scar, Emily thought.

She knew the story. Everyone on Earth did.

It had happened on the last day of the war.

Katyusha—the dreaded premier of Red Dawn. She had led her troops across the red plains of Mars, meeting the Alliance on the field. As millions perished all around, Katyusha battled Ulysses King, the great general of the Alliance. Out of bullets, she grabbed the general's knife from him, then stabbed him in the chest, slaying him on the red dust.

A great cry rose then. A cry of anguish from the black smoke and red sandstorms.

A young captain charged forward, howling in grief. James King, a son grieving.

Katyusha bested him in battle that day. She sliced open his throat and left him to die.

Through sheer force of will, and the pluck of a nearby medic, the young officer survived. He returned to Earth, a war hero. The bulldog, they called him. The soldier who never gave up.

And there he stood before her now. Commander James King, son of Ulysses. The old bulldog himself.

He was older than the holograms and hallucinations Emily had seen. Those were all from World War III. Commander King was an old man now. But when he turned toward her, when he stared into her eyes, Emily saw that same hero. That same son grieving. That same determination that shielded old pain.

There was intensity in those eyes. There was great strength like unyielding stone, but like all strength earned in war, sadness flowed through it. There was raging fire and cold steel and everything in between. There before her, Emily thought, stood a leader.

All those thoughts and memories flashed before her in an instant.

King bowed his head to her. "Your Highness, welcome aboard the starship *Freedom*. It's my honor to host you aboard our ship."

His voice! His voice was barely more than a rasp. It sounded like sandpaper scraped over asphalt. The wound, Emily realized. It had never fully healed. She wondered if it still hurt.

She held out her hand. The commander kissed it.

"The honor is mine, sir." She smiled. "My grandfather thinks the world of you."

King smiled thinly. "He's a good friend."

The commander looked at the flock in the lounge, who were still standing at attention.

"At ease," he said.

The soldiers relaxed, but everyone still stood in place.

At ease means to remain in place, just more relaxed than at attention, Emily remembered. Her grandfather had taught her some military terms.

The pilots glanced around nervously. Emily guessed that it was rare for Commander King to visit the aerie. Maybe he was a little like King Robert, mostly keeping to his chambers, never hobnobbing with the hoi polloi. Her grandfather had been gregarious once, they said. Long before Emily had been born. In the old videos, Robert was always smiling and laughing and chatting.

Not since the war. Not since whatever . . . happened.

Whatever Spitfire is so angry about, Emily thought. *What did my grandfather do? What secrets will I uncover on this ship?*

King cleared his throat and spoke to everyone in the lounge.

"This morning, we detected concerning signals from the Rubicon, a space station on the edge of the solar system. It's the farthest point of human presence in space. The signals were unclear, but they suggest the destruction of the station. We also received a snippet of a voice message. It came from the Rubicon before the station's destruction."

The commander raised a minicom, a computer the size of a playing card. He tapped a button.

A frightened voice emerged, speaking with an American accent.

"Beverly, I love you. It's me, Mike. Aliens are real, Beverly. Monsters are real. A fleet. An enemy fleet, heading to Earth. Tell the army! Tell them to get ready. I love you. I love—"

A scream.

A sound like shattering glass.

A screech.

The recording ended.

Emily shivered. She glanced toward Darjeeling. A true Englishman, he stepped forward to shield her, though if there was any threat, it must be deep in space.

Aliens are real.

Could it be?

Niles hovered closer to her.

"I'll protect you, Princess," the robot whispered. "With my life if I must."

"As would I," said Darjeeling, chin held high, and clasped the ceremonial saber that hung from his waist. "You have my saber, my strength, and my soul, Your Highness."

King cleared his throat, drawing their attention. "This is probably nothing," the grizzled commander said. "Probably just an astronaut suffering from space sickness. Seeing things. God knows we've dealt with their type before. For centuries, humanity has been flooded with false reports of aliens. Hoaxes, every last one. This probably is too."

Spitfire laughed. "Of course it's a hoax, sir. I mean, c'mon. What's next, a Bigfoot sighting on Pluto? Ignore it."

"Ignore it?" King rasped. "No, we can't do that. Odds are this is another hoax. But our duty calls for caution. This warning came from the Rubicon, an outpost with a clear mission: to report threats from outside the solar system. We take warnings from the Rubicon seriously on this ship. I'm ordering a full yellow alert to all military personnel. The flock will remain in their hangar, ready to deploy if ordered."

Spitfire saluted, a crooked smile on her face. "Sure thing, sir. If any aliens invade the solar system, we can dazzle them with a stunt show. Want me to grab a cane and top hat and dance the ragtime too?"

A few smirks rose among the pilots. The commander wiped them off with a glare. He kept speaking. "Meanwhile, all civilians—both tourists and staff—will be restricted to their cabins. Sergeant Major Darjeeling." He turned toward the Englishman. "You'll be responsible for evacuating the entertainment decks. Casinos, spas, dance clubs, the whole damn circus—I want them all shut down. Summon what resources you must from the crew, but get it done within an hour."

Darjeeling hesitated. He glanced at Emily, then at King again. "Sir, with all due respect, as a proud Englishman and servant of the crown, I believe I should remain at Princess Emily's side. I must protect her at any cost."

Emily smiled soothingly. "It's all right, Mr. Darjeeling. I can take care of myself."

Darjeeling looked back at her. "Ma'am, how can I abandon you? I have a duty to this ship, true, but also to the crown."

"Sergeant Major!" King said, voice rising louder. "You are an NCO of the Free Alliance Fleet. While you wear the uniform, your duty is to this ship and to your commanding officer. Is that clear?"

Darjeeling spun toward the commander. "Sir, I—"

"Oh, cease your fretting, Mr. Darjeeling!" Niles interjected, floating forward. "Tend to your duties about this ship. I am perfectly capable of defending our princess myself."

A click sounded inside the hovering drone. Dozens of knives, pistols, and even a blowtorch sprang out from his body. Hovering in the air, Niles looked like a cross between a blowfish and a Swiss army knife.

"Dear God, man!" Darjeeling said, eyes wide. "You carry enough firepower to take down a Red Dawn phalanx."

"I was programmed to educate, chaperone, and protect the princess of Great Britain with my life," Niles said. "That I shall do. Tend to your duties, fellow soldier of England. Your princess is in good hands." The drone paused. "Metaphorically, of course. Thank goodness I don't have actual hands. Dreadfully inelegant things. I don't know how you humans get anything done with them."

Darjeeling nodded, turned toward Commander King, and saluted. "Sir, forgive my lapse of duty. My full loyalty is to this ship and her fine commander."

King smiled thinly and squeezed Darjeeling's shoulder. "I

know, Oliver. We've been friends for forty years. I know. See to your duties. We'll get through this."

Oliver Darjeeling saluted again, bowed to Emily, then rushed out the aerie.

There goes a fine Englishman, Emily thought. *Among the finest I've seen.*

"Princess Emily," King said. "During our lockdown, you may remain in the royal suite aboard deck 28. It's a cabin for dignitaries. I would say that you qualify. I'll assign a guard to your door, of course. I'll have my ship's computers upload a map to your drone."

"Don't you dare let any computer touch my circuits," Niles said. "I'm likely to get a virus. I can find my way around a starship on my own, thank you very much."

King nodded. "Very well. I would accompany you there, ma'am, were this a different time."

"You have duties to attend to, sir, I know." Emily bowed. "Thank you, dear commander. May God bless you."

As she hurried down the corridor, following Niles, Emily shook her head in wonder. Back on Earth, the tabloids said that Commander King was a setting star, a lion who was once mighty, who had been declawed, defanged, and locked in a floating cage. That was not the man Emily had met.

I met a leader, she thought. *I met a soldier. I met the hero who saved the world long ago. If Earth is truly in danger again, James King is a man we can trust.*

As Emily entered the royal suite, she wondered if she should actually worry. If she believed in aliens. Believed they were invading the solar system.

She scoffed. Of course not. What, because of some snippet from space, the ravings of a spacer gone mad? Ridiculous. Just a hoax! Soon enough, the lockdown would end, and Emily would fly back to England, and everything would be fine.

Of course everything would be fine.

Yet as Emily sat on the embroidered armchair, a princess in a starship far from Earth, she trembled.

CHAPTER FIFTEEN

Nebraska
15:18 Christmas 2199

"Finally you're here! Jesus Christ, Bastian, I almost missed the last aero-cab. Goddamn you."

Stacy was waiting on the patio, holding a suitcase. The sound of cartoons came from inside the house. Rowan must be inside, watching the holofeed.

Bastian halted the robotic horse and dismounted. During the ride there, he had practiced several different apologies. But seeing Stacy, they all faded from his mind. Her crossed arms, her angry eyes, her sharp mouth—they reminded him of too many arguments. Too much pain. The old rage rose in him. They had always been so angry together.

"If you hadn't sold my shuttle, you could have flown yourself to Bemidji."

Stacy rolled her eyes. "You know I don't fly. And it was *my* shuttle. The judge gave it to me. Piece of junk anyway."

"It was a classic Falcon-class cherry-red speedster, not a piece of junk!"

"I wasn't using it, and Hunter needed money to open his second health food store."

Bastian's eyes widened. "*That's* why you sold my shuttle? To give the money to goddamn Hunter?"

She shoved him aside. "I don't have time for this. I ordered a shuttle service. It'll be here soon. It's already late. Dammit, why is everyone late today?"

"Maybe the cab driver's wife sold his shuttle," Bastian said.

"Hilarious." Stacy tapped her fingernails against her thigh, glanced back toward the house. The cartoon's lights flashed through the window. Stacy looked back at Bastian. "Let her come with me to Bemidji."

"*What?*" Bastian exclaimed, almost shouting. "Are you crazy, Stacy? She's my daughter. She's gonna spend the second half of Christmas with me."

"An army base is no place for a little girl," Stacy said.

He gritted his teeth. He was close to losing it. "If you hadn't taken my house, maybe I wouldn't have to bring her to an army base."

"If you had been a better husband—"

"Enough!" Bastian snapped. "Rowan is coming with me and that's that."

"Daddy?" The voice came from the doorway. "Are you and Mommy arguing again?"

Bastian turned around and his heart melted. Whenever he saw Rowan, all the anger flowed away. She was the only good thing in the mess of his life. The only reason he kept going. The little girl even looked like him—the same brown hair, same gray eyes. Nothing like Stacy, who had blond hair and blue eyes. Bastian took a little satisfaction in that. Stacy took everything from him, but at least the kid would never look like her.

He knelt by his daughter.

"Hey, Row. You ready to spend Christmas with Daddy?"

Rowan pouted. "Mommy said I can go to Bemidji."

Goddamn Stacy.

"Aww, come on, Row," Bastian said. "We're gonna have

way more fun at Fort Liberty. They have a tank. A real tank! Do you want to ride it?"

It was actually just an armored Jeep, but a machine gun rose above the hood. Close enough.

Rowan sniffed. "I want to go to Bemidji with Mommy. She's going to go to the lake and skate on the ice, and I want to go too. She said if you're late I can go, and you were late, so can I go to Bemidji, Daddy? Please."

He took a deep breath. Inside his chest, his heart shattered.

"Sweetie, I promise you. We're going to have so much fun. Maybe there's no beach, but there's ice cream in the commissary! What say first thing when we get there, we eat ice cream?"

"She already had a treat today," Stacy said, still tapping her thigh.

Bastian clenched his jaw, forcing himself to keep his smile. "Come on, Row. Let's get on my horse. We get to ride a horse all the way there!"

"It's a robot," Rowan said. "I don't like robots. I want to go with my mom." She ran to Stacy, clutched her leg. "Mommy, I want to go with you."

Bastian stood there, helpless. He was almost ready to give up. To let Stacy take the girl to Hunter. To walk away, defeated.

But no.

He could not back down. He wanted to have a relationship with Rowan.

I have no relationship with my father, Bastian thought. *I want better for Rowan.*

"Stacy?" he said softly. "A little help?"

Stacy looked at him, anger still in her eyes. But then she sighed. She knelt by Rowan.

"Rowie, go with your dad. You'll have tons of fun! And you can eat ice cream again." Stacy winked. "I'm jealous. I wish I could go to Fort Liberty. It's so much fun there."

Bastian nodded at her.

Thank you, he thought.

That was the Stacy he had married. That was the woman he had fallen in love with. Before the anger tore them apart.

Rowan sniffed and wiped her eyes. "I want to go with you, Mommy. I don't care what's more fun, I don't care about ice cream—I want to be with you."

Stacy lifted the girl, carried her toward the horse. "We'll be together again soon, Rowie. In just two days."

"I can't wait that long!" Rowan said, tears flowing.

Bastian climbed onto the horse. He had to hug Rowan tightly, practically restraining her. As he galloped away, the girl wept, reaching back toward her mother. And with every step the robot took, Bastian's heart broke into smaller pieces.

As he rode to Fort Liberty, his daughter crying in the saddle, Bastian forgot all about giant spiders and old tales of demons.

* * * * *

It was afternoon, and most of Christmas was gone already, when Bastian and Rowan reached Fort Liberty.

"We have a few hours until bedtime, Row," Bastian said, riding into the base. "You can stay up late. We're going to have lots of fun."

Rowan sat on the saddle before him, pouting. Her tears had dried during the ride there, but her arms were still crossed. Bastian understood. Divorce was hard for everyone. Especially for a five-year-old girl.

"Why can't we all be together for Christmas?" Rowan said. "You, me, and Mommy?"

Bastian sighed. "Sometimes kids have parents who live separately, and they get to celebrate Christmas in two different places."

"I know, Daddy, it's called divorce. I'm five. Don't talk to me like I'm four."

Bastian laughed. "My mistake."

"I don't know why you and Mommy had to get divorced," Rowan said. "Why can't we be like before? Last year we had Christmas all together."

Bastian remembered last Christmas. The tension. The angry looks. They had hidden it so well from Rowan. The marriage had fallen apart the next month.

They rode the robotic horse toward the main gate. Snow swirled around the metal hooves. The guard, a scrawny private in an oversized coat, gave them a sullen look. He wasn't happy to be working on Christmas, especially not outside in the cold. But when he noticed the insignia on Bastian's shoulders, marking him an officer, the guard snapped to attention and saluted.

Bastian returned the salute. He queried his MindLink for the guard's name. It hovered up before him. Private William Reynolds, third battalion, nineteen years old.

"Merry Christmas, Private Reynolds," Bastian said. His breath frosted with every word.

"Merry Christmas, sir. Nice horse."

He seemed like a good kid. Too bad he was stuck here.

Bastian didn't know everyone at Fort Liberty by name. Not without his MindLink. But he recognized many faces, maybe even most of them. Five thousand soldiers were stationed there—the entire Freedom Brigade.

Of course, most of them were home now, relaxing by the fireplace with presents and candy canes. Lucky bastards. The base was a ghost town today.

Bastian rode through the gate and across a snowy courtyard,

passing by the armory, mess hall, and chapel. He dismounted his horse by the barracks where the troops lived. He held Rowan's hand, and they stepped into the concrete building.

A stench hit his nostrils. He groaned.

"Eww, it stinks here!" Rowan said. "Can we go to Bemidji now?"

They kept walking down the hallway. Bastian waved his hand, trying to scatter the stench. He recognized the oily, meaty smell. He had smelled it on the hilltop.

A voice rose from around a corner. "Careful, chief! You're going to snap off its leg."

Bastian recognized the voice. Alice.

Another voice rose behind the corner, deep and rumbling.

"I told you, Alice, I'm not a chief. Just because I'm Native American doesn't automatically make me a chief."

Bastian recognized that voice too. Charging Bear.

A *crack* sounded.

"Bear, careful!" Alice cried. "See? You banged its leg against the wall."

"Lift your side higher," Bear said. "We need to pivot around the corner."

"I *am* lifting it higher. It's not my fault I'm not a seven-foot freak like you."

Bickering, Alice and Bear emerged around the corner. They were carrying the corpse of the giant spider.

Bastian and Rowan stood in the corridor, staring.

Rowan blanched. "Daddy . . . what is that?"

"I wish I knew, Row."

"It looks like a giant spider." The girl covered her eyes. "I'm scared."

"Don't worry, Row, it's dead." Bastian glared at Alice and Bear. "Will you please carry that thing to the lab? It's stinking up the barracks."

"We have a lab?" Alice said.

Bastian nodded. "You know, the building in the back. White walls. Big red cross on the front."

Alice tilted her head. "The infirmary?"

"Yeah, part of it is a lab," Bastian said. "The room where they analyze our blood and urine samples."

"Bas!" Alice adjusted her grip on the spider. "The lab where they do our drug tests isn't exactly equipped to study an alien lifeform."

"A lab is a lab! Just take it there. Get it out of here. It's scaring my daughter. And it's stinking up our barracks."

Grumbling, Alice and Bear carried the spider into the courtyard. The damn thing was the size of a horse. Luckily, so were Alice and Bear.

Alice, the bear, and the spider, Bastian thought. *Sounds like a children's book.*

Rowan was still covering her eyes. "Is the giant spider gone?"

"It's gone, sweetie."

She opened her eyes. "Daddy, was it an alien?"

"The lab will find out."

"The lab where they do your drug tests?"

"A lab is a lab!" Bastian exclaimed. "Everyone's a critic. Come on, Row. It stinks here. Let's head to the commissary. They've got ice cream!"

Rowan poked his belly. "Should you really be eating ice cream, Daddy?"

He groaned. "It's muscles! I have big stomach muscles."

Rowan giggled. "Daddy, you're silly and playing tricks."

Good. She was giggling. At his expense, but still giggling. That beat the tears. The sound of her laughter, the sight of her smile—it made everything seem okay. Even with a giant spider on base, which had probably escaped from a Russian lab.

They were sitting in the mess hall, eating peanut butter ice cream, when his MindLink rang.

It was another call from the starship *Freedom*. It was labeled urgent.

* * * * *

"I told you, Dad, I'm not coming onto the *Freedom* for Christmas," Bastian said. "So stop calling."

He stood in the mess hall, his ice cream forgotten. Rage pounded through him. The old man had not called him all year. And now he was pestering Bastian twice in one day.

Amazingly, King was actually using his MindLink this time. Not a phone. An actual telepathic connection. Incredible. Commander James King, embracing new technology? A Christmas miracle! The old bastard was finally learning.

Bastian's MindLink created a vivid hallucination of the commander. The old man seemed to be sitting in front of Bastian, right here in the mess hall. The implant crafted the hallucination from cameras and microphones aboard the starship *Freedom*, using artificial intelligence to fill out the blanks. The illusion was complete.

Sitting at the table, face covered with ice cream, Rowan gasped. "Is that Pop Pop? Can I talk to him?"

She couldn't see the apparition. The call was to Bastian's implant only.

"Is that you, Rowan?" King said.

"She can't hear you, Dad," Bastian said. "Only I can hear and see you. Hang on. I'll patch Rowan's MindLink into the call."

King frowned. He rose from his seat, and his face flushed with anger. "You gave Rowan, a five-year-old girl, a brain implant?"

"Calm down, old man. It's like giving kids a toy car these days. She has the kiddie implant. I can control it from my end. Hang on, I'm patching her in." He looked at Rowan. "Ready, sweetie?"

The girl tapped her skull. A year ago, she had gotten the surgery. She used her implant to hallucinate cartoons and telepathically play with friends. An hour a day, that was her limit.

"Ready!" she said.

Bastian patched her in. At once, her brain received the signal and created the same hallucination that Bastian was having. Rowan too daydreamed James King, her grandfather, standing in the mess room.

"Hi, Pop Pop! Want some ice cream?" She held out the bowl.

"She still doesn't know that you can't share food through the MindWeb," Bastian explained.

"I missed you, Rowie," said the hallucination. "Merry Christmas. I plan to come visit you real soon. As soon as I can."

"Pop Pop, there's a giant spider here at Fort Liberty, and it stinks real bad, and my dad said he isn't fat!"

The two talked for a moment. But King seemed distracted. The commander finally said, "Rowie, I gotta talk to Daddy for a sec, all right?"

"Love you, Pop Pop!"

"Love you too, sweetie." The commander turned toward Bastian. "I didn't call to keep bugging you about Christmas, son. I have news to share. Can we talk in private?"

Bastian took Rowan off the line. The girl focused on eating ice cream. King talked for several moments. He described strange signals from Rubicon Space Station. A strange warning. The admiralty blowing him off, and the *Freedom* going into lockdown.

Finally he played Bastian the Rubicon message.

"Aliens are real, Beverly. Monsters are real. A fleet. An enemy fleet, heading to Earth. Tell the army! Tell them to get ready. I love you. I love—"

A screech. Then silence.

"Jesus," Bastian said.

"I wanted to let you know," King said. "You serve in the Freedom Brigade. You might be down on Earth, but you're still part of the starship *Freedom*. It's probably nothing. But if there's trouble, you need to prepare."

"Dad." Bastian gulped. "It's not nothing. I have news too."

He talked for a while, describing finding the spider in the forest, Hannah Allenby dead inside a cocoon, and battling the alien.

Yes, it is an alien, Bastian thought.

"Before he died, the alien spoke a little," Bastian said. "The son of a bitch could speak English. He called his species the rahs. At first I thought it was some mutant created in a Red Dawn lab. But damn it, Dad. It's gotta be whatever blew up the Rubicon. Shit! Dad, is this for real? Are we dealing with actual aliens here?"

"I don't know," King said. "This whole thing might just be an elaborate Red Dawn hoax. But I'm taking the threat seriously. Listen to me, Bastian. I need information on the specimen you've captured. It was likely a scout or a spy. This is a chance to learn about their biology before more arrive. I need you to send me photos of the alien, reports on its biology, all the details you can glean. Send them to my ship."

Bastian nodded. "Way ahead of you. I've got the alien in the lab. My best people are studying it right now."

Rowan looked up from her ice cream. She somehow managed to activate her MindLink on her own and leaped into the call. "Alice and Bear took the spider to where Daddy gets tested for drugs!"

"Get off the line!" Bastian said, cutting her off again. He'd have to tinker with her chip's settings.

Rowan giggled.

"All right, son," King said. "I have duties to attend to. Continue your research on the alien. And if you speak to Colonel Holt, tell him everything. We've been trying to reach him from the *Freedom*, and we'll keep trying. Get your base on full alert! I know it's Christmas. But this is urgent. Recall the brigade."

Bastian nodded. Colonel Harry "Hound Dog" Holt was the commander of Fort Liberty. He was a good man, honorable and brave, but he also had an ongoing feud with King. Something about being left on Earth while his brigade's old billets, located aboard the *Freedom*, were now a hotel. Bastian wasn't surprised that he was filtering King's calls.

"I'll talk to Holt," Bastian said. "Goodbye, Dad. Stay safe."

"Goodbye, son. Goodbye, Rowan. I love you."

"Love you, Pop Pop!" Rowan said, waving.

"How did you get back on the line?" Bastian said to the girl. She only giggled. The call ended.

Well, this is certainly shaping up to be an interesting Christmas, Bastian thought.

"Daddy," Rowan said, "I'm having fun. This is way better than Bemidji."

Normally Bastian would laugh. Today he just stood there, somber. He wanted to feel the same old hatred toward his father. To let the rage consume him.

You drove my mother to her death, he thought. *You ruined our family. I hate you.*

The same old words. He had uttered them many times.

They felt hollow now. The rage fizzled away. Maybe it was seeing King as a kindly grandfather, laughing with Rowan. Maybe it was the fear of the spiders. Maybe the pain of his mother's death was simply fading to a dull throb. Bastian didn't know.

I used to love you so much, Dad. You were my hero. Like you were a hero to everyone on Earth. And now I need your guidance. Now I feel alone.

He took a deep breath.

He would call for help. He would muster the Freedom Brigade.

* * * * *

"Sir, this is Captain Bastian King, calling from Fort Liberty. I'm sorry to disturb you at Christmas."

Bastian sat in his office. A hallucination of Colonel Holt appeared in the chair before him. The colonel was tucking into turkey, mashed potatoes, and gravy. The feast appeared in the hallucination too—right on Bastian's desk. The MindLink even replicated the smell.

"Nonsense, Bastian! Don't worry about it." Holt waved dismissively, then wiped his lips with a napkin. "I'm sorry that you're stuck on the base at Christmas. Bad luck."

"Yeah. Bad luck." Bastian didn't feel like sharing that he had nowhere else to go. Not since Stacy had kicked him out. Right now there were more important matters. "Colonel, I have some news. It came from Commander King."

Holt was preparing to bite into a dinner roll. He put the bread down. "Commander James King called, did he?" The colonel snorted. "I presume he didn't call to give us back our bunks in the starship *Freedom*, did he? No. I suppose it's much more important to run that minigolf course with the animatronic dragons."

"Dinosaurs, sir. They're dinosaurs. You have to hit the golf ball between their legs."

The colonel stared at him, eyes dark. "I know he's your father. But the man gives me indigestion." Holt grimaced. "What did he want?"

Bastian spent a while describing the message from the Rubicon and the dead creature on the base. He was breaking some protocol here, going straight to the colonel. Normally Bastian would have contacted his battalion commander, who was lower in the chain of command. But Holt, who led the entire brigade, was like a father to him. They had a good enough relationship that Bastian could call him directly.

As Bastian spoke, Holt listened carefully, his food forgotten.

"I'm sending you a photo of the creature, sir," Bastian said. "Hang on. And . . . here you go."

Holt grimaced. "Nasty bugger. I lost my appetite." He tossed down his napkin and rose to his feet. "I'll tell you what, Captain. First thing tomorrow morning, I'll get the boys down at Biodefense Labs on the phone. I know the guy who runs the place. A real smart fella. We've gone fishing together, and let me tell ya, the guy talked my ear off about all sorts of crazy stuff the Russians are doing. Whether that bug you caught is an alien, mutation, or Red Dawn freak that escaped from a lab, the Bio Boys will figure it out."

"Tomorrow . . . morning," Bastian said. "But sir, what about the message from the Rubicon?"

Holt snorted. "A spacer gone crazy. Happens all the time out there. What are we gonna do about that? Bring our brigade back to the *Freedom*? Now, after all this time? And what, billet among the animatronic dragons?"

"Dinosaurs," Bastian said.

"No, that ship has sailed," Holt said. "Literally. Our days in space are over, aliens or no aliens. Keep holding down the fort, Captain. I'll look into this."

"Sir, maybe we should recall the brigade back to the base?" Bastian said.

"Of course we will. First thing tomorrow, we'll all be there."

Bastian pursed his lips. "Sir, with all due respect, maybe today would be—"

"Captain, it's Christmas," Holt said. "My grandson is throwing a tantrum because I bought him the wrong halluci-game. My in-laws are staying over at my house, complaining about everything, from the lumpiness of my mashed potatoes to the roughness of the hand towels. I have enough to deal with right now. If I recall the brigade over some dead bug, I'd have five thousand angry moms calling me, whining that I pulled poor Private Billy, their precious little angel, away from home on a holiday. Not to mention that Mrs. Holt would have me sleeping on the couch for a week. I'll see you tomorrow morning, Captain. Merry Christmas."

Holt hung up.

Bastian stood there in his office.

He blew me off. He totally blew me off.

He walked into the mess. Alice was there, playing checkers with Rowan. Bear stood nearby, his rifle slung across his back. The giant was a civilian, but he had decided to stay and keep them company.

Bastian stood at the doorway for a moment, looking at them.

Alice Allenby—his company sergeant, his right-hand woman, his most loyal soldier.

Bear—his best friend.

Rowan—the light of his life.

Bastian didn't have much left in his life. No more wife, no more house, maybe no future. But he had them. Three people he loved. Here with him at Christmas.

He vowed to protect them. If he could not protect Earth, at least he could protect three people he loved.

He knew what to do.

"I'm a commissioned officer in the Freedom Brigade," he said, perhaps speaking to himself more than to them. "Only a junior officer, yes. I don't have the authority to summon the entire brigade, let alone alert the generals at the Alliance headquarters. But I command a company. I command two hundred brave soldiers. And I'm calling them here. We will defend this base." He grimaced. "They might hate my guts for recalling them at Christmas, but it must be done."

Alice slapped his shoulder. "If it makes you feel better, we all hate your guts already."

Rowan poked his belly. "And you have lots of guts to hate."

"Very funny, guys. All right, Alice, let's start making calls." He heaved a sigh. "I hope this is nothing."

* * * * *

An hour later, they were all at Fort Liberty. Two hundred marines.

They stood in the snowy courtyard, not exactly happy about being recalled at Christmas but ready to do their duty. They called themselves Bastian's Badgers—the brave soldiers of Fourth Company, Second Battalion, Freedom Brigade.

Frost covered their battle fatigues, armored vests, and helmets. Each soldier boasted a Gideon assault rifle, a bandoleer heavy with magazines, and a belt jangling with grenades. They were decked out for war.

The Freedom Brigade, Badgers included, had a proud history. They were forged in the flames of World War III, a marine force to strike the enemy anywhere in the solar system. It was the Freedom Brigade that led the fabled Martian Charge, breaking through the Russian lines and liberating the planet. They still remembered their history with pride. Theirs were the first boots on the red soil. They won the war.

Today? Well, today the Freedom Brigade was a mere echo of past glory. These marines had never fought a war. Never even been to space. To them, the starship *Freedom* was something from the history books.

A few World War III veterans did serve at Fort Liberty. But the old-timers served higher up in the hierarchy, overseeing the brigade. Right now those veterans were home with their families, enjoying Christmas afternoon.

It was only the young Badgers here on base. Their average age was nineteen. Bastian was thirty-three, and he felt like an old man among them. His soldiers were all local Nebraska kids. They had joined the Alliance fresh out of high school, preferring to live at Fort Liberty than plow the fields. Their battle experience came down to the odd bar fight. They were not heroes. But they were good kids. Bastian was proud of them.

Right now, however, his soldiers were *not* happy. In fact, they were quite pissed off.

Bastian stood in the snowy courtyard, facing the soldiers. They stood in a neat formation. They did not complain. But Bastian saw the scowls. Heard the angry breathing. Saw the clenched fists.

He addressed his troops with a booming voice. "Nobody wanted to be here today. I get it. You were all enjoying Christmas at home, and the last thing you wanted was your officer calling your MindLinks, telling you to haul ass back to base. But right now I need you here. We received a warning. And we must defend Fort Liberty."

A few soldiers glanced at one another.

"Sir?" asked a private. "What's going on?"

"You don't need to know!" snapped Alice. "Your job is to follow orders and shut up."

Alice wore full battle gear too. With her body armor, helmet, and hefty Gideon rifle, she looked like she could take on a Red Dawn division. By herself. Her towering height and muscular frame made her look even fiercer. Her two blond braids spilled out from under her helmet, and war paint adorned her cheeks. The company's senior NCO, Alice was older and tougher than the other enlisted marines. She knew how to keep her troops in line. Bastian could think of no one better to command at his side.

"Sir, there are rumors going around," said a soldier, a scrawny farm girl with freckled cheeks. "Something about aliens. I saw it online." She gulped. "Are the aliens coming here, sir? I'm worried about my mom. She's alone on the farm."

Alice approached the young private. She placed a hand on her shoulder. "I'll send a drone over to your farm. We'll watch over your mother. Don't worry."

"So it *is* aliens then?" asked another soldier, this one a corporal with big ears and crooked teeth. "When do we get to kill 'em?"

Alice spun toward the corporal. "First kill the lice in your hair, Harrington. I can hear them chirping from here."

A few soldiers laughed.

"All right, all right, knock it off!" Bastian said, but he was stifling a smile.

Every good officer needed a strong NCO at his side. Bastian commanded the company, but without Alice, it would fall apart. She was the glue that held the Badgers together. He gave the orders. But Alice kept things running. She made sure the troops were disciplined, trained, well armed, always at the ready. If you missed target practice one week, Alice would show up and give you hell. If your gun wasn't oiled, your boots not polished, your hair not trimmed, you had Alice Allenby to deal with.

But she did more than yell. She took care of her troops. If somebody had trouble at home, showed up after a weekend with an empty belly, Alice made sure they got first dibs at the mess hall—and she gave them battle rations to take home next weekend. If a soldier had no home to go to, Alice made sure there was always a weekend bunk with a warm bed, a meal cooking in the galley, and a listening ear. To her, the troops were like younger siblings. She was tough on them. Sometimes she made their lives hell. She also loved and protected them.

Bastian was proud of all his soldiers. But deep in his heart, he was most proud of Alice.

"All right, split up into your platoons," Bastian said. "We're a bit understaffed today. But we're going to guard this base. First platoon will guard the main gate. Second platoon—you guard the armory. Third and fourth platoons—you walk patrols along the outer walls. I hope you got your beauty sleep last night, because we're on duty until tomorrow morning."

A few grumbles rose, but Alice silenced them with a glare.

"All right, get to work!" Bastian said.

He left the courtyard. His platoon commanders would take things from here.

They would have to defend Fort Liberty alone. And Bastian had something even more precious to protect. Rowan.

* * * * *

As troops moved into defensive positions around the base, Bastian walked toward the barracks.

Fort Liberty was reasonably fortified. It wasn't exactly Fort Knox, but they could hold their own. A concrete wall surrounded the complex, topped with barbed wire. Guard towers rose at regular intervals. There was only one gate, facing south. Within the walls lived the Freedom Brigade, outcast from space.

This wasn't just a military base. It was a second home. To all of them. Fort Liberty often felt like a town. There was a basketball court, a mess hall, a chapel, even a movie theater—at least if a big concrete room with a projector and folding seats could be called a movie theater. Bastian had spent his childhood hopping between the starship *Freedom* and the King family ranch. But since joining the marines, he had spent most of his days here. Twelve years now. Ever since he flunked out of flight school, breaking his father's heart.

He entered the concrete building in the center of the base—the troop barracks. Normally thousands of people moved up and down these halls. Today the place was eerily silent.

He approached his personal bunk. The room was even smaller than his office, and that was saying something. But it was his and his alone. For a marine, privacy was a luxury. As a company commander, he enjoyed this privilege. Most marines shared a room with several other soldiers, sleeping in bunk beds.

But hey, they have homes to go to for Christmas, Bastian thought. *I'm not shedding any tears for them.*

He entered his room, where he found Rowan sitting on the bed, playing with a plush octopus. Charging Bear stood guard beside her, his rifle hanging across his back.

"I couldn't get the full brigade," Bastian said. "But we got two hundred of the toughest soldiers on Earth along the wall. Whatever the hell is going on, we're safe."

"Daddy, you said a bad word," Rowan said.

"Sorry, sweetie." He scooped her up into his arms. "You're being very brave. Are you protecting Bear?"

The girl rolled her eyes. "Daddy! Bear is a giant. He's even bigger than you. Even bigger than a dinosaur."

"I know, but you need to protect him, because even though he's so big and strong, he gets really scared."

Bear said nothing. His facial expression remained stern.

Rowan giggled.

"Daddy, you're silly."

Bastian put her down, then turned toward Bear.

"You all right, bud?" Bastian said.

Bear's eyes remained dark. "Let's step into the hall."

Bastian nodded. Leaving Rowan in the bunk, they stepped outside. They stood in the corridor.

"What is it?" Bastian asked.

"What you said was true, Bastian. I'm scared. Yes, I'm a big, strong man, but that spider scared me. Something is coming. A great evil."

Bastian shuddered. "I feel it too."

"I don't know if these are demons, aliens, or something created in a lab," Bear said. "But the words of the old stories return to me, and yes, I'm scared. We're facing a long night, Bastian. The long, dark night of humanity."

Bastian looked through the door into his bunk. Rowan was watching a cartoon. *Danger Dogs.* Her favorite. He could hear the familiar theme song. An image flashed before his eyes like a waking nightmare: a spider wrapping her in webs, ready to feed.

"I must man the wall with my troops," Bastian said. "When this long, dark night comes, I must stand on that wall. I must cast back whatever evil comes." He looked at Bear. "I can't stay here with Rowan."

The giant squeezed Bastian's shoulder. "I'll guard her. With my life. Nobody will get past me."

Bastian nodded, then pulled his friend into an embrace. "Thank you. You've always been there for me and my family. You *are* my family, Bear. You're my brother."

The giant nodded. "Always. Now go man that wall, brother. I'll stay here and watch the little one."

It broke Bastian's heart, but he walked away from the bunk. Away from his daughter.

He left the barracks, crossed the courtyard, and climbed onto that wall. As he stood guard, a chill ran through him. He could still smell the spider. He could still hear the thing's dying words.

"We . . . are . . . the rahs. You . . . are . . . meat. Humanity will fall!"

CHAPTER SIXTEEN

The Starship *Freedom*
High Earth Orbit
17:35 Christmas 2199

King walked through the winding corridors of his starship, heading toward the bridge.

Around him, the ship was in chaos.

Soldiers bustled back and forth. Yellow lights flashed along the bulkheads. Speakers kept announcing: "Yellow alert, yellow alert. All military personnel report to your stations, all civilians return to your bunks. Yellow alert, yellow alert . . ."

Back in the war, they could enter lockdown within moments. Now it took an afternoon. Seeing the ship's lackadaisical response to an emergency underscored how far they had fallen. Truly, the *Freedom* was no longer a warship.

As King walked the ship, soldiers stopped, pressed themselves against the bulkheads, and stood at attention. Once he walked by, they rushed onward. Tourists filled the corridors too, gawking.

"That's him!" whispered a tourist in a Hawaiian shirt. "There, that's Commander King!"

A few tourists took photos.

"Is there a problem, sir?" asked a woman. She held a plush Freedom the Frog doll; you could win them at the carnival on deck 31. "Sir! I paid good money for this trip. Why must we return to our bunks?"

"Oh, give it a rest, Karen," said her husband, a potbellied man with a bushy beard. "We're getting our money's worth here. A proper military drill! Just the way they used to do 'em." He gave King a brisk salute. "Wonderful show, sir! Wonderful."

King grunted. He had asked Darjeeling to send the tourists to their bunks. But it was a large ship. Thousands of tourists clogged the *Freedom* this Christmas. Darjeeling was facing a monumental task.

"Return to your bunks," King rasped at the tourists. "This is not a drill."

A helpful corporal happened to be walking by. Thankfully, the young soldier approached the tourists, soothed them with soft words, and began accompanying them to their bunks.

"I'll take care of this, sir," said the corporal.

King nodded. "Good man."

He kept walking. The metal labyrinth coiled onward. In a ship as large as the *Freedom*, it took a while to get anywhere.

It was both the blessing and bane of the ship—her sheer size. A commander couldn't simply pop down from the bridge to engineering. The two departments were a kilometer apart. That was assuming you could travel between them in a straight line. Which you could not. A labyrinth of corridors and shafts, twisting and turning, ran through the ship like ant burrows. It could take an hour to cross the ship by foot.

They had developed workarounds. The MindWeb let them talk anywhere on the ship. And there were seven Mimori units aboard, ready to help in different stations. In recent years, King had rarely left the prow. He didn't need to. Roaming these halls today reminded him of how massive the *Freedom* truly was.

And of how she had declined.

He passed by the Dinogolf. Ignoring the wailing alarms, teenagers were putting golf balls between the legs of animatronic dinosaurs. Two teenagers were making out under the brontosaurus. King walked by a Middle Eastern restaurant where androids were belly dancing on stage. One corridor with broad windows afforded a view of the wave pool. A few tourists were still swimming.

King could still remember when all these decks were military. When soldiers lived and worked in these cabins and caverns. Heroes.

How has this happened to my starship? King wondered.

He too had declined, perhaps. Withered away. Become something he was never meant to be.

The decline had been so easy to ignore, to pretend it wasn't happening. A series of compromises. Every compromise another cut.

One day, three years after the war, the order had come. Turn the *Freedom* into a museum. King had agreed. It would save his ship from being scuttled and sold for scrap metal. Instead, he could share his beloved *Freedom* with the world. He could show the people what honor and courage meant, show them the halls of glory. He rejected positions at Alliance Headquarters, rejected the command of other ships. A captain should stay with his ship. So he had stayed.

A year later, another order. Open a restaurant. After all, the tourists needed something to eat. All right then. King had compromised. Let them grill burgers and serve ice cream aboard. Even commanders liked burgers. Why not?

A year after that, they asked him to open a movie theater. Only to show reels of the war, of course. Fine.

After that it never ended. The flood gates had opened. Civilian investors came up, gobbling up ownership of deck after deck. Then it was spas, haunted houses, even a strip club. A goddamn strip club on his beloved ship. Freedom the Frog appeared in commercials on Earth. He also walked around the ship, signing autographs and taking photos—a teenager in a fluffy green suit.

A series of compromises. A thousand cuts. And now King was dying.

He wondered: Was this why, on his last day, he had ordered a yellow alert? Was it less about the warning from the Rubicon, more about wanting to salvage whatever remained of his dignity? To be a true soldier one last time?

King didn't know.

These days, he didn't even know himself.

But one thing he had to admit. This felt good. This felt right. As he marched down the corridors, a soldier again, he felt twenty years younger.

I hope that's not why I'm doing this, he thought.

* * * * *

He entered the prow of the ship, and the crowd of tourists thinned out.

Finally.

Goddamn, I hate walking the midsection, he thought.

Normally he avoided the place. Hell, even the stern, with its roaring engines and punishing heat, beat the midsection. But the aerie, where he had visited the pilots, was located on the bottom of the midsection. To get there and back, King had traveled through thirty decks of tourism.

But now, ah—relief. He was back in the prow.

All of the *Freedom* was his home, but the prow was special to him. If all the *Freedom* was a sprawling castle, the prow was its central tower, the haunt of the king.

The *Freedom*'s prow was built around the Fist of Freedom. The railgun sprouted from the midsection, thrusting out its mighty rails. Science labs, ops rooms, war rooms, ATLAS stations—they all sprang up around these prongs like mushrooms around tree trunks. The railgun was five hundred meters long. But for three hundred and fifty meters, the prow hugged them.

There were no tourists here. The prow was dedicated to science and command. It was true during the war. It was true now.

The prow was bustling today. Officers ran back and forth. Machines hummed inside war rooms. Gears turned. ATLAS sensors swept the sky, displaying information on countless screens.

Finally King stepped onto the bridge.

"Commander on deck!" cried the guard at the door. The man saluted.

King returned the salute and marched across the bridge, heading toward his station.

The bridge was built deep inside the prow, safe behind several layers of armored bulkheads. Along with engineering, it was the most protected section of the *Freedom*. It would take several nuclear torpedoes to breech the ship this deep.

The *Freedom*'s design was revolutionary. Back during World War III, older warships had flown to battle with bridges built near the outer hull. Some of those bridges even had windows. Windows! None of those ships came home. A single enemy blast was enough to breach the hull and kill the bridge crew. The Alliance had learned quickly. Aboard the *Freedom*, the bridge was the safest place on the ship.

The *Freedom* was revolutionary in another way. In the old days, warships had separated the bridge and CIC. The bridge was dedicated to navigation and helm control. The CIC, or Combat Information Center, controlled battle operations. The commander and XO split their duties, one officer manning the bridge, the other overseeing the CIC. In a bold move, the *Freedom* combined

209

both navigation and combat operations into a single hub, allowing the commander and XO to work in perfect concert. This reorganization proved itself in World War III. Today most modern warships followed that standard.

Across the *Freedom*'s bridge, King's officers were busy at work. Some were wearing their parade whites, complete with gloves, bow ties, and ceremonial sabers, all ready for the Christmas gala. Others still wore the simpler blue service uniforms. Aside from the guard at the door, they did not snap to attention nor salute. During yellow alert, they were to focus on their tasks, avoiding normal courtesies such as salutes and attentions.

They knew the rules. But most of the crew had never experienced a yellow alert. The *Freedom* hadn't gone to an elevated alert status since World War III.

"Give me an update," King said, reaching his station.

The bridge was purely utilitarian. Aside from a coffee machine, it was all business. The deck was diamond-plated steel. Cables and pipes ran along the bulkheads. Computers hummed. A dozen officers stood at their stations, busy at work. There were no potted plants, no bright colors, no carpets—just metal and plastic and glass. The bridge was about getting work done. Even the coffee maker, the single luxury, was deemed essential to full crew functionality.

Monitors glowed everywhere. They covered the bulkheads and hung from the deckhead. Some displayed stats from the starship—life support, crew positions, shield strength, and more. Other monitors displayed ATLAS stats; the telemetry system connected to probes and sensors across the solar system. Real monitors. Green font. Black backgrounds. Good and simple data without the frills. No need for fancy holograms, splashy interfaces, or hallucinations.

Some modern ships no longer used monitors. The crew

relied purely on their MindLinks. The neural implants connected to MindWeb, downloaded the data, and displayed it as a floating hallucination. Even that might soon be obsolete. In a few years, they said, a new generation of MindLinks would download knowledge directly into the brain, bypassing the visual cortex. You'd simply *know* what you needed to know.

But the *Freedom* was an old ship, built before neural implants became a military standard. Everyone aboard the *Freedom* could access MindWeb, but the bridge still kept the old monitors, a system considered downright antique. ATLAS and MindWeb were the old and new, finding an uneasy alliance aboard the starship.

When King said "Give me an update!" it wasn't just an order. It was also a rebuke of neural tech. Even with his ruined voice, he was talking aloud instead of communicating telepathically. He was making a statement.

I let my ship succumb to the tourist industry, he thought. *I'll be damned if it succumbs to the goddamn MindWeb too.*

Lieutenant Commander Jordan approached. The XO had been manning the bridge during King's tour of the ship. He was wearing his parade dress. Golden buttons shone on his white coat, and his saber hung at his side.

"We're still entering full yellow alert mode," Jordan said. "Eighty percent of the crew are at their stations across the ship. Power has been diverted from the upper midsection decks to engineering and weapons. Shields have been enhanced with electromagnetic boosters. ATLAS system is doing a level-5 diagnostic sweep of our surroundings. We've got ten sensors awaiting more info from the Rubicon, twenty performing an inspection of deep space, and the rest monitoring the fleet orbiting Earth."

"And the tourists?" King said.

Jordan grimaced. "That's the last piece of the puzzle. So far, we've only moved about half into their bunks."

King lifted his minicom and called Darjeeling.

"Sergeant Darjeeling, this is Commander King calling from the bridge. Give me an update."

The Englishman's voice came across the line. "Begging your pardon, sir. But these tourists are a rowdy bunch. I've got a hundred enlisted men working on rounding them up. But it's like herding cats in heat, sir. I've got teenagers lighting fireworks in the skating rink, and there are gamblers who refuse to leave their slot machines."

"Double your crew," King said. "Pull soldiers off cannon duty. It's not like we have ammo anyway, and the Christmas fireworks display is canceled. Will a hundred more soldiers help?"

Darjeeling could be heard arguing over the line. "Hey, you kids! Put down that statue!"

Laughter sounded. Kids could be heard repeating the words in a mock English accent.

"Trouble, Darjeeling?" King said.

"No sir, I can handle them. Though yes, a hundred extra spacers would come in handy."

"Get it done, Sergeant. I want every last tourist in their bunks."

"Yes, sir!"

King hung up and turned toward Jordan. "Nice outfit. You should always dress up for the bridge."

Jordan glanced down at his parade whites, then looked back up at King. "Why, thank you. At least one of us doesn't look like a slob." He grinned. "I was rather looking forward to singing at the gala tonight. I suppose that's the true reason you called a yellow alert. Just to ruin my plans."

King chuckled. "Maybe if you'd sing some old country music, I wouldn't mind so much."

Jordan gasped. "Me, a trained opera singer? You wound

me."

A few bridge officers heard the banter and stifled smiles. That was an intentional move on King's part. Some light banter told the crew that while this was serious, things were under control. There was no need to panic.

Jordan leaned closer and lowered his voice. These words were for King alone. "You know, Jim, if this is nothing, we'll be the joke of the fleet."

"We're already the joke of the fleet," King said. "We became the joke of the fleet when we allowed the minigolf course to open."

Jordan raised his eyebrows. "You don't like the dinosaurs? Not even the brontosaurus who eats the golf balls? My daughter loves those. Well, she used to when she was younger." He patted King on the shoulder. "I know, Jim. You're being careful. I would do the same thing."

Mimori approached the two men. She was Model 1, the original android. The bridge model. Like Jordan, she wore her parade whites.

"Sirs?" the android said.

"What is it, Mimori?" King said.

"I have an update. ATLAS is reporting suspicious activity deep in the solar system."

King's stomach sank.

"Elaborate," he said.

Mimori frowned. "It's hard to explain, sir. It's a bending of spacetime. An echo in the very fabric of reality. And—" She gasped. "Another anomaly! Just reported! This one is in low Earth orbit, sir!" She clasped his hand. "Sir, there's something happening just above Earth."

Her grip was tight. She was trembling. King knew that the android—the ship herself—was artificially intelligent, aware, and could experience emotions. But he had never known Mimori to seem this scared. Not even during the war.

"What's happening?" King said. "Mimori, put it on-screen. Main viewport."

The main viewport dominated the prow-side bulkhead. It was bigger than King's dining room table back on his ranch. The screen began displaying streams of raw data, green text on a black background. Everyone stared.

King was not a scientist. He had his bachelor's degree in English literature, his master's in history. But decades aboard the starship *Freedom* had taught him a thing or two. He understood the data racing across the screen. So did the other officers. A few officers gasped.

My God, King thought.

There were massive disruptions in Earth's orbit. Gravitational waves. Agitation of the Higgs field. A storm of gravitons. A bending of electromagnetic radiation. King couldn't explain it. He had never seen anything like this. Physics was going crazy.

"What the hell is going on?" he said.

"I don't know, sir," said Mimori.

"Get me a live video feed. Not from the *Freedom*'s sensors. We're in deep orbit, too far from Earth. Tap into a lower orbit telemetry satellite and show me the view."

"Right away, sir. I'm accessing a video feed from one of MuskLabs' science satellites in geosynchronous orbit. It's only thirty thousand klicks from Earth, so we should get a good view. And we should be getting the video . . . now."

The text vanished from the main viewport. The screen now showed a view of space. Earth appeared on the left, a sphere the size of a beach ball. Thousands of satellites, starships, and space stations were orbiting the planet. On the eve of the twenty-third century, Earth's orbit was always cluttered.

For a moment everything seemed normal. Captions

appeared on the screen, labeling important vessels. A handful of warships were orbiting over Europe. Some were frigates. A few were modern dreadnoughts, smaller than the *Freedom* but newer, faster, and deadlier. Other starships belonged to Earth Patrol, the police fleet that maintained order in space. But most ships were civilian. Cruise ships, space racers, freighters, tankers, and many others.

Starships were affordable these days. Millions flew across the solar system. Three centuries ago, cars took over the surface of Earth. Today starships dominated space. There was plenty to visit. A century ago, Talaria drives had opened up the solar system to human imagination. A journey from Earth to Mars, which would once take a year, now took a day. Casinos, hotels, theme parks—they popped up on every planet or moon with a solid surface. And if there was no solid surface, you could always build a space station. World War III was a distant memory. The wounds had healed. Half a billion souls had died in that brutal war, but now . . . now peace had come.

Peace was what King loved. Peace was what he had fought for. Yet peace came with a cost. Peace softened the soul. Softened him.

Or maybe he wasn't soft. Maybe that was the problem. Maybe he was just a grizzled old soldier who didn't know how to survive peace. Maybe war was all he knew.

He watched the panorama of starships for a moment, trying to understand the source of the irregularities.

And then it happened.

Right before his eyes.

He could barely believe what he was seeing.

* * * * *

Above Earth, holes tore through space.

The starlight bent, swirling around a thousand black holes. Shadowy rings rippled outward like dark water. Caverns gaped open like hungry mouths, swallowing all light. The strange dark circles appeared all around Earth. Chunks of the galaxy seemed to disappear.

"What the hell?" King growled. "Starboard monitor A, zoom in on one of those holes."

A side monitor came to life, featuring one of the holes in space. When King looked more closely, he could see a strange landscape inside the hole. Lightning forked between splotches of purple shadows like bruises. Strange shapes moved in the murk.

"They're portals," King whispered. "Portals through spacetime. Wormholes."

"There's no such thing," Jordan said. "Scientists have been hunting for wormholes for centuries."

"Human scientists," King said in a low voice.

They all remembered the message from the Rubicon.

"Sir, ATLAS reports more portals opening across the solar system!" Mimori said. "Several over Mars, one over the moon, and—more reports coming in, sir. They're all over!"

"Get the Alliance headquarters on the line," King said. "Mimori, can you—"

"Sir!" Mimori pointed at the monitor. "Look!"

King spun toward the front monitor.

"God save us," a lieutenant whispered.

Another lieutenant fainted.

King stared, face hard, clenching his fists. Jordan took a step closer to him, staring with dark eyes.

Starships were emerging from the portals. Starships such as King had never seen.

They were spiky, jagged things of dark metal. They looked

like the exoskeletons of monstrous marine animals, strange urchins or crabs from the depths. Claws thrust out from the ships, curving, irregular. Hundreds of claws grew from each vessel, all pointing at the same direction. At Earth. Some claws were small and serrated. Others were the size of skyscrapers.

The monitor HUD displayed the size of the ships. They were gargantuan. Many were as big as the *Freedom*. Many were larger.

They kept coming, thousands of them, pouring from God knows where into Earth's orbit. They floated in space, hulking, menacing, predators crouched and ready to pounce.

"Jim, what are those?" Jordan whispered. "Could they be Red Dawn ships?"

"Those are no human ships," King said. "Earth has just made first contact. This is an alien invasion."

CHAPTER SEVENTEEN

The Starship *Freedom*
High Earth Orbit
18:17 Christmas 2199

King stood on the bridge of the *Freedom*, watching it happen. Helpless to stop it.

From his starship, seventy thousand kilometers away, he watched the destruction of Earth.

"The rahs," King whispered, remembering what Bastian had told him. "They're called the rahs."

Thousands of alien ships hovered around Earth, their claws facing the planet. Slowly the rings of claws expanded, blooming like metallic petals. They revealed pits of molten, swirling metal. The ships suddenly seemed like hideous steel flowers with centers like dying stars. The cauldrons of energy churned, gullets to hell. The red light was blinding. Radiation alarms blared across the *Freedom*. The ship thrummed as the shields automatically increased their electromagnetic radiation dampeners.

"The radiation levels are insane," Jordan said, watching stats on the monitor. "Those are fusion reactors! I've never seen anything like this."

"Mimori, engage our Talaria engine," King said. "Take us to Earth. We're entering this fight."

"Jim!" Jordan grabbed his arm. "We don't have ammunition."

"We can still ram into enemies. We will not stand by while

Earth is threatened. Mimori!" King raised his voice as much as his throat would allow. "Why aren't we flying?"

"Sir?" the android said, eyes wide and face pale. "The Talaria reactor is powered down to idle mode. The guests said they didn't want noise during the Christmas gala. You approved it, remember?"

Goddammit. He had overlooked this. How could he have overlooked this? He wouldn't have made this mistake during the war.

"Get the reactor back up and running!" King barked. "How long until we can fly?"

"Ten minutes, sir. Fifteen at most."

"Get it done in five," King said.

Mimori closed her eyes and began to whisper urgently. She was communicating telepathically with her counterpart in engineering. Deep inside the ship, gears turned, motors hummed, and pistons pumped. Even here on the bridge the deck vibrated. The Talaria drive was priming. But it would take a while.

And every second counted.

For a moment they were just a rock in space, floating aimlessly. King could only stand and stare.

The alien ships were now fully dilated. Their claws, which had pressed together at the tips only moments ago, now flared open like rings of swords. Their molten cores churned.

The *Freedom* was dead in the water. But she was not the only Alliance starship.

Several warships, which were closer to Earth, opened fire.

Torpedoes and photon bolts flew toward the invaders.

"Get 'em!" King blurted out, leaning forward and balling his fists.

The fusillade streaked through space, etching white lines, racing at hypersonic speed toward their targets.

Instants away from impact, the torpedoes and photon bolts

hit . . . something.

Suddenly space lit up. Glowing orange webs appeared around the rah ships. They looked like laser beams, crisscrossing into a webbed pattern, enveloping each enemy vessel.

The torpedoes and photon bolts plowed into these glowing webs—and exploded.

Shrapnel flew through space. Plasma sprayed. The glowing webs quivered, then went dark again.

The rah warships had survived without a scratch.

"Those were shields," King said grimly. "Energy shields such as we've never seen. These clawed ships have technology we can't even understand."

And then the alien ships attacked.

And then Earth's history changed forever.

And then this day went down in infamy.

From the churning cores of these steel flowers roared pillars of flame.

Lines of searing red light filled space. Thousands of flaming columns constructed an unholy cathedral. They were like tornadoes of fire. Like the swords of titans. Each pillar was longer than cities, brighter than nuclear devastation, as hot as the center of stars.

Alarms blared across the *Freedom*. Gauges spun and shattered. The radiation warnings leaped off the charts. Even here, so far away, the radiation bathed the *Freedom*. Light flooded the bridge.

King remained standing. In the blinding inferno, he stared, squinting, grieving.

Just ahead of him, magnified by the ATLAS sensors, he saw it happen.

A pillar of fire plowed into the FAS *Templar*, the flagship of the Alliance fleet, a mighty dreadnought. The *Templar* cracked open. Another blast shattered her into a million pieces.

Alliance frigates charged to battle, mighty warships the size of city blocks. Blasts of enemy fire ripped them apart as if they were merely twigs. Dreadnoughts, starfighter carriers, destroyers, frigates—around Earth, they burned.

The Alliance fleet was crumbling.

At the same time, some of these spinning, crackling pillars of flame descended through space—and slammed onto the surface of Earth.

One pillar plowed into New York City.

Another carved through Beijing.

A raging inferno crashed into London.

It was happening all over the world. Over every major city, the aliens were raining fire. Their searing beams drove holes into the world.

On the *Freedom*'s bridge, people cried out. Somebody screamed. Somebody wept. An officer fainted.

"A nightmare," whispered a tactical officer. "A nightmare. It can't be real. It can't be real . . ."

King remained standing, staring with dry eyes.

No. This was not a nightmare. This was very real.

"Mimori, is the Talaria drive ready?" he said. He forced himself to speak calmly. He must remain calm for his crew.

"Five more minutes, sir, and we can fly," the android replied.

Jordan stepped closer. The light from the monitors bathed him. Horror filled his eyes like ghosts haunting dark chasms. He was from Los Angeles, one of the cities hit.

"Jim, we can't win this," the XO said softly. "Even if we were armed, even at the height of our power, we could not withstand this enemy. We have civilians aboard. Thousands of them. We have to run."

"I will not run from a fight," King said. "There is no safe place for civilians anymore. And this ship is now part of the war."

He swept his eyes across the bridge, staring at his officers. One after the other. Some officers were weeping. Others were praying. All were terrified. Aside from him and Jordan, none of them had known war.

"Sir, they're destroying Earth!" said a navigator. "We have to run. Oh God, we have to—"

"Get ahold of yourself!" King snapped. "All of you. Stop your whimpering. You are soldiers! Stand at your stations! Prepare for battle!"

"Jim." Jordan held his arm. "We don't have ammo."

"But we have our mass," King said. "We're flying in a ship the size of a town. We'll ram into the enemy. We'll use our bulk to destroy them."

Jordan spoke in a low, urgent voice. "Jim, how long do you think we'll last in there? I want to fight too. But we need to arm ourselves."

King growled deep in his throat. He leaned toward his XO, speaking in a low voice. "There are armories on Earth. We'll carve our way through."

"We'll never reach Earth without our cannons booming," Jordan said. "The enemy would destroy us like a piñata. Jim, Mercury is a hundred million kilometers from Earth tonight. We can be at Alliance Mercury Armory within ten hours. We can stock our bays with missiles, torpedoes, and bullets, then fly back."

Alliance Mercury Armory. Nicknamed Merc Mory by the troops. King remembered it. A rickety old space station, orbiting Mercury. *Freedom* had docked there once during the war. It was a good armory. But far.

King clenched his jaw. "It's a long flight. Even once we're there, filling our armories can take a full day or two. By the time we're back, Earth might be gone."

"If Earth can fall within two days, Jim, then the *Freedom*

won't make any difference, weapons or no weapons."

King looked back toward Earth.

A rah ship shot a pillar of flame. An Alliance frigate burned. Farther out, corvettes were cracking, falling down to Earth like so many dry leaves.

King watched them fall. He watched the fleet crumble. He watched the cities of Earth burn.

"It breaks my heart to run from this fight," he said softly.

"We will return," Jordan said. "Stronger than we are. Ready for war. And it's war again, old friend."

King heaved a long, painful breath. Everything hurt. He knew that Jordan was right.

I let my emotions get the better of me, King thought. *I nearly killed us all.*

"You were always the smarter officer," King said.

"And you were always the hothead. Nothing's changed."

"Everything has changed," King said, and he felt a great weight on his shoulders.

"Our Talaria drive will be ready in sixty seconds, sir," Mimori said. "Should I chart a course to Earth through the destruction? Where should we enter the battle?"

King looked at his crew. At Mimori. At his navigators, helmsmen, gunners, technicians. Everyone was staring, awaiting his orders. The firelight through the monitors painted them red.

"You all see what is happening on Earth," King said. "An alien invasion has hit us. Our fleet needs our help. Our people need our help. Our families need our help. And we will not let them down. But we're not flying to Earth right now. We will fly the *Freedom* to Merc Mory, an armory orbiting Mercury, which supplied us during World War III. We will prepare ourselves for battle."

"We can't just fly away from Earth!" said a tactical officer.

"You will obey your orders," King said. "I know it hurts. To leave our friends, our families behind, if only for a day. But right now the starship *Freedom* is helpless. That is why the enemy is not attacking us. They realize we're not a threat. Just a museum. They're right. Right now, if we fly to battle, we would die with the others. I will not lead you on a suicide mission. I will lead you to victory!"

"Victory!" Jordan cried, his deep voice booming.

King raised his fist. "For freedom!"

His officers raised their fists. "For freedom!"

"*For freedom!*" King shouted.

"*For freedom!*" they cried back.

"Sir, the engines are primed," Mimori said.

King faced the main viewport. He stared at the fire and devastation engulfing Earth. His heart broke. It might never mend.

He gave the order.

"Mimori, turn us away from Earth. Fly to Mercury. Fly as fast as you can."

The great engines of the starship *Freedom* rumbled. Clanging machinery sounded in the depths. The engines grew hotter, hotter, fusing atoms within magnetic fields, then blazing out their energy. Pistons the size of grain silos rose and fell, rose and fell, hammering, pounding. Electricity raced through cables, and particles charged through pipes. The gargantuan Talaria drive, a triumph of engineering the size of a cathedral, roared to life.

Outside the ship, anyone watching would see the three great exhaust ports—each larger than a football field—blaze out their fury.

The starship flew slowly at first. Then she gained speed. Soon she was racing.

They flew away from Earth. Away from an enemy they did not understand. Away from their families. From people who needed them.

But they flew for freedom.

They flew away from Earth and for Earth.

So much for retirement on the farm, King thought. *So much for running a museum. I thought that World War III was the big one. But here is the great war of my life. Of all our lives.*

The starship *Freedom* blazed through the night, leaving a trail of luminescence like a shooting star.

CHAPTER EIGHTEEN

**The Starship *Freedom*
Leaving Earth orbit
19:04 Christmas 2199**

Deep in the stern of the starship *Freedom*, the legendary Talaria engines hummed.

Talaria was old technology these days. Antiquated. Some said obsolete. Too large, too noisy, too expensive. As the engines roared, the entire starship vibrated and grumbled. Bulkheads creaked, cables thrummed across the corridors, and static electricity turned every doorknob into an endurance test. People swayed on their feet. Dishes rattled on tables. These were not like the modern engines with their graviton tech. You could barely feel yourself moving with those. No. With Talaria drives, when you were flying fast, you *felt it*.

They were massive machines, the Talaria engines, like cities for mechanical giants. A great ring spun, full of radial beams, moving faster and faster like a propeller, like a Ferris wheel that could dwarf the London Eye, like God's eye gazing upon the cosmos. Power surged through pipes so large you could drive a car through them. Nuclear fusion churned in a chamber the size of an arena, clutched within an electromagnetic fist. Energy shone blue, blasting out the exhaust ports, showering the cosmos with isotopic rain.

The starship *Freedom* surged through the darkness, moving faster and faster. Soon they were moving fifty thousand kilometers per hour. Then a hundred thousand. Then they doubled speed again.

Finally the Talaria drive reached its maximum power. The *Freedom* surged forth at one percent the speed of light.

It was a staggering speed. A wonder of physics and engineering. They were flying thousands of times faster than a speeding bullet. A century ago, starships would need a year or two to reach Mercury. Thanks to Talaria tech, the *Freedom* would get there tomorrow morning.

At Merc Mory, the *Freedom* could rearm, then fly back to Earth with weapons to win this war. A day of flying. A day to rearm—if they hustled. It seemed so long to be away from the fight. But King had no choice.

Earth shrank behind him.

For the first time in his life, King was running from battle.

But not for long, he swore. *I will return, stronger than ever before.*

The bridge bustled around King. Some crew members had their eyes closed, mumbling under their breath. They were communicating telepathically with other departments aboard the *Freedom*, as well as with other starships, those in the thick of battle. A few crew members were arguing loudly. Some kept running from station to station.

Monitors across the bridge kept displaying information from ATLAS. The system was pointed at Earth, attempting to paint a picture of the battle in orbit. Some ATLAS sensors were sweeping the rest of space, searching for more enemy ships. Portals were opening across the solar system—notably above Mars, Titan, and Europa—spilling out more aliens. Red warning signs kept flashing. Alarms kept sounding.

To add to the chaos, King had his MindLink turned on. He hated the damn implant, but right now he needed it. Information from the MindWeb kept feeding directly into his brain. He hallucinated floating numbers, maps, and video clips. The information hovered all around him, bluish and translucent like ghosts.

Data kept flooding in, too fast to process. Other starships, battling the rahs in orbit, kept sending updates. Alliance bases on the ground were transmitting too. Most were begging for aid.

King could hear them.

"Oh God, they're breaking in."

"They're boarding us!"

"They look like spiders. What the hell are those things? Send reinforcements! We need ai—"

Gunfire rattled.

People screamed.

Aliens screeched.

Every moment, another warship went silent. Another monitor aboard the *Freedom* went dark. Starship after starship—gone. Base after base—destroyed.

The picture was incomplete. ATLAS couldn't see everything. The updates from Earth were scattered. Aboard the *Freedom*, they scrambled to arrange the data into a meaningful picture of the war.

But everyone knew that humanity was losing.

King looked at the monitors around him, the old physical ones and the new telepathic ones. He saw the starships burn. He heard the voices cut silent. He knew many of those starship commanders. He had mentored some. He had fought with others in the war. He watched them fall. He watched his beloved Alliance tear apart.

He watched Earth burn. The rahs were landing. The spiders were swarming.

King saw all this. And he was out here, flying into deep space, unable to help.

He picked up a comlink. He opened a communication channel to every speaker on the starship. Thousands of people aboard the *Freedom* heard him speak.

"Attention, all crew and passengers. This is James King, commander of the starship. An hour ago, a fleet of alien starships attacked Earth and her colonies. Until tonight, we did not know if aliens existed. Tonight we learned that aliens are not only real, they are an enemy.

"The aliens belong to a species known as the rahs. We do not know their origin planet. We do not know why they attacked. We know only that they are predatory, technologically superior to us, and hostile. On the surface, they resemble arachnids, though we have not studied their biology.

"The rahs fly clawed starships, which my crew and I have been referring to as clawships. We've witnessed two types of clawships. Some are small, agile, and deadly, with a single rah pilot. We've called them clawfighters. Other enemy ships are larger, even larger than the *Freedom*. We've called them warclaws. Both types of vessels have unleashed unimaginable violence and destruction.

"The rah attack was planned in advance. We know this due to its sophistication. The attack caught us off guard. It caused terrible loss of life.

"An hour ago, the rahs attacked the Alliance fleet in orbit around Earth, destroying many of our starships. Our greatest dreadnoughts were hit first, with many destroyed. Much of the fleet is gone, and the rest are still engaged in bitter combat.

"An hour ago, the rahs also attacked the Red Dawn and the Desert Thorns. Those two unions of nations have joined the war. The enemy does not distinguish between humans. They do not take sides in our squabbles. They see us all as prey.

"An hour ago, the rahs struck many targets on the surface of Earth. With beams of focused plasma, like swords of fire from the sky, they destroyed many of our landmarks. The Statue of

Liberty. The White House. The Kremlin. The Forbidden City. The Alliance Headquarters. Buckingham Palace. These targets, some symbolic and others military assets, have all been destroyed. The president of the United States is believed dead. So are the leaders of many other nations. We've been unable to contact High Commander Archer, the head of the Alliance, and we know his bunker was struck.

"Battles rage across Earth and her orbit. The brave soldiers of the Alliance, as well as soldiers from the Red Dawn and the Desert Thorns, are fighting the enemy. Many are giving their lives to defend our homeworld.

"I regret to tell you that many lives were lost. The number of casualties, civilian and military, is not yet known. But the number is staggeringly high.

"I know this news is difficult. I know our hearts are all broken. But tonight we must set aside grief. Tonight we must summon our courage and strength—and fight the enemy.

"The starship *Freedom* is a museum. A tourist attraction. A resort. Recognizing this, the enemy spared us. While many warships burned, the *Freedom* escaped destruction. But decades ago, the *Freedom* was a mighty warship. That she will become again.

"As commander of the *Freedom*, I've ordered the starship to fly to Mercury. The Alliance maintains an armory orbiting that planet, ready to equip the starship *Freedom* for war. At Alliance Mercury Armory, we will stock up with torpedoes, railgun projectiles, Eagle missiles, bullets, and all the other weaponry we will require.

"Once we return to Earth, civilian guests aboard the *Freedom* will be given a choice. You may depart the *Freedom*, return to your homes on Earth, and seek safety there. Shuttles will be provided. Or you may remain aboard the *Freedom* where you will be classified as refugees, and thus under Alliance protection. The

Freedom will be flying to battle. But I believe that everywhere that humans live is now a war zone. We don't know the full situation on Earth, but we know the rahs have landed ground troops. Perhaps no place is safe.

"My guests—this is a difficult choice. Our trip to Mercury and back will take two days. By then, you must decide. Depart our ship. Or stay, hope for safety within our armored hull, and fly with us to battle.

"The path ahead will be long. The battle will be hard. And the starship *Freedom* will be part of this war. Thirty-five years ago, we fought a great war among humans. Now we will begin to fight in the great war of all humanity.

"With the determination of our fleet and her brave spacers, with the courage of our forces on the ground, with the unrelenting spirit of humanity, we will triumph against the rahs—so help us God.

"Tonight we enter the great war of our lives. For Earth. For humanity. And for freedom!"

King ended his transmission. For a moment everyone on the bridge was silent. Maybe everyone across the starship. For a moment only the sound of the machinery filled the bridge.

They all looked at him.

Jordan, his second-in-command and best friend. Jordan—tall and somber, forever the voice of reason that tamed King's fire.

Darjeeling. Dear old Darjeeling, the backbone of the ship, forever stalwart and loyal.

Mimori. Personification of the *Freedom*. Woman and machine. Muse and goddess. Mimori, beloved above all others.

Spitfire. Spitfire of so much flame and anger and sadness. Spitfire, commander of the starfighters, mistress of the stars, who was like a daughter to King.

Navigators. Technicians. Engineers. All those on the bridge. All those who served on this ship. A crew that ran a resort, that now carried the hope of mankind.

They looked at King. At this time of crisis, they turned to him for leadership, for strength, for hope. King did not know if he had any hope to give them.

He looked at his bridge crew. He spoke to them alone.

"I believe in you. I'm proud of you. None of us expected this. But I have full confidence in your abilities. There is no better crew in the Alliance. And there is no better starship than the *Freedom*."

Jordan stepped forward. The tall XO raised his chin. He began to sing with a mellifluous baritone. He sang the "Song of Freedom," the anthem of the starship. Spacers had sung this song during World War III. Jordan himself, back then a young starfighter pilot, had composed the music, while Prince Robert had written the lyrics. Today every human knew the words, knew the legend of the *Freedom*. Standing on the bridge, the crew joined the XO. Even King joined in, raspy voice and all. They sang together.

Let all free souls salute her flight
Let her engines bathe the dark with light
Let her cannons sing the song of freedom
The fleet will gather; she will lead them
Our flagship sails into the flame
As poets weep and sing her name
For liberty's light! For glory's hymn!
Praise the Freedom, she will win!

The song ended. They stood in silence. Many of them had tears in their eyes.

Darjeeling stepped toward King. Tears glistened on his

mustache.

"Sir," the Englishman said. "Has there been news of the royal family? Have they been able to evacuate the palace, or . . ."

King put a hand on Darjeeling's shoulder. "Oliver, I'm sorry. They're gone."

Darjeeling tightened his lips. Even to remain standing seemed a struggle to him. "Sir, may I depart the bridge? I must see the princess. If there is any comfort I can give, I must."

King nodded. "Of course, Oliver. Be there for her. She needs you now."

Darjeeling saluted, lips quivering, then spun on his heel and marched off the bridge.

We all need you now, Oliver Darjeeling, King thought, watching his friend go. *We all need strong men, loyal soldiers, and good friends.*

Daniel Arenson

CHAPTER NINETEEN

The Starship *Freedom*
7 million kms from Earth
19:59 Christmas 2199

Princess Emily was sitting in the royal suite, holding Niles in her lap, when she heard the commander's speech over the speakers.

When the speech ended, she sat in silent terror.

The royal suite aboard the starship *Freedom* was luxurious, fitting for a princess. Oil paintings hung on the walls—original works by Renaissance masters, depicting scenes of Greek mythology. A Titian hung over the fireplace, featuring a lounging Venus with flaming red hair. Giltwood furniture, Italian marble tiles, silver statues of cranes and ibises—it was all elegant, priceless. A suite for the most pampered and powerful of guests.

But none of this opulence could comfort Emily now. She barely noticed it. She sat in an upholstered armchair, struggling to breathe.

In his speech, the commander had said many things. But just two words echoed in Emily's ears.

Buckingham Palace.

Her home.

It was among the targets destroyed in the assault.

Tears flowed down her cheeks, and she trembled.

"Oh, Niles," she whispered, holding the drone.

"Emily, I'm . . . I'm sure your family rushed into the bunker," the drone said, but his voice shook. "As soon as the attacks began, I'm sure they fled to safety."

Emily nodded. She had seen the bunkers below Buckingham Palace, constructed during the third world war. The royal family had plans to deal with doomsday threats. There were not only bunkers below the palace, but also shuttles ready to rush the family out of London entirely, if deemed necessary, and to countryside hideouts. But had her family evacuated in time? The attacks had been so sudden.

"Niles, I'm scared." She hugged him even closer.

A knock sounded on the suite door.

Emily leaped to her feet. Niles flew through the air, then steadied himself and hovered at her side.

She stood there, trembling. Suddenly she felt like a little girl. Just a weak seventeen-year-old child, lost in space, so afraid. A little bird in a gilded cage, trapped as the house burned around her.

She took a deep breath.

Steady yourself, Emily, she told herself. *Whatever happens, be strong. You are a member of the royal family of Britain. You are a steadfast Englishwoman. Whatever terror comes your way, you will face it with courage and dignity. Besides, if it were a rah outside, I doubt he'd knock.*

"Come in," she said.

Darjeeling entered the suite. He still wore his parade whites. He had not had a chance to change.

"Your Highness," he whispered.

And she knew at once.

She saw it in his eyes. In the tears that dampened his white mustache. She heard it in his voice.

"They're gone, aren't they?" Emily said. "My family. They're all gone."

Darjeeling was pale. He met her gaze steadily. "I managed to contact the royal steward. He confirmed the terrible news. They're gone, ma'am. The royal family is gone. All of them but you."

Hovering nearby, Niles gasped.

Emily nodded. A tear trailed down her cheek. "Thank you for letting me know, Mr. Darjeeling."

The aging sergeant held his cap to his chest. "Your Highness, I was and remain your loyal servant. I vow to dedicate my life to protecting you. I will not stop fighting until your enemies are defeated, until we rebuild the throne of our proud nation, and until you are crowned and sit upon it. My life, my honor, and whatever strength remains in me—they are yours, Emily, princess of England."

She nodded. "Thank you, Mr. Darjeeling. You will best serve all of us now by returning to your post. You are a sergeant major aboard a warship. And the *Freedom* is a warship again. Godspeed, Mr. Darjeeling."

He bowed deeply to her, and when he straightened, fresh tears shone on his cheeks. He backed out of the room and closed the door behind him.

Niles spun toward her. "Oh dear. Oh dear. Emily, it can't be true. It can't. How can they be gone?"

The drone began to make strange, discordant sounds. Robotic weeping, she supposed.

She sat back in her armchair. She stared at the hovering, jeweled drone, the last piece of her home. And finally Emily let out a great sob, lowered her head, and wept.

CHAPTER TWENTY

Fort Liberty
Nebraska
23:58 Christmas 2199

It was two minutes to midnight when the sky blazed with fire.

For hours now, the soldiers of Badger Company had been guarding their fort. Waiting. Staring into the darkness. The night was cold. The kind of cold that cut through the thickest coat, that sliced down to the bone. The wind moaned. The stars seemed distant, their light scattering in the frost that filled the air.

Bastian had spent these long, cold hours with the company. He manned the southern guard tower, gazing at the shadowy farmlands of Nebraska. Remembering. Seeing again his life, growing up the scion of a great military family. Growing up with stories of war. Growing up and dreaming of becoming a pilot, ending up a grunt. A good life, overall. A life among golden wheat under the blue sky. But now everything was darkness and ice and fear.

Rowan was inside the barracks, asleep in a bunk. Charging Bear was guarding her, a rifle in his hands.

Out here on the wall stood the soldiers.

Still. Silent. Watching. Waiting.

Alice stood at Bastian's side. She leaned over the guard tower railing, peering into the dark.

"I can't see shit. We need more lights. A spotlight or something."

"The lights on the gate are all we got," Bastian said. "I can see fine. Eat more carrots."

But he was lying. He couldn't see much either. Standing here, it felt like gazing into a black ocean. Just endless miles of shadow, spreading to an unknown horizon, to an unseen terror.

What is out there? he wondered.

His soldiers were still and silent, guns loaded. Some stood here on the southern wall. Some at the gate below. Others were patrolling the rest of the camp. Just two hundred troops. Two hundred from a brigade that should be five thousand. On Christmas, it was all he could muster. If trouble came tonight, they would have to be enough.

And then, with two minutes before Christmas ended, it happened.

The fire blazed, lighting the darkness.

The pillars of fire crisscrossed the sky. Bastian had never seen anything like it. He gazed upward, jaw dropping. Enormous roads of flame stretched overhead.

"What the hell?" Alice shouted.

Bastian stared grimly. An explosion blazed far above, about the size of the moon, then vanished. Then another explosion. Another. More lines of fire raced across the sky. More blasts lit up the night.

"Are those comets?" Alice said. "The biggest damn comet shower in history?"

Bastian shook his head. "That's a battle. The fleet is under attack."

They heard it then. Booms above. There was no sound in space, of course. But great chunks of starships must have been falling into the atmosphere. Blobs of light spread above like glowing watercolor stains. Boom after boom shook the world. Shrapnel shrieked downward, etching trails through the night.

And then—

Bastian gasped.

"Look!" Alice said, pointing.

She didn't need to point. Bastian saw it. People probably saw it for thousands of miles around.

A pillar of fire plunged down from space and slammed into Earth just beyond the horizon.

A second later, another tornado of flames touched down. This one was closer.

All around, lines of flame descended, forming columns like a fire god's cathedral. The red light painted the fields and danced on the faces of soldiers.

Cries rose from across the base.

"What's going on?"

"It's aliens! Check the news, it's an alien invasion!"

"It's war! It's goddamn war!"

"We're gonna die. Oh God, we're gonna die."

"I gotta go home. I gotta go to my family. Oh God."

With a thought, Bastian activated his MindLink. The chip in his brain came to life. MindPlay, the implant's hallucinatory interface, floated before him. It displayed the positions of his troops across Fort Liberty, as well as various other stats and notifications.

News headlines raced across the bottom of the MindPlay interface.

ALIEN WARSHIPS ATTACK EARTH

ALLIANCE FLEET BATTLING ENEMY FORCE IN SPACE

STATUE OF LIBERTY SINKS

ALLIANCE HEADQUARTERS DESTROYED

ALIEN ATTACKS ON ALL MAJOR CITIES

Snippets of videos hovered in MindPlay. Bastian caught a glimpse of a great battle in space. He gasped to see the alien starships—big, nasty machines covered with claws. Just watching a few seconds of the video told Bastian enough. The Alliance fleet was crumbling.

A voice rose through his MindLink. A soldier in his company was reaching out.

"Sir, I'm scared."

Another soldier called to him telepathically. "Captain King, what do we do?

"We have to run!"

"Oh God, I can see the explosions above. That's our fleet burning. Oh God. Oh Jesus."

This has to be a dream, Bastian thought. *How could this be real? An alien invasion? The world burning? This has to be a nightmare.*

But he couldn't wake up.

Panic rose in him. A tingle to his fingers. A churning sea in his belly. He shoved the panic down. He refused to succumb to the enemy or to his own fear.

Bastian spoke, letting his MindLink carry his words to every brain in his company. "Badgers Company, collect yourselves! I know you're scared. I know this is new. But you are soldiers of the Alliance! You are *my* soldiers! You are soldiers of the Freedom Brigade, and you will overcome your fear!"

"What do we do, sir?" asked a lieutenant—a pale, trembling young man.

"We defend this base!" Bastian said. "We stand at our posts! And if we must, we fight. Whatever enemy comes at us tonight—you will kill it. Is that understood?"

Two hundred voices rose through the MindLink. "Yes, sir!"

He heard the terror in their voices. Many of those "yes, sirs" were shaky. Bastian himself was shaking. His knees felt weak. Cold sweat dripped down his back, and his hands trembled when he clutched his rifle.

But he remained at his post.

He had never fought in a battle. But these soldiers

depended on him. Rowan, hiding inside this base, depended on him. Earth depended on him. He would do his duty. He would fight.

He steadied his grip on his Gideon. He aimed the heavy assault rifle at the shadows.

"Daddy?" Rowan's voice came through the MindWeb.

Somehow she had activated her chip again, overriding the parental controls. For once, Bastian was thankful.

"I'm here, sweetie. I'm nearby. Guarding the gate."

"Daddy, I'm scared," she whimpered. "I see fire out the window. Are the monsters coming? Come back, Daddy. I'm scared. Please."

"I gotta stay in this guard tower, sweetie." Bastian sent his words telepathically. With the lump in his throat, he didn't trust himself to speak aloud. "Bear will look after you until I'm back. Isn't that right, Bear?"

The giant's voice came over the MindWeb. "Absolutely, Bas. I'm here. If any monster wants to mess with Rowan, it would have to get through me first."

No sooner did Bastian hang up when movement caught his eye.

He inhaled sharply. He leaned over the guard tower railing, staring at the shadowy fields.

Shadows were moving in the darkness, stirring the snow.

Something was heading to the base.

Bastian made a telepathic call to Colonel Holt.

"Sir, we need backup!" Bastian said. "There's something coming. I believe we're under attack. I need backup."

A video feed appeared, floating before Bastian. He was seeing through Colonel Holt's eyes, hearing through his ears.

The colonel was at home. The leftover Christmas turkey was still on his table. Two enormous spiders filled his dining room, lashing their claws. Blood covered their teeth. Mrs. Holt hung from a hook on the wall, disemboweled, while a spider was gnawing on her legs.

"Oh God, oh please don't, mercy!" Holt was screaming.

A claw swiped toward him. Holt raised his hand to block the attack. The claw severed his hand. The rah laughed, then drove a claw into Holt's stomach. The colonel gave a final scream, and then his MindLink went dark.

Bastian found himself back on the tower, facing the oncoming storm.

"Bas," Alice whispered. She had seen the video too.

"Be strong, Sergeant Allenby," Bastian said. "We will defend this base."

He stood in the tower. Alice stood at his side. Across the base, the other soldiers manned other positions.

They all stared at the dark fields.

The shadows were moving faster. Countless creatures were racing in the dark.

"We need a spotlight!" Alice whispered urgently. "I can't see a damn thing."

The creatures kept moving closer.

"Alice?" Bastian said.

She looked at him. "Yes, Bas?"

"I'm proud of you, Alice. I've always been proud of you. Stay strong tonight."

She nodded and gulped. "Let's kill some aliens."

And there they came.

Hundreds of them, racing across the snow, shrieking for blood.

Giant spiders the size of horses. The rahs.

The battle for Fort Liberty began.

CHAPTER TWENTY-ONE

Motherclaw *Hunger*
18 Billion kms from Earth
38th night of Hunter's Moon
576th Imperial Millennia
Earth time: Midnight, Dec 26, 2199

Skel'rah, High Huntress of the Sixth Rah Fleet, lurked in her mothership on the edge of the solar system. Hanging on her web, she watched the great hunt begin.

Good.

Overall, things were good.

Her clawships had bombed their targets, taking the humans by surprise. Her hunters were swarming. Her orbweavers were weaving webs. Claws were being sharpened.

Yes, quite good.

They were an interesting species, the humans. So young. So afraid. Surprisingly warlike for a species that had evolved from prey animals.

Yet perhaps not so surprising. Humans were prey animals, yes. You could tell from their soft skin, small teeth, and lack of claws. Prey animals were fearful by nature, angry and chaotic when trapped in a web. Somehow these humans, lacking claws or horns or exoskeletons, had built the weapons to hunt, to eat meat like the predators they feared, to dominate their planet. But their minds still stormed with the fear of their prey ancestors.

This would be an interesting hunt. They made interesting

meals, these humans. They fought like predators, yes, but their meat was so soft. They were no crunchier than maggots. At the end, trapped in the web, stripped of their weapons—just prey animals after all.

Skel'rah had hunted many species across the galaxy. To feed, a rah must hunt. Must fly stretch strands from world to world. Must seek new enemies to fight. Must continuously sharpen the claws. *Sheertone ash keresh*. They lived it every day.

That was the great curse and blessing of the rahs. That was *Ishar*, the Right Path. Eternal warfare.

The gazers, like her mother, had forged this path long ago. Gazers were small spiders, smaller even than orbweavers, but their many eyes saw far. They understood the great dilemma of the rahs.

If they were to domesticate prey, to raise insentient animals merely for their meat, the rahs would become farmers. Farmers! They would grow fat, weak, decadent. The empire would stagnate. One of the Great Evils from beyond the darkness would topple them. Those demons were forever seeking weak strands in the web.

It was therefore the greatest sin in *Ishar* to eat meat grown on a farm. A rah would rather starve. A rah would rather eat her own eggs.

They could, some factions of hunters observed, become cannibals. No farming necessary. Just pit rah against rah and feast! But that would lead to chaos, claimed the gazers. The entire civilization would cannibalize itself. The Great Evils would watch in delight, then rise to consume whoever remained.

And so Elder'rah, the great gazer, queen of the web, created *Ishar*. Their faith. Their way of life.

There were many rules in *Ishar*, much wisdom, much punishment for sins. But one central concept guided all its followers: The Great Weaving.

It was their purpose in this universe.

They wove this web across the galaxy, stretching invisible strands from star to star, hunting and eating along the way. Growing strong. Sharpening their claws. Planting their eggs in the wombs of species deemed strong enough to nurture a new generation. When the web stretched across the entire galaxy, the gazers taught, the fabled Glass Spider would descend from above and usher in a utopia, an era of endless meat and fleshy wombs.

Skel'rah was no gazer. She had hatched into the hunter class. That was a stroke of luck. Only one in a thousand eggs hatched a hunter. Even fewer hatched gazers. Even the best of wombs mostly just yielded orbweavers.

Hunters were practical. They lived for fighting, hunting, eating, and laying eggs. They did not build. They did not question. They followed *Ishar* and never doubted its wisdom.

But Skel'rah was no typical huntress. Her mother was the great gazer herself, leader of all rahs. Maybe some of that wisdom had passed into her. Deep down, Skel'rah wondered. She questioned. She did not know if she believed in the Glass Spider.

Still, the prophecy kept them hunting. Kept them conquering. Kept them sharpening their claws. *Kata hel anak*, the dance of war, continued.

Mother probably invented the Glass Spider just to keep us from growing fat and slow, Skel'rah thought.

So Skel'rah played along. She went on these crusades. She led these great hunts. She wove this galactic web. Dutifully, she prayed to the Glass Spider.

But she was playing a game of her own.

My mother is a million years old. She has lived for too long. If I conquer enough worlds, earn enough eresh, *I will become the first huntress to lead the Great Web. The long reign of the gazers will end!*

It would take much *eresh* to convince the Old Ones to accept a huntress, but at least she wasn't an orbweaver.

Skel'rah turned her gaze away from the future and toward the hunt of humanity.

Inside her starship, the orbweavers had woven her a great web where she now hung. Iron pulleys were connected to every strand. The pulleys, in turn, were attached by cables to sensors on the motherclaw's hull. Whenever something interesting happened outside, the pulleys tugged on her cobwebs, delivering the information.

Skel'rah closed her eyes, sensing the vibrations on her web. Billions of years ago, when the rahs had been small spiders hunting in the jungles, they had learned to sense the movements of other animals on their webs. Later, the rahs had learned to communicate among themselves by tugging on gossamer, delivering simple messages. One quick tug on a strand—food in this direction! A strumming on another strand—watch for danger. A violent yank on two strands together—I desire to breed!

Over time, they had developed web vibrations into a complex language. The same vibration could mean something completely different depending on the strand, be it radial or circular, near the center of the web or on its perimeter. The combinations allowed for millions of words and concepts. Web-language was more complex than the hisses and grunts they used when hunting. The pulleys continuously vibrated the web where Skel'rah hung, updating her on the great hunt.

Through the vibrations, she gazed far. She sensed Earth. She sensed the starships that flew around the planet. She sensed the other planets that orbited this star. The trembling cobwebs painted the picture in her mind.

Everything was going well. Her troops were hunting much prey, earning much *eresh*.

But then came a strange vibration on a radial strand. A frequency that disturbed her.

She inhaled sharply and scuttled higher up her web.

Well, this was interesting.

Was this a concern? Maybe. Maybe . . . But she would deal with it.

She tugged a strand that connected to a cable in the wall.

"Hel'rah!" she cried. "Come to me, my spawn."

A shriek sounded deep inside the motherclaw. "I don't want to!"

Skel'rah growled. She tugged the strand again. "Come to me, spawn. I will not ask you again."

The shriek echoed, even louder this time. Claws clattered in the depths of the ship. He scuttled into the Grand Cave from which Skel'rah oversaw her ship. The humans, she knew, called such starship chambers bridges.

"What do you want, Mother?" Hel'rah said. "My new claw hurts. Leave me alone, you withered old hag!"

She stared down at him. He was a male, and males were small and weak, even those born into the hunter class. But Hel'rah was no ordinary male hunter. He was twice the size, and his colors were odd too. Most hunters were completely black aside from their crimson eyes. But Hel'rah had a gray body like a gazer, and his legs were red. Only one in a billion rahs was ever born with red legs, and they were always particularly vicious.

She had ripped off one of those red legs recently. Punishment for him destroying the Rubicon, compromising their element of surprise. The leg had grown back, but new legs were always sore for a while.

"Are you done sulking, spawn?" Skel'rah said. "I have a mission for you."

His eight eyes lit up. "May I finally hunt and feed? Oh, I'm so hungry. Send me down to Earth! I will gorge myself on human flesh."

Sometimes hunters are so stupid, Skel'rah thought.

"No, yours is a different task," she said. "There's a human

247

vessel that fled the fight. A dreadnought-class starship. It's heading to the innermost planet in this system, where I've detected a base. Perhaps an armory. You will intercept this ship—and destroy it."

Hel'rah sniffed. "A dreadnought? I thought we destroyed all the dreadnoughts in the initial assault."

"We spared this one," Skel'rah said. "We did not detect any munitions aboard it. It was only a museum."

"What is that?" Hel'rah hissed.

"A place where humans collect artifacts to remember past heroism. Like the skulls of vanquished foes we wear on our backs."

Hel'rah snorted. "That sounds harmless. There is no *eresh* in destroying a museum ship."

"This ship is unarmed, but there is something about her master. A human named James King, commander of the starship *Freedom*."

"The humans have such silly names." Hel'rah laughed.

Skel'rah ignored him. "Among the human leadership, only this James King recognized the destruction of the Rubicon. Only he took measures to protect himself. He tried to warn the others, but most humans are stupid, blind creatures. They ignored him, mindless beasts that they are. But King . . . he is not like the others. He sees too far. He is cunning. If he arms his ship, we will face a terrible foe."

"Let him arm himself!" Hel'rah rose on his back legs and raised his front claws. "I desire a good fight."

"You act as stupid as a human," Skel'rah snapped. "You must stop this museum ship now—while it is unarmed. That is my order to you. You will obey or I will pull off all your legs!"

The young male hesitated. His legs twitched. He remembered the pain.

Finally he snorted, feigning nonchalance. "Very well. Give

me a skullfighter. I'll fly over, destroy this human, and then proceed to Earth."

"Take a warclaw," she said.

"A warclaw?" Hel'rah bristled. "An entire armored warship with enough plasma to destroy a planet? To fight a museum? Where is the *eresh* in that?"

Skel'rah considered for a moment. "Take three warclaws. He is cunning, this James King. Take your personal ship, the *Bloodlust*, and choose two more. Destroy the *Freedom*. Feed upon King for your *eresh*. Then come back to me, and perhaps I will let you descend to Earth."

He snapped his teeth at her. She growled, scuttled closer, and loomed above him. She raised her front legs, and her claws gleamed.

He was big, yes. But she was larger and she could rip him apart. If he died, well, she had a thousand more children, and on Earth she would find wombs for a thousand more. And Hel'rah knew it.

Finally the young hunter huffed. "Very well. I'll destroy this starship with its silly human name, and I'll devour its pathetic commander. You'll see, Mother. I'll grow strong. I'll fertilize many eggs that will hatch into great phalanxes. Someday I'll be the one to rip off *your* legs!"

With a last snap of his teeth to save his dignity, he scurried out of her cavern.

Impudent slitherpup.

Not long later, Skel'rah felt vibrations in her web. Three warclaws detached from her fleet. The *Venom*. The *Wandering Widow*. And finally the *Bloodlust*, which Hel'rah flew, a ship with a gray hull and red claws.

She had built him this clawship for his first hunt long ago. A ship to match his own colorings. He had seemed such a promising heir then. So much for that! Now a fear filled Skel'rah.

What if she succeeded in her plan and usurped the withered Elder'rah?

This wild beast will become heir to an empire, Skel'rah thought. *My spawn is a great hunter. And once he is a step from the center of our Great Web, he will stab me in the underbelly.*

She must find good wombs on Earth. She must lay many eggs in fertile flesh. She must hatch wiser offspring. The future of the rahs depended on it.

CHAPTER TWENTY-TWO

Fort Liberty
Nebraska
00:18 Dec 26, 2199

The rahs roared toward Fort Liberty like a tidal wave.

Standing on the southern guard tower, Bastian gazed upon hell.

He had fought one of these creatures before. That one had been a spy. Now he saw warrior rahs. They were larger. Faster. Spikes rose from their backs, impaling the skulls of vanquished foes. Their red eyes blazed in the darkness like torches of hellfire. Their legs sliced through the frozen ground. Their jaws opened, full of gleaming teeth, and they screeched.

"Grab the humans!"

"Flay them alive!"

"Eat their skin!"

"Drink their blood!"

They were screaming in English. They knew English, the bastards. Bastian realized what they were doing. This was psychological warfare. These aliens were trying to break his spirit.

It was working.

His hands trembled. Somehow he managed to aim his rifle.

"Soldiers, open fire!" he howled.

He pulled the trigger.

A single bullet flew into the army of rahs. It drowned in the sea of claws and fangs.

Alice let out a battle cry and unleashed hell, firing on full automatic. Below on the field, her bullets shattered the impaled skulls, tore off one spider's leg, cracked another's abdomen.

But the beasts kept charging. Not a single one fell.

There was only a single gateway into Fort Liberty. From up here in the guard tower, Bastian had a good view of it. The gate was just a few meters away from the tower. Concrete walls topped with barbed wire surrounded the base. The gateway was the weakest point—a doorway of steel bars.

Right now fifteen marines were guarding that gate, all armed with Gideons and grenades. Corporal Martelle led the squad. He was a good kid. Only twenty years old. He had moved down from Alaska a few years ago, Bastian remembered. Something about the family business going under, his older brother dying, and starting a new life on the prairies. Hell, they were all good kids. Everyone in the squad below. Everyone in this company. They all had their stories. They were all scared. And not everyone would survive the night.

Below at the gate, Corporal Martelle was trembling. He saw the oncoming horde. He took a few steps back.

"Corporal Martelle, fire your weapon!" Bastian cried.

The rahs raced closer, shrieking for blood.

The young soldier's Gideon shook in his hands. But he managed to open fire. His bullets drowned in the darkness. Seconds later, his squad began to fire too. The bullets streaked through the gate's bars toward the surging nightmare.

Bastian kept firing from the tower. But all their bullets drowned in the surging dark wave.

The creatures scuttled closer in the night. Hissing. Clattering. Claws tearing the ground. Jaws open. Fangs shining. Eyes burning. A sea of evil, risen from hell, hungry for human flesh.

And then it happened.

The rah army slammed into the walls.

The battle for Fort Liberty began.

* * * * *

From his position on the guard tower, Bastian kept firing his Gideon, but it seemed so pointless. He watched in a daze, knowing this enemy was beyond him.

Several rahs slammed into the gate, twisting the metal bars. It only took a second. The bars snapped like toothpicks.

The rahs surged.

Corporal Martelle screamed and fired his weapon on automatic. His muzzle lit up the night. The aliens plowed over him. Blood splashed, gushed upward, a geyser. A severed arm flew. A foot tumbled into the darkness. The gunfire died. So did Martelle's screams.

The rest of the squadron stood before the mutilated gates. They saw their commander fall. They saw the enemy charge.

A few privates turned to run. Others stood and fought, but the rahs rolled over them. The privates fell, praying, begging. One soldier called out to his mother. The aliens tore them apart. Severed limbs flopped onto the snow.

Bastian could only watch from the nearby tower, helpless.

"First Platoon, we need you!" Bastian shouted, transmitting his orders through MindLink. "Southern gate—now!"

Howling for war, new soldiers stormed toward the broken gate. Their guns roared.

The rahs leaped toward them. Claws met bullets. Blood splashed the snow. Soldiers crashed down dead. Kids. Just kids. Teenagers. Privates dead in the dirt, eyes still full of terror, mouths open in silent screams.

Those who still lived screamed too. In rage. In terror. In madness. A few fled. But most charged at the enemy, killing, dying. At the broken gateway of Fort Liberty, so many soldiers fell.

Screams rose from across the base. On his MindLink, Bastian glimpsed videos from other locations. The rah army surrounded Fort Liberty. They were assaulting the northern, eastern, and western walls, scrambling up the concrete, tearing at barbed wire. Soldiers roared and fired their guns.

Across the base, the two hundred fought. But soon they were down to a hundred and eighty. Then, only moments later, a hundred and seventy-three.

And more kept dying.

Bastian could only spare the rest of the battle quick glances. A second later, a host of rahs came scuttling across the snow, racing toward the guard tower where he and Alice stood.

The creatures were enormous, but they moved incredibly fast. They began climbing the guard tower, their claws grabbing the metal framework.

"Humans, humans, humans to eat!" one shrieked.

"Come, humans, feed us!"

"Suffer, humans. Suffer and die!"

Alice took a step back. She hit the railing, stared with wide eyes. Her face was pale.

"So many," she whispered. "Bas, we're going to die."

"Recharge and fire!" Bastian shouted. "Alice, fire!"

He flipped his Gideon to automatic and let loose. Within a second, he emptied his magazine into a rah. One of its eyes burst. It fell to the ground, twitching.

"They can be hurt!" he said. "They can be killed! Soldiers of Freedom, fight them! Aim for the eyes!"

Alice finally snapped out of it. She leaned over the railing, firing her Gideon down at the climbing beasts. Another eyeball burst. The rah fell.

Briefly, Bastian felt hope. But dozens of the spiders surrounded the tower. The beasts kept climbing.

Other spiders were now making their way through the shattered gate. A few soldiers still fought there, desperate to hold back the enemy. But the human defenders were falling fast.

Dammit! The rahs were entering the base. Neither bullets nor grenades were holding back the storm.

Rowan, Bastian thought. *I must protect Rowan.*

"Alice, cover me," he said. He had to telepathize the message along with speaking. The gunfire was just too loud.

Alice nodded, firing downward all around the tower, desperate to knock off the climbing rahs. Bastian, meanwhile, unhooked a grenade from his belt, pulled the pin, and hurled it toward the mangled gateway below.

The grenade burst. Smoke filled the air. Severed claws and skulls flew, pattering against the guard tower. A rah twitched in the dirt.

The explosion held the rahs back for a moment. But they would soon keep swarming into the base.

"We need to secure the gate!" Bastian said. "We—"

A rah reached the top of the tower.

The spider leaped toward Bastian.

The alien slammed into him. Bastian was a big guy, tall and beefy. That spider knocked him on his ass. It felt like getting hit by a train. Bastian lay on the tower top, stunned, as the spider roared above him.

"Daddy, I'm scared!" Rowan cried over the MindWeb. "I can hear monsters coming. Help, Daddy!"

Bastian couldn't even answer her. He found himself facing the gaping jaws of death. The rah had a mouth like a shark, lined with rings of teeth, leading to a gullet full of sizzling acid. It was like staring at a portal to hell. The mouth widened, ready to devour him, to pull him into the abyss.

"Bas!" Alice cried.

She leaped and slammed into the spider, knocking it off Bastian. The alien slammed onto the metal floor. But within a second, it rose again and lashed its claws.

Bastian swung his rifle, knocking a claw back. Another claw sliced across his side. Bastian screamed. His blood dripped. Alice stepped toward him, raising her rifle like a club.

"Alice, shoot the rahs at the gates!" Bastian shouted. "Stop them from entering! I got this one."

Reluctantly, Alice slung her Gideon over the railing and bombarded the mangled gateway with bullets. Bastian couldn't see if any rahs had gotten past the courtyard yet. He was busy dealing with the enormous arachnid on the tower.

The creature stepped closer, claws scraping the metal floor.

Another rah climbed onto the tower.

And a third.

Alice couldn't help. She was tossing grenades at the gate now.

"Daddy, they're coming closer!" Rowan cried. "I can hear them!"

"I love you, sweetie," Bastian whispered. "Stay strong."

He stood, staring at the three spiders on the guard tower. They were bigger than him—and people joked that Bastian made bulls seem dainty.

"We have conquered ten thousand worlds," hissed one spider, taking a step closer.

"Earth has already fallen," said the second.

"Die now . . .," hissed the third. "Your daughter will be next!"

More rahs came climbing up. The tower shook under their weight.

Bastian unhooked all the grenades from his belt, pulled the

pins, and dropped them onto the floor.

"Not today, fellas," he said, grabbed Alice, and pulled her off the tower.

They tumbled down into a sea of war.

* * * * *

Bastian thumped into the snow. Alice landed on top of him. Their guns clattered. Their helmets banged together.

Above them, high in the guard tower, the grenades detonated.

A massive explosion rocked the tower. The metal foundation twisted and bent. The rahs across the tower screeched. Severed spider legs flew. A claw landed by Bastian, slicing through the snow. Several alien skulls, rah trophies ripped off their spikes, thumped down around him.

Bastian shoved himself up, groaning. "Ow, Alice, you fell on me, and you weigh a ton."

She rose too, covered in snow. "Shut up, Bas, you're twice my size."

Thanks to the pile of snow and their body armor, they had survived the fall with mere bruises and scrapes. The guard tower creaked, and then its foundation snapped. It crashed down, burying several rahs.

Down here was no safer. The aliens were everywhere. More kept coming, mobbing the shattered gateway. Human soldiers lay dead across the courtyard. Some soldiers were still fighting on the wall, but the spiders kept climbing, tearing men and women apart.

Thankfully, Bastian and Alice had fallen inside the camp. Just a few yards away, rahs stormed through the broken gateway, trampling over dead marines. The aliens were racing across the snowy courtyard, heading deeper into the base.

Toward Rowan.

Bastian glanced at the video feeds streaming through his MindLink. The rahs had breached the western wall, but a platoon of marines was holding them back. The other guard towers were being overwhelmed. The rahs were climbing in. But for now, no spiders had reached the inner buildings. Rowan was still safe inside the barracks. As safe as she could be in this hell.

Bastian glanced at news headlines scrolling below.

ALIENS DESTROY WHITE HOUSE

PRESIDENT CONFIRMED DEAD

RED DAWN ARMY JOINS BATTLE IN EUROPE

ALLIANCE FLEET BURNS IN ORBIT

Bastian shut the headlines off. Right now the world might be burning, but his task was to defend this base.

Everything hurt. Bastian's shoulder was aching, maybe dislocated in the fall. Blood dripped down his side. The tooth marks on his arm blazed with fresh pain. But Bastian let out a battle cry, slammed a new magazine into his Gideon, and charged toward the enemy.

"For freedom!" he cried, bullets flying.

"For freedom!" Alice shouted, running at his side.

Their bullets plowed into spiders. Several rahs fell. Other aliens spun toward them and pounced.

Bastian and Alice stood their ground, pounding the enemy with bullets. The spiders bellowed. A few fell, their limbs mangled. But they kept storming forward, the living climbing over the dead. Their red eyes blazed in the night.

One spider leaped toward Bastian. He clubbed it down with his rifle.

Another rah lunged at Alice. She drove her shoulder into the beast, knocking it back.

Both soldiers reloaded. They kept firing.

Bastian took a step forward. Then another step. Alice advanced at his side, roaring as she fired on full automatic.

They were pushing their way forward. Carving through the beasts. Trudging toward the shattered gates.

"We will hold the enemy back!" Bastian said as he fought. He broadcast his words across his company's MindWeb. "We will not fall! We will not die! We will win!"

Across the base, soldiers heard him. They were scared. They were wounded. Some lay dying. Others were already dead. But the survivors rallied. They fought on.

"Second Platoon!" Bastian said, contacting the platoon's lieutenant telepathically. "Send me two squads. Southern gate."

"I don't have men to spare!" the lieutenant replied. The kid was twenty-one, fresh out of officer school. His hand was a bloody, mangled mess. He only had two fingers left. But he still managed to hold his Gideon up, to fire on the enemy. His troops stood around him, guarding the eastern wall, as the spiders kept coming.

"Send one squad then," Bastian said. "You still have a damn wall. My gate here is breached."

The young officer nodded, gave the order, and one squad of soldiers abandoned the eastern wall. They ran across the base, heading toward Bastian at the southern gate.

For a few moments, Bastian and Alice stood alone. Behind them spread human corpses. Before them the rahs kept racing through the breached gateway. Just two soldiers—facing the horde.

A claw thrust into Bastian's shoulder.

He roared, fell to one knee, and pushed himself up. He kept firing.

A spider vaulted toward Alice, teeth gleaming. Its jaws snapped shut around her Gideon rifle. Alice refused to release the weapon. She managed to keep firing. Bullets filled the spider's mouth. The alien screamed and stumbled back. Drool covered the gun, and a tooth had ripped Alice's arm. Her blood dripped. But she kept firing until the rah fell.

They cut down the beasts.

They did not let them in.

"Daddy, please . . ."

Rowan's voice came through his MindLink as he fought.

"Daddy, I'm scared."

And Bastian stayed standing. Kept fighting. For her. Even as he bled, he held back the enemy.

It only took the eastern squad a few minutes to arrive. Those minutes felt like an eternity.

"For freedom!"

They were here. The eastern squad. Ten men charged toward the gateway, shouting, firing their guns. Bullets streaked through the dark. Rahs screamed and fell back. The red blood of men and the black blood of spiders drenched the snow.

All across Fort Liberty, the Badgers Company fought that night. Two hundred soldiers. Falling. Dying. Cut down to a hundred.

But they held the gate.

They held the walls.

They defended their freedom.

The gate had fallen, so they formed a new blockade with their bodies. The walls were breached, so they formed a new wall with their bullets and their courage.

And they held the enemy back.

All that night, they fought. The Badgers Company of the Freedom Brigade. For long hours in the dark, they stood and bled and punished the enemy. They fought alone.

The moonlight revealed the devastation. Scores of soldiers—dead. Scores of rahs—twitching, stinking in the killing field.

And the enemy kept coming, and the battle raged on.

Until finally hope came to Fort Liberty.

Bison Company came first. Two hundred farm boys and farm girls, roaring back from their Christmas vacation. Then came Wolf Company, another two hundred soldiers, a little hungover, stuffed full of turkey and wine, but ready for war. More and more kept coming. Company after company. Battalion after battalion.

The marines of the Freedom Brigade.

They had gone home for Christmas. They had heard the news. They had fought their way here. Some marines had remained home with their families, vowing to protect them. Others had lost their families. Not everyone arrived today. Some had died along the way. Some fled.

But many came.

Thousands came.

At the hour of need, they all knew where to go. To their home. To Fort Liberty.

And Badgers Company, two hundred souls, had held down the fort. They welcomed their fellow soldiers with cries of joy.

With thousands of soldiers, the tide turned. Christmas was over. The moonlight spilled over blood, corpses, despair. But with its light shone hope.

CHAPTER TWENTY-THREE

The Starship *Freedom*
79 million kms from Earth
03:17 December 26, 2199

King stood on the bridge, staring at data coming in from Earth.

"Look at that," he said. "The Desert Thorns managed to destroy a clawship. Not bad for the new kids."

Jordan stood beside him, dour. "We'll have to join forces with Red Dawn too. If there's any hope for victory, humanity must unite."

King spun toward his XO, glowering. "Join the Red Dawn? I don't think so. They're no better than the goddamn aliens."

His throat blazed with pain. The pain always reminded him of Red Dawn's evil.

But maybe Jordan was right.

For the first time, humanity's three great powers—the Alliance, Red Dawn, and Desert Thorns—would have to unite.

King was proud to fight for the Free Alliance. To him, it was the only force of civilization in a chaotic world. The Alliance was created in 2133 to combat the rising threat of equalism. Alliance nations were diverse. They came from around the world. Most shared Judeo-Christian values. Others—like Japan, South Korea, and India—did not share that cultural heritage, but they believed in other ideals that united the Alliance. Democracy. Capitalism. And most importantly—freedom. Yes, that was the central tenet of the Alliance. Freedom.

Starship Freedom

The Red Dawn hated freedom. They fought for equalism, the nefarious ideology that had nearly crushed the world. It was often said that equalism was the bastard child of communism and fascism. Its proponents claimed the ideology brought true equality and justice to mankind. If you asked King—bullshit. To him, equalism meant tyranny, the individual crushed under the heel of the government. Russia, China, and North Korea formed the central axis of the Red Dawn, but many other nations had joined them. With sweet words and empty promises, equalism had spread across South America, Eastern Europe, and large swaths of Asia. At one point, they had even seized Mars—at least until the *Freedom* knocked them back down to Earth.

The Desert Thorns were a new pact, only formed after the war, uniting most Middle Eastern and North African nations. During World War III, some of these nations had fought for the Alliance, others for the Red Dawn. When the war ended, when everyone was licking their wounds, they decided to eschew both the Alliance and Red Dawn. They formed their own union, creating humanity's third great power. Queen Laila, hailing from glittering Dubai with its floating skyscrapers, led the Desert Thorns. Laila had been a baby during the third world war. She would have to fight her first war now.

Was it possible? To unite the three superpowers?

King didn't know. He had no grudge against the Desert Thorns. But the Red Dawn was another matter. Even an alien invasion couldn't make him forget Katyusha's sins.

The woman murdered my father, he thought. *I'll be damned if I join her.*

"Commander, may I see you for a moment?" Mimori said, pulling him from his thoughts.

King approached the android. "Speak your mind, Mimori."

"I've been analyzing the data from the battle on Earth," she said. "Specifically the electric shields around the rah clawships."

King nodded. "The ones that appear like electric webs."

"Yes, sir. I've discovered a vulnerability to exploit. The clawships generate a complex, grid-shaped electromagnetic pattern. With the right photon burst, we can disrupt their shields. Maybe disable them entirely."

King inhaled sharply. "That would be a game changer."

"Indeed, sir," Mimori said. "Without their electromagnetic shields, they'd still have the protection of their armored hull. But at least one line of defense will be gone. However, we can only use this trick once. As soon as the rahs discover the weakness, they can easily patch the security hole."

King nodded, his excitement souring a bit. "All right. Well, that's better than nothing."

Jordan, who had heard the conversation, approached them. "Jim, we should transmit this information to the fleet."

"I would caution against that, sir," Mimori said. "From this distance, the rahs will intercept our transmission. It's true that our transmissions are encrypted. But if the rahs have seized any human starships or military bases, they can find the encryption keys. And then they can patch their security hole before we can exploit it."

King considered for a moment. "All right. We'll sit on this information for now. Mimori, I want you to program a shield disruptor into our ATLAS photon broadcasters. Can you do that?"

"Already done, sir." She smiled. "I'm very good at my job."

"And humble," King said.

Her smile widened. "Humility is a human frailty. As a superior life form, I—" She paled. She clutched his arm. "Sir! ATLAS reports a portal opening ahead!"

* * * * *

King wheeled toward a monitor. A plan position indicator filled the screen. The *Freedom* appeared in the center of the display—a luminous green icon with two prongs. Concentric circles spread around the icon like ripples in a pond, marking distance. Each circle was ten thousand kilometers farther from the ship. The ATLAS sensors kept sweeping space around the *Freedom*, constantly updating the PPI. A few green dots appeared on the diagram, denoting small asteroids and comets. Debris was a constant threat in space. At this speed, even a grain of sand could cause serious damage to a ship's hull.

ATLAS's interface was crude, even ugly to some. Just basic green and red graphics on black backgrounds. None of those fancy MindPlay hallucinations, which were so lifelike King wanted to shoot them. ATLAS was old and clunky, a little like him. King loved it.

"I don't see it," King said, staring at the display.

Mimori pointed. "There, sir."

He noticed it then. A part of the ATLAS display was . . . rippling. A green circle bent. Just in one section. Then it straightened again.

"That's a disturbance in the spacetime fabric," Mimori said. "An enemy portal."

Three red dots suddenly appeared on the screen. Right where the display had rippled.

"Three clawships," King said. "Thirty thousand klicks away. They're heading right at us."

Thirty thousand kilometers was more than twice the diameter of Earth. In space, that was nothing. The enemy was right on them.

We might need to use those shield disruptors earlier than expected, King thought.

"Sir, they're broadcasting their identification signals using standard Alliance protocols." Mimori frowned, tilted her head. "The enemy clawships are identifying themselves as the *Venom*, the *Wandering Widow*, and the *Bloodlust*."

King glowered at the monitor, watching the three red dots fly closer. "Psychological warfare. They learned our language, and they translated the names of their ships to intimidate us. I won't play that game. What stats can you give me on those ships?"

"Still parsing ATLAS data, sir," Mimori said. "Preliminary data confirms all three are warclaw-class vessels. If they were human starships, we would classify them as dreadnoughts. They're roughly two kilometers long, half a kilometer wide. No report yet on their armaments or complement. Wait. Updating. One ship, the *Bloodlust*, is larger than the other two. Almost three kilometers long."

"All three are bigger than us," King said. "And we can assume that, unlike the *Freedom*, they're armed. Can ATLAS get us a visual of the ships?"

Mimori closed her eyes, which she sometimes did when scanning the streams of data in the *Freedom*'s central computers. "ATLAS sensors are still parsing the data, and . . . yes, we're picking up a visual of the clawships now. Should I send it to your MindWeb?"

"No. Display on main monitor."

Everyone stared at the large screen, which dominated the prow-side bulkhead. A live video appeared, feeding from telescopes on the prow.

A portal floated in space, revealing a strange, shadowy realm beyond, a place of smeared lights and dark shapes that glided like whales in the murk. Three clawships had emerged from the portal. They were charging toward the *Freedom*. Behind them, the portal faded away like a bad dream.

The clawships were coming in fast. They looked hungry for

war.

Dammit.

"Mimori, are there any Alliance ships nearby who can assist?" King said. "Hell, I'll even take help from Red Dawn ships." That hurt to admit, but that's how far things had come.

"No, sir," Mimori said. "Everyone else is fighting the battle in Earth's orbit. We're here alone."

The bridge crew was silent for a moment.

The three clawships slowed down and hovered ahead. Three colossal dreadnoughts, covered with spines and claws. Some of those claws were as long as the *Freedom*. They could slice them open like a katana.

The two smaller clawships, the *Venom* and the *Wandering Widow*, looked identical. They were both black with swirling red centers. But the gargantuan *Bloodlust* had a gray hull, and her claws were blood red. At three kilometers long, she was twice the *Freedom*'s length.

The *Freedom* and the three clawships floated in space, sizing one another up.

Alone, King thought. *We're alone out here. Unarmed.*

He took a deep breath.

"Mimori, open a channel. Hail the clawships. We're going to have a little chat. I want to know more about these creatures."

"Yes, sir." The android concentrated for a moment. "Sending out a communication request, sir. Their ships are attempting to respond. Their technology is . . ." She frowned. "Definitely alien. I'm not sure we can establish a video call. Wait." She gasped. "One of the clawships is accepting our call, sir! Their technology can understand ours. It's the *Bloodlust*. The big one with the red claws."

"Put it on the front monitor," King said.

"Yes, sir. Beginning call in three, two, one . . ."

A video feed appeared on the central monitor, coming from

inside the clawship.

Across the *Freedom*'s bridge, crew members gasped or cursed. A tactical officer swayed, nearly fainted.

King stared, jaw clenched, fists tight at his sides.

For the first time, he got a good look at a rah.

Ugly sons of bitches, he thought.

* * * * *

The clawship's bridge—if that was the right word for it—was a cavernous place. The walls were craggy, irregular, carelessly cobbled together with chunks of raw iron. Cobwebs filled the cavern, trapping several victims. Most of those victims seemed alien—strange creatures, some scaled, others insectile, and some that seemed amphibian. One of the victims in the cobwebs was human. She still wore an Alliance uniform. Her belly had been slashed open, the innards removed, and eggs placed inside.

King only spared these victims a glance. He could not help them now. He focused his attention on the creature who hung in the center of the web.

A rah.

The spider was enormous. As large as a rhino. A spiny gray exoskeleton enclosed its abdomen. Each spine impaled a severed head. Eight blood-red legs thrust out, tipped with claws like swords. Eight red eyes stared at King. Slowly a grin spread across the creature's face, revealing rows of sharp teeth. Not a spider's mouth. A shark's mouth. A mouth made for ripping flesh.

King's crew members were trembling. A few cowered. But King stood his ground, staring at the beast on the monitor. He stared into its hideous red eyes.

"I am James King, commander of the starship *Freedom*," he

said. "You've encroached on human territory. Turn back now or—"

"Hello, Commander King," the creature hissed. "Ah, so you are the famous war hero, yes? I've heard about you. You're so much smaller and older than I imagined."

"You have me at a disadvantage," King said, not taking the bait.

The creature bristled, spikes rattling. "You don't know me? Truly you humans are ignorant little parasites. I am Hel'rah, warlord of the clawship *Bloodlust*, prince of the Great Web. You speak to the son of Skel'rah, the Midnight Huntress, High Mistress of the fleet. I am the storm that rises from the void between stars. I am the devourer of lost souls. I am your doom."

"Nice to meet you," King said. "Can I call you Helly for short?"

The creature laughed. Drool dripped between his fangs. "Normally I would have destroyed you by now. But I'm so curious." He squinted his eight eyes. "What manner of ship is this *Freedom*? You have thick shields like a warship. Yet you're unarmed. You're supposedly a great warrior. Yet you're clearly a miserable maggot. My mother claims you are . . . What did she call it? A *museum*? Some ape foolishness." The rah snorted. "What is this trickery?"

"Get used to living in ignorance, Helly," King said. "I give you one last chance. Turn back now. Or get your answers the hard way."

The rah laughed—a terrible sound. A sound like crunching bones. "So you choose death. Very well. I will gladly destroy your miserable ship, Commander King. And once I'm done, I will pay Earth a little visit. I will devour your granddaughter, King. I will eat little Rowan. Yes, we know all about your family. I will make it hurt. I will—"

"Get this crap off my screen!" King said.

Mimori nodded. The video feed vanished. Instead, the monitor now showed a view of space. The three clawships hovered ahead.

The clawships began to accelerate.

They came storming toward the *Freedom*, raring for war.

"Mimori, how long until they reach us?" King said. The monitors were zoomed in. The clawships were farther than they appeared.

"At their current speed," the android replied, "they'll reach us in seventy-three seconds."

"Change course!" King barked. "Get us out of here, Mimori. We must choose our battles. We can't fight our dear friend Hel'rah. Not yet. Not without weapons."

"Sir." Mimori winced. "The three clawships are accelerating at incredible speed. I don't think we can outrun them. Not all the way to the armory."

"Then give us whatever time you can," King said. "If Hel'rah wants a fight, delay it as much as possible."

Mimori nodded. "Yes, sir. Yawing the ship, sir. The enemy is adjusting course to intercept us."

"Give our engines a boost of afterburner," King said. "Even while we're yawing."

"Yes, sir."

The deck thrummed as the *Freedom*'s engines roared. Everyone swayed on their feet. The ship blasted forward while yawing, carving a curved path through space. And the clawships followed.

King gritted his teeth. "How long before they catch us now?" He had to speak loudly over the roaring engines.

"I don't know, sir. Depends on their maximum speed. Judging by their current acceleration rate, if we push our engines hard and divert all power to our Talaria drive, we can delay the battle by thirteen minutes."

"Do it," King said. "Keep running. As fast as you can." He turned toward the rest of his crew. "In thirteen minutes or less, we'll have a battle on our hands. We need to prepare. If anyone has a brilliant plan, speak up now."

* * * * *

The crew was silent.

The *Freedom* charged across space, but the clawships kept pursuing. They were gaining on them.

King turned toward his XO. "Jordan, what do you think?"

Jordan's eyes were dark. "We have no weapons. Only one Goliath projectile for the Fist of Freedom, and it's a dummy. Hollow. Just a fake for the tourists to snap photos of."

"Then we'll have to get creative," King said. "I was hoping to reach the Mercury armory before we had to fight. But we're gonna have to fight at least one battle unarmed. We have fireworks. We shoot them for the tourists from the Angels of Liberty."

Jordan tilted his head. "You're not suggesting we shoot fireworks at them, Jim? Even if Mimori can disable their shields, they still have armored hulls. Fireworks won't even scratch them. We might as well shoot spitballs."

Maybe we should shoot out the tourists, King thought.

"Fireworks are not lethal, but they can blind the enemy," King said. "And the Fist of Freedom is more than a railgun. It's a ramming weapon too. Two rails of solid metal, hundreds of meters long—they can rip through an enemy hull." He smiled grimly. "Remember the battle against the *Xiaoping*?"

Jordan nodded. "Of course. We rammed her. Tore right through her. But Jim, that was a Red Dawn frigate. Much slower, much weaker. These clawships . . ." He shook his head. "I've never seen ships fly like this."

"That's why we'll blind the bastards," King said. "If we can blind 'em, we can ram 'em."

Jordan nodded. "All right. It's a crazy plan. But it sounded crazy back in World War III too. I'll begin coordinating things with the gunnery boys. We'll get those fireworks loaded in time. We'll put on a show."

"Mimori, how long do I have?" King said.

"Nine minutes, sir," the android said. "They're accelerating faster than I thought. I've shut down everything but life support in the tourist decks, and I'm diverting that energy to our Talaria drive. But our acceleration is slow compared to theirs, and—"

"Got it," King said. "Mimori, send out an ATLAS probe. Have it hover five hundred klicks above us. I want an eye up there."

"Launching probe now, sir," said the android.

A device the size of a coffeepot soared into space. The probe offered them an extra camera, which they could connect to from the bridge, giving them a bird's-eye view of the battle. Such probes had proved themselves priceless in the last war.

"Probe in position, sir. Seven minutes until the enemy reaches us."

King turned away from the android. "Colonel Levy!"

The Israeli fighter pilot looked at him, chin raised. She had stayed up drinking late last night. Her flight suit was wrinkled. Her eyes were red. But she snapped to attention right away. "Yes, sir!"

"There are two hundred Eagle starfighters on this ship. I want them launching within the next eight minutes. I want your Eagles to attack two enemy clawships while we ram the third."

Spitfire frowned. "Attack them with *what*, sir? My Eagles don't have missiles. And we're not equipped for shooting fireworks either. Do you want us to perform stunts for them?"

"Eagle starfighters come with a compartment for firing chaff at enemies," King said. "During World War III, the Red Dawn would often attack our Eagles with heat-seeking missiles. So we'd open our back hatches, and we'd release clouds of chaff. Screws. Strips of aluminum. Any scrap metal we could find."

Spitfire nodded. "I know. We store snacks in those compartments now."

"Well, fill them with chaff!" King said. "Grab whatever you can. Anything metal. Hell, fill bins with cutlery and dump that in. Whatever you can get in eight minutes! Seven minutes now. At high enough speeds, chaff can severely compromise a hull. Go! Get to work."

Spitfire hesitated. "Sir, we're just stunt pilots."

"Not today. Today you're all fighter pilots. Now go, Colonel! Get my starfighters flying."

"Yes, sir!" She ran off the bridge.

"Five more minutes, sir," Mimori said. "They're gaining on us. I can't go any faster."

"Jordan, how are the Angels of Liberty doing?" King said.

There were fourteen Angels in all—cannons that thrust out from the starship, seven on each side.

"The gunners got three loaded with fireworks, all on the starboard side," Jordan said. "They're working on the rest."

"Three minutes, sir!" Mimori said. "They're moving faster than I expected."

King cursed. "Mimori, begin to position our starboard hull toward the enemy. We'll hit 'em with fireworks, then yaw so our prow faces them, charge them head-on, and ram the bastards."

"Should I stop fleeing?" Mimori asked. "Two more minutes until they reach us."

King nodded. "Yes. It's time. Slow to a halt and prepare for battle. And get those shield disruptors ready to fire."

"Understood. Beginning our yaw, sir."

It could take a dreadnought the size of the *Freedom* a while to yaw under the best conditions. It also required massive amounts of energy diverted from other systems to the side thrusters.

The deck plates creaked. Motors rumbled. King could feel the massive starship turning. The Talaria drive began to hum down, slowing the ship as they turned. The side thrusters roared, surging with energy. Power rumbled and clattered through pipes and cables. The lights dimmed as the *Freedom* sucked up all the energy she could.

King stared at his bridge crew. "Godspeed, everyone."

He looked at the main monitor. The three enemy ships were coming in fast, almost on them now. A hundred steel claws sprouted from each vessel, pointing at the *Freedom*. As King watched, those claws began to extend, blooming open to reveal centers of glowing plasma.

"Sir, we're now in position to aim the Angels and fire," Mimori said. "Should I launch the shield disruptors?"

The alien ships bloomed wider. Their centers blazed, furious and blinding.

"Not yet," King said. "Mimori, cut our engines. Divert all available power to starboard shields."

It was a risk. There was no fleeing this fight now. They were in this to take the punches—and hopefully dish out some punishment too.

"Diverting full power to starboard shields," Mimori said. "Stern engines powering down. Sir . . . waiting for your order to disrupt their shields."

"Not yet, Mimori!"

King just hoped his own shields would hold. These shields had withstood Red Dawn torpedoes, even a nuclear blast. But could they take rah plasma?

"Jim, we need to disrupt their shields now!" Jordan said.

"Wait for my order," King whispered. "Wait . . ."

The enemy stormed closer.

Their plasma crackled white-hot.

"Mimori, disrupt their shields!" King shouted. "Now!"

The *Freedom* thrummed. Waves of photons blasted outward and washed over the enemy.

Shields blazed to life around the three clawships—orange webs of electromagnetic energy. The shields flared, trembled—and vanished.

"Their shields are down!" Mimori cried. A few officers cheered.

Jordan raised his eyes from a control panel. "All starboard cannons loaded with fireworks! Awaiting your order, Jim." The XO grimaced. "I hope this works."

The three alien ships were fully dilated now, displaying their swirling, flaming cores.

Plasma surged forth.

"Fire!" King shouted.

CHAPTER TWENTY-FOUR

**The Starship *Freedom*
79 million kms from Earth
04:01 December 26, 2199**

King's voice echoed across the bridge.

"Fire!"

The *Bloodlust*, one of the enemy clawships, had gotten off a shot first. The plasma was storming toward the *Freedom*—a spinning, crackling stream of death.

"Five seconds to plasma impact!" Mimori cried.

A ship the size of the *Freedom* was too slow to dodge an assault at such close range. Definitely not with the power flowing to their shields and cannons, leaving their Talaria drive to idle.

"Four seconds!" Mimori said.

"Why aren't we firing?" King demanded.

"The enemy is moving fast, and we need to re-aim our cannons," Mimori replied. "Three seconds to impact!"

King saw it on the monitor. That flaming stream of death charging toward them, closer and closer, devouring the distance.

Motors hummed. Atop the *Freedom*, the Angels of Liberty were moving, readjusting their aim. The bridge vibrated as the enormous cannons rotated.

"Two seconds to impact!"

"Fire, dammit!" King shouted. "Fire now!"

The *Freedom*'s mighty cannons fired.

Silvery canisters flew into space, streaming toward the

enemy. They were full of fireworks, which had not yet detonated.

"One second to—" Mimori began.

The jet of plasma hit.

A locomotive of fury plowed into the *Freedom*'s starboard hull.

The ship shook.

Klaxons blared.

Smoke filled the bridge. Red lights strobed.

"Our shields held, sir!" Mimori said, and a few officers cheered.

A few thousand klicks ahead, right by the enemy ships, the fireworks burst.

They were special fireworks the ship was saving for the annual Fourth of July Freedom BBQ Bash. It was always a hit with the American tourists. Now the red and blue fireworks lit up space. The red ones streaked in every direction, painting stripes through the darkness. The blue fireworks sparkled like ten thousand stars.

The grand display, with all its American glory, flowed over the three rah clawships. It draped them with flags of light.

"Yaw toward them and charge!" King shouted, ignoring the agony in his throat. "Full power to thrust! Ram the middle one, the one that burned us. GO!"

Mimori had already begun the yaw. She deflected power from shields back to the Talaria drive, which was still primed and red-hot.

The *Freedom* charged like a bull.

She stormed toward the blinded enemy. Faster. Faster.

"Sir!" came Spitfire's voice over the MindWeb. "I still need a few minutes to grab chaff, I—"

"Hold on to something, Spitfire!" King said.

The *Freedom* blazed through the red and blue fireworks.

The enemy fired again. All three clawships were firing now.

Plasma washed over the *Freedom*'s prow, searing the shields, melting several sensors. Warnings flashed. The *Freedom* kept flying, roaring through the inferno. The flames blazed around them, forming a hemisphere of light. And still the *Freedom* flew. Proximity alarms screamed. One thousand klicks away. Five hundred. And—

The mighty rails of the starship *Freedom* plowed into a clawship—a vessel twice her size.

King fell and banged his knees on the deck. Monitors shattered. Control panels ripped free. Mimori slammed down beside King. Crew members flew, hit the bulkheads, the deck, the railings.

And still the *Freedom* flew. King *felt* them moving.

Half the goddamn ATLAS monitors were down. King pulled up MindPlay and connected to the telemetry probe, which was still flying five hundred klicks above the *Freedom*. He hallucinated a monitor, which hovered in the air before him. It displayed a video from the probe, showing him a bird's-eye view of the *Freedom*.

King lost his breath.

His starship had slammed into the *Wandering Widow*, one of the black clawships. The railgun's two mighty prongs, each the size of a skyscraper, had impaled the rah dreadnought. The *Freedom* was like a fork stuck in a piece of meat. And the ship was *still* flying, shoving the enemy back through space.

"Mimori, fire the railgun!" King said.

"Commander?" Mimori tilted her head. "You mean . . . fire the Fist of Freedom?" They had not fired it since the last war. "I would need confirmation from the XO. But sir, there's barely any power in the rails. And no Goliath projectiles loaded."

Lieutenant Commander Jordan pushed himself up. The tall XO was bleeding from his forehead.

"Jim, you know we don't have any Goliaths to fire," he said.

The two other clawships, the ones not impaled, came flying in fast. They flanked the *Freedom*. Plasma crackled inside them.

"Fire the goddamn railgun!" King shouted. "Just turn the damn thing on and fire a blank. Now!"

Jordan nodded. He seemed to understand. "Do it, Mimori."

"Yes, sirs!" said the android.

Enormous, unimaginable power surged through the starship, streaming toward the railgun.

The two clawships flanking them opened fire.

Electricity raced across the bridge's deck, the bulkheads, raising everyone's hackles, racing to the prow. Vast electromagnetic fields pulsed out the hulls, rocking the flanking clawships.

For the first time in decades, the Fist of Freedom turned on.

Plasma slammed into both the port and starboard sides of the *Freedom*.

The Fist was only at seven percent power. It had no projectiles to hurl. But it roared, and its two rails lit up with furious white electricity.

The hull shields heated, heated, began to crack, to melt. The plasma was unrelenting. The klaxons wailed in protest. Mimori screamed.

The electricity surged from the rails into the clawship they impaled.

The *Wandering Widow* burst open like a black dragon egg.

The mighty clawship, a vessel the size of a town, tore right in two.

Claws the size of city blocks flew through space. Chunks of craggy black hull scattered every which way. Some pieces of the destroyed clawship pounded the *Bloodlust* and *Venom*, the two surviving rah vessels.

Both *Bloodlust* and *Venom* reeled in space. Their jets of

plasma spurted harmlessly into the distance, giving the *Freedom* some respite. Just in time too. The port shield was down to forty percent, the starboard to thirty-five percent.

The rails were free.

One clawship down. Two to go.

* * * * *

"Spitfire, where are my Eagles!" King shouted into his MindLink. The bridge smoked around him. The two clawships were raring for more brutality.

King hallucinated Spitfire running across the starfighter hangar, shoving a cart of cutlery.

"Getting chaff, sir, as you ordered!" Spitfire said. "Had to stop by the galley. Needed to grab a ton of cutlery, as you suggested."

"Get those Eagles into the fight, dammit!"

"Yes, sir! One more minute, sir. Two tops. Definitely no more than five."

King shut off the hallucination. "Mimori, how long until you can charge the rails again? Even five percent is enough to shock the enemy."

The android winced. "I can't charge them, sir. Not if we want the shields to stay up. The Fist of Freedom is out of commission for at least seven, eight hours. Longer if we want a full charge."

That had always been the downside of the gargantuan railgun. The damn thing took so long to charge. To charge it enough to cause serious damage took a full day, even under the best conditions.

When fully charged, when hurling its legendary Goliaths,

the Fist of Freedom could destroy worlds. That was why the XO needed to authorize its use; even the commander of the ship could not wield such power alone.

Well, the Fist was down for now. The Eagles were still in the hangar. The Angels of Liberty, the Freedom's secondary weapons, were out of fireworks. During the war, the Angels had fired the dreaded Maccabee torpedoes, but they had none today, not until they reached the armory. A hundred machine-gun nests sprouted across the *Freedom*'s hull, but what use were they without bullets?

Out of weapons. Out of options. And two clawships came charging right at them, one from each side.

Perfect.

Not how King had imagined his first day of retirement.

"We should try another ram," Jordan suggested.

King shook his head. "No. Without a charge in the rail, we'll get lodged inside one clawship. The other clawship would rip us apart. Spitfire?"

"Two more minutes, sir!" she replied through MindWeb.

King's upper lip twitched. He sent a telepathic transmission to everyone in the gunnery department.

"Gunners! This is your commander. Load the Angels of Liberty with whatever you can. Anything heavy. Chunks of loose bulkhead. Metal furniture. Railings. Helmets. Anything you can grab! We'll fire what we can."

Several dozen tiny icons hovered before King—the crew responsible for the Angels of Liberty. They all saluted and sounded their yes sirs. One of them was a Mimori model, one of the three midsection units.

"Jordan, stay on their asses," King said. "Let me know when the Angels are ready."

"Got it, Jim." Jordan summoned his own MindPlay interface, overseeing the work on the cannons.

But they were out of time.

The *Venom* opened her metal jaws and unleashed hell.

"Mimori, evasive maneuvers!" King barked.

"Yes, sir!"

The Talaria engines roared. The *Freedom* shot forward. She barely dodged the stream of plasma.

Meanwhile, the *Bloodlust* yawed and charged toward the *Freedom*. Her red claws thrust forward. She was the largest of the enemy ships, dwarfing the *Freedom*. Hel'rah was aboard that ship, no doubt cackling away.

"She's going to ram us!" King said.

"Not today," said Mimori, yawing hard and rolling toward their port side.

The two ships shot toward one another.

The *Bloodlust*'s claws gleamed. The Fist of Freedom thrust out its rails. The claws were longer.

King braced himself for impact.

"Mimori!" King cried. He wasn't sure the *Freedom* could take another collision. Not with those claws aimed right at them.

Those things will rip us open like a can of sardines, he thought.

"Yawing as hard as I can, sir. I . . ." The android strained. "Hold on . . ."

The ships raced by each other.

Only a few klicks apart now.

Too close. Too close!

One of *Bloodlust*'s enormous steel claws, a weapon the size of the Burj Khalifa, scraped across the *Freedom*'s starboard hull.

Mimori screamed and clutched her side.

The *Freedom* jolted.

The bridge crew swayed on their feet.

What monitors were still active flashed red.

Mimori fell to her knees, holding her side. "It hurts. Help. Help me. It hurts."

King stared at one monitor, but it flickered, then died.

"Somebody give me a damage report!" he barked.

Jordan looked up from a workstation that was still operational. "The claw ripped our midsection open along decks 23, 24, and 25."

"Tourist bunks," King said.

"The ship is venting air fast!" Jordan said.

King knelt by the android, who was still holding her side. "Mimori, are you with me?"

She looked up at him, pale. She nodded, still holding her side. "Yes."

"Seal off decks 23 to 25 in the midsection," King said. "All hatches, vents, everything—seal them off!"

Jordan stepped closer. "Jim, there are hundreds of tourists in there. They'll suffocate."

"Most are already dead," King said. "The rest are dying. If we don't seal the breach, the entire ship will depressurize."

"We need time to evacuate tourists from those de—"

"Sir, they're coming in for another assault!" cried a tactical officer, interrupting the XO.

"Mimori, evasive maneuvers!" King said. "And seal those decks *now*. That is an order, Mimori."

A MindLink message appeared on high priority, hovering before King, drawing his attention at once. Only senior officers had permission to do that.

"Sir, this is Mimori Unit 3 in the midsection." A hallucination of a Mimori unit appeared before him. Her uniform was torn and charred. A gash on her cheek revealed whirring electronics. "I'm working on sealing the breaches. My bridge counterpart will focus on evasive action."

The hallucination vanished. Mimori Unit 1, here on the bridge, was still kneeling on the deck. She had her eyes closed, and her arms were moving like a conductor. She was still piloting the ship.

The beloved *Freedom* was hurt. But she was still flying.

They soared, dodging more claws.

"Sir, it's Spitfire, calling from the Eagle hangar!" came a call on the MindLink. "We're all loaded up here with chaff and ready to fly."

The *Freedom* swerved, dodging a plasma spray. Both enemy clawships were coming in fast. The *Venom*, the black clawship, was spurting plasma. Meanwhile, the *Bloodlust* seemed determined to ram the *Freedom* and claw her apart. Dear old Hel'rah probably got a kick out of it.

The *Freedom* flew faster, yawing, rolling, desperately trying to avoid death by fire or steel.

"Spitfire, fly!" King said. "Focus all Eagles on the *Venom*! Launch everything you got at the *Venom*! Go!"

The Bloodlust is mine, King thought, fists clenched. *I'm taking you down myself, Hel'rah. You threatened my granddaughter. You hurt my ship. You murdered hundreds of my passengers. I'm going to crush you under my boot like the bug that you are.*

"Here we go!" Spitfire shouted and laughed. "If we don't make it, see ya in hell, Commander! Woo!"

King watched the video feed from the probe. On the starboard hull, the hangar airlocks opened. The Eagles emerged to fight.

CHAPTER TWENTY-FIVE

**The Starship *Freedom*
79 million kms from Earth
04:27 December 26, 2199**

Spitfire shoved down the throttle. Her starfighter stormed out the hangar, flying to battle.

Two hundred more Eagles soared with her, etching trails of white light.

They left the *Freedom* behind. Before them loomed the beasts. Two gargantuan clawships. The Eagles were like a swarm of hornets flying toward two charging bulls.

Oh hell, Spitfire thought.

Terror flowed over her like icy waves. Her hands shook on her yoke.

She had clocked countless hours in her Eagle, the best starfighter in the galaxy. But only as a stunt pilot. Never in battle.

None of them had ever fought a battle.

She directed the flock toward the *Venom*, the black clawship. *Venom* was smaller than the *Bloodlust*, but at two kilometers long, she was still colossal, larger than any starship humans had ever built.

The *Venom* yawed in space, turning toward the starfighters. Her ring of claws bloomed open, revealing a flaming gullet. The alien dreadnought almost seemed to be smiling. It was the sort of smile a predator gave its prey—just before feasting. It seemed to Spitfire less like a starship now, more like a god of the dark.

I'm going to die, Spitfire thought. *I'm going to die out here in space, far from home. We all are.*

Visions flashed before her eyes. Not MindLink hallucinations but memories. Her little hilltop apartment in Haifa, overlooking the sea. Her mother, collecting fallen pine nuts in the garden. Her grandfather, fixing his little machines. Her pet dog, a mutt named Schnitzel, wagging his tail. Her nephews and nieces playing in the yard, laughing, leaping onto Spitfire.

She would never see them again.

MindPlay hovered before her, showing the positions of her pilots. Their voices rose, filling her mind.

"What the hell are we supposed to do, loop-de-loops?"

"We have to get out of here. We have to run!"

"We're not fighter pilots! We're gonna die here. Oh God, we're all gonna die."

Spitfire took a deep breath. She gripped the yoke more steadily.

Calm yourself, Gal Levy! she thought. *You are a colonel in the Alliance Fleet. Your father was a fighter pilot. His father was a fighter pilot. Your family has flown in battle for centuries. You will face this enemy!*

"Freedom's Flock!" she said. "This is Spitfire, your flight commander. I know you're scared. But today you are all warriors! Charge that clawship and fire your chaff! With me—fly!"

"Let's rock!" somebody cried. It was Pickles. Sarcastic Pickles with his bionic eye and sardonic smile.

"Let's kill these sons of bitches!" roared Meatball, the beefy pilot with the pink cheeks.

"Come on, charge with Spitfire!" cried Katana. The Japanese pilot laughed. "For death and glory!"

The Eagles soared. All of them. Babyface. Honey Badger. Dingo. Razor. Snoopy. All the rest of them. They knew one another by their call signs. They were a family. Today they were warriors.

Facing them, the *Venom* spewed her plasma.

"Scatter!" Spitfire cried. "Peacock formation!"

The Eagles branched apart, each starfighter drawing an arc through space. They often used this move in the shows, drawing an enormous peacock tail in space, every starfighter etching another feather.

The plasma jet stormed between them, tearing through their luminous wakes.

From a distance, the plasma jet had seemed slender, a flaming blade in the dark. But now, flying so close, Spitfire saw that the torrent was thick and engorged. It could swallow a starfighter like a fire hose washing over a fly.

"Zebra formations!" Spitfire said. "Fly toward the enemy!"

The Eagles yawed toward the clawship. They charged.

As they flew, the Eagles rose and fell, zigzagged and bounced, drawing lines through the sky like zebra stripes. The formation was meant to dazzle the audience, drowning the eyes in optical illusions of crisscrossing wakes. Spitfire just hoped it would distract the enemy.

The *Venom* yawed left, then right. She seemed unsure where to attack.

"It's working!" Pickles cried. "We're bamboozling the heck out of—"

"Watch out!" Spitfire cried.

The *Venom* rolled, spraying plasma, swinging her blade of fire through space.

The crackling torrent tore into a starfighter.

Pickles screamed, ejecting just in time. His starfighter exploded. Pickles tumbled into the distance, still strapped into his seat. His MindLink went dark. He was either dead or unconscious.

"Pickles!" Meatball cried.

One starfighter broke out of formation. Meatball charged at

the enemy. The *Venom* turned toward him.

"Meatball, get back in formation," Spitfire snapped.

"I've had enough with these spiders!" Meatball cried. "I'm gonna—"

The plasma washed over him.

His Eagle exploded.

Another avatar went dark. But this time they saw no pilot eject.

"Meatball?" Spitfire whispered. Nobody answered.

Fear washed over Spitfire. Her fingers began to shake, her pulse to quicken.

From the corner of her eye, she saw the *Freedom* far away, battling the *Bloodlust*, the other clawship. The *Freedom* was hurt, still leaking air. Plasma was spraying her hull. She was taking a pounding.

A third starfighter burned.

Curly's starfighter this time.

Curly—silly Curly with his jokes and cigars and wide smile.

Curly—gone.

Spitfire began to pant. Her breath shook. Panic was setting in.

Be calm, Spitfire, she told herself. *Be cool. You are the child of warriors. You are a daughter of Earth. You can do this.*

"Bumblebee formation," she said. "Swarm and attack!"

The Eagles swarmed.

Bumblebee formation basically meant—charge like hell.

It was an in-joke among the flock. What to do if a tourist shuttle annoyed them too much? Fly like bumblebees! Swarm, swarm! Just a joke.

Now it meant life or death.

The *Venom* stormed toward them, plasma spurting. Another Eagle exploded.

But scores of Eagles still flew. Swift starfighters. Legendary machines. The famous starfighters that won World War III. They were now painted red and blue. They were now stunt vessels, unarmed.

But they were still damn fast.

They swerved around the plasma.

The fiery jet arched toward Spitfire.

She executed a spiraling barrel roll, dodging the assault.

The *Venom* flew closer.

A claw extended, sweeping toward Spitfire. That claw was a kilometer long. Spitfire soared in a straight line, then looped around the claw, dodging the gargantuan blade.

Yes. They were fast. They were agile. These pilots were daredevils. And maybe, after all, that wasn't a handicap.

Spitfire flew in spirals around the plasma beam, corkscrewing closer toward the *Venom*.

She had no missiles. No bullets. No bombs. But she had a trunk full of chaff. Forks. Spoons. A few butter knives. It wasn't much. But in space, flying at these speeds, objects carried immense kinetic energy. Every starfighter pilot had heard horror stories, some maybe just urban legends—a single grain of sand in space or maybe just a fleck of paint peeled off some hull, slamming into a starfighter, shattering the hull, and killing the pilot inside. Many times, when flying her Eagle, Spitfire had looked back toward the *Freedom*, had seen the scars on the starship's armor. Some of those scars were a meter deep. Just tiny fragments of junk, floating in space, slamming into the ship at hypersonic speed. It turned even specks of dust into bullets.

Well, Spitfire had more than dust in her trunk.

She roared closer toward the *Venom*. Closer. Closer still.

The clawship yawed toward her, sweeping her claws, ready to slice Spitfire's starfighter apart.

Spitfire kept flying, heading toward that craggy black hull.

At the last second, she executed a quick, perfect dime flip.

Within an instant, she was facing the other way.

Dime flips were tough moves, impossible in the air, hard even in space.

Spitfire did it perfectly.

"Eat my dust," she muttered, opened her back hatch, and hit the thruster.

Her engine roared.

She blazed on full afterburner, leaving a trail of flame.

From her back hatch, she released the chaff. Cutlery flew toward the enemy ship.

At the sight of spinning spoons and forks, Spitfire had to laugh.

The chaff hatch was meant to confuse heat-seeking missiles. These starfighters had used it successfully in the war. Now, instead of aluminum strips, cutlery flew toward the *Venom*—and impacted.

The cutlery plowed into the clawship's hull.

Knives, forks, spoons—they carved into the metal armor like maggots burrowing into old wood.

All around the *Venom*, the Eagles were unleashing their chaff. Eagles? Next to this alien dreadnought, they seemed as small as bees. And they kept stinging the great, lumbering beast.

Unfortunately, none of the chaff did serious damage.

The *Venom*'s hull was damn thick.

A claw came swinging toward Spitfire.

She cursed and tugged the yoke. Her heart leaped. Too slow. She was too slow! Why had she paused to look at the hull? The claw came closer, streaking toward her, she pulled hard left, and—

The claw clipped her wing.

Spitfire screamed.

The wing shattered. Her Eagle careened through space. Alarms blared through the cockpit.

"Spitfire!" a pilot cried.

"Spitfire is down! Our colonel is down!"

"I'm fine, I'm fine!" Spitfire said. "Close one."

She struggled with the yoke, steadying her flight. Thankfully, she didn't need wings. They were only necessary when flying in an atmosphere. In space, they normally just carried missiles, but she didn't have any of those anyway.

She flew back toward the *Venom*. The plasma beam was slicing downward, carving through a formation of Eagles.

Spitfire executed another flip, exposing her rear to the *Venom*, and released more chaff. The cutlery slammed into the clawship, driving into the hull. Again—it did no significant damage.

This just isn't going to work, Spitfire thought.

She watched a claw slice an Eagle in two. The pilot screamed, then fell silent. A pilot Spitfire had trained with, laughed with, drank with.

They were all her friends. Her soldiers. Dying.

They kept badgering the *Venom*, hurling the only weapons they had. Just cutlery. Scarring the hull but doing no more damage.

The *Venom* turned in space. She began accelerating toward the *Freedom*, which was battling the much larger *Bloodlust* in the distance. Apparently, *Venom* was bored with fighting the Eagles, realizing they were no threat.

The *Freedom* was barely hanging on. A second clawship would tip the balance.

I must stop this clawship, Spitfire knew. At any cost.

She shoved down the throttle, lurching forward on a spurt of afterburner. She raced alongside the *Venom*'s scarred hull. Spitfire shoved the throttle down as far as it would go. She gained speed. She outflew the clawship, speeding toward its prow.

A hidden claw burst out from the *Venom*'s hull like a

switchblade.

Spitfire screamed and yawed hard, desperately trying to dodge the weapon.

The claw slammed into the tail of her Eagle. She careened. She gripped the yoke, tightened her lips, and kept flying.

"You will not destroy the *Freedom*," she vowed, flying faster.

Claws took down another Eagle.

"I am Gal Levy. I am Spitfire. I am a soldier of Earth. And I will stop you!"

In her Eagle, missing a wing and tail, she shot past the *Venom*'s prow. The great plasma beam crackled at her side, wider than her starfighter, racing toward the *Freedom*. The heat bathed her. Her Eagle creaked as the heat expanded its components.

Spitfire hit the afterburner. She was almost out of fuel now. She jolted forward at hypersonic speed, racing alongside the plasma torrent, moving farther, farther ahead of the *Venom*. She left all her other pilots behind.

Finally, halfway between the *Venom* and the *Freedom*, Spitfire spun around.

She faced the incoming *Venom*, this gargantuan vessel. The clawship suddenly seemed to her like a beast. Like the head of a dragon. The hull was all craggy black skin. Portholes blazed like red eyes. The claws thrust out in a ring of horns. The jaws opened, spurting flame. A dragon. A dragon of the depths. Before this reptilian goddess, Spitfire was so small. Just a speck of dust.

But even a speck of dust, at the right speed, at the right angle—it could topple dreadnoughts.

"I am Gal Levy. I am Spitfire. I am a soldier of Earth. I will win!"

She let out a battle cry, shoved her throttle all the way down, and charged toward the beast.

The dragon roared in the darkness.

The stream of fire arced toward her. A whip of flame.

Spitfire yawed.

She rolled.

She executed loops, dives, barrel rolls, flips. Wherever the plasma blade sliced, she dodged it. She kept charging. A medieval knight on a horse, charging toward the fire-breathing dragon. She would slay the beast.

She flew closer.

Closer still.

She dodged every assault. She flew faster than she had ever flown. All her aerobatic moves—she executed them one after the other, moving like lightning, swerving over and under the plasma jet.

The *Venom* unleashed more firepower. Jagged black missiles like shards of obsidian flew at Spitfire. She dodged them. Photon bolts hurled at her. She swerved around them. Spinning saw blades rolled toward her starfighter. She rose, fell, whipped between them.

She was putting on a show.

She was performing for a crowd.

The moves were natural. She heard the applause.

She saw them die. The faces of her friends. Her flock.

She stood at her father's grave.

She was Gal Levy, the little girl with skinned knees, with angry eyes, with bruised little fists. The little girl from the hills with so much rage.

Today she was a soldier.

Today she was lightning.

The *Venom* unleashed everything at her. And Gal Levy flew through the gauntlet, streaming toward the flaming gullet in the center of the beast.

Among the ring of claws it shone, swirled, gurgled. A collapsing star. A cauldron of molten souls. A portal to a land of endless fire and dark, beautiful agony. The core of the *Venom*. Her mouth. Her pulsing heart. Her Achilles' heel.

From this pit, *Venom* spewed her dragonfire. Spitfire flew closer. Closer. Skimming the blade of fire. The heat melted her remaining wing. It grazed the side of her Eagle. The paint burned off. The hull dented. The canopy creaked. She kept flying. Faster.

She was a blade.

She was a bullet.

She was Jael with a nail.

She was Ahab's harpoon.

She was David's sling stone.

She was Spitfire.

She let out another burst of afterburner, exhausting her fuel.

Leaving a streak of light, flying faster than it had ever flown, her Eagle shot into the flaming maw of the dragon.

Spitfire ejected.

She tumbled through space, still strapped into her seat.

Below, her starfighter flew into the caldera of swirling plasma.

"From the depths of hell, I stab at thee," she whispered.

Fire blazed deep inside the *Venom*. Tongues of flames licked through cracks in the hull. Her starfighter was still flying, carving through the beast. More explosions rocked the clawship.

Spitfire flew on her ejected seat. The momentum hurled her into the distance at breakneck speed.

She watched it happen.

The center of plasma heated, turned blue, then white.

And then the *Venom* burst open.

A massive explosion lit up space. A supernova. A nuclear storm. It was like the birth of a star.

A huge claw flew by Spitfire. It nearly sliced off her head. Another claw spun beneath her. Fragments of the clawship were flying everywhere. A shock wave of debris blasted into the distance.

Then it was over.

The enemy ship was gone.

Sitting in her seat, breathing from her oxygen tank, Spitfire shut her eyes.

You were a great pilot, Dad, she thought. *What Prince Robert did to you I cannot forgive. If you're watching me now, I hope that you're proud.*

Cheers sounded in her MindLink.

"You took the bastard out!" a pilot cried, laughing.

"Woo, Spitfire did it! Spitfire killed the ship!"

"Spitfire! Spitfire!"

"You're a major badass!"

Spitfire laughed, blinked away tears. "Actually, I'm a colonel, not a major. Somebody come pick me up. I'll squeeze into your Eagle. There's still one clawship left. This battle ain't over yet."

Neither was the war.

This war would be a long one, Spitfire knew. But she vowed to fight this war every day until victory. She was no longer a stunt pilot. She would never be one again. Today Spitfire was a warrior.

CHAPTER TWENTY-SIX

The Starship *Freedom*
79 million kms from Earth
05:04 December 26, 2199

On the portside monitor, the *Freedom*'s bridge crew saw it.

An Eagle flying into the *Venom*, as small as a wasp flying into a campfire. The alien clawship exploding. Steel claws hurtling into space, spinning like scythes.

Aboard the *Freedom*, everyone cheered.

"You did it, Spitfire!" Jordan cried, raising his fist.

"Two clawships down, one to go!" somebody added. A few people clapped.

King stared at the monitor, heart nearly stopping.

That had been Spitfire's Eagle.

"Spitfire!" he said. "Spitfire, are you there?" King could barely breathe. "Gal?"

For a second—nothing.

Then Spitfire's voice came over the MindWeb. "I'm all right, *Freedom*! I ejected just in time. Got that son of a bitch for ya."

Everyone on the *Freedom* cheered again. King exhaled in relief.

I almost lost you, Gal. I couldn't handle that.

But they couldn't celebrate for long. The *Freedom* was still engaged in bitter battle.

There was still one clawship in the fight—the largest and meanest one. The *Bloodlust*. Red stripes marked her gray hull. War paint. Her claws glinted, eager to carve up more of the *Freedom*.

King stared at the enemy dreadnought.

Hel'rah's ship.

The bastard who had gutted their hull, killing hundreds. The bug who threatened Rowan.

King sneered. Pure, raging hatred blazed inside him.

"Fire everything you have at that son of a bitch!" he shouted. "Turn our portside toward him, and fire everything!"

Mimori stood at the head of the bridge, facing the main viewport, gazing out at the enemy ship. She moved her arms and tilted sideways. Motors hummed. The *Freedom* rolled around her horizontal axis, matching her movement, raising the port hull toward the incoming enemy. The Angels of Liberty wheeled atop the starship, facing the clawship.

The *Bloodlust* came swooping hard and fast, claws at the ready.

The Angels of Liberty fired.

They had no actual torpedoes to fire. But the crew had loaded the bores with everything they could find. Old refrigerators. Scrap metal. Broken chunks of machinery. Even parts ripped out of the amusement decks—gondolas, golf clubs, carousel horses, anything that would fit.

The Angels fired this collection of junk at hypersonic speed. It was like firing a thousand little asteroids.

The *Bloodlust* fired her plasma, trying to burn the oncoming fusillade. The flaming spray disintegrated half what the Angels had fired. Tongues of plasma licked the *Freedom*'s hull, searing through armor, melting sensors and machine-gun turrets. A monitor went dark, its sensor burned out.

But the *Bloodlust* could not stop all seven portside cannons. Chunks of scrap metal slammed into the clawship, digging into the hull. One claw dented, nearly tore loose.

For a second, King dared to feel hope. But unfortunately,

the damage was skin-deep. The *Bloodlust* came charging closer. She pulled her claws together, hiding her churning core, her Achilles' heel.

Hel'rah learned from his comrade's mistake, King thought. *He won't expose his plasma core again. He'll claw us apart.*

"She's coming in fast!" Jordan said.

The *Bloodlust* was seconds away.

"Mimori!" King said.

The android had her eyes closed, swaying on the bridge. The *Freedom* rolled and swerved. The *Bloodlust* rushed by them, narrowly missing them. They were like two jousting knights.

But we have two dead rails, and they have a hundred claws, King thought. *We can't win a jousting match.*

"She's turning around and coming back at us!" Jordan said. "Gunnery station—why did you stop firing?"

The gunnery officer's voice came over the MindWeb. "We're all out of scrap. We need time to collect more."

"We don't have time," Jordan said. "Fire whatever you have. Yank out the goddamn deck plates and fire them if you must."

The Angels swiveled and fired again. But not much came out the cannons. A few pieces of scrap metal. Most missed. A few grazed the *Bloodlust*, scraping her hull but doing no significant damage.

"This isn't going to work," King said.

Jordan took a deep breath, nodded. "Agreed. We need another plan."

King stared at a viewport. A severed claw from the *Venom*, the clawship the Eagles had destroyed, was spinning through space a hundred klicks above. It was the length of the *Freedom*. King stared at it, frowning.

The *Bloodlust* charged again.

Mimori swerved. A claw scraped across the *Freedom*'s underbelly, slicing off a radio dish. The entire ship jolted.

"Oliver!" King said. "I need you."

Darjeeling stepped forward and snapped a salute. "Sir!"

"Head down to hangar 5. Get the tugs. You fly one, Oliver. Have your people fly the other four." King pointed at the viewport. "I want you to connect to that flying claw, which Spitfire blasted off the *Venom*. Understood?"

Darjeeling nodded. "Yes, sir."

The sergeant raced off the bridge, already barking orders through his MindLink, summoning his soldiers.

King remained on the bridge, waiting.

The *Bloodlust* charged at them again. Mimori cried out, managed to rise above the enemy, trying to roll away from the claws. But another claw nicked their starboard hull. Alarms blared. More air whooshed out, along with the corpses of several men. The ship shook as hatches slammed shut, sealing off the breach.

The tugs were small vessels, barely larger than starfighters. The *Freedom* had five of them. They were designed to attach onto starships with dead engines, then haul them to safety. The *Freedom* sometimes used tugs to stabilize and guide the dreadnought while docking at space stations.

"If the tugs can grab that giant severed claw . . .," King rasped.

Jordan nodded. "We'll wield a mighty sword."

"But we need to distract Hel'rah. Or he'll shoot the tugs just as they launch." He turned toward a communication officer. "Get me on the line with the *Bloodlust*."

The officer tapped a few buttons. "Yes, sir."

A monitor came to life.

Hel'rah appeared there. The hideous spider cackled.

"Had enough, King?" The rah roared with laughter, shaking his web. "I'm gutting you like a tunnel worm!"

King took a step closer to the monitor. He stared at the creature with its gleaming, bulbous red eyes.

"Hel'rah, I call on you to surrender now. Before we destroy you."

Hel'rah laughed harder. His trapped victims jangled on the cobweb. "*You* destroy *me*? Your ship is unarmed! Burnt! Breached! You are moments from death. And yet you threaten me?" He tossed his spiky head back, roaring with laughter. "No, King. You do not get to threaten a rah prince. Kneel! Kneel before me and beg for your death to be quick."

On his MindPlay hallucination, which was invisible to others, King watched the tugs launch. Darjeeling flew one, and four of his men flew the rest. The boxy vessels raced toward the spinning claw in the distance. The severed claw was now thousands of klicks away and still flying fast. Darjeeling and his boys needed a few more moments.

Keep talking to the bug, Jordan telepathized. *You're getting it angry. You've always been good at annoying people.*

I learned from the best, King thought back.

Hel'rah was still cackling. King cleared his throat.

"Are you done giggling?" King said. "Good. Now listen to me, you bloated, festering cockroach. I just destroyed two of your dreadnoughts. I might consider sparing you, if—"

"Dreadnoughts?" Hel'rah laughed. "Isn't that the name you humans give your largest starships? You haven't seen our large ships yet. Our mothership will make your precious *Freedom* seem like a fly!"

King glanced at his hallucinatory monitor. A few thousand klicks away, the tugs had caught up to the spinning claw. They were busy attaching their tethers to the gargantuan blade. They needed more time.

"Well, why not run along to your precious mothership?" King said. "You can hide behind her skirt. Or are you so dumb you prefer to keep jousting with me?"

"I could destroy you in an instant!" Hel'rah said. "I chose to keep you alive for a while. Because I enjoyed toying with you. But now it's your time to die, King!"

The tugs began dragging *Venom*'s severed claw back toward the duel.

"Wait!" King said. "Hel'rah, one moment! Listen to me. There's one thing you don't know."

The spider narrowed his eyes. "What is this? More trickery? Speak!"

The tugs flew closer. Closer. The blade gleamed.

King smiled thinly. "There's something behind you."

Hel'rah laughed. "Do you truly think you can distract me with such trickery? I—" The spider went silent. He spun around. His eyes widened.

The transmission died.

"Seems like he finally noticed the giant claw bearing down on him," Jordan observed.

The *Bloodlust* began evasive maneuvers. Darjeeling and his tugs kept pulling the blade. The colossal claw dwarfed the tugging ships. But they were powerful little beasts, and the tugs pulled the claw faster, pointing the tip at the *Bloodlust*. They were like ants carrying a steak knife.

The *Bloodlust* yawed, began flying away.

"Mimori, ram it!" King shouted.

The android nodded.

The *Freedom* charged.

The rails were cold. But they still delivered a punch. They slammed into the *Bloodlust*.

The *Freedom* shook. King swayed on his feet.

At this speed, the rails couldn't penetrate the *Bloodlust*'s thick hull. But they did shove the clawship back through space.

Right into the path of the tugs and their blade.

The enormous severed claw, a blade the length of the Freedom Tower in New York City, plowed into the *Bloodlust* and burst out the other side.

The mighty clawship split in two like a coconut.

Cheers erupted across the *Freedom*'s bridge.

"Gotcha!" King said, clenching a fist.

Thousands of rahs spilled out from the halved clawship. They tumbled into space, legs twitching, jaws snapping. The Angels of Liberty had fun with them, firing chaff at the aliens. Without a hull to protect them, the chaff made minced meat of the bugs.

Spitfire and her Eagles came streaming back. The pilots cheered as they flew through the devastation, firing more chaff onto the floating spiders.

"Woo, Commander, this is fun!" Spitfire cried, zipping between the marooned spiders. "Bug hunt!"

King suppressed a laugh. Almost losing Spitfire had shaken him badly. He realized how much he loved her, how much he loved all his pilots. They were all like his children.

"All right, Spitfire, bring your flock back home to roost," he said.

The Eagles turned like a school of fish, heading back toward the *Freedom*'s hangars. If any rah were still alive in space, they were tumbling into the distance, harmless. King would let the vacuum take care of them.

He took a deep, pained breath. He realized his knees were shaking. He had not slept all night, had not eaten since yesterday morning. The adrenaline began to wear off, leaving him feeling weak and dizzy.

"Good work, everyone," he said. "Now we can proceed to Merc Mory, patch up our hull, and get some real ammunition in us. You all performed magnificently today. I'm proud of—"

Then he saw it.

He stared at the monitors.

In space, the thousands of rahs were still alive. They began to sling webs.

The strands stretched out and grabbed the *Freedom*'s hull. Thousands of strands.

"Cut them down!" King shouted. "Cut those strands down!"

A few Eagles, who had already landed in the hangar, burst back into space. One Eagle slammed into a strand, but instead of severing it, the strand hurled the starfighter back. The Angels of Liberty fired chaff. But whatever they tossed at the strands just got caught.

"We can't cut the damn things!" Spitfire cried.

King watched from the bridge, helpless.

Thousands of rahs reeled themselves in, gripped the hull, and began scuttling over the *Freedom*. On the bridge, Mimori twitched and pawed at her clothes.

"They're all over me!" she cried.

A few rahs found an airlock. They began clawing at the metal door.

King growled deep in his throat.

"They're boarding us," he said. "It's time to draw our sidearms. This is about to get ugly."

CHAPTER TWENTY-SEVEN

The Starship *Freedom*
79 million kms from Earth
06:07 December 26, 2199

Emily sat in the royal suite, listening to the battle through the bulkheads.

Every few moments, the ship jolted. Booms sounded. People screamed. The royal suite shook with every blast. Priceless Ming-dynasty vases fell and shattered. The original Titian crashed to the floor. Emily sat in her upholstered armchair, holding her drone, very still. There was little else she could do.

From here, she couldn't see what was happening, and nobody was bringing her any news. But she knew that *Freedom* was engaged in a great battle in space. Every few moments, a crew member ran just outside her door. She heard the footsteps. Heard them shouting.

"We got one! We got one rah ship! The railgun did it!"

"The bastards are ramming us!"

"Three decks are lost. Head up to deck 22. We gotta seal another hull breach."

"Those goddamn spiders!"

Throughout it all, Emily sat in her armchair, holding her jeweled drone. Listening. Wanting to help. Not knowing how.

She was not a soldier nor spacer. She knew nothing about fighting nor operating a starship. All she could do was wait and hope and pray.

"We should never have come into this godforsaken ship," Niles whined, trembling in her grip.

"If we had remained in Buckingham Palace, we'd be dead now," Emily replied. "Along with the rest of my family."

"Oh, don't say such horrible things." Niles's jewels clattered as he shook.

"It's true, Niles. The royal family is dead. I'm the last. And I must be she who rebuilds the throne." She took a shuddering breath. "I just hope I don't die here in space."

Another boom shook the starship *Freedom*. An alarm blared in the deck above them. Machinery creaked and clattered in the deck below. An African tribal mask fell off the bulkhead. It cracked against the Italian marble tiles.

"Oh, this is intolerable!" Niles said. "What is going on? Why won't anyone tell us? We can't see anything from here. I demand that Commander King comes here and updates us."

"They don't have time to keep updating us," Emily said. "They're busy fighting. Even Mr. Darjeeling was called out to fight."

"Well, the least they could do is invite us onto the bridge," said Niles. "Maybe we'd actually see what's going on."

"Niles! We'd just get in the way. Now calm down. You're making me nervous."

The drone gasped, looked up from her lap. "*I* am making you nervous? I, your loyal companion? Not the alien starships pummeling us, but I, your dedicated robotic chaperone? Well, I never! You wound my deepest sockets. To think, after all the years I've served your family, that during our hour of need, you should—"

"Shut up or I'll turn you off," she said.

Niles huffed, but at least he stopped talking.

Still, neurotic as he was, the drone had a point. Emily did feel isolated in here, and maybe there was some way she could help. She was only seventeen, yes, but so what? Her uncle, the Prince of Wales, had been only eighteen when he had fought in the third world war.

This was a new type of war, a galactic war, and here in the royal suite, with priceless artwork shattering around her, Emily decided that she would fight in this war. She would not simply be a passenger of history. She would be a participant. A soldier. The royal family was gone, and the palace lay in ruins, but Great Britain still stood, and so did Earth. So long as there was something to fight for, Emily vowed that she would fight.

A scream came from the deck above.

"Oh my God! They're breaking in! The spiders are breaking in!"

Screams rose from all around. From this deck. From above and below.

"The aliens are boarding us!"

People wailed. Screeches sounded. A roar echoed. Alien noises. Clattering feet.

Niles whimpered. "Oh, we're done for!"

"We will fight!" Emily said.

She looked around the room for a weapon. Shards of broken pottery? No. Useless. A fireplace poker? That was better. Maybe that African spear on the wall?

Then she saw it.

On the mantle.

An authentic Samurai sword. According to a little plaque, it was centuries old but still sharp.

Emily took a deep breath. Her legs trembled. Her heart pounded against her ribs. She reached out, gripped the katana, and drew the blade. It hissed free. Ripples gleamed across the folded steel.

"Emily!" Niles hovered backward. "What do you think you're doing with that? Put it away before you cut yourself."

A screech sounded somewhere in the ship. Nearby. A man screamed, then fell silent. A gunshot rang. Deep laughter rolled through the decks.

"Niles, stay here in the suite," Emily said, stepping toward the door.

He huffed. "Where do you think you're going, young lady? To fight? You're not a soldier."

"We're all soldiers now, Niles." She glanced at him. "Well, maybe not fussy little drones. Stay here. Hide in the closet. I'll be back. I hope."

"Fussy little drones?" he exclaimed. Something clicked inside him, and an array of blades, muzzles, and hooks sprouted from him. "Does this look like a fussy little drone to you? You forget that I'm designed to protect you, Princess. And protect you I shall." His voice softened. "You're the last of the House of Windsor. The last hope of Great Britain and the Commonwealth. I was made for times such as these. Come now, Emily. If fight we must . . . then let us fight with courage."

She looked at him. "I've never heard you speak so eloquently before."

He harrumphed. "Of course you have. I am always the paragon of elegance and eloquence." He spun, and his blades flashed. "Tallyho then, good princess! To war!"

Emily raised her katana. "To war."

She opened the door, left the royal suite, and stepped into a nightmare.

* * * * *

Emily walked down the corridor, katana held before her.
Leaving the royal suite was like stepping into another world.

The opulence ended at the door. Diamond plate steel covered the deck. Pipes and cables ran along the curved walls. Fluorescent bulbs shone pitiless white light. The royal suite was just an illusion, an oasis of comfort aboard a military warship. A corner of heaven in hell.

For the *Freedom* had become hell. Screams echoed in the distance. Somebody ran by, barely sparing her a glance. His arm was gone, ending with a spurting stump. Blood speckled the deck.

A roar sounded deep in the distance. Somebody or something was cackling. A mighty *boom* shook the ship. The corridor whipped from side to side. Emily swayed and caught the bulkhead for support. The overhead lights flickered and died.

Darkness filled the corridor.

Emily gulped.

"Oh crumbs," she whispered.

The blast had cracked open a bulkhead. Cables spilled out, sparking, offering the only source of light. Emily kept walking, each step slow and cautious. She gazed into the darkness. Niles hovered beside her, his jewels reflecting the sparking light.

The corridor stretched ahead like a tunnel. Emily remembered herself as a girl, traveling the Chunnel under the sea, heading from England to France. She remembered being afraid of monsters in the dark, of how the tunnel never seemed to end.

"There's no such thing as monsters," her mother had told her.

But there was. Monsters were real. Monsters had always been real. And now they were here aboard this ship.

A scream sounded ahead.

Emily froze, hackles rising.

A shadow came lurching toward her!

Emily gasped and raised her blade, and Niles made a whirring, angry hissing sound.

But it was not a monster. It was a man. A soldier. He came

running, and the sparkling light reflected in tears on his cheeks. His belly was gashed open. His insides were spilling out. The man was holding the gash, trying to keep his entrails inside, and as he ran, he called for his mother. He didn't even notice Emily. He ran by her, delusional with pain.

"Emily?" Niles whispered. "Perhaps we should return to the suite. We can both hide in the closet."

She gulped. "Maybe you're right."

Her courage fled. She was not ready for this.

She spun around, intending to rush back to her suite.

It was there.

It had been stalking her.

It loomed before her, grinning a terrible white grin in the darkness.

A rah.

Emily gasped and took a step back. She waved her blade before her.

"Step back!" she cried.

The enormous spider scuttled closer. It straightened its eight legs, rising taller. Its dorsal spines scraped the ceiling. The creature filled the tunnel, so large it could have swallowed her whole. Its grin widened, a vicious moon in the night, a Cheshire grin, a predator's grin. Multiple eyes like pools of blood blinked above the hellmouth.

"Ah, the princess . . .," it hissed. "My lord told us to kill the soldiers. But you . . . ah, you will decorate my web. Your womb will carry many eggs."

Emily stood, paralyzed, as it loomed above her. She could barely see it in the darkness. Just that horrible, grinning mouth, with its white teeth all slick with saliva, and the red eyes like balloons full of blood, and the tips of those terrible claws, long and black and reaching toward her. A spider? This was more than a spider. It was a demon. A dark god. It was darkness taken form, the most perfect of predators, hatched in the interstellar void, and she was its prey.

Emily could only stand before it, frozen in terror.

Then Niles shot forth.

The drone buzzed toward the rah, weapons flashing, thrusting every which way like the spikes of a blowfish.

"Have at you, scoundrel!" the robot cried.

Like a sphere of light, he flew toward the bulky dark form of the beast. With a great battle cry, Niles sank one of his blades into the rah's head. Just below an eye.

The blade couldn't have been longer than Emily's index finger. It didn't seem to bother the rah very much. With a swipe of a mighty claw, the alien knocked Niles down. The drone crashed onto the deck, and the rah slammed down its leg. Jewels spilled across the floor. Niles let out a pitiful mewl.

"Niles!" Emily cried.

The rah kicked the mutilated robot aside, then scuttled closer to Emily. For a big creature, it moved with incredible speed, its *patter patter* on the deck beating with the rhythm of a much smaller animal. The sparking cables flashed, lighting its form, revealing the forest of spines on its back. Upon every spike was impaled an enemy head, leering at Emily with dead eyes. All but one spike. One spike was waiting for her.

Join us, the severed heads seemed to say. *Rot with us.*

The rah rose before her again, its grin a celestial light, a crescent moon, hanging above Emily and washing her with its sickly, milky white. The teeth parted, and a red tongue slithered out, as long and thick as her arm. It licked her. From navel to forehead, that bloated tongue caressed her body, tasting, and the alien shivered with delight.

"Yes, you taste delicious," it hissed. "After my eggs hatch inside you, I will enjoy your flesh."

The tongue reached out again, dripping and sticky.

Emily let out a great cry, a howl, a torn scream, the cry of a girl who was dying in this ship, of the woman being born from her shattered shell. With the cry of childhood's end, Emily swung her katana downward.

The blade sliced clean through the alien tongue.

The hideous red muscle slapped onto the deck. It wriggled there, leaving trails of slime, a wounded worm.

The rah screamed. Blood spurted from its mouth. It tried to say something, could not, and instead let out a terrible squeal, a sound like pigs being butchered.

Emily swung her katana through the air. "Back, back!"

But it charged at her.

The mighty jaws widened, nearly filling the tunnel, a portal to agony. The tongue's stump bubbled with black blood.

Emily leaped back. The jaws snapped shut before her like a bear trap, nearly slicing off her arm. The beast roared again, scuttled closer. Even swinging the katana did not hold the beast back. She slammed the blade against its face, but it bounced off the exoskeleton. It was like hacking at a boulder.

She tripped over something. A cable, she thought. She fell to the deck. Cables snaked out from the cracked bulkhead, stirring, hissing, tips sparking with electricity. The rah slammed down one claw, and Emily squirmed aside. The claws slashed across her arm, drawing blood. She screamed.

The spider raised its claw again, then a second claw, a third, and the rah grinned, ready to slam down those claws and impale her.

Emily lifted the sparking cables and thrust them upward.

The severed tips of the cables touched the spider's underbelly. Electricity leaped into the beast, branching across its body in fractals of light.

Emily hurried backward to safety. Electricity raced across the rah like luminous serpents, and the alien screamed, a pained cry, high-pitched. It wobbled, fell onto the cables, then burst into flame.

Heart pounding, Emily raced around the burning alien, careful not to cut herself on those long claws. Behind the spider, she knelt on the deck, and her heart broke.

"Oh, Niles."

The drone lay on the deck, his hull cracked open, revealing gears and flashing microchips. His weapons had retracted. He still seemed to be alive. His twin cameras moved from side to side on their stalks.

"I've been savaged!" he said. "Oh Lord. Oh, look at me now! No. No! Actually don't look. Look away, Emily! I'm a monster now."

"Oh shush, Niles," she said. "You're just a little broken. We can fix you."

"I'm done for. Done for! Leave me behind, Emily. Keep going! Leave me to die. Make sure that they write songs about my sacrifice. Make sure they mention my jewels."

"You're not going to die, Niles. But I might if I must listen to any more of your whingeing." She laughed and wiped tears from her eyes. "My dear Niles, it was rather brave of you to charge at the beast like that. Foolish but brave."

She lifted the broken drone, tucked him under her arm, and kept moving down the corridor.

CHAPTER TWENTY-EIGHT

Fort Liberty
Nebraska
07:20 December 26, 2199

Dawn rose over Fort Liberty. The morning light spilled over a scene from hell. Corpses lay across the courtyard and beneath the defensive wall. Blood stained the snow. The battle still raged, and the guns still boomed.

But hope rose with this dawn.

Where two hundred guns had fired now roared five thousand. For hours, the brave Badgers Company had held the fort alone. Now the full brigade was mustered. Now they showed the enemy their true might.

The rahs shrieked in fear. Bullets pounded them, cracking exoskeletons, taking eyes, shattering legs. The aliens kept fighting. Not a single rah retreated. The humans trapped them—some companies inside the fort, the others pushing from the fields. Squeezing. Squeezing the aliens and making them bleed.

Now we're even, Bastian thought.

He stood on the wall, facing the southern fields. They had raised a great barricade where the gate had stood. Sandbags, pieces of scrap metal, and two armored trucks blocked the entrance, all topped with barbed wire. A hundred soldiers stood in the courtyard behind the barricade, and more topped the wall like medieval archers defending a castle. They had built makeshift guard towers from scaffolds and ladders. More soldiers stood atop them, armed with Gideon rifles and enough bullets to last for days.

One battalion was fighting in the field, driving the rahs against the walls, where the fort's defenders shot them down. The alien army screeched and clattered among the two human forces. Slowly, spider by spider, the humans were cutting them down.

"The rahs caught us with our pants down," Bastian said. "But now we're hitting them hard."

"Maybe your pants wouldn't fall down if you could find a belt that fits you," Alice said.

A bandage was wrapped around her head, red at the temple. Another bandage covered her arm. Bastian too was wounded. His arm was a bleeding mess, and his side was bandaged and aching. But both soldiers could still stand, still pull the trigger, so they still fought.

"Very funny," Bastian said. "You know, you could lay off the donuts in the rec room yourself. You're no—" He frowned. "Alice, what is that?"

They stared together toward the southern fields.

New spiders were arriving, scuttling through the snowy fields toward the base.

Just three. But Bastian had never seen anything more terrifying.

"They're huge," Alice whispered.

The smaller rahs, the ones Bastian had been fighting all day, raised their claws and chirped and grunted and hissed. It sounded almost like cheering. Those ones were about the size of horses. But the spiders approaching now dwarfed them. They were the size of woolly mammoths.

"What are those?" cried a sergeant.

"Jesus, we're screwed!" shouted a corporal.

"Why are they so big?" somebody said, pale and trembling.

Bastian stared, and his fists balled at his sides. "Among

spiders on Earth, the females are larger. The female black widow makes the male look as insignificant as a larva. I believe we've been fighting only males so far." He slammed a fresh magazine into his trusty Gideon. "Well, that's about to change."

The three female spiders let out terrible shrieks. Bastian had never heard anything louder. He grimaced. Some soldiers dropped their guns and covered their ears. Icicles cracked, falling off the barbed wire and guard towers.

The beasts stormed forward, jaws open wide, full of fangs like swords.

"It couldn't be wrinkly little ETs from space," Bastian muttered, gripping his gun with weary fingers. "It had to be goddamn giant spiders."

Gideons roared all across the walls. Thousands of bullets flew at the spiders. But the females kept charging. It was like firing bullets at rumbling tanks. Pointless.

"Grenades!" Bastian shouted. "Tear them down with grenades!"

He himself was out of grenades. He scanned his surroundings, saw a dead corporal, and knelt by the young woman. He knew her. Valerie Bowie. A girl from a nearby farm who loved dogs. She went to his church. Bastian ripped grenades off her belt, then returned to his position. He stared off the wall.

The female rahs were closer.

With a small attachment, Gideon rifles could be converted into grenade launchers. Bastian screwed on the launching tube, then loaded the grenade. He aimed at one of the females and fired.

His grenade flew at the enemy.

From the walls, a dozen more grenades arced toward the spiders.

The three females paused, opened their jaws wide, and hissed. Strange organs extended from their mouths. Not tongues.

These organs looked like black tubes.

Spinnerets, Bastian realized.

A second before the grenades could hit, the spiders spat sticky webs.

The webs caught the grenades in midair. Explosions shook the landscape, tearing the webs apart. The females kept charging, unhurt.

"Great," Bastian muttered. "They can sling webs. Of course they can."

"I always told you, dude," Alice said. "We females are way tougher than you males."

She was bantering, but Alice was pale and trembling. That head wound was nasty. She was possibly suffering from a concussion.

Under a hailstorm of bullets, the three females reached the southern wall. On Bastian's MindLink, he saw more females attacking the walls in different locations. All around, the male spiders were celebrating.

"Die, humans, die!"

"Kill them, sisters!"

"Drink their blood!"

"Earth is ours!"

"Eresh, eresh!"

One female was approaching the gateway. From his position on the wall, Bastian fired another grenade. The female whipped her head toward him, shot a strand of webbing, and caught the grenade. It exploded in midair only meters away from Bastian.

The shock wave slammed into him. Shrapnel flew, pattering the wall.

Bastian groaned, stumbling backward, and bumped into Alice. She grabbed him before he could fall off the wall. His ears rang. Smoke filled the air. His body armor had absorbed the blow, sparing his organs, and his earplugs protected his eardrums from rupturing. But everything hurt. He looked around, dazed. For a moment he could just stare in shock, not sure if he was alive or dead.

Alice groaned beside him. "You okay, Bas?"

He blinked. He looked at a piece of shrapnel embedded into his armored vest. Another piece had cut through his sleeve and was stuck in his skin.

"I . . . think so?" he said. He could barely hear himself, and it wasn't just the earplugs. His ears rang. He shook his head madly, struggling to clear the haze.

The female spider was firing more strands, blocking more grenades. Explosions rocked the sky. Bullets kept pounding the female, but they just bounced off her armored abdomen. The spider reached the barricade protecting the camp—that pile of metal, sandbags, and armored trucks.

With long, thick legs, the massive spider lifted one of the armored trucks.

Bastian stared in wonder. That truck weighed many tons. The spider struggled. Her back legs drove into the ground. Her body was shaking, and bullets kept sparking against her abdomen. One bullet took an eye. But the spider kept at it. She managed to lift the truck overhead—then hurl it.

Bastian and Alice ducked.

The truck flew over their heads, then crashed into the courtyard, plowing through a squad of marines.

The female spider lifted the second armored truck.

Bastian ran off the wall, raced across the courtyard, and faced the spider.

She towered over him. God, she was huge. Those legs rose taller than Bastian, and the abdomen loomed like a craggy asteroid. The beast still held the truck overhead with two claws.

Red eyes like bags of blood turned toward Bastian, wet,

blinking, filled with malice. The creature hissed, jaws opening, jaws that could devour worlds.

A goddess, Bastian thought. *A spider goddess from beyond the dark. Charging Bear was right. These are deities.*

Bastian froze. He tried, failed to move. The terror was too great.

Earth will fall, he thought. *Humanity will end.*

Then he thought of Rowan. Her smile. Her tears.

He howled and opened fire.

He emptied a magazine, focusing all his bullets on the same spot—one of the legs holding up the truck.

The enormous, gleaming black leg *cracked.*

For a second, the armored truck swayed. Then it fell, slamming onto the spider.

A marine armored truck weighed twenty-five tons. As much as a family of elephants. All that weight crashed into the spider and cracked the abdomen open like a bad egg. Blood and ooze spilled across the courtyard. Trapped under the truck, the alien squealed and whimpered. Her legs twitched.

She looked up at Bastian with one red eye. It gleamed, a bead of swirling red evil.

"She will die, Bastian . . .," the creature hissed. "Your daughter will be ours to eat . . ."

They knew about Rowan.

How the hell did they know about Rowan?

Bastian knelt by a dead soldier, took a magazine from his vest, and recharged his Gideon. He aimed at the spider's red eye.

"Off you go to hell, bitch."

He opened fire on automatic. His bullets tore the eye apart and plowed into the brain. The female spider thumped down dead.

*****

But more females rose from the snow.

Soon a dozen of them surrounded the base, attacking the walls.

Bastian saw it happening on his MindLink. The gargantuan arachnids climbed the walls, stomped through the base, and slaughtered all in their path.

They were moving closer to the center of Fort Liberty. To where Rowan hid.

The girl sent a telepathic message. "Daddy, I hear them coming closer!"

"I'll hold them back, sweetie, I promise," Bastian said. "Meanwhile, Bear will look after you."

Through the MindWeb, Bastian saw the giant there, standing guard over Rowan. At seven feet tall, muscular and armed with a damn big rifle, Bear struck an imposing figure. But even he could not take down these female rahs. Not alone.

"Second Platoon, with me!" Bastian cried. "Charge! Tear her down!"

They ran toward one of the towering females. The rah spun toward them, screeching. She swept her claws across the courtyard, mowing through soldiers like a scythe through wheat. Soldiers fell, sliced in half.

The survivors stood all around the spider, roaring, firing their bullets. One man fell to friendly fire—the son of a local apple farmer. Bastian had often taken Rowan apple picking on his farm. The other soldiers kept shooting.

"Focus on the lower leg!" Bastian shouted. It was almost impossible to hear anything over the roaring bullets, but he telepathized the words too. "The front left leg. Yes, there, concentrate your fire!"

It took several Gideons working together to rip that leg apart. The spider dipped, swaying on her remaining legs.

"The other front leg!" Bastian shouted.

The marines concentrated their fire. The second leg buckled. The spider thumped down.

The soldiers cheered and kept firing, taking out her eyes. In her death throes, the spider cast a web, trapping several soldiers—a final, desperate move before the bullets finished the job.

Bastian cursed, pulling sticky cobwebs off his limbs. The things stank.

He surveyed the battle through MindWeb, tapping into the MindLinks of his fellow Badgers. He could see through their eyes. What they saw appeared as little video feeds, hovering before Bastian.

He sent telepathic messages to a few fellow captains, who were fighting elsewhere on the base.

"Where's our battalion commander?" Bastian asked.

The battle was still raging, but he had a moment—just a moment—to talk.

"Nobody knows!" replied Captain Anderson, commander of the Wolf Company, which was currently defending the northern wall.

"Are there *any* senior officers here?" Bastian said.

He sent the telepathic message to all officers in the brigade. A few ignored him. They were busy battling the spiders. But a few answers came back.

"I haven't seen any damn battalion commander," replied a lieutenant.

"What about the colonel?" asked an ensign. "Has anyone seen Colonel Holt?" The colonel commanded the entire base.

"I did," Bastian said. "Through the MindWeb a few hours ago. Last I saw, a spider was munching on his severed hand and poking through his guts. Holt was a good man. But I think he's gone."

Silence fell over the MindWeb.

"Who's in command?" Captain Anderson finally asked.

Bastian thought for a moment. "Nobody. We are. Together. The senior officers are dead or missing. Junior officers and NCOs—we will hold this brigade together. Our troops need us more than ever. Keep fighting and keep your MindLinks on. Let's keep communicating throughout the battle."

"Gotcha."

"You got it, boss."

"Let us know if you need help at the southern gate."

"Oh, I need help," Bastian said. "But you guys do too. Let's hang on. I've been trying to contact other bases. We could really use some air support, let me tell you. No luck so far. Nobody's answering. Everyone's fighting for their lives."

Normally a few hundred noncombat soldiers served at Fort Liberty. One department was in charge of communication with other bases and corps. None of them had reported back from Christmas. Hell, there was no way for them to get here. Not with rahs surrounding the base on all sides.

Bastian spent a moment on MindPlay, trying to reach somebody, anybody, outside the base. He needed air support. Armor support. More infantry. Anything would help right now.

Nobody was answering. The Freedom Brigade was cut off.

Then three more rahs, males this time, ran toward Bastian. He minimized his MindLink windows and kept fighting.

* * * * *

"They're breaching the wall!" rose a cry through the MindWeb. "This is Captain Anderson from the north wall.

They're breaking in! I need assistance."

Bastian was still in the south. He was helping reconstruct the barricade of armored trucks and sandbags, sealing the broken gate. A hundred troops from his company were on the wall, firing into the countryside, holding the enemy back. The spiders kept clawing at the barricade, trying to climb the walls. They just kept coming.

Bastian dumped a sandbag into place, then paused, drenched with sweat. His left arm ached so much he could barely move it. Black spider blood covered his uniform. He raised his MindPlay HUD and connected to Captain Anderson. He stared through the captain's eyes.

Dammit.

With her mighty claws, a rah female had managed to crack the northern wall. The gargantuan arachnid was now widening the crack, allowing the smaller males to pour in.

"Anderson, hang tight," Bastian said. "I'm bringing a platoon to reinforce your position."

His company was already cut down to half its size. His beloved Badgers had suffered the heaviest losses in the brigade. That was not surprising; they had defended the fort alone most of the night. Only a hundred Badgers still fought, half their original size. Reluctantly, Bastian divided them in two.

"Alice, stay here with fifty marines and defend the barricade," Bastian said. "I'll lead the other fifty north and save Anderson's ass."

Alice was leaning against a refrigerator taken from the galley. She was shoving it onto the barricade, adding to the pile of heavy objects. Sweat dripped down her forehead, and blood stained her two blond braids, but despite her wounds and weariness, she was still fighting. God bless her.

She nodded. "Come on, Bas, I know you're sneaking off to have a nap."

"You got me. See ya soon, Alice. Oh, and try not to kill all the spiders while I'm away. Save me some."

"You wish!"

They were both battling exhaustion. Bastian could barely use his left arm now, and he needed to replace his bandages, drink, and eat. And yes, a nap would be nice. He'd have time for all that later.

Breathing hard, he ran through the base, leading fifty men. They raced by the armory, and Bastian sent one squad inside to grab as many bullets as they could, then catch up with them at the north wall. They raced by the kitchens, the latrines, the barracks, and the training yard. Finally they reached the northern wall.

By the time they got there, it was a mess.

The rahs had widened the crack in the wall. A truck could drive through the damn thing. The aliens were pouring into Fort Liberty. A dozen or more were already inside, and more kept coming.

"Anderson!" Bastian said, scanning the battle. He couldn't see his fellow captain. "Anderson, where are you?"

Bastian brought MindPlay back up. Icons representing every officer in the brigade floated before Bastian, little hallucinations the size of golf balls. Anderson's avatar was grayed out.

"Anderson?" Bastian said. "Come in. Bob! Bob, are you there?"

A rah screeched.

A severed head flew and slammed down at Bastian's feet.

It was Bob Anderson, his mouth open in a silent scream. Bastian stared down at the head. The two had gone to the same high school. He remembered them once fighting over a girl, then deciding their friendship was more important and sharing a beer. Now little Bobby, who knew how to ride his bike on its back wheel, who always got more girls than Bastian, who was always better at darts—now this boy, this soldier, this officer—he lay there in the dirt. A head. Unceremoniously discarded. A piece of Bastian's childhood. Of his soul. A head in the dirt.

Bastian looked up. He saw the rahs pour through the breach. A hundred, maybe more. His platoon was falling fast. One spider was eating a headless body.

There is no victory here, Bastian thought. *Not at Fort Liberty. Not on Earth. They will kill me. And my soldiers. They will keep going and they will kill my daughter. How did this happen? How could this nightmare be real?*

A *boom* sounded in the distance. The ground shook.

The rahs froze, spun back toward the plains.

A rumble sounded, distant, coming closer. Rahs screeched.

Another *boom* shook the world.

Bastian frowned, ran across the bloody ground, and climbed the northern wall. A rah leaped at him. He shot it, knocking it off the wall, and stared at the prairies.

A cloud of snow and smog was racing down the road.

A tank. A tank was roaring toward Fort Liberty.

Rahs charged at it. The tank fired again, clearing a path through. Rahs flew, limbs snapping off. The tank crushed one of the spiders beneath its treads, then kept roaring forth. The banner of the Alliance fluttered from its turret—a proud eagle with golden wings.

It was just one tank. Bastian would have preferred to see an armored division. But even one tank lifted his spirits. Whoever was driving that thing had some serious brass balls.

A rah female, the one that had cracked open the wall, spun toward the tank and screeched.

The tank fired.

A shell slammed into the rah. The gargantuan spider burst open. Black blood splattered the yard. Organs slapped onto the ground, still pulsing. The tank kept charging, plowing through the enemy, and finally lodged itself in the cracked wall. With its armored bulk, it sealed the breach.

For a moment the battle died down. Bastian and the other soldiers stood, covered in blood and dust, staring in wonder at the tank.

An icon popped up on Bastian's MindPlay HUD.
NEW CONTACT ONLINE
The tank's hatch opened, and out crawled Colonel Holt.

* * * * *

He was hurt. Badly hurt.

Bastian could see that at once. Colonel Harry "Hound Dog" Holt, commander of the Freedom Brigade, was dying.

The colonel was missing one hand; a tourniquet was constricting the stump. Bandages wrapped around his midsection like a mummy's shroud. The injury was bad. A deep stomach wound.

Bastian had seen it happen over the MindWeb. Seen the spider sink the claw in.

Somehow Holt was alive. Those injuries would have killed any other man within seconds. Holt had managed to ride a goddamn tank back to the base.

Covered in blood, pale and shaking, Holt climbed down the tank and stumbled across the yard.

Bastian ran toward him. He caught the man just as he collapsed.

"Hey there . . . Captain," Holt managed to rasp.

"Sir." Bastian held his commanding officer. "Let me get you to the infirmary, sir."

Commanding officer? Holt was more than that. Bastian barely spoke to his father anymore. Holt had become a surrogate father. A lump filled Bastian's throat. He had to save this man's life.

Holt coughed. Blood speckled his lips. "Wait. Bastian. I have only a few seconds left. I'm dying. They tore up my insides, the bastards. Let me die out here. On the battlefield, among the corpses of my enemies. Not in some infirmary bed."

"You're not going to die," Bastian said.

The battle resumed. Bullets whistled and rahs shrieked. But here in the dirt, Bastian focused on his dying commander.

"The bastards . . . knew where I lived," Holt said. He was shaking now. His skin was gray. "They came right to my house. They hit all the senior officers at home. Every lieutenant, colonel, and major. They're gone, Bastian. The spiders knew to hit us at Christmas. Knew where the leaders lived. They're doing it all over the world. They've been watching us, studying us. You were right, Bastian. You tried to warn me. I didn't listen. You were right." A tear rolled down the dying man's cheek. "Forgive me."

"Sir, I forgave you the moment you rode that tank into our base," Bastian said. The lump in his throat grew. He was struggling not to cry. "Now where the hell did you get a tank?" They were an infantry brigade with no armored attachment.

Holt laughed, coughed, laughed some more. "I kept it around my farm, parked right behind the chicken coop. Every man needs a tank, son."

Bastian laughed too, and now his tears were falling. "It took guts to ride here alone in a tank."

"And I only have half my guts. The damn rah ate the rest."

Bastian wondered how the colonel was still alive. That stomach wound could have killed a wild boar. Holt was high on stims, Bastian realized. He saw the dilated pupils, the pulsing veins. He was drugged up. And it would wear off soon.

"There's one thing I don't get, son," Holt said. "If the spiders are so damn smart, why didn't they just nuke us from orbit?"

Bastian knew the answer. "They want to eat us." He wiped tears away and barked a laugh. "It sounds ridiculous, but I think they landed on the ground because they want to eat us. They've been eating the corpses. This isn't war for them. It's a hunt."

"Goddamn." Holt shook his head. "You're right. They're predators, not conquerors." He coughed for a long moment. There was a lot of blood. "Son, don't let them eat me. Burn me when I'm dead. Burn me down to ashes. Don't let the bastards eat me." He grimaced. "Any more than they already ate, at least. I hope my hand gives them indigestion."

"I promise," Bastian vowed.

"Captain," Holt said, voice weaker. "I want you to record my next words on your MindLink. Are you recording? Good. The other senior officers of the Freedom Brigade are all dead. I'll be joining them soon. Bastian King, I promote you to colonel, and I name you the new commander of the Freedom Brigade. Win this war for me, Colonel. Win this . . ."

His voice faded.

His heart stopped.

Bastian lowered his head, holding his commanding officer, his mentor.

Then he rose to his feet and pulled up MindPlay. His software was upgrading. His promotion to colonel was being pushed through. New stats came to life. Suddenly Bastian didn't just see his own company on the hallucinatory interface. He saw the entire brigade. Thousands of marines.

The Freedom Brigade was his to command. And Bastian vowed to honor his mentor, to lead wisely, and to win this war.

CHAPTER TWENTY-NINE

The Starship *Freedom*
80 million kms from Earth
07:47 December 26, 2199

I cannot fight alone, Emily thought. *I must find soldiers. Brave soldiers like Mr. Darjeeling. With them I will find . . . not safety, no. But a position to stand at. A place to swing my sword. To be one in a formation, one in an army, not a single light in the darkness but part of a great flame.*

So she walked onward, but she saw only bodies. Savaged bodies on the corridor floors. Most were tourists. A man in a Hawaiian shirt lay by the bulkhead, his glass shattered. A young woman lay in the corner, still holding a Freedom the Frog plushie. Her belly had been slashed open, and eggs gleamed inside her.

Darkness closed in. Emily could barely see. It was as if the corridor was contracting, becoming a tunnel, leaving just a small circle of light, then a pinpoint. She gasped for air, and the veil lifted. She was close to fainting.

Be strong, Emily, she told herself. *Your grandfather faced the Red Dawn in war. Your ancestors faced the scourge of Nazism. You are a single leaf, trembling in the wind, but you grow from a mighty English oak, and your roots run deep.*

She walked by the bodies, chin held high, her blade held before her. Niles was feeling a little better, and he even managed to fly, but he complained relentlessly about aching screws and sparking circuits.

Gunshots sounded in the distance.

A screech rose. Then men shouted and more gunshots rang out. A battle was raging ahead!

Emily burst into a run. She wasn't sure where to go. Wasn't even sure the sound came from this deck, not a deck above or below. The fluorescent lights were still off. Only the backup lights, pale little dots along the floor, glowed faintly. The ship was a labyrinth. The corridors twisted and turned, never ending.

She passed by many doorways to bunks. A few doorways were open, revealing the tourist cabins. They were quite a bit humbler than the royal suite—simple rooms like one might find in a hotel on Earth.

Inside one cabin, Emily saw a family lying across the bed, heads removed. The mattress was red with blood. When she passed by another cabin, she saw a rah inside. It was cocooning an old man. The man's wife already hung from a web, skin ashen. She had been drained of blood. Emily hurried by before the rah could see her.

A nightmare, she thought. *This has to be a nightmare. Yesterday morning, I was in Buckingham Palace, a pampered princess. Now I'm trapped in a labyrinth in space with monsters all around.*

She wanted to wake up, to find herself back home with her family. To go out riding with her mother. To listen to her father's tales of history. To stroll through the gardens and read away the hours in the library.

But that life was over. Her family was gone. The library, the gardens, those places of opulence—they had burned. Her life had changed. Overnight, she had been transported to another reality. She thought of people throughout history given horrible news. Your cancer has spread. Your spouse is cheating on you. Your newborn son will never walk. A moment—and life is tossed upside down, never to be the same. Now she had faced such a transition. They all had, every human on Earth and in space. They had woken from a dream and found themselves in a nightmare.

Lights shone ahead, purple, blue, and yellow. Emily followed them. Any place with light was a good place.

As she walked, the corridor expanded, and Emily found herself racing across a promenade. The chamber was enormous, easily the size of a sports arena, spanning the ship from port to starboard. You could fit thousands of people in here. Walkways, escalators, and elevators led to dozens of tourist attractions. Each attraction boasted neon signs, begging for attention. The lights flashed around Emily, spinning her head.

SEA OF FREEDOM AQUARIUM

CARNIVAL OF FREEDOM: KIDS HALF OFF!

DRACULA'S MANSION HAUNTED HOUSE

LADY LUCK CASINO

CABARET DINNER AND SHOW 19+

"It's all dreadfully American," Niles said. "Not a single teashop to be found. I don't know how Mr. Darjeeling tolerates it here."

There were dozens more signs, none for teashops. Emily raced by them. Apparently, she had found the *Freedom*'s entertainment district. Or at least one of them. With the tourists all recalled into their bunks, the promenade was deserted.

Clattering claws sounded behind her.

Emily froze and stared. An eight-legged shadow moved along the wall.

She ran across the promenade.

She raced by a vintage arcade, a laser-tag maze, and a gift shop, seeking an exit. She wanted to find soldiers—or at least a dark place to hide. With all this neon, any rah who happened by would see her.

The claws sounded again. Closer now. Emily ran faster, heart pounding.

By chance, her path took her toward a towering animatronic brontosaurus. A doorway was set between its legs. A neon sign hung across the dinosaur's side, spelling the word DINOGOLF.

Can I find safety here? Emily wondered.

The mechanical dinosaur held a golf club in its mouth, but when it saw Emily, it still managed to speak. The words seemed to be coming from a speaker on its neck. The dinosaur's mouth moved clumsily with every word, trying and failing to lip-synch. The golf club wobbled like a cigar.

"Welcome to Dinogolf! Step between my legs and enter a land before time! Explore a world where dinosaurs roam! No outside food or drink allowed. Visitors will be charged one dollar per missing golf ball. Freedom Resorts and Entertainment Limited is not liable for any injuries incurred while climbing its animatronic attractions. Dinogolf! Where minigolf meets prehistory!"

Niles stared at the animatronic brontosaurus. "That is the *worst* robot I've ever seen. An insult to my kind."

Screeches sounded behind them. Emily turned and saw rahs racing onto the promenade.

She froze and tightened her grip on her katana, but the aliens hadn't noticed her yet. One rah overturned a table in the food court, and soda and french fries spilled across the deck. Another rah was carrying a half-eaten tourist. One rah had a Freedom the Frog plushie embedded on a dorsal spike; the doll was drenched in blood. A few other rahs leaped onto the tables, and one alien slammed into a carousel, knocking over the unicorns. The aliens were laughing, slurping, feeding.

"Where are you, humans?" one rah cried out. It was speaking English. The bastards knew English.

"Come out, come out, humans!" another rah said. "Come out, come out wherever you are! We just want to talk."

The other spiders laughed.

Emily ran toward the plastic brontosaurus. "We'll hide in there."

"*What?*" Niles said, clearly affronted. "Inside a miniature golf course? I'd rather die."

"I would rather live," Emily said, racing among the stanchions that formed a line to the brontosaurus.

The clatters and screeches rose louder behind them. Any moment now, the rahs would see her. She raced between the brontosaurus's legs, pushed her way between some plastic ferns, and entered the miniature golf course.

* * * * *

The ticket booth was abandoned. Emily ran into a plastic jungle. Fake palm trees, ferns, and grass rose all around. Eighteen animatronic dinosaurs rose from the prehistoric landscape, their jaws opening and closing, their tails swishing. The T-Rex, who wore big purple sunglasses, was moving his little arms as if doing the robot dance. Every once in a while, one of the dinosaurs unhooked its lower jaw and let out a prerecorded roar. It was dim in here, but thankfully the dinosaurs glowed.

Each dinosaur guarded another hole in the course. Players had to putt the ball between dinosaur legs, past sweeping tails, even into the mouth of one ravenous triceratops.

"Hi, I'm Terry the Pterodactyl!"

The voice came from above. A pterodactyl whooshed overhead, swinging from a cable. Emily didn't think it was part of the game.

As it dived over Emily's head, the pterodactyl opened its beak and squawked: "Buy your own glow-in-the-dark dinosaurs. Only at Dinogolf Gift Shop!" It flew onward, then came swooping back. "Remember to try our Dino Donuts at the Dinogolf Café! They're dinomite!"

"Can I shoot it?" Niles said.

"No. Be quiet. Or those rahs outside will hear us."

A screech sounded outside the golf course. Hisses and grunts followed. The aliens were talking in their own language. Claws clattered across metal deck plates, moving closer.

"They know we're here!" Niles said. "We're done for!"

"Shh!"

Emily grabbed the drone and pulled him into a thicket of plastic ferns. An animatronic stegosaurus rose nearby, guarding the first golf hole. You were meant to putt the ball between its legs, past its swinging tail, and into the hole. A few abandoned golf clubs littered the putting green. Golf balls lay around Emily, knocked into the ferns and forgotten.

For a moment—silence.

Emily crouched among the ferns, waiting, hiding.

Then—a clatter.

A hiss.

Peeking between the ferns, Emily saw a shadow move into the golf course. Eight long legs. A bloated abdomen covered in spikes. Something sniffed. Smelling. Sensing. Hunting.

Suddenly, all around Emily, the lost golf balls lit up like Christmas ornaments. They began to play jaunty calliope music.

The animatronic stegosaurus swung its neck toward Emily. Its metal jaw clattered open and closed, and a voice emerged from a speaker inside.

"Please return your lost balls to the front desk!"

Behind the stegosaurus, a rah screeched. It was a terrible sound. A sound like fingernails along a blackboard. A sound that could shatter glass.

Claws clattered. A shadow scurried.

Emily leaped from the ferns and ran.

She heard it behind her. A shriek tore across the golf course. Emily ran past a display case which held, according to a plaque, a real dinosaur bone. She saw the rah reflected in the glass, claws raised and ready to strike, jaw open to reveal rings of teeth.

Claws lashed, ripping plastic ferns. A claw tore into the animatronic stegosaurus. The crude robot crashed down. Its bottom jaw detached, but it still tried to speak.

"Please return . . . your . . . lost . . . balls . . ."

The rah stepped on it, crushing the machine's head, and kept scuttling toward Emily.

Emily panted, tripped on a ball, and hit the Astroturf. The alien squealed in delight, preparing to feast.

Heart pounding, Emily lifted a fallen golf club. She hurled it at the alien. The rah screeched, that terrible sound like shattering bones. With a swipe of its claws, it knocked the club aside.

Emily leaped up and kept running. But the beast was faster. She had to kill it somehow, but her katana could not penetrate that thick exoskeleton. She'd have better luck hacking at these animatronic dinosaurs.

That gave her an idea.

She ran toward the second hole. A fake cave rose there, made of hardened plastiform painted to look like rocks. An animatronic Neanderthal family stood inside, moving their arms and heads, cooking a plastic steak. The golf hole lay at their feet.

A red dinosaur stood outside the cave. It kept dipping its neck toward the putting green, rising again, bowing again. A golfer would have to time things right to putt his ball into the cave. Timed wrong, the golf ball would roll into the dinosaur's mouth.

A grainy voice emerged from a speaker on the dinosaur's neck. It had a thick Russian accent.

"I am Oleg the Allosaurus, the Red Dawn dinosaur. I hate freedom!" The plastic jaws opened wider, revealing several golf balls inside. "I'll eat your balls!"

The rah let out a bone-piercing cry.

Emily ran toward Oleg the Allosaurus. The giant spider

followed, tearing through the putting green. Strips of Astroturf flew through the air. Golf balls scattered, glowing blue and red. Emily glanced over her shoulder, saw the spider pounce. She hurled another golf club. The rah snapped its jaw shut, mangling the club, and spat out the bent metal.

"Back, beast, back!" Niles cried, stabbing at the rah. The spider waved its claws, trying to knock the drone aside, but Niles kept dodging the blows. His lights flashed, blinding the beast. "Run, Emily! Run!"

Noble drone! Emily thought.

Using the distraction, she raced behind the animatronic allosaurus. While the rah was busy swiping at Niles, Emily shoved herself against the back of the dinosaur. She pushed with all her strength.

"I am Oleg the Allosaurus!" the machine said. "The Red Dawn dinosaur."

Emily groaned, giving it a mighty shove, digging her heels into the Astroturf.

"I hate freedom!" said the dinosaur. The tip of its tail rose off the ground. The dinosaur began to tilt forward.

"Niles, watch out!" Emily cried and gave one last mighty push.

The drone zipped aside.

The rah looked up.

The animatronic dinosaur fell down hard, crushing the spider. The rah squealed. Its legs flailed. But Oleg the Allosaurus was a big, heavy machine, and it pinned the spider down.

"I'll eat your balls!" Oleg warned, snapping his mechanical jaws.

The spider squealed, tried to shove the dinosaur off, but could not.

Emily drew her katana, stepped forward, then leaped back from a swiping claw.

"Filthy human," hissed the trapped rah. "I will devour your soul."

"Eat balls," she said.

With a swing of her katana, Emily sliced off Oleg the Allosaurus's lower jaw. All the golf balls in his mouth cascaded out, slamming into the rah, blinding the beast.

With a great cry, Emily thrust her katana.

The spider was too busy batting away the spilling golf balls. It never saw the blade. Emily stabbed the creature's eye, popping it like a boil. She shoved the sword down to the hilt.

The spider twitched and died.

* * * * *

Emily pulled her katana free from the dead rah. The blade dripped black blood. Niles hovered at her side.

"Oh, Emily, look at your dress." The drone gave a sniveling sound. "It's all such an awful, awful mess. Not just the dress. This whole sad situation."

A shadow stirred ahead, eight-legged. Emily took a step back, her katana raised. Another rah moved among the plastic palm trees. She ran toward the third hole, where a group of velociraptors raced back and forth along the putting green, their legs attached to rails. A third rah burst from behind a waterfall, roaring.

Emily fled, leaping over a stream, around a plastiform boulder, and over a nest full of colorful dinosaur eggs. As she vaulted over the nest, the eggs cracked open. Tiny animatronic dinosaurs emerged and began to sing "It's a Small World After All."

Rahs lunged from all sides. Emily swiped her katana,

desperate to hold them back. A dozen or more now chased her, their claws destroying the fake trees, boulders, and singing baby dinosaurs. Soon those claws would rip through her flesh. Emily ran for her life, making her way to the center of the golf course.

A plastiform volcano rose in the center, as big as a house. Fake lava trickled down its sides, lit by small LEDs.

More spiders emerged from ahead. Their teeth snapped at Emily. A claw slashed her thigh, cutting the skin. Her blood dripped. Emily screamed, slicing, stabbing, unable to hold them back. They drove her toward the volcano. Desperate, with nowhere else to go, she clambered up the slopes.

She rose to the top of the volcano. A smoke machine was built into its vent, releasing a few weak puffs. Some tourists had tossed candy wrappers and empty soda cans inside.

Emily stood on top of the volcano, katana in hand, looking from side to side. The rahs were climbing the mountainsides all around, closing in on her.

"We're trapped!" Niles cried, floating beside her. "Oh, Emily, this is the end for us."

"Fly off, Niles," Emily said. "You can fly. I can't."

"Were that I were strong enough to carry you!" Niles said. "No. I prefer to die at your side."

A rah leaped toward them.

Emily swung her katana. The rah slid down the volcano. Another rah leaped from behind. Niles drove into it, knocking it down. But more of the giant spiders kept climbing, too many to defeat.

"Hi, I'm Terry the Pterodactyl!"

The voice rang across the golf course.

The animatronic pterodactyl, the same one Emily had seen when first entering Dinogolf, came swinging toward her from a cable.

The rahs looked up, hissing.

As the pterodactyl swung overhead, Emily reached up and caught its legs. The robot kept flying, pulling her off the volcano. She clung on with all her might.

"Buy your own glow-in-the-dark dinosaurs!" the pterodactyl said. "Only at Dinogolf Gift Shop."

It swung through the air, flying over all eighteen holes. The other dinosaurs were moving robotically below, aside from Oleg the Allosaurus, which still lay on his side, burying a rah.

"They're dinomite!" the pterodactyl cheerfully added.

From up here, Emily got a bird's-eye view of Dinogolf. Aliens filled it, all seeking her.

She spotted the exit. The small doorway stood behind a dinosaur skeleton with big novelty sunglasses. A neon sign shone. EXIT THROUGH THE GIFT SHOP.

As the pterodactyl swung over the exit, Emily released its legs. She tumbled down and landed hard, banging her knees. A pained cry fled her lips.

"Princess!" Niles said. "Quick!"

The drone nudged her. The rahs were racing close. Ignoring the pain, Emily rose and ran with a limp. She raced into the gift shop.

* * * * *

Rows of shelves stretched before her. Some shelves held toy dinosaurs, copies of the larger animatronic beasts in the golf course. Other shelves held more generic merchandise: models of the starship *Freedom*, World War III action figures, Freedom the Frog plushies, and an assortment of puzzles, key chains, and T-shirts.

A rah burst into the gift shop behind Emily. Then another.

She ran between the shelves, swinging her katana, knocking over merchandise. A rah slipped on a toy Commander King.

"For the Alliance and for freedom!" the little action figure said before the rah crushed its head.

A great rah leaped up before her, grinning. More rahs came from behind. One of the giant spiders knocked over a shelf of model starships, then stepped toward Emily, licking its chops. She was surrounded.

Just then, a ventilation grate opened on the ceiling.

A pale arm reached down from above.

"Grab on!" came a voice. "I'll pull you up."

"The hand of God!" Niles whispered in awe.

Emily reached up and grabbed the proffered hand. Her mysterious savior pulled her toward the deckhead. A few rahs leaped, slashing their claws and snapping their teeth. Emily curled her legs upward, narrowly dodging the assault.

The hand pulled Emily into an HVAC duct. Eyes gleamed in the shadows. Human eyes.

The rahs shrieked below. The spiders leaped. Claws scraped the vent.

"Hurry!" came a voice from the shadows.

The hand pulled her along. Emily followed. The duct was just wide enough that they could crawl. Niles hovered with them. The aliens roared in fury below. A claw punched through the duct, nearly slicing Emily. She screamed. The claw retracted, and she raced onward. Another claw burst through the steel, and this one scraped her shoulder. Emily yelped but kept crawling.

Finally the duct took them away from the gift shop, and the sound of aliens faded behind.

Emily allowed herself to collapse and tremble.

Daniel Arenson

CHAPTER THIRTY

The Starship *Freedom*
80 million kms from Earth
08:30 December 26, 2199

King stood on the bridge, holding his drawn firearm, waiting to kill and die.

A dozen ATLAS monitors rose around him, displaying security videos from across the starship. On every video, the rahs were attacking, savaging tourists, hotel workers, crew members. King also had his implant turned on. Ten hallucinatory schematics hovered around him, translucent and glowing, mapping out the various decks and sections of the *Freedom*. On every schematic, glowing red dots showed the positions of the rahs.

Hundreds of aliens had boarded the *Freedom*. They were ripping through the ship, slaying everyone in their path.

King imagined that right now they were doing the same thing on Earth, and Hel'rah's warning echoed in his mind.

I'll devour your granddaughter.

"The bastards are making their way to the stern," Jordan said, watching one of the glowing schematics. They were sharing the same hallucinations, pulling the data from the ship's sensors.

"They want to blow our engines," King rasped. He scrolled through spherical avatars, found Darjeeling. He sent him a telepathic message. "Sergeant, are you seeing this?"

Darjeeling had just returned from flying the tugs. He was now in the stern of the ship, leading a group of soldiers. Alien screeches and gunshots sounded over the MindWeb connection.

"Yes, sir, I see the beasties," Darjeeling said. "We're tracking the enemy's movements. I've reinforced all hatches and access points."

The *Freedom* didn't have a real security force. They had a few guards. That was it. They were there to redirect curious tourists away from sensitive areas of the ship, not repel an alien army. Over the past hour, every soldier aboard the ship—gunners, warehouse workers, janitors, science officers, the lot—was called to join the security force. Some had firearms. Most just picked up pipes and swung them as clubs.

You go to war with the army you have, King thought.

"Darjeeling, I've received information from the midsection Mimori units," King said. "Some rahs have been moving through the HVAC ductwork, popping into various cabins from the vents above. I want you to guard all HVAC grates."

Darjeeling inhaled sharply. "They can fit into the ducts, sir? I've tried to chase Stowy there before. Even I can't fit in there."

King smiled wryly. Stowy had been a pain in Darjeeling's backside for three years now, ever since the girl smuggled herself aboard. King himself didn't mind her. Stowy had become something of a mascot for the crew. Sometimes the girl even popped out of hiding and joined the crew for poker or beer. But to Darjeeling, she was an archenemy. The old man probably hated her more than he hated the rahs.

King put Stowy out of his mind for now.

"Apparently the rahs can detach their abdomens like lizards detaching their tails," King said. "It makes them small enough to fit into tight spots. They retain their claws and teeth and are as deadly as ever."

"Understood, sir," said Darjeeling. "Nasty buggers they are. We're understaffed back here in the stern, but we'll do what we can. These are good boys and girls under my command, and we're giving the enemy hell."

"I'm going to try to find you reinforcements," King said. "Hang tight. And Godspeed, Sergeant Major."

"Godspeed, sir," Darjeeling replied, then returned to the fight.

King stared at the schematics and video streams, seeking a spare security unit. The few guards aboard the *Freedom* had their hands full. The rahs were concentrating their attack on the hotel, which spanned several midsection decks. The glowing maps showed the rahs as sterile red dots. But in the video feeds, King saw the true horror. He watched, helpless, as the enormous spiders burst into hotel rooms. As they ripped people apart. As they fed on flesh, chortling and slurping. In some rooms, they were laying eggs inside the women.

King knew what he had to do.

It broke his heart.

"We must divert security forces from the hotel to the stern," he said. "Jordan, oversee the redeployment. Leave one security squad in the hotel. Send the rest to help defend the *Freedom*'s Talaria drive."

Jordan spun toward him, frowning. "Jim, the spiders are tearing the tourists apart. There are thousands of civilians in the midsection, still alive, still under our protection. We need our forces there."

King gave his XO a hard stare. He then passed his gaze across the rest of the bridge, staring at his crew, one officer at a time. They were all looking at him, shocked.

"If the rahs reach the Talaria drive, they can blow this entire ship to kingdom come," King said. "Then every tourist dies. Then we all die. Then the *Freedom* is gone and out of the fight. Our ship must survive and reach the Mercury armory. Earth needs us! If we must sacrifice a few thousand lives now but potentially save millions—we must."

"Jim." Jordan spoke softly. He put a hand on his shoulder. "Are you sure about this? If we survive, we still need to live with ourselves."

A growl rose in King's throat. "You have your orders, Lieutenant Commander. Execute them."

Jordan nodded, a slight frown creasing his brow. "Yes, sir." He got on his MindLink. He began connecting to security forces in the hotel, to divert them to the stern.

We've been best friends for a long time, King thought, looking at his XO. *But right now we are officers on a warship. We must act like it.*

King watched the monitors. He watched as guards left the hotel. As rahs swarmed in. As tourists died.

A few bridge officers began to weep.

What they did not see, could not know, was that King's heart shattered.

This has always been the burden of command, he thought. *That we must sacrifice the few to save the many. And sometimes we must sacrifice the many to save the world. This is a weight I will always carry. We all will.*

"I can feel them inside me," Mimori whispered. The android was shaking. "I can feel them move through my veins. Parasites. Digging. Clawing." She fell to her knees. "It hurts."

King approached her, held her hand. "Hang in there, Mimori. You're going to be okay. We're fighting the infection."

She looked up at him. Fear filled her mechanical eyes. "It hurts, sir. Why did they program me to feel pain?"

Of course there were no parasites inside the android. Mimori was feeling her true body. The *Freedom*. When the ship hurt, she hurt.

He patted her hand. "You can disconnect your interface, Mimori. The androids feel more acutely than the ship. You can turn off. You can sleep."

The android shook her head, hair swaying. "No. You need me. I—" She gasped. "Sir! The rahs! I can feel them. Moving fast.

Moving here! They're heading to the bridge." She pushed herself into the corner, trembling. "Death. Death is coming."

* * * * *

King stared at the floating schematics. He saw them. A cluster of red dots moving through the corridors, racing toward the bridge.

The bridge was located deep inside the *Freedom*'s prow, far from the external hull. Pre-World War III starships had their bridges located right along the outer hull, only a thin wall separating them from space. But the *Freedom* was a warship through and through, born in the crucible of war, and her bridge was like a bunker.

Yet the enemy had broken through. They were moving fast.

"They'll be here in moments," King said.

Darjeeling, I could sure use you and your boys here right now, he thought.

He drew his sidearm, cocked the loading handle. The gun clicked. The dots on the map moved closer. Closer still. King could hear them now. Terrible banshee shrieks and scraping claws.

King looked at his bridge crew. They stared back, pale, eyes sunken. None of them had slept last night. They were nearing exhaustion. Other than Jordan, none of them had ever seen combat. Some had been only babies during the last big war. Others had not been born yet. They were all, King knew, thinking of their families back home. He had to motivate them. To lead them.

"We did not choose this war," King rasped. "And you did not choose to be fighters. When you took this job, you thought you were going to manage a museum. Well, that's over. Over the past two days, you've all proved to me that you are brave. That you are warriors. I'm proud of every one of you. The enemy is about to break onto our bridge. And when they come storming in . . . we will give them hell."

Jordan raised his own firearm. "Just like the good old days, huh, Jim?"

"Except we're twice as old," King said.

"And in your case, twice as ugly," Jordan said.

The red dots moved closer on the schematics. The screeches grew louder, vowing agony and death.

King and Jordan stood back-to-back, guns at the ready. There had been many times like this during World War III, just the two of them, back-to-back, as the enemy closed in. King wondered if this was how they would die.

"Hey, dumbass," King growled.

"What, ugly?" Jordan said.

Claws began pounding the bulkheads, the hatch, trying to break in. The spiders screamed.

"If we gotta die now," King said, "I'm glad to die by an old friend."

"Not me," Jordan said. "To have them find my body by a corpse as ugly as yours? It's embarrassing." He softened his voice. "Let's live today, Jim."

"I'll certainly try."

The door to the bridge burst open.

The rahs stormed inside.

* * * * *

King fired his gun.

His bullet hit one rah in the eye. The creature fell. At once, several more rahs charged over the corpse.

King fired again. Again. At his sides, his crew were firing their own firearms. They tore another rah down. More kept coming.

For the first time, King got a good, close look at the bastards. He had seen Hel'rah on video, and that had been bad enough. In real life they were even worse. They stank. A stench like bad meat and worms after rain. Their eyes were like red boils full of blood, and their saliva sizzled when it hit the deck. Claws swiped through the air, graceful in their deadliness, claws like birds of prey made from onyx, like katanas forged in collapsing stars, like shards of a broken black mirror, reflecting King a hundred times.

He aimed at one rah at random, emptied his magazine. Most of the bullets hit the rah's exoskeleton and ricocheted. But one bullet hit an eyeball. It burst, splattering red juices. The rah tossed its head back and screeched. Despite losing an eye, it was still alive. The bullet must not have gone deep enough to hit the brain.

King loaded a fresh magazine. He shot the beast with the mutilated eye. Again. Again. He tried to reach the eye socket, to drive another bullet into it, but the rah still had its head tossed back, protecting its eyes. Instead, King shot its roaring jaws. Bullets tore into the palate. Still the alien refused to die.

The creature leaped at him.

King raised his arm, deflecting the blow. Pain roared up his arm.

The rah knocked him down. King fell onto his back, grunting, and the beast roared above. Its drool sizzled over King. Its claws rose high, ready to rip King apart.

King kicked one of its back legs.

The spider buckled and fell onto King, nearly crushing him.

But at least the front claws hadn't torn him apart.

One of King's arms was still free. He planted his pistol against the ravaged eyeball and pulled the trigger.

His bullet drove through the socket and into the brain. The rah gave a pathetic mewl, then died, still crushing King beneath its girth.

King shoved the alien off and spat. Damn things weighed a ton.

All around him, the battle raged across the bridge. One crew member, a young nav officer, already lay dead. A rah was ripping out her innards. A tactical officer stood against a wall, one arm severed. He was firing with his remaining hand.

Jordan shot a rah through the eye, slaying the beast. Two more dead rahs lay at his feet.

"Three already, Jim!" the XO said. "You're slowing down."

A ventilation grate opened above Jordan.

"Above you!" King shouted and fired his gun.

A rah emerged from the vent, leaping down onto Jordan. King kept firing, knocking the beast back. He finally hit an eye. The creature mewled and twitched, kicking the air. It had detached its bloated abdomen to fit into the vents. It was all claws and teeth—just what it needed to kill.

"More coming through the vents!" King said. "Guard the vents!"

They came from above. From below. Through the door. Through the walls. They were everywhere.

Another crew member fell.

King reached for another magazine of bullets, but he was out. He pressed his boot against one dead rah, gripped a claw, and tore it free. Just like ripping a claw off a crab. He swung the severed limb like a blade, holding the enemy back.

Jordan ran out of bullets next. He was still wearing his parade uniform, complete with the ceremonial saber. He drew the sword. The two men stood back-to-back, wielding their blades.

"Jim?" Jordan said. "It's been an honor."

"We're not dying yet," King growled. He thrust the claw at a rah, aiming for an eye. The beast roared and lashed its own claw. King parried. Another spider leg swung, and King grunted in pain. Blood spurted from his arm.

Another claw thrust.

Pain blazed on King's leg. He roared and fell to his knees.

He looked around him, saw dead crew members lying across the deck. The rahs were eating some. One woman was already gone up to the navel. The spiders had eaten the rest.

Mimori stood among the carnage, eyes shut. The rahs were ignoring her, perhaps recognizing her as a machine, not flesh to consume. The android seemed to be in shock.

"Mimori!" King barked. "Mimori, do you hear me?"

"It hurts," the android whispered.

"Mimori, activate your combat mode."

Her eyes snapped open. She looked at him. "I'll have to untether myself from the ship's mainframe. I won't be able to fly anymore."

"Do it," King said, swinging his severed claw, desperate to hold the enemy back.

A rah laughed before him.

"I won't kill you, Commander King," the alien said. "I have orders to bring you to my mistress. She has special suffering planned for—"

King rose from his knees, thrust his claw, and impaled the creature through the eye. The rah twitched and fell, yanking the weapon from King's hands.

He looked up at Mimori.

The android's eyes began to glow white.

Her hair buzzed with electricity. The strands rose as if she floated underwater. A crooked smile touched her lips.

King had not activated Mimori's combat mode since the last war. When in this mode, Mimori was detached from the starship. She could not see through the sensors, hear through the microphones, or feel space around her. She lost nearly all the grand body she normally had, remaining small, alone.

In combat mode, she was lost. She was broken. She was insane.

Every time she entered combat mode, Mimori lost something of her soul. A part of her mind never recovered.

At this time, she was no longer the beloved starship avatar. All her processing power was dedicated to one purpose: slaughtering the enemy.

A rah, noticing the changes in the android, lunged toward her.

Mimori ducked.

The rah's claws swung over her head.

Almost casually, Mimori grabbed one of the claws and twisted. The exoskeleton cracked. The leg came free.

The rah, still alive, opened its mighty jaws in a roar. Those jaws could swallow Mimori whole.

The android thrust the severed claw, driving it through the rah's palate and into its head.

Another rah leaped at her.

Mimori tossed the dead spider at the new threat. Both aliens tumbled to the deck. A third rah lunged at her. Mimori sidestepped, dodging the claws, and thrust her hand forward, fingers forming a spearhead. She drove her hand into an eye, then her entire arm. She pulled her arm free, scooping out brains.

Across the bridge, the rahs turned toward Mimori, abandoning the humans. They recognized that here was the real threat.

Several rahs leaped at Mimori from all sides.

And then the android began to fight in earnest.

She ducked, swerved, leaped, spun. She lunged over a workstation, kicked off a wall, somersaulted through the air. She kept grabbing claws, pulling them free, stabbing, killing. Alien corpses piled up on the deck.

King and the others helped, killing whoever they could. But the android put them all to shame.

Finally it was over.

The android stood atop a steaming pile of dead spiders. She looked at King. Her face was expressionless, her eyes haunted. Glowing eyes. Insane eyes.

One day I might send you so deep that you can't come back, King thought.

He got on his MindLink.

"All Mimori units!" he said. "Stop whatever you're doing and go into combat mode. Destroy the enemy."

Jordan inhaled sharply. He was bleeding from a cut on his side. Black spider blood covered his saber. "Jim, we'll be flying blind, tumbling through space like an asteroid. We've never taken all Mimori units offline."

"We've never needed to," King said. "We do now."

He watched them on the monitors.

Across the ship, the androids' eyes became white. And they began to kill.

* * * * *

The lights dimmed across the *Freedom*. The engines died. Even the air stopped flowing through the vents. The ATLAS monitors shut down across the bridge. The ship floated aimlessly.

The Mimori units normally handled so many of the ship's basic functions. Now all her copies were offline, and the human crew was busy fighting too—at least those who were still alive.

The ship tumbled through space, a dead chunk of metal.

But the MindWeb was still online. That technology had been retrofitted onto the *Freedom* only a few years ago. The Mimori units did not operate it. King's telepathic abilities were still intact.

He hallucinated a few video feeds. They floated around him. He watched the Mimoris fight. Seven of them served aboard this ship, ranging from prow to stern. Now their eyes shone like neutron stars, and they became berserkers, charging at the enemy.

In the midsection, the rahs had overrun a mess hall. A Mimori unit let out a battle cry and leaped into the sea of spiders. She slaughtered many, but the aliens swarmed over her. One rah tore off the android's left arm. Then they took her legs. Still she fought. With one arm, she tore at them, killing them until they ripped off her head.

That video went dark.

The other Mimoris kept fighting. The alien corpses piled up at their feet. The androids were the starship herself, and they were furious. They were like white blood cells, protecting their body. If the starship *Freedom* was a great living being, a whale the size of a town, the androids were her immune system. They rose in battle, cutting back the enemy, scouring the ship's twisting halls. The *Freedom* was fighting back against the parasites.

Screams rose from one video feed. Telepathically, King scrolled through a carousel of videos. They shuffled by before his eyes, showing different battles aboard the ship.

The scream had come from a gunnery station. It was a cavernous chamber, full of gears the size of houses. From that chamber, the crew could control one of the Angels of Liberty. There were fourteen such chambers, all identical, to fire the fourteen cannons.

This particular gunnery station, the one in the video,

controlled the Libertas. King had just been there yesterday. It was where he had entered a mecha and shot the fireworks.

The Libertas was a special cannon. Among the fourteen, she was perhaps the greatest. The enormous gun, the length of a football field, was located atop the starboard hull, overlooking the prow. During the Battle for Mars, the Libertas had shot down the mighty RDS *Mao*, opening a path to the red planet—and ultimately to victory in the war.

Right now, as King watched from the bridge, an enormous rah was tearing through the gunnery crew. It was the largest rah King had seen so far, twice the normal size. Corpses lay around the colossal spider. There was just one spider in the chamber, but it had slaughtered twenty people.

This rah was different from the others, and not just in size. The other rahs were all black. This one had a gray body and red legs.

"Hel'rah," King growled, staring at the video.

As if Hel'rah could hear him, the rah looked up at the security camera.

"Hello, Commander King," the spider hissed. He raised a severed head. "I hope you won't miss this one too much."

He hurled the head at the camera. Blood splattered the lens, and the camera jerked sideways. It now pointed at a wall.

Tourists hung on the wall.

Girls.

They hung from meat hooks, eggs in their stomachs. A few were dead. The others were dying.

Hel'rah's voice rose to a shriek. "I will do this to Rowan! I will do this to your granddaughter as you watch, King!"

King realized that everyone on the bridge was looking at him. They had their MindLinks on too. They had seen the same thing.

"Somebody get me a full magazine," King rasped. "I'm

going to crush that bug."

"I'm going with you," Jordan said.

King shook his head. "No. You're my XO. I need you on the bridge. The ship is yours until I come back."

"Jim." Jordan held his arm. "Send a security team down. It doesn't have to be you."

"All our forces are protecting the engine. This is between me and the spider." King accepted a magazine from a lieutenant. He loaded his gun. "I'm going to take back my damn ship."

As the starship drifted aimlessly, as the aliens swarmed through her halls, King left the bridge.

I'm coming for you, Hel'rah. This is between you and me. I'm going to make you regret the day you saw the starship Freedom.

CHAPTER THIRTY-ONE

**The Starship *Freedom*
81 million kms from Earth
08:52 December 26, 2199**

Emily collapsed in the duct, breathing heavily, bleeding from her leg and arm. The shadowy figure paused ahead, eyes gleaming. Emily still couldn't see who had saved her.

"Whoever you are," Emily whispered, breathing heavily, "you saved my life. I thank you."

Niles's exposed circuits cast a dim glow. The figure wriggled closer, coming into the light.

She was a teenage girl. Her long brown hair lay across her face. Curious hazel eyes peered between the tangled strands. The girl wore a raggedy dress with many pockets, no shoes, and just one striped stocking. Oddly, an expensive-looking pendant hung around her neck from a shoelace. A gust of air moaned through the duct, blew back the girl's hair, and revealed an elfin face. Freckles sprinkled her upturned nose, and soot covered her cheeks.

"Stowy's the name!" The girl held out her hand to shake. "Stowaway extraordinaire, rescuer of damsels in distress, slayer of spiders! Well, to be honest, I've only ever slain one spider, a tiny thing that crawled onto my leg. Them big alien ones are a doozy!"

Emily tilted her head. "I know you. We met. Briefly. At the Fist of Freedom."

Stowy grinned. "That's right! I remember! How silly of me

to forget." She slapped her head. "One runs into so many princesses here in the HVAC ducts that they all kind of blend together."

"All right, very funny." Emily rolled her eyes.

The stowaway laughed. "You're silly. I like you." She giggled. "I'm sorry. It's just all funny! Isn't it? Giant spiders and princesses and talking dinosaurs eating your balls." Her giggling intensified. "I know I shouldn't laugh. Lots of people died. My mother always told me that. Stowy, she said, don't just laugh at dead people! Show some empathy! But I can't, you see. I have none! I don't think so. My mother said that the doctor said that I might even have autism, and that's why I'm so rude. I just blew that doctor a raspberry. Oh, by the way, she didn't really call me Stowy. My mom. I have a real name, but I left it somewhere. I can't find it now." She shrugged. "Maybe it'll pop up eventually." She began giggling again.

Emily watched all this in silence. Niles leaned toward her.

"I don't think she's quite right in the head, that one," the drone whispered.

Shrieks echoed down the ductwork.

A stench of oil and rancid meat filled the recirculated air.

Both girls tensed. Stowy cocked her head, listening, and Emily gripped the hilt of her katana.

Another shriek—closer.

Claws clattered.

Suddenly the entire duct was shaking.

"They're coming into the ducts!" Emily whispered.

"Impossible," Stowy said. "Those bugs are the size of baby elephants and even stinkier. They can't fit in here. They gotta just be making a racket above us."

They listened for a moment longer. The screeches grew closer. Closer. The ducts rattled. The stench wafted. The shadows of long legs stretched around a bend in the duct.

"Oh crumbs," Emily whispered.

The creature emerged around the bend.

For a moment Emily froze in terror. She stared.

The rah had no abdomen. It must have detached that big, bloated part of its body like a lizard detaching its tail. The giant spider had essentially become a head with legs. Without the abdomen, the spider could squeeze into the ducts. It dragged itself forward, claws scraping the steel plates. The alien's jaws opened wide, ready to feast.

"Oh, how dreadful!" Niles cried.

More rahs scuttled behind the first one. They too had detached their abdomens. More alien cries rose, echoing. There were scores of them.

"Come on, Emily!" Stowy cried. "Run! I mean—crawl! Hurry!"

The girls crawled through the duct, and the spiders followed. The jaws snapped behind them, coming closer, meat grinders hungry for their limbs. Emily forgot about the pain in her wounds. All that mattered now was crawling.

Even without their abdomens, the rahs were big creatures. If Emily curled up into a ball, she'd probably be smaller than those horrible heads. Their size slowed them down. The disembodied creatures dragged themselves through the ducts, banging their big hairy heads against the walls, scraping the steel, clumsy and cumbersome but still moving forward. They reminded Emily of bingo balls tumbling through tubes. That was, if bingo balls had jaws that could shame Oleg the Allosaurus.

"We're done for!" Niles cried. "It's like I always feared. We're going to die in the darkness, devoured by spiders."

"We're not dying yet," Emily said. "I have an idea."

As she crawled, she reached into her pocket. She pulled out the folded map of the starship *Freedom*, the one she had picked up when first docking inside the starship. She unfolded it, tried to read it as she crawled forward.

"Niles, shine a light on this," Emily said.

The drone hovered above, casting his dim light onto the map.

"Hurry up, princess and robot!" Stowy said. "Stop reading and crawl faster."

"We need to make our way to the engine room on this deck," Emily said. "According to the schematic, there's a deuterium reactor powering the promenade."

"I know the way," Stowy said. "But why?"

"I have an idea. Just trust me."

Stowy nodded. "All righty. Forget the map. Just follow me. I know better than any map—trust me—my brain is full of maps and baby crocodiles. I'll take you to the engine room. If we're all gonna die anyway, we might as well be warm."

They kept going and the spiders kept chasing.

One of the rahs got close. Claws reached out, nearly grabbing them. Emily had to curl her legs inward, and she lost a shoe. The rah clambered closer, slobbering. Niles cried out and began stabbing at the spider, suffering a blow from a claw. The drone crashed into the duct wall. His jewels dislodged and spilled across the duct. The rah roared in rage.

Emily lifted the fallen gemstones and hurled them.

"My gems!" Niles cried. "Not my precious gems!"

Emily ignored him and kept tossing the precious stones. She got a few in the rah's eyes. One gemstone lodged into an eyeball. The beast bellowed and stumbled back. More rahs were clambering behind it, desperate to reach the humans.

"We're almost there!" Stowy said.

They kept crawling, moving at a mad pace. Emily could feel the heat now. The duct rattled. The steel was getting so hot Emily winced. She could hear it below. The grinding, crackling inferno of the deuterium reactor. According to the ship's schematics, this engine powered the entire entertainment district. Dinogolf and all.

The rahs scampered closer. They felt the heat too. It enraged them. They moved faster. Their legs reached out. One claw nicked Emily's heel, and she yowled. Stowy pulled her along. The engine rumbled below. The heat bathed them. Emily thought she would burn here, that she was cooking inside the ducts. Even the rahs cried out in pain. But they only moved faster.

It was time.

Emily stopped fleeing.

She turned to face the rahs.

The creatures filled the duct, craggy heads with ravenous mouths, red eyes and grinning sneers, dripping tongues and hungry maws. Horrors from deep space. Demons awoken into the world. Incubi in a nightmare she could not wake up from. Emily, a princess, a girl, a human—she knelt before them in the duct, and she stared. And the rahs stopped. She held them back with her gaze.

"I am Emily, the Lady of the White Rose, the uncrowned Queen of Great Britain," she said. "In the name of my throne, of my nation, of my planet—I send you bastards to hell!"

She thrust her katana.

But not at the rah.

Instead, she drove the blade into the duct. A hole gaped open in the steel plate. Emily began to saw, carving the ductwork open like a can.

The heat blazed from below. Red light filled the duct. The engines churned below.

Emily kept carving the steel.

A rah leaped at her, trying to vault over the pit she had sawed open.

Emily lashed her sword. The blade clanged against the alien's head. Sparks flew. The creature roared, raised its claws to strike . . . and then the duct crumpled beneath it.

The alien tumbled into the jaws of the waiting engine. Gears grabbed the spider, crushed it, and pulled it into the mechanical depths.

Another rah lunged.

Emily swung her katana again. Another section of the duct ripped open. The rah tried to reach her, but the duct swayed. The opening widened. The entire structure was falling apart. Metal sheets detached. Screws came loose.

The rah scrabbled for purchase, then slid down too. Screaming, the alien crashed into a magnetic field. The forces ripped it apart. Its scream died.

Many spiders remained inside the duct, gazing across the pit at Emily. The lead rah opened its jaws wide, revealing a spinneret, and shot a strand of cobwebs at Emily. She sliced through it, then slashed her katana at a screw above. A screw that was holding the duct in place.

The entire duct twisted, bent, and began to collapse.

Rah after rah slid down the mangled chute. The churning, glowing, pumping engine grabbed them with gears like teeth, crushed them with its magnetic field, and digested them within its churning cauldrons of fusion.

Emily fell with them.

As the duct fell apart, she tumbled.

A hand grabbed her.

Stowy!

Stowy still clung to what remained of the duct. Which wasn't much. Just a few slats of steel and some loose beams. But Stowy held on to the rickety bits of metal, and she pulled Emily up.

"Saved ya again!" Stowy said and giggled.

Emily climbed into what remained of the ductwork. A few more screws came loose. A beam bent. The two girls hurried, racing along the buckling duct until they left the engine room.

Niles hurried behind them.

Finally they crawled out a vent, finding themselves in an abandoned control room. Large windows overlooked the reactor chamber. Many rahs had fallen in, were burning, screaming as the great engine consumed them. They reminded Emily of souls tortured in hell, mutilated and strange.

This starship has become hell, Emily thought.

She swayed and slumped to the floor. Her wounds were bleeding, and there was something broken inside her. All around she heard the battle raging. Many rahs still filled the starship *Freedom*, and millions swarmed across Earth, and life had become a nightmare.

"Emily? Emily!" Niles was nudging her.

"Emily? You good?" Stowy was shaking her. "You good, Emily? You good?"

But Emily could barely hear them. The darkness rolled over her, her head rolled back, and she drowned in an endless black sea.

CHAPTER THIRTY-TWO

**The Starship *Freedom*
82 million kms from Earth
09:32 December 26, 2199**

King marched down the corridors of the *Freedom*, passing by devastation.

People lay dead everywhere, their bodies mangled. Some were Alliance soldiers. Many were civilian employees—the staff who cleaned the hotel rooms, cooked food, served tables, operated the amusement park rides, and did a hundred other jobs.

But most of the dead were tourists. Many were women and children.

King passed by a rah devouring the body of an old woman. The spider raised its eyes, glared at King, huffed, then lowered its head and kept eating. King walked by. He would not waste bullets on this creature.

He was saving every bullet in his magazine for one particular spider.

I'm coming for you, Hel'rah.

As he stomped down the corridor, King sent out telepathic orders.

"This is James King. Anyone in the midsection who can fight, track my beacon and join me."

A security guard ran up, paunchy and mustached. Blood

covered his uniform. He was a civilian contractor, one of the guys who guarded the amusement park. But he stood at attention and saluted. He held a smoking pistol in one hand.

"Here to help, sir."

"What's your name?" King asked.

"Dennis, sir. Dennis Pibbs."

"Where are you from?"

"The Freedom Carnival, sir. I make sure the teenagers don't steal any of the plush animal prizes or hog the rides. Oh, you mean, where I'm from on Earth? New Jersey, sir. Well, born in Philly, but . . . yes, a Jersey boy."

"Well, Dennis Pibbs from New Jersey, today you are a soldier. Today we go to war."

Another man ran up. A tourist, judging by his Hawaiian shirt and flip-flops. He too saluted.

"Here to help, sir! I found a gun on a dead soldier. I hope it's all right that I took it."

The three of them walked down the corridor, and more joined them. A few were Alliance soldiers. Most were not. Some carried guns. Most did not. Soon thirteen of them were marching down the hallway, heading toward the Libertas control room. Toward the terror that awaited there.

Toward Hel'rah, prince of the alien empire.

A rah came scrabbling down the corridor. They opened fire. They shot it down. They kept going.

They fought their way through the ship. They stepped over corpses. Over severed limbs and pools of blood. They passed by a warehouse where a Mimori unit was battling twenty spiders or more. They raced by a pool where corpses floated and spiders swam through the red water.

Finally they rose in an elevator, walked down a corridor, and there it was.

The gunnery station.

They stepped into a chamber the size of a church nave. Their footsteps echoed.

When people saw the *Freedom*, it was usually on postcards, T-shirts, or posters. Sometimes they bought plastic models of the starship. Small images. Small toys. It was easy to underestimate the *Freedom*'s true size. The fourteen cannons on top, the famous Angels of Liberty, perhaps looked small on the souvenirs. Just little guns jutting out from the hull like cannons from an old sailing ship. The sheer size of those cannons rarely sank in. Stand an Angel of Liberty up like an obelisk, and it would rise taller than the Statue of Liberty.

The Angels' control rooms were appropriately enormous. Gears, valves, and hydraulic pumps covered the walls—the machinery to aim and fire the cannon. A chute dominated the room. It sloped from the hull toward the deck like a slide. At the bottom of the tube, gunners used to load the famous Maccabees—torpedoes larger than some small starships.

King had been here just yesterday. He had stepped into Samson, the great mecha, and loaded fireworks into the chute. He never imagined he'd see this room again. Once more, Samson stood behind velvet ropes, his yellow paint peeling. Stowy was gone, but her apple core was still on the deck.

The gunnery crew, who had spent the past thirty years shooting fireworks instead of torpedoes, lay dead across the chamber. Dead tourists hung from the wall. Eggs festered inside their slit stomachs.

In the center of the station, he stood.

King's nemesis. A warty gray spider with red legs. A spider larger than the mightiest grizzly bear. He was busy chewing on a dead woman, ripping off strips of her skin, sucking them up like noodles.

"Hel'rah!" King called out.

The rah raised his head from his meal. A grin spread across

his face. King hated the way the damn things were always grinning those psychotic Cheshire cat grins.

"Hello, Commander King!" the rah said. "I've been waiting for you. Join me for dinner? I've saved you the choice cuts." The spider cackled, blood in his mouth.

"Hilarious," King said, aimed his gun, and opened fire.

On cue, his crew opened fire with him.

A storm of bullets slammed into Hel'rah. They bounced harmlessly off his exoskeleton. The alien just stood there, laughing as the bullets shattered against his armored body.

King tried to hit an eye. But transparent eyelids like glass visors snapped shut, covering the alien's swirling red eyeballs. The bullets bounced off those goggle-like shields.

Apparently, Hel'rah was a rare breed of rah. Not only was he larger and colored differently. He also had nictitating membranes, able to protect his eyes, a rah's weak spot. And who knew what other abilities the bastard had?

"Yes, King," the rah hissed. "I am no mere hunter. I am a prince! I am the son of Skel'rah, Warweaver of the Fleet. I am the grandson of Elder'rah, Empress of the Great Web. You cannot kill me with bullets or blades." He laughed. "You can only die, King. And I will make sure you die so slowly."

The spider prince pounced.

David Pibbs, the paunchy carny, ran forward and shielded King with his body.

"You will not touch Commander King!" Pibbs cried.

The spider plowed into him.

Claws lashed with incredible speed like the needles of some deranged sewing machine.

The claws perforated Pibbs. They ripped him apart. He collapsed in several pieces onto the deck.

"Let's kill this son of a bitch!" shouted the tourist with the Hawaiian shirt. He ran toward the spider, swinging a pipe. And then everyone was running. Soldiers. Carnies. Tour guides. Tourists. The whole makeshift squad of them. Their guns were useless. They wielded blades, clubs, or just fists. Thirteen men and women, they did not flee, even as they saw the carnage. They ran toward the enemy.

And King made a choice.

Another choice he knew would haunt him forever.

He ran away from the spider.

He left the others to die.

Behind him, he heard them scream. Heard Hel'rah laugh. Heard the skin rip, the blood splatter, the wet pieces of people slap onto the deck. King did not look back. He kept running.

At his age, King didn't run much anymore, but now he raced as if the world depended on it. Which in a very real sense, it did.

He ran until he reached the mecha at the back of the chamber.

The machine rose there, as tall as an oak. During the last war, Samson had loaded the heavy Maccabees into the chute. The mecha had seen better days. His paint was peeling. His gears and pistons were rusty. Tourists had etched rude drawings into his steel frame. But Samson's forklift hands were still strong.

As the screams rose behind him, King climbed a ladder toward Samson's torso, which contained the operator's seat.

"What are you doing, King?" rose a screech from behind. "Hiding as I kill your lackeys? How cowardly!"

The spider laughed, a high-pitched, demonic sound. King heard the claws scraping across the deck, racing toward him.

He still didn't look back. He concentrated on climbing the ladder. He hurried into the cockpit, which filled the mecha's torso. He sat on the plastic seat and pulled down the metallic harness. Two steel bars held him in place. It reminded him of the roller-coaster rides on the upper deck.

From here, sitting inside the mecha, he saw Hel'rah racing across the deck toward him. Behind the spider lay his victims. King had led a dozen warriors into this chamber. Within seconds, the spider had killed them all. Their mangled bodies lay across the steel deck, blood pooling.

The spider charged like a bull, shrieking.

King shoved down a throttle.

Motors grumbled. Servos hummed. Pistons chugged. The smell of motor oil and exhaust filled the air.

Samson woke up.

Hel'rah leaped through the air, soaring toward King in his mecha.

King pulled a joystick. Samson swung his left arm. His forklift hand slammed into Hel'rah, knocking the spider down.

The rah shook his head madly, pushed himself back up, and glared at King.

King shoved a lever. Samson took a step. His footfall shook the mighty chamber.

Hel'rah rose onto his back legs, grinning savagely. His legs lengthened, new joints emerging from his abdomen. The creature rose higher and higher, extending his sharp red legs. Soon the spider stood even taller than the mecha. He swung one of his front legs like a scythe.

King moved another joystick. The mecha's right arm rose, parrying the spider's attack.

The mecha took another step, reached down, and grabbed Hel'rah with his mechanical hands. Samson squeezed the spider between the metal fingers.

The alien shrieked, a deafening sound. King growled and kept squeezing the spider. The mecha was designed to lift torpedoes the size of trucks. It could certainly crush a damn bug.

Caught in the machine's grip, Hel'rah screamed. He stretched out his front legs, extending them like retractable pointing sticks. More and more joints emerged from the body. Then Hel'rah thrust one leg like a sword.

King leaned sideways. The claw whooshed over his shoulder, impaling the back of his seat.

Hel'rah thrust another claw. King leaned the other way. This claw scraped against his arm, slicing the flesh. He roared.

"I will carve you up, King!" Hel'rah said. "I'll skewer you like a tunnel maggot!"

King extended the mecha's arms as far as they'd go. But the spider's claws were longer. Hel'rah thrust another leg.

King squirmed aside in his seat. This claw tore across his shoulder. He bellowed in agony.

But he kept moving the joysticks.

The mecha kept walking, its mighty feet shaking the deck.

"Die now!" Hel'rah screamed, thrusting more claws.

King moved the joysticks. Samson's arms swung to the side, slamming the spider into a beam. The alien shrieked, opened his jaw, and revealed his spinneret. He shot a bundle of cobwebs at King. The sticky glob slammed into his right arm, binding it to his seat. King tried to free his arm but could not.

His left arm was still free, but it was an ugly mess, slashed twice and bleeding badly.

With his wounded arm, King kept operating the mecha, still gripping Hel'rah with Samson's mighty hands. He moved his own hand from joystick to joystick, controlling the machine's hydraulic limbs.

"We are done, King!" Hel'rah screamed. "Die now!"

He thrust a claw, aiming at King's head.

Before the claw could hit, King released the spider, hurling him downward.

Hel'rah crashed onto the deck, and King slammed the mecha's foot down.

"I will crush you like the bug that you are!"

Samson's enormous foot landed on the spider.

Something *cracked*.

Hel'rah screamed.

King shoved down with all his strength, leaning the mecha's great weight against the spider, intending to flatten him.

Hel'rah was pinned down. He wrapped his red claws around the mecha's leg, tightened his grip like a vise, then hurled the mecha aside.

The machine weighed several tons. And the damn rah tossed it through the air.

Samson slammed down hard, cracking the deck. The *clang* could probably be heard across the starship. Dangling from his harness inside the torso, King grunted. His blood soaked his chair.

Before he could rise, Hel'rah leaped into the air, then came swooping down.

Those red claws gleamed.

King rolled aside in the cockpit. The claws drove into the blood-soaked seat. One claw slashed King's thigh. He bellowed in rage. The spider crackled above him, drooling. The sizzling saliva burned King's skin. In frustration, King fired his sidearm, but the bullets did nothing.

"Goodbye, Commander King," the spider hissed, then thrust his jaws into the cockpit. His mouth opened wide, revealing a gullet ringed with teeth, hungry for flesh.

King finally managed to free his right hand from the webs. He grabbed the joystick. Samson's massive metal hand grabbed Hel'rah, pulling him out of the cockpit.

He shoved another joystick.

The mecha rose to its feet.

Hel'rah struggled, caught again in the mecha's grip.

Ahead King saw it. Waiting. Ready.

He took several more steps, moving the mecha at a run,

until he reached the chute. The same place where Samson would insert torpedoes during the war.

King shoved the spider into the chute.

The alien struggled, claws slashing, lacerating the tube's entrance. But King kept shoving him deeper. Finally the spider's body disappeared into the metal tunnel.

"What are you doing?" Hel'rah screeched from inside, clawing madly, desperate to escape.

With the mecha's metal fists, King kept shoving the spider deeper inside. "This chute connects to the barrel of Libertas, an Angel of Liberty, the great starboard cannon of the starship *Freedom*. The tourists love when it fires."

"I will devour your soul!" Hel'rah screeched from the chute. "I will rip your granddaughter apart! I will destroy your son! You are doomed, King! Doomed!"

King reached down with one of Samson's forklift hands. He gripped a lever the size of a gallows.

"Get the hell off my starship, you goddamn piece of filth!" he growled and shoved the lever.

Deep inside the chute where the great metal tube connected with the starship's hull, a hatch opened.

Vacuum grabbed everything inside the tube.

Which, right now, meant Hel'rah.

The spider was sucked down the metal tunnel, shrieking.

Gears spun across the chamber. Cables thrummed with energy. The lights dimmed. And the great Libertas fired.

King connected his MindLink to the drone which still hovered above the starship *Freedom*. He watched through the drone's camera. The Libertas boomed, and out flew Hel'rah. The spider had seemed enormous inside the starship, but flying out the great cannon's bore, the alien seemed like any old spider. Just a bug after all. Limbs flailing, jaw open in a silent scream, Hel'rah flew into the distance and disappeared into the darkness.

"Good riddance," King muttered.

He climbed out the mecha and down the ladder. He kept bleeding. Once he hit the deck, King tried to take a step, but his leg buckled. He fell into a puddle of blood. For a moment, he knelt, wheezing.

Don't die yet, he told himself. *This war ain't over. You stay alive until you win the damn thing.*

He took a raspy breath and scrolled through videos on his MindLink, checking on the rest of his starship.

The tide was turning.

Across the *Freedom*, the rahs were looking from side to side, dazed. They paused from fighting, began speaking in their language. King couldn't understand them, but he understood one word. *Hel'rah.*

They were looking for their master.

A few rahs pointed toward the outer hull. Others ran around in confusion. Without their leader, they were lost. It seemed that unlike humans, the rahs had little individuality. Without a strong commander, their army fell apart.

The Mimori units, still in combat mode, kept chewing through the aliens. Thousands of humans, soldiers and civilians alike, rallied behind the androids. With guns, knives, sometimes just pipes or wrenches, they beat back the enemy.

King took a shuddering breath. Everything hurt. His throat. His wounds. His damn bones hurt.

The war was not over. But this battle was won.

He sent a MindLink transmission. "This is Commander James King. I need a medic. Track my beacon. I . . ."

He didn't realize he was falling. But the next thing he knew, he was lying in blood. He stared across the deck, and he saw the dead. The brave souls he had led here. The warriors who had died for humanity. He did not know all their names, but he would find out, and he would remember them forever.

A while passed in a haze.

And then medics were rushing into the chamber. They knelt around him, tended to his wounds, lifted him onto a stretcher. Finally King allowed himself to lose consciousness.

CHAPTER THIRTY-THREE

**The Starship *Freedom*
Approaching Mercury
12:21 December 26, 2199**

When King awoke, he bolted up in bed.

His MindLink was offline.

"Give me an update! Somebody update me, dammit."

He was in the infirmary. An IV was attached to his wrist, and bandages covered his left arm and leg. Nothing hurt.

He tried the MindLink again. Reluctantly, it began to boot up, then fizzled away. They must have given King potent painkillers. Those were known for interfering with the neural implants. Coursing through the brain, the drugs blocked the pain but also messed up access to the MindWeb.

Grunting, King rose from the bed, slammed his feet against the cold floor, and took a step.

"Hey there!" came a cry. "James King, you lie back down right now."

Dr. Annie Jordan barged into the room, her green eyes flashing. She had the same mahogany skin and commanding presence of her father, Lieutenant Commander Larry Jordan. But her green eyes came from her mother, an Irishwoman who still lived on Earth. The young doctor was only thirty, but King knew her to be fiercely intelligent and capable.

"I need to get back to my bridge," King growled. "Get out of my way."

Annie placed her hands on her hips. She was a slender woman and several inches shorter than him, but when she raised her chin, and when her green eyes flashed, she seemed an impassable force.

"Not so fast. Let me look you over one more time first. You took a beating in this battle, Commander. I won't let you walk until I'm sure you can. Now sit down so I can take a proper look."

"Get me a comlink at least," he said. "Whatever damn drugs you gave me are jamming my MindLink."

She huffed, pulled a device from her pocket, and handed it to him. "Keep yourself busy and don't bother me."

She began to scan him with a variety of medical devices, checking his blood pressure, heart rate, and other stats. As she worked, King placed a few calls. First to Jordan on the bridge, then to Darjeeling, then to Spitfire, then a few other of the ship's commanders. The picture came clear.

The *Freedom* was clean of rahs.

All the invaders were dead.

So were several hundred crew members and tourists.

Meanwhile, the *Freedom* was still flying toward Mercury. Beaten. Battered. Her hull carved open. But still flying fast.

"Jim, the war down on Earth is looking bad," Jordan said over the comlink. "Only three clawships attacked the *Freedom*, but thousands of clawships have been ravaging the Alliance fleet. Our dreadnoughts are all gone. The frigates are barely holding up. And millions of rahs are swarming across the planet, overwhelming our ground troops."

"The dreadnoughts are not all gone," King rasped into the comlink. "The *Freedom* is a dreadnought. The first dreadnought ever built. And still the greatest. We will turn her into a warship again." He clenched his fist and spoke through a tight jaw. "And then we will return to Earth and defeat the enemy."

He then tried to call Earth.

The planet's communication networks were down.

He didn't know if Bastian and Rowan were alive.

"Doctor, now get these damn gadgets off me," King growled, gesturing at the sensors and tubes attached to him. "I've got a goddamn ship to run."

Annie rolled her eyes. "Still as stubborn as a mule." She sighed, put a hand on his shoulder. "We nearly lost you, sir. If the medics hadn't gotten there in time . . ."

He nodded. "Annie, your dad and I are best friends. You've known me all your life. But you weren't born during the last war, so there's something you didn't know until now."

The doctor tilted her head. "What's that?"

"I'm damn hard to kill." He winked.

She laughed. "Must say, sir, launching that bastard out the cannon? Brilliant."

He looked into her eyes. "Thank you, Annie. For saving my life. I know this is a busy day. I know the wounded are flooding the medical bay. Thank you."

She nodded, wiped away a tear. "We've lost a lot of people."

"And we will lose more," King said. "This war is not over."

He pulled on his uniform and left the infirmary.

* * * * *

As he marched through his ship, he saw the devastation. The blood on the decks. The claw marks on the bulkheads. The shattered machines. Crew members ran back and forth, not even pausing to stand at attention, racing to seal more hull breaches. A few tourists huddled in a corner, weeping. One old man had a bloody bandage wrapped around his head. One boy lay on a stretcher, missing his legs, as medics fought for his life. A woman wandered in a daze, asking people where the medical bay was. Half her body was burnt red and black.

This was the aftermath of a victorious battle. King had learned long ago that victory always came with a cost. It never got easier.

On his way to the bridge, he passed by Spitfire. The pilot still wore her flight suit, and she carried her helmet under her arm. But when she saw King, she dropped her helmet and ran toward him.

She crashed into his embrace. They held each other for a long moment.

"You kicked butt out there," King said. "Spitfire, I'm damn proud of you."

She smiled, tears in her eyes. "I guess watching all those videos of you flying in World War III finally paid off. I learned a thing or two."

He chuckled. "Soon you'll be giving me lessons."

"No way, sir." Spitfire wiped away her tears. "Next time, you fly with us. You're still the best damn pilot in the fleet, I bet."

He smiled thinly. "Maybe someday. Now go on! Get down into the hangar. I want double shifts and full rosters. We're still in yellow alert."

She saluted, eyes damp. "Yes, sir."

He returned the salute. "Spitfire, you are no longer a stunt pilot. You're a fighter pilot."

Sniffing, the pilot ran off, and King continued walking down the corridor.

He marched onto the bridge.

"Commander on deck!" Darjeeling cried, snapped his heels together, and saluted.

King paused, looked his friend in the eyes, and returned the salute. Then he stepped to the center of the bridge.

"As you were, everyone," he rasped.

The crew got back to work, bustling around their monitors. Not the whole crew. Several of them had fallen.

King stared at the central monitor. Mercury shone ahead, as wide as a wagon wheel. The monitor's heat maps painted the planet in purple and golden hues, all swirling like a psychedelic brew. The sun shone farther back, dazzling and flaring. The solar wind blazed across the *Freedom*. They flew through the photon storm, their hull sparking.

They were almost there. At Merc Mory. At the armory that could refit the *Freedom* into a warship, that could transform a dying old bird into a mighty eagle.

"Perhaps we had to pass through fire," King said softly. "Perhaps like a phoenix we can only rise again from the ashes of destruction. This ship is hurt. But she is being forged anew. She will rise like a steel blade to strike down our enemies."

Jordan approached him, put a hand on his shoulder. "You led us to victory in this battle, Jim, and you will lead us in the great war ahead. But Jim . . . when the rahs stormed onto the bridge, I still killed more of them than you." He winked. "You're slowing down, old man."

King did something he rarely did.

He laughed.

* * * * *

Battered and bruised like a boxer after nine rounds, the starship *Freedom* limped into orbit around Mercury.

Mercury was unique among the planets. It was tidally locked to the sun. The planet did not rotate around its axis. One side blazed in a constant inferno. The other side remained eternally dark and bitterly cold. Because of the extreme temperatures, the surface was inhospitable. Merc Mory was a space station, orbiting the planet, staying always on its dark side. This close to the sun, you definitely wanted to stay in the shade.

The *Freedom* settled in a low orbit, only a thousand klicks from the dark, frozen surface. The ship glided through the night, heading toward the station. The planet's horizons blazed around them, crackling with sunlight like a halo of fire. From afar, the *Freedom* would seem to be flying inside a flaming corona.

They were fifteen minutes from the armory when they saw it.

King stared, fists clenched at his sides.

No. God, no.

A portal opened in space, obscuring the stars.

From inside they emerged. Three clawships.

They came storming toward the *Freedom*.

Jordan walked closer to the monitor. He inhaled sharply. "We have to turn and run. We can't fight three more. Not without ammunition. Not with our shields all battered and our hull cracked open."

King knew his XO was right. Last time, they had been lucky.

"Sir, the enemy are charging toward us at incredible speed!" Mimori cried.

King nodded. "All right. Mimori, turn us around, kick up the Talaria drive to full power, and—"

"Jim!" Jordan grabbed his arm. "Look!"

The XO pointed.

They all stared.

From beyond Mercury's horizon she rose.

A dreadnought. A human-built dreadnought. A ship even larger than the *Freedom*. Her hull was painted red. A golden equal sign glittered across her prow, the symbol of equalism, the cursed ideology that had dominated the twenty-second century. The ideology King had fought a world war to beat back.

The dreadnought rose from the fiery horizon, flying fast, prow lifted in pride. The enormous letters on her hull, spelling out her name, were Russian letters. But King could read them.

Here flew the RDS *Lenin*, flagship of the Red Dawn. The personal starship of Premier Katyusha herself.

The *Lenin*'s cannons boomed.

"Shields to full power!" King barked. "Prepare for impact!"

But the impact never came.

The *Lenin* wasn't aiming at the *Freedom*.

The mighty photon bolts, rolling balls of energy the size of houses, plowed into a clawship.

The alien starship exploded, scattering metal claws every which way.

The *Lenin* fired a great laser beam.

The second starship exploded.

Finally the *Lenin* fired a storm of torpedoes.

The third and last clawship shattered into a million pieces.

Shrapnel pounded the *Freedom*. The old ship rocked in space.

It's a good thing I ordered the shields to full power, King thought wryly.

"Sir, we're getting a neural call request from the *Lenin*," Mimori said.

A chill flooded King's stomach. The scar on his neck blazed in sudden pain. He knew who was calling.

"Accept the call," he growled. "Feed it to my MindLink."

A hallucination appeared on the bridge, life-sized.

It was her. Katyusha. Premier of the Red Dawn.

She wore a fine military uniform. Tall black boots. A red coat with golden buttons and a braided aiguillette. A saber hung from her side, and her chin-length black hair spilled out from under her cap.

"*Zdravstvuyte*, Commander King!" She gave him a crooked smile. "So nice to meet you out here. And to save your American ass."

King growled at her. "We can handle ourselves."

Katyusha tossed back her head and laughed. "You still have your sense of humor, James King! Even now, in these dark times, you make jokes."

He glared at her. They were both sixty years old, but King looked his age. Katyusha did not. She still looked like a woman of thirty, same as she did during World War III. He had heard the rumors. That the Red Dawn was growing her clones in labs. That every few years, she sliced a clone's head open, scooped out its brain, and planted her own brain inside. That way she kept young forever, but with every implant, she became a little madder.

King believed those rumors.

Suddenly he saw it again.

The battlefields of Mars.

The Red Dawn troops closing in—Russia from one side, China from another, the North Koreans from behind.

He remembered how Katyusha had laughed when slicing his throat.

Instinctively he touched his scar.

"Ah yes, it still hurts, doesn't it, James King?" Katyusha said. She *tsk*ed her tongue. "So sad."

"What do you want?" he snapped.

She laughed. "Oh, Jamechka! You are always so direct and to the point. What does Katyusha want? Call it . . . an alliance. No, not an alliance. Bad word. That is the word for that group of rogue nations who joined against us. Instead, call it . . . a truce. Between you and Katyusha. Between your precious Alliance and Katyusha's glorious Red Dawn. Today we have a common enemy."

"Contrary to popular opinion, the enemy of my enemy is not my friend," King replied.

"A lovely American truism," she said. "But we Russians are more practical." She gave a mock pout. "You do not want to be Katyusha's friend, Jamechka? Not even after Katyusha saved you?"

King felt everyone on the bridge staring at him. He took a ragged breath.

I cannot let my personal feelings interfere with my duty, he thought. *Katyusha took my father from me. I hate her as much as I hate the rahs. But that is my hatred. That is my burden. And mine alone. The world needs us to unite.*

"For now, until the rahs are defeated, we'll work together," King said. "Not as friends but as allies." A growl fled his throat. "Now get that dreadnought of yours out of my way."

Katyusha laughed heartily. Her hallucination leaned forward and patted King's cheek. The implant generated the feeling of her hand—soft but cold. She wasn't really there, but he could feel her.

"Goodbye, James. Try not to fly into any more ambushes while Katyusha is away." She winked, and her avatar vanished.

King took a deep, grainy breath. He turned toward his XO. "I hate that woman."

The *Lenin* yawed in space, then her engines flared. The mighty dreadnought blasted into the distance, leaving a streak of light. King watched her fly away. She was heading back to Earth.

Jordan patted his shoulder. "Come on, Jim. Let's get to the armory. We've got a bunch of missiles to load. Not to mention a lot of repairs."

"And not a lot of time," King said. "Every moment we linger here, the rahs are gaining ground on Earth. We must rejoin the fight as soon as possible."

Starship Freedom

* * * * *

Scarred, dented, still leaking some air, the *Freedom* arrived at the Merc Mory.

A cylinder formed the station's axis, three kilometers long. Seven rings spun around the central axis, offering docks for Alliance starships. The *Freedom* was too large to dock directly at the station, so the ship entered a matching orbit five klicks away. They would use shuttles to go back and forth.

There was a lot to do.

Standing on the bridge, King talked to the station crew.

"I need my ship's hull repaired," he told them. "I need Maccabee torpedoes, as many as you have, for my cannons. I need bullets for my machine guns. I need Goliath projectiles for my railgun cannon. I need medical supplies for my wounded. And I need any men and women you can spare. If they can fix a machine, if they can fire a gun, if they can face the rahs without turning to flee—send them to me. I'll get them into the fight."

On the bridge monitor, the station technicians spoke to one another in hushed tones. Their leader turned toward King.

"We can do all that, Commander. We need three days to load you up with ammunition, about three weeks to repair your hull, and as for finding fresh soldiers, we'll need to—"

"I need it done in twenty-four hours," King said. "That is not negotiable. Repair what you can. Give me what weapons you have. Give me any man or woman willing to face the rahs in battle. Twenty-four hours from now, the starship *Freedom* is flying to Earth and reentering the fight. Get my ship fixed and armed!"

He cut the call.

Jordan sighed. "You've always been a charmer, Jim."

King turned toward him. "I don't need to charm people. I expect them to step up in times of war and do their damn job."

He turned to look at the rest of the bridge crew. "Which you all did. In the war so far, you've all made me proud. I know that you will keep making me proud in the battles ahead."

A nav officer saluted, her eyes damp.

A comms officer saluted next. Then everyone was saluting. Most of them had tears in their eyes.

King looked at them, and he saw children. His children. Children who had never known war. Who had, within two days, become proud men and women. Officers of the Alliance. Soldiers.

"None of us asked for this war," King said. "None of us loves fighting. If I could, I would much rather see the *Freedom* as a museum ship, not a warship again. But this war was thrust upon us. And you all stood up to the task. We fought a great battle today. We fought without ammunition. Without hope. Without any aid. And we won. The cost of victory was high, and many of our brothers and sisters gave their lives for this victory. We will forever remember the fallen. Let us stand a moment in silence and honor their sacrifice."

They stood, silent. They thought about those they had lost. King also thought of those he had lost in the war long ago.

Then he spoke again. "We defeated three clawships, including one that bore a rah prince. But thousands of clawships still attack Earth and her colonies. Long ago, in a different great war, Winston Churchill said: 'This is not the end. It is not even the beginning of the end. But it is, perhaps, the end of the beginning.' Many battles still await us, and the road to victory seems long and uncertain. Hope barely shines. But when I look at my crew, I see this hope. I see it in your eyes. In your hearts. In your courage. We will continue this fight with relentless determination and belief in our cause." King raised his fist. "For freedom!"

Jordan raised his fist too. "For freedom!"

Darjeeling raised his fist next, tears on his mustache. "For freedom!"

"For freedom!" cried Spitfire, fist raised.

Everyone on the bridge raised their fists. Their voices rang out. "For freedom!"

"*For freedom!*" King repeated, louder now.

Their voices filled the bridge. *"For freedom!"*

* * * * *

Emily stood in the royal suite, looking around at the devastation.

The battle had rocked the starship *Freedom*, knocking priceless artifacts off the shelves and walls. Ming-dynasty vases, an ancient Greek statue of The Three Graces, the Titian painting, African tribal masks—they lay shattered on the floor. A rah had entered the room at some point, slashing the furniture and ripping out the rug.

The royal suite, once a place of opulence, lay in ruin, a perfect metaphor for Emily's life.

"Oh, this is such an awful, awful mess!" Niles said.

The drone was still damaged. A hole in his silver shell revealed the gears and microchips inside. Most of his precious jewels were missing. Darjeeling had promised to find a technician to repair Niles, but Emily had turned him down.

"Right now, Mr. Darjeeling, every technician we have must work to repair the *Freedom*," she had told the sergeant. "We must get back into the fight."

Niles had not liked that. He had been sulking since.

"Oh, it's my lot to suffer!" the drone said, flying around the trashed suite. "Look at this painting. Look at it! This is an original Lord Leighton. Ruined. Ruined like our lives. Oh woe!"

"Niles, please," Emily said. "Calm down. It's only a

painting."

"Only a painting?" The drone bristled. "That's like saying that *Hamlet* is only a play, that England is only a country, or that you, Princess Emily, are only a girl."

"No," she said softly. "I'm not only a girl. I'm the last of the House of Windsor. The heiress to the throne. I am all that remains of Great Britain's royalty. And from here, in exile aboard this starship, I must be a symbol to our people."

Niles stopped fretting, hovered toward her, and nuzzled her. "The princess in exile. And someday—our queen."

"That must be my mission, Niles. To return to England. To rebuild the throne. To be crowned queen. Until that day, yes, I am the princess in exile. I will fight in this war. And however I can, I will lead our people."

Her dress was tattered, covered in soot and blood. She had lost a shoe in her flight through the ducts. Her hair was a fright. She didn't mind. She left the royal suite, walked through the starship as people stared. A few mumbled blessings. Others bowed. This was an Alliance ship, and people from many nations served here, not only nations of the Commonwealth. But they all showed her respect.

As she walked by an ATLAS control room, Emily ran into Spitfire, who was walking the other way.

Emily froze, and her heart pounded. She remembered her confrontation with Spitfire in the aerie.

It was only yesterday, she thought. *But it feels like a lifetime.*

The tall Israeli pilot froze too. She glared down at Emily and placed her hands on her hips.

Emily took a deep breath. "Spitfire, I'm sorry for what my grandfather did. I did not know the tale. I only learned it today when reading through the ship archives. He . . ." Emily took a deep breath. "He got scared. He turned tail and fled from a battle. He left your father alone, facing the enemy. He left him alone to die." Emily stared steadily into Spitfire's eyes. "I believe that it haunted King Robert until the day he died in the alien fire. I hope that now, with my grandfather dead, you can find it in your heart to forgive my family. As the last scion of my house—I'm sorry."

Spitfire's face softened. A sad smile touched her lips.

"Hey, you're all right, Emily. I saw the footage of you and Stowy taking on those rahs. You're a badass bitch, Princess. Just don't expect me to bow and kiss your ass." She winked. "I don't serve no one but Commander King."

Emily laughed. "I wouldn't expect you to. I heard how you destroyed the clawship *Venom*. Spitfire, you yourself are one badass bitch." She gasped, then covered her mouth. "I can't believe I just said that."

"Clearly I'm a bad influence." Spitfire grinned. "I'm sort of proud of that."

"Maybe, when all this is over, we can share some tea?" Emily said.

"To hell with tea!" Spitfire said. "You join us at the aerie for poker and beers tonight. Cool? One last party before we return to war."

Niles hovered closer. "Princess Emily will certainly *not* join you for such debauchery!"

"Princess Emily most certainly *will*," Emily said. "It would be my honor." She glanced at Niles. "And I must keep up my reputation as a badass bitch."

If robots could pale, Niles certainly did.

Spitfire laughed.

Emily continued walking until she reached the starship bridge. As she entered, everyone bowed their heads. Darjeeling bowed deepest of all. A janitor was mopping blood and shattered glass off the deck. He paused to bow too. Emily walked across the bridge, barefoot, her dress tattered, but she kept her head high and her shoulders squared.

A princess must always be elegant, her tutors had told her. At least one lesson stuck.

She approached King.

The steely commander nodded at her. "The ATLAS broadcasting antennae are in position, Your Highness. The ship is ready to broadcast your words to Earth."

He handed her a comlink. She took the little device. It looked like a cigarette lighter from one of those antique automobiles her grandfather had collected.

I suppose all those cars are gone now, she thought. *Melted into metal globs.*

She took a deep breath. It shook slightly. "May I begin now, Commander?"

He nodded. "When you're ready."

Emily closed her eyes, composing herself, then spoke into the comlink, broadcasting her message from Mercury to Earth.

"To the people of Great Britain and the Commonwealth, and to all humans wherever they may be. This is Princess Emily of Great Britain. I'm speaking to you now at the most difficult time in my kingdom's history. Indeed, in our world's history.

"We have faced challenges before. We have fought in world wars. We have faced plagues and economic collapses. Yet the challenge today is different. Today we Britons, and all people of Earth, face a terror we never thought was possible.

"The rahs caught us off guard. They thought we would fall easily. Yet we will stand. We still resist.

"Buckingham Palace has burned, along with the White House, Parliament Hill, the Rashtrapati Bhavan, the Alliance Headquarters, and many other centers of leadership. Many of our leaders, including my family, are dead.

"Yet I remain, though I cannot disclose to you my location. And many great leaders still fight. This is a dark hour. An hour of spiders. An hour of fear. But not an hour of despair. In this darkness, hope shines all the brighter.

"We are facing this invasion together. With our courage, our resolution, and our strength, we will overcome. We will meet again."

She finished her speech, returned to the royal suite, and began collecting the broken shards of an old life.

* * * * *

The shuttles flew back and forth between the *Freedom* and the station, hauling munitions. Some shuttles delivered medical supplies; the *Freedom*'s infirmary was overflowing with the wounded. Technicians began welding the cracks in the hull, then installing new sensors. Dock workers operated cranes and mechas, guiding torpedoes the size of grain silos into the starship's hangars. They were moving at breakneck speed. They all understood the urgency. They all had family back on Earth.

So did King.

I'll be home soon, Bastian and Rowan, he thought. *Hang on just a little bit longer. I'm coming home.*

"Mimori, you have the bridge," King said. "Everyone else—get some rest. You're gonna need it."

They all left the bridge. Most of them headed to the galley for some food; many had not eaten anything in two days. Others headed to the showers. Some headed to the infirmary to treat minor injuries. But King walked to his quarters.

He stepped inside and closed the door. For a moment he stood there, staring at his little sanctuary aboard the starship. The bridge was utilitarian, military, a ruthless machine. His quarters could be a cabin on Earth. Hardwood planks covered the deck, hiding the original diamond plate. Bookshelves spanned the bulkheads, holding leather-bound books, antique astrolabes, and sailing ships in bottles. A dozen history books and novels covered his desk; he always read multiple books at once, hopping from one to another.

He took a deep breath. This room could normally soothe him, but not today. Something hurt inside him. Old wounds ran deep, and today their poison filled him.

He sat in his leather chair and lifted the framed photograph he kept on his desk.

The photograph of his dead wife.

"I'm sorry, Diane," he whispered hoarsely. "I drove you away. It's my fault. Bastian was right. What happened to you . . . it's my fault."

He closed his eyes.

He had saved newspaper clippings of the story, read them over and over, seeking answers. He might never know the full story.

"But some things I do know," King whispered, voice like sandpaper. "I spent too many years on this starship. I loved the *Freedom* and I drove you away. I drove you into his arms. The arms of another man. A man who loved you, who showered you with attention, who gave you what I could not. A man who took you on a trip to Europe . . . and murdered you."

A tear fled King's eye.

When Diane went missing, it was Bastian who traveled to Europe, who went from hotel to hotel, who finally found her in Prague. Shot ten times. Her lover had then put the gun in his own mouth and pulled the trigger.

The press had a field day, of course. The story was juicy, just the way they liked it. A murder-suicide. A sexual affair. The wife of a World War III hero, cheating on him. Journalists waited years for a scandal like that.

But nobody ever learned why the bastard did it. Why the

son of a bitch took Diane away.

"I'm sorry, Diane," King said to the photograph, tears falling. "I won't let anyone else in our family die. I will find Bastian. I will find Rowan. I will protect them. I won't lose anyone else."

He looked at the second framed photograph on his desk. A photograph of Rowan riding on Bastian's shoulders. Both were laughing.

Please, God, he prayed silently. *Don't let this photo become a memorial too. Watch over them, God. At least until I can take over.*

He opened his desk drawer, and he pulled out his bottle of Martian ale. He poured a glass. Drained it. Poured another. He had a day before they sailed back into battle. He intended to get good and drunk.

A knock came on his door. A voice spoke outside.

"Jim? It's me, Larry."

"Come in."

Larry Jordan entered the room. He raised an eyebrow. "Did you start drinking without me, Jim? This is a new low, even for you." Then he noticed the tears on King's cheeks. "Jim! Are you all right?"

King nodded. "Yes. I am now. Sit down, you old bastard. Don't let me finish this bottle alone."

Jordan sat down. But King did not yet pour his friend a cup. He picked up his comlink again.

"Sergeant Darjeeling?" he said. "Join the Lieutenant Commander and me for a drink?"

Darjeeling's voice emerged from the speaker. "I would be most honored, sir."

The sergeant major entered the cabin and saluted. Oliver Darjeeling was an enlisted man. He had not gone to the academy with Jordan and King, had not flown Eagles with them in the war. But he was an old friend. A good friend. A war friend.

King poured them all drinks.

Jordan raised his cup. "We did all right today. For a few old farts."

Darjeeling laughed. "That we did, sir."

But King remained somber. "We're not just old farts. We're old war dogs. The three of us fought in World War III together, and we won. I don't know if we're going to win this one. But I do know we're going to give the enemy hell."

"I'll drink to that, sir," Darjeeling said.

They all drank. The ale burned down King's throat. Outside the porthole, the shuttles kept flying back and forth, arming the *Freedom* for war.

CHAPTER THIRTY-FOUR

Earth
Evening
Dec 27, 2199

For two days, Bastian fought the enemy, not sleeping, not eating, just giving the bastards hell.

It was his brigade now.

The Freedom Brigade. The bravest marines in the world. He was their new colonel. Their new commander. The man who would lead them in this war.

But when the battle of Fort Liberty ended, when victory was theirs, Bastian delivered no inspiring speeches. He left his troops. He ran through the base toward the bunk where Rowan was waiting.

Alien blood filled the room. It covered the floor, the walls, even the ceiling. Charging Bear stood in the center of the carnage. Dead rahs lay around him, limbs sticking every which way.

Rowan sat on the bed, covered in blood.

Bastian froze for a moment, staring.

"They broke in," Bear said in his deep, rumbling voice. "I took them down. I protected her."

Rowan rose from the bed. The blood covering her was black. Rah blood.

She was unharmed.

Bastian scooped her into his arms, held her close, and screwed his eyes shut.

"I've got you, Rowan. Thank God. Thank God you're all right."

"I love you, Daddy," she whispered.

Bastian just stood there, holding her, tears flowing down his cheeks.

* * * * *

After a long moment, Bastian turned toward Bear. He pulled the dour giant into an embrace too.

"Thank you, friend. Thank you."

Bear held him in mighty arms like the trunks of trees. "I'm proud to fight with you, old friend."

Bastian looked up into the giant's eyes. "Bear, this will be a long war. Join us. As a soldier. Enlist in the Alliance. Put on the uniform. Help me win this war. I can't do it without you."

Bear was silent for long moments, considering.

"I'm a proud member of the Meskwaki tribe," he said. "My loyalty must be to my tribe. Not to any foreign army. But today things are different. Today all men are brothers. All humans face a common enemy." He nodded. "I'll join you, Bastian, my brother."

Bastian fought back tears. "Then the enemy truly doesn't stand a chance."

The door opened.

Alice burst into the room. Bandages wrapped around her arm, her uniform was tattered, and blood stained her blond braids.

"Bas! Hurry!" Alice was panting, and fear filled her blue eyes.

Rowan whimpered and clung to Bastian.

"Alice, what is it?" Bastian said.

"An alien starship!" Alice said. "It's descending into the atmosphere right above us."

Icy claws clutched Bastian's heart.

"Then we'll shoot it down. Alice, get every soldier with a grenade launcher into the courtyard."

She nodded and ran out the room, shouting, "Grenade launchers! I need grenade launchers!"

Bastian hurried outside, holding Rowan in his arms. If a clawship was flying above, no place on the base was safe. Bear ran with him.

Hundreds of soldiers were already in the courtyard, aiming their Gideons at the sky. Those with grenade launcher attachments were screwing them onto the guns. Bastian joined them, loading a grenade of his own.

The sky rumbled. The clouds churned. The falling snow melted, pattering down as rain.

It emerged from the cloud cover, descending toward Fort Liberty. A clawship.

The alien vessel was huge. It was the size of the entire infantry base. Blades grew from its craggy hull, all pointing downward. It looked like a god's claw ready to grip the base and crush it. Between the bundle of those blades churned a cauldron of fire.

Bastian's head buzzed.

He groaned and grabbed his head. Something was vibrating inside his skull, burning him, deafening him.

The MindPlay operating system appeared, floating before his eyes. The hallucination was imperfect, jittery, bleeding out at the edges. The icons flickered.

Somebody was hacking into his MindLink.

Somebody was calling him.

A video feed appeared, floating before Bastian in the courtyard.

Bastian gasped and cursed.

"What is it?" Alice said, hurrying toward him. She could not see what he saw.

"A rah," Bastian said, clenching his jaw. "Calling my MindLink."

He stared at the hallucination. The rah towered before him, as large as an elephant. A female. Around her, Bastian caught fuzzy glimpses of her location. The spider hung from a web inside a cavernous room. Humans hung from the web all around her. The males were dead. The females were still alive, their mouths gagged. Eggs pulsated inside their bloated bellies.

The spider spoke, voice like shattering glass. "Is this Colonel Bastian King, commander of this military installation?"

"Last time I checked," Bastian said. Cold sweat trickled down his back.

The spider licked her lips. "You probably noticed my clawship hovering above you. My spawn attempted to feed upon you. They have decided that you are inedible."

"You mean we handed your asses to you, and you lost your appetite?" Bastian said.

The spider laughed. "What do you understand of *eresh*, human? You are an honorless species. We believe in *sheertone ash keresh*. The sharpening of the claw. Only through eternal war can we grow strong. Only by culling the weak can our web thrive. You served your purpose. You were the stone against which we sharpened our claws. That is *Ishar*. The Right Path. That is *kata hel anak*. The dance of war. But you are too foolish to understand. All you know is killing and dying. And today, human, you die."

The transmission ended.

The ship's claws bloomed like a steel flower, revealing more of the blazing eye in the center. The caldera pointed downward at the base. It began to heat up, to churn madly, to rumble.

Bastian had seen these weapons in video feeds from across

the world. The clawships could blast down pillars of fire that destroyed anything they touched. With these terrible weapons, they had destroyed the White House, the Forbidden City, Buckingham Palace, and many other centers of power.

Now they were going to destroy Fort Liberty.

They ate a few of us, sharpened their damn claws, and now they're bored, Bastian thought.

He raised his rifle, aimed it at the swirling plasma sun above.

"Shoot this damn ship down!" he cried and fired his gun.

Across the base, his soldiers fired with him. They unleashed grenades and bullets alike. But the flaming eye devoured everything they shot at it. The inferno heated, heated, turning blue, then white.

Bastian knew there was no point in running. There was nowhere to run.

This was the end. Here in white fire.

He held Rowan tightly.

"Rowan, I love you."

She pointed at the sky. "Daddy, look!"

"Don't look at it, sweetie. Look away from the fire. I'm here with you. I—"

"*Daddy.* Look there! Behind the spider ship!"

Bastian looked, squinting, and gasped.

Fire blazed high in the sky.

A new starship was entering the atmosphere, ionizing the air.

A massive starship. A dreadnought.

According to his MindLink stats, it flew a hundred klicks above, skimming the blue sky. It blazed like a comet.

Bastian directed his MindLink to zoom in. His contact lenses changed shape. The starship above grew.

She was the starship *Freedom,* wreathed in light.

The clawship yawed away from Fort Liberty, turning its claws toward the *Freedom*. It was about to launch its plasma at the starship.

The *Freedom*'s railgun lit up.

Thrusting out from her prow, the two prongs blazed white, blinding. For the first time since World War III, the Fist of Freedom was about to fire a projectile.

A streak of light blazed across the sky.

The line carved right through the clawship.

The rah dreadnought exploded.

Thunder boomed.

The earth shook.

The sky burned.

Chunks of debris slammed down around Bastian. Soldiers ran for cover. An enormous steel claw, torn free from the clawship, slammed into the ground. The shock wave knocked soldiers back.

Bastian fell to his knees, holding Rowan, shielding her with his body. He squinted up at the sky, and he saw the *Freedom* soar. Her engines shone blue, and she rose, leaping from the atmosphere back into space.

For a moment silence filled the air.

Then dead spiders began to rain. Thousands of rahs—mutilated, slamming down onto Fort Liberty and the surrounding countryside. All were dead before they hit the ground.

* * * * *

A dropship rumbled down from above.

Bastian stood in the courtyard, watching it descend.

It was a RAD. A Rhino Armored Dropship. Spacers just

called them rhinos. They were heavy machines, covered in thick armored plates, and their powerful engines roared. At thirty-three meters long, they were formidable vessels, straddling the line between shuttle and starship. With their wings, treadmill tracks, and powerful engines, they could operate in air, on land, or in space.

Not many starships carried rhinos anymore. They were considered too crude, too bulky, too damn loud. They didn't even fit into most modern hangars. But the starship *Freedom* carried twenty-five of the beasts in her lower decks. During World War III, the rhinos had transported marines onto the surface of enemy worlds. Each had room for a fully armed heavy infantry platoon.

A symbol was painted onto the rhino's hull. A blue star with three red stripes on each side, spreading out like wings. Symbol of the starship *Freedom*.

Motors grumbling, exhaust ports puffing out smoke, the rhino thumped onto the courtyard. It shook the fort.

A hatch opened, and a ramp extended to the ground.

Commander James "Bulldog" King stepped onto the courtyard.

For the first time in many years, he wore battle fatigues—the simple beige combat uniform of the space corps. It was strange to see him without his formal blues, that fine uniform with its polished buttons and medals. A Gideon hung across his back, and an armored vest covered his torso, heavy with magazines. The commander stared across Fort Liberty, taking in the dead spiders. And the dead soldiers. His eyes were hard, his craggy face inscrutable. He could have been carved of granite.

I never knew him as a soldier, Bastian thought. *I only heard the stories. But there he is. The man from those old tales. The bulldog. The killer.*

The commander's eyes landed on Bastian and Rowan. And finally some humanity touched his face.

He began marching toward Bastian and Rowan. Then he

was running.

Bastian ran to meet him, moving between the dead rahs. He held Rowan in his arms.

A few feet away, the two men paused.

They stared at each other.

Bastian remembered their call a few days ago. The anger. The hatred. The old, cutting pain. Diane's ghost still stood between them.

It was Rowan who broke the awkwardness.

"Pop Pop!" she cried in delight, reaching out to him.

King's hard, craggy face cracked with a smile. He pulled Rowan into his arms, hugged her close. She began kissing him, mussing his hair, and laughing.

"I missed you, kiddo," King said. "You've grown so big."

They haven't seen each other in a year, Bastian remembered. *Not outside the MindWeb.*

He looked at his father.

King looked back.

"Hello, Bastian," he said.

Bastian pursed his lips, then took a deep breath. "Dad, I'm sorry. For what I said before." He wiped his eyes. "I love you."

King's lip twitched. It almost looked as if James King himself, the grizzled old war dog, was going to cry. Then he put down Rowan and pulled Bastian into a crushing hug.

"I love you too, son." He stared into his eyes. "I want you on my ship. On our ship. You and your brigade. You wear the insignia of a colonel now. You command the Freedom Brigade. Long ago, your brigade served aboard the starship that gave it its name. Your brigade fought in many battles. It won a world war. Today you will fly in the starship *Freedom* again, and you will deliver the might of humanity wherever we choose to strike. The enemy will speak of the Freedom Brigade in fear."

"Is that all this is about?" Bastian asked softly. "A military decision?"

King snarled. He gripped Bastian's arms, digging his fingers. "You are my son. My only son. I'm proud of you. And I love you more than my starship, more than this planet we stand on, more than the stars. Come home, Bastian. I know you think the ranch is our home. And maybe someday it will be. But right now our home is wherever the war takes us, be it in space or on the ground. Let's be a family again. Come home."

Bastian nodded. He picked up Rowan. "Is there room on the ship for this little one?"

"Of course," King said. He lowered his voice. "What about Stacy?"

"Last time I saw her, she was heading north for Christmas," Bastian said. "Before the enemy attacked. Dad . . . I need to borrow a shuttle. I need to find Stacy."

* * * * *

They didn't have much time. Thousands of clawships still surrounded Earth, battling the human fleet in space. Millions of rahs still swarmed across the planet, hunting, eating. More would be here soon.

Within minutes, twenty-five rhino-class dropships landed at Fort Liberty. Alice began to herd the troops inside.

"Move your asses, you lazy sons of bitches!" she cried. "Faster, dammit, or I'll shoot your legs off and leave you for the spiders!"

In his first act as colonel, Bastian had promoted Alice Allenby to sergeant major. She was now the senior NCO in the brigade. It was already going to her head.

Oh, you're loving this, aren't you, Alice? Bastian thought.

He remained on the ground, waiting until everyone was in the starship *Freedom*. Rowan traveled up with Commander King, her beloved Pop Pop.

Then Bastian took a shuttle. Not a rhino—those beasts were built for more than one man. He flew in a Sparrow-class shuttle instead. The *Freedom* kept a handful of the small transporters, which contained only six seats. They were normally used for transporting officers or civilian dignitaries; a Sparrow had carried Princess Emily into the *Freedom* a few days ago. At twenty meters long, they were just slightly larger than Eagle starfighters.

Bastian flew over the prairies of Nebraska, and his heart broke.

His beloved homeland lay in ruins.

Scars covered the earth. Craters pockmarked the fields. Rahs swarmed across the plains like black puddles. Here and there, Bastian saw the signs of human resistance. The streak of a missile through the sky. The blast of a tank's cannon. Fighter jets roaring across the land. Bastian flew in the atmosphere, but high above, he saw explosions too. Lights flared atop the sky like watercolor stains. Every moment, a piece of broken starship blazed down like a comet. A battle was raging in space, visible even down here.

He scrolled through reports on his MindLink, learned that the Alliance fleet had lost a thousand starships, that the Red Dawn and Desert Thorns were joining forces, that battles raged across all world cities. That most world leaders were dead. That Earth was bleeding.

Finally Bastian reached his destination. Bemidji, a town in Minnesota, the next state over. The town Stacy had flown to for Christmas, hoping to spend the holiday with her new boyfriend and his family.

When Bastian glided his Sparrow down, he saw the devastation.

The fallen buildings. The corpses on the snowy streets. The feeding rahs.

A few soldiers were racing down the streets, firing machine guns, and a tank rumbled along one road. But there wasn't much military activity here compared to other places. After all, this was just a backwater. And it seemed like there was nothing left to save.

As he gazed down from above, Bastian flashed back to a day years ago. To arriving in Europe, searching city by city, desperate to find his mother. That old pain clutched his throat and squeezed.

Before leaving, Stacy had given Bastian the address where she was staying. Bastian landed and stepped out of the Sparrow.

A rah leaped at him.

Bastian fired a grenade from his Gideon, tearing it down.

He stared at the house ahead. An old wooden house, its white paint flaking, overlooking a lake.

And in his mind, Bastian was back in Prague. He was climbing the hotel staircase. He still remembered how those stairs had creaked.

He entered the wooden house by the lake. A rah crouched in the living room, feeding on somebody. It was impossible to tell who. The corpse was little more than a skeleton by now.

The spider hissed and snapped its jaws. Bastian emptied a magazine into the damn thing until it died.

He remembered entering the hotel room, seeing her there on the bed. Shot several times, but still graceful, her face peaceful. He remembered pulling his mother into his arms.

He walked through the house with flaking paint. He found more corpses.

Stacy had not been mutilated. A hole in her chest had killed her. She hung on a web, still whole, perhaps a meal for later in the day. Bastian cut her down. He carried her body into the Sparrow; he would give her a proper funeral aboard the starship *Freedom*.

He flew into space, lips tight, eyes hard, and allowed himself a few tears.

I love you, Stacy. Whatever happened between us . . . it doesn't matter anymore. I love you. I'm sorry I couldn't protect you. I'm sorry I drove you away.

And he felt that the sins of his father had passed into him. The guilt and grief battled inside him.

As he rose into space, he flew through a great battle. Everywhere in orbit, clawships and starships were fighting. Lasers shot back and forth. Torpedoes streaked. Plasma bolts exploded against enemy hulls. Corpses and debris floated through the void. Thousands of starships lit up space with war.

The starship *Freedom* was firing her cannons, blasting an enemy warclaw. Bastian piloted his shuttle around a laser beam, under a stream of bullets, and around a cluster of Eagles battling enemy clawfighters. He made his way into the *Freedom*'s hangar.

He walked down the corridors. Crew members ran back and forth, shouting orders. A blast shook the ship. A klaxon blared. The lights went dark, then came back on with a thud. Electric cables sparked. A bulkhead cracked.

Bastian walked in a daze.

He tracked Rowan's location on the MindWeb. She was in the royal suite, the best room in the starship. It took Bastian a good fifteen minutes to walk there, and he walked fast. The battle seemed to be dying down. Or maybe he was just so deep inside the ship now he couldn't feel the blasts anymore.

He entered the royal suite without knocking.

It looked like a room plucked out of a European palace, completely out of place inside a warship. Rowan sat on a luxurious rug, playing with toy cars. Smashed artwork lay around her. Princess Emily—yes, the same Princess Emily from the tabloids—sat beside the girl.

Rowan leaped up. "Daddy! I met a real princess! Pop Pop is

busy on the bridge, fighting the bad spiders, so Princess Emily has been playing with me. Do you want to play with us?"

Emily rose to her feet too. She smiled at Bastian, but her smile faded. Maybe she recognized the tragedy on his face. She mumbled something about wanting some tea, and she left the room.

Bastian sat on an embroidered couch with golden legs. At least to him it looked like a couch. It probably had some fancy name like *divan* or *ottoman* or something. He didn't care. He didn't care about meeting a princess, about being in a palatial room, about any of it. This all seemed like a dream.

"Rowan, sit beside me," he said softly. "I have to tell you something."

She blinked at him. "Daddy, where's Mommy?"

She sat beside him. She listened carefully as Bastian told her. He hugged her as she shed silent tears.

In the suite's kitchen, Emily lowered her head, and her own tears fell.

Across the starship *Freedom*, ten thousand people fought, wept, prayed, grieved.

Across Earth, billions of souls tore apart.

Across the solar system, this little corner of humanity in the vastness of space, a species mourned. Everyone had lost somebody. Everyone was scared.

In this great darkness, through this infernal fire, the starship *Freedom* flew. Her cannons sang the song of war, and her commander stood on the bridge, staring the enemy in the eyes. Wherever she would fly, the *Freedom* would bring hope, and the courage of her crew would not falter even in the darkest shadows.

James King stared at the main viewport. Ten clawships were charging toward him, ready to fire. Around him, alarms blared, smoke rose from cracked workstations, but his crew still stood at their posts.

"We are the starship *Freedom*," King said as the enemy came closer. "We are the light in the dark. We are the pillar of fire that leads the armies of men. We are hope when all other hope is gone. Today we are a warship again."

The clawships shrieked toward them, plasma crackling.

"Charge at them!" King cried. "Damn the plasma! Full speed ahead!"

The *Freedom*'s mighty engines roared. The starship flew toward the enemy, cannons booming, lighting the darkness.

The story continues in
STARSHIP FREEDOM II
The Cost of Freedom

NOVELS BY DANIEL ARENSON

Starship Freedom:
Starship Freedom
Starship Freedom II: The Cost of Freedom
Starship Freedom III: We Fight for Freedom

Earthrise:
Earth Alone
Earth Lost
Earth Rising
Earth Fire
Earth Shadows
Earth Valor
Earth Reborn
Earth Honor
Earth Eternal
Earth Machines
Earth Aflame
Earth Unleashed
Earth Remembers
Earth in Darkness
Earth, Our Home

Soldiers of Earthrise:
The Earthling
Earthlings
Earthling's War
I, Earthling
The Earthling's Daughter
We Are Earthlings

Children of Earthrise:
The Heirs of Earth
A Memory of Earth
An Echo of Earth
The War for Earth
The Song of Earth
The Legacy of Earth

Alien Hunters:
Alien Hunters
Alien Sky
Alien Shadows

Kingdoms of Sand:
Kings of Ruin
Crowns of Rust
Thrones of Ash
Temples of Dust
Halls of Shadow
Echoes of Light

The Moth Saga:
Moth
Empires of Moth
Secrets of Moth
Daughter of Moth
Shadows of Moth
Legacy of Moth

Dawn of Dragons:
Requiem's Song
Requiem's Hope
Requiem's Prayer

Song of Dragons:
Blood of Requiem
Tears of Requiem
Light of Requiem

Dragonlore:
A Dawn of Dragonfire
A Day of Dragon Blood
A Night of Dragon Wings

The Dragon War:
A Legacy of Light
A Birthright of Blood
A Memory of Fire

Requiem for Dragons:
Dragons Lost
Dragons Reborn
Dragons Rising

Flame of Requiem:
Forged in Dragonfire
Crown of Dragonfire
Pillars of Dragonfire

Dragonfire Rain:
Blood of Dragons
Rage of Dragons
Flight of Dragons

Misfit Heroes:
Eye of the Wizard
Wand of the Witch

Standalones:
Firefly Island
The Gods of Dream
Flaming Dove
Utopia 58
Star Stuff

KEEP IN TOUCH

www.DanielArenson.com
Daniel@DanielArenson.com
Facebook.com/DanielArenson
Twitter.com/DanielArenson

Made in United States
North Haven, CT
05 January 2022